C000262246

The 11th Percent

The 11th Percent

T.H. Morris

Dedication

This book is dedicated to my lovely wife, Candace. If it weren't for her, this book would have remained a wild dream that I had one random night in 2011. Her tireless editing didn't hurt either! Thank you for all your support, darling, and also for never letting me give up. Thank you, also, for being my very first fan and one-woman cheerleading squad.

Contents

Blue

Jonah Rowe killed the ignition in his car and shook his head. To call this routine stressful would be a compliment.

He had just parked at the office complex where his job was located, but he remained as stationary as the car. He had no desire to drag himself the twenty feet it took to get to the front door. He looked at his reflection in the mirror and sighed at what he saw. The hazel eyes that stared back at him already drooped. The slightly round face with the persistent stubble already looked worn out. He slowly ran a hand through the brown hair he also saw in the mirror. He was in need of a haircut, but that was a worry for a different day.

The question in his mind at the moment was the same one that had been there since the very first day he'd parked in this very same spot several months ago: Was it possible to feel *this* down this early in the morning? Before he had even set foot into the office? He found it increasingly difficult to convince himself each morning that his job was worthwhile. Come to think of it, he found it hard to convince himself that his life was worthwhile.

When he completed graduate school with a Master's Degree in Accounting, his favorite instructor, Professor Rohn, gave him what he must have thought was sage advice: "Jonah, you have always said that you wanted to assist people. This diploma is your pass into a very highly chosen and polished fraternity of people who do just that. These next years will be exciting and fulfilling for you."

God, if that hadn't turned out to be a joke.

Jonah's days usually consisted of everything *but* assisting people. So far, his accounting job at Essa, Langton, and Bane, Inc. included being a gopher, transporting files, printing copies, correcting and re-correcting errors in the files, and more billing reports than he cared to tolerate. Jonah's experiences in this "high-chosen" field proved to be nothing more than a waste of time. He should have read the fine print.

It doesn't matter, he thought to himself. *This day can't be that bad. Just coast through the staff meeting, finish all of your work, and be happy that 5 p.m. will be here before you know it. That'll be the end of the day.*

"Five p.m.," he said aloud. "The best part of the day. Just make it to 5 p.m."

"Excuse me?" said Jonah. "What did you just say?"

Jonah's boss, Anders Langton, smiled. "I know that it's a shock, Mr. Rowe, but you heard me. The office will be open until 6 p.m."

"For how long?" asked Jonah's friend and co-worker Nelson Black. He scratched at his stubble, which he always did when he was irritated. He scratched his stubble a lot at this job.

"I don't think we should restrict ourselves to a timeframe, Mr. Black," said Mr. Langton with that stupid smile still on his face. He didn't seem to realize that his announcement about extending the office hours by one was about to incite a small-scale riot.

"Business is down," he continued. "We need to build up the business that we have coming in, and the board does not see that occurring with the normal eight-hour format. As such, we have agreed that accept-able gains can be achieved only if we all hunker down and implement a longer work day. I know that it will be an adjustment, but this is something that will benefit everyone."

Jonah looked at Nelson and saw that the grimace on his face mir-rored his own. He knew that most of his other colleagues thought the same thing they did: Mr. Langton was overselling this. Everyone knew that when he used the term "we," that meant *him* almost exclusively. Langton was surrounded by yes-men (and women), and they usually went along with anything he said because if they voiced their own opinions, it would likely stunt their career growth. Jonah didn't even want to focus on Langton's point about business being down. That was a very difficult thing for him to believe when Langton's burgundy Lexus, visible through the blinds, gleamed in the morning sun and caused an unpleasant glare in the meeting room.

"These changes will rejuvenate the company," declared Mr. Langton, oblivious to the mutinous eyes that glared lasers through him. "Do not believe for one second that this doesn't inconvenience me as well."

Again, Jonah locked eyes with Nelson and made a wry face.

"We are all in this together," Langton continued. "I would not ask anything of you that I wouldn't do myself. Meeting adjourned, and thank you all in advance for your cooperation!"

The staff rose from the tables and didn't dare grumble about this new foolishness. They didn't have to because their opinions were written on their faces. Jonah couldn't blame them; everyone knew that Langton would check out at 3 p.m., if he even bothered to wait *that* long. He was just about to reach for Nelson's shoulder when he felt a tap.

"Mr. Rowe, a quick word if you please!" It was Mr. Langton.

Jonah turned to him slowly, using as much time as he dared to make his face an impassive mask. "Sir?"

"Do sit down!" said Langton, still so jovial that Jonah wanted to vomit. He lowered himself into his chair and interlocked his fingers, prompting Jonah to make himself comfortable. If the man locked his fingers, this word was going to be anything but quick.

"I must ask you something, Jonah," said Langton, some of the heartiness fading out of his voice. "How do you like your job?"

Jonah's brain immediately went to work attempting to conjure the most acceptable answer to Langton's inquiry. The obvious answer of, *"Which part? The making copies or the hours hidden in the file room?"* was on the tip of his tongue, but he settled on a much more respectable one. "There are good days and not so good ones, sir," he said. "One has to roll with the punches and be willing to adapt. I believe that I manage myself well with every ebb and flow."

Mr. Langton knit his brow, obviously trying to find something in Jonah's statement to criticize. He must not have succeeded because his expression cleared, and he resumed that ridiculous smile. "I must agree with you, son," he said, "which is why I had to speak with you. I've noticed recently that you have appeared to be coasting through your work."

"Excuse me?" said Jonah, frowning.

"You don't appear to be pleased with your responsibilities," said Langton. "I've seen you going to your cubicle, appearing very glum and, dare I say, miserable. This brings down office morale, Jonah. I'm not the only one who thinks so."

Jonah had no idea what to make of that. He was fully cognizant of the fact that the company was rife with Langton's informants. *Snitches*, if one called a spade a spade. There were several times he had seen people complain about their job only to have an impromptu staff meeting where Langton repeated, almost verbatim, what had been said. Jonah had picked up on this rather quickly and had begun to keep his opinions to himself. Since there were no verbal weapons with which to arm themselves, it appeared that Langton's rats were attempting to criticize Jonah's mood.

"Mr. Langton," he said with caution, "I was not aware that my demeanor had been bothering anyone. I keep my head down. I come here, I do my work, and I go home. I have never heard of anyone having a concern with my mood, whatever you have been told."

"I never said anyone told me anything," said Langton, who must have forgotten that he had just said that he wasn't the only one who thought so. "I'm simply saying that we must support each other with a kind word, a congratulatory pat on the back, or with a pleasant smile. Positivity is infectious, after all. You never know who is watching!"

Amen to that one, thought Jonah, irritated. Apparently his face betrayed him yet again because Mr. Langton looked reproachful. "See that face there? That could be remedied with a nice smile! You might benefit from improving your posture as well, and a little exercise could take care of that! It isn't like it would kill you to lose about ten pounds."

Jonah eyes narrowed. "I'm sorry?"

Mr. Langton flashed that stupid grin. "Sorry is not a good way to be either, son!"

Jonah had to get out of there. Langton's comments had pissed him off. That man had some nerve to say that someone was overweight when he probably hadn't seen his own toes in years. The ones going on about his "miserable" demeanor were revealed the minute he exited the conference room as they were the ones that stared hungrily at him before they looked in opposite directions: Jessica Hale, an unabashed sycophant who successfully distracted people from her snarky and devious nature with her perfect figure, and Anthony Noble, a useless slacker who couldn't seem to grasp the fact that the fun-loving, devil-may-care days of high school and college were behind him, no matter how youthful his wavy hair, boyish features, and slim frame made him look. In Jonah's opinion, his looks didn't make him appear ageless. They made him look immature, vapid, and precocious. What was worse was the fact that Anthony might have actually been tolerable if he didn't cater to Jessica's every whim. He did whatever she asked in a fruitless hope to obtain a date, a compliment, or simply an acknowledgment of existence.

"Hello, Jonah!" said Jessica with false brightness. She brushed her strawberry-blonde hair out of her face and stood to meet him. "He didn't tear you down too badly, did he?"

Remembering that he was under tight scrutiny, Jonah replied, "Nah, Jess … he didn't. Just got some pointers."

"Nothing wrong with getting a leg up, man," chimed in Anthony, eyes toward Jessica and nowhere near where he spoke. "We all need to remember when to put on a happy face."

"How do you—?" Jonah began, but Nelson appeared behind him.

"How about the new hour, Jonah? Guess we will have to need an extra hour of sleep to balance out the universe!"

Even though he was still annoyed at Anthony and Jessica's nosiness, Jonah couldn't help but smirk at Nelson's joke. It was just like him to diffuse a situation, and Jonah didn't want to bother with the snitches. He allowed Nelson to steer him away. When they reached their cubicles, Nelson's smile faded, and he suddenly looked tense.

"You know better than to let those two get to you, Jonah," he told him. "What did the big man want, anyway?"

Jonah told him Langton's ridiculous remarks. Nelson glared at the conference room and scratched his stubble again.

"You don't need to worry about that, man," he told him, "nor do you need to worry about his little stooges either. What you need to do is ditch this place and finish up your books!"

Jonah merely smiled. He was an aspiring novelist and loved to write from a very early age. A few people said he had a way with words, but in his own mind, his largest problem was that he could never bring any books to completion. He never could understand why his ideas would start out white-hot in the beginning and then always fizzle out somewhere near the halfway point. In his apartment right now, there were four "novels" that had been all but abandoned. Out of all the people who were privy to his writing aspirations, Nelson was the one who was the most supportive and actually entertained the notion that Jonah could go somewhere with it. This opinion, however, was not shared by all. Several detractors had described his talents as "amateur" and said he needed to focus on a "real" job. For that reason, Jonah couldn't bring himself to be too vocal about it and usually kept it close to the chest.

"I would love to complete a novel, man," he told Nelson, "but I can't seem to make it work. Maybe it's just a pipe dream. Not reality, you know?"

Nelson shrugged. "Who knows, Jonah? You could be a great author. And I don't mean one of those who are lost in the shuffle. I mean one that changes the world."

Jonah looked at Nelson, who was worked up with excitement just thinking about possibilities for Jonah's future. Jonah couldn't help but allow glimmers of the same vision to permeate the negative cloud that shrouded his mind. It'd be great to have the safe haven of a padded chair, a comfortable table, and mounds of paper just waiting to be covered with spellbinding tomes, all-encompassing verses, and thrilling tales that would etch their place in history and remain undeterred in the annals of time.

The exhilarating fire was extinguished when he saw the portly figure of Langton, who heartily inquired about people's days in a thinly veiled attempt to determine how much work they had done. He plopped down into his chair, refreshing the page on his computer.

"It's a nice thought, Nelson, believe me," he said. "But until 6 p.m. tonight, these reports are the only things I'm authoring."

At 5:54 p.m., Jonah could swear that the clock had slowed simply to spite him. He had finished all of his work but kept the page up on his laptop to maintain the facade of working. He had learned early on that if you finished your duties early, it did not result in gratitude. It resulted in further work. And he did not want another chore added on, lest he suffer further time in this hell hole. He chanced a glance at the clock once more.

5:55?! Seriously? He knew for a fact that it had been *at least* five minutes since he last looked at that thing!

He closed his eyes and recited the alphabet with three breaths in between each letter. It was a trick he started in elementary school. It always worked wonders for making time pass, and better yet, he rarely ever finished. It was sure to work. Sure enough, before he had even reached the letter P, Langton called, "Alright, my friends! The workday is now completed! I would like to thank you all for being troopers. Remember, you are helping ALL of us keep our jobs! Good evening."

Jonah packed his laptop gratefully. That tactic worked every time. He headed for the door, grateful to hear the exit signal's rhythmic chimes.

It was on the third chime that it happened.

Jonah blinked, a natural occurrence that he had done a billion times. Only in *this* momentary closing of his eyes, he opened them to bear witness to a very strange phenomenon. The world around him—the office, the parking lot, the cars, everything—looked *blue.*

They were perfectly normal in every other regard, but it seemed as if someone had shaded his vision with cerulean. Alarmed, he glanced around and blinked hard. It made no difference. The blue veil remained.

His eyes shot up to the sky, which now had an even darker hue because of the blue veil over his eyes.

What the hell is going on? he wondered wildly. What had happened? Had he damaged his eyes? Had he suddenly contracted some rare disease that had polarized his eyes and resulted in a permanent tinge of blue?

"Jonah Rowe," said a voice.

He whirled around. A woman stood there, swaddled in what looked like fading lights. Her hair was dark, made darker by the bluish tinge. Her eyes were wide set and full of fear. She might have been pretty if she didn't look so horrified and desperate.

"Jonah Rowe," she repeated again.

"What is going on?" demanded Jonah. "Why is everything blue? Who are you?"

"Jonah Rowe," she said for a third time. Her voice was as strange as her appearance; it sounded like a two or three-part harmony. She also sounded like she spoke to him from several yards away, though she stood right in front of him. "You must help us all. You have the power. Help us. Please."

Jonah was more confused than ever. "What power? What are you talking about, lady? And tell me why everything is *blue!*"

"You are the one," said the woman. "You must help us cross on. He has blocked the path."

Jonah backed away from her. "Lady, I don't know who you are or who *he* is, and I don't know anything about any paths! Now tell me what's going on!"

"You must help us! Please, Jonah Rowe! You have the power. Please—!"

She disappeared. It looked as though it had been against her will, like she'd been yanked into thin air. The silence left in her absence seemed even more frightening than her disconnected voice.

Then a cat's meow whipped Jonah around once more, almost like his body was moved in response to the sound.

He now saw, if possible, an even stranger sight. A calico stared at him while pawing at the shin of a tall man that Jonah could have sworn had not been there moments before. He looked to be in his late thirties and was as calm as could be. He looked like this scene was entirely normal. Although the blue color shaded everything, Jonah could tell the man had a ruddy complexion and brownish black hair. His penetrating eyes looked like they could be grey. He had aquiline features and a demeanor that was almost regal. His casually dressed and cloaked form appeared to be shrouded in lights, just like the woman's form had been.

"Yes, Bast," he said quietly, "I see now. It is indeed him. You have done well."

His eyes rose to Jonah. "Jonah Rowe," he said in an ominous tone, "I will be seeing you again. Go home now. Do not leave. I know who you are now. Unfortunately, *he* does too."

Jonah stared. Was this some kind of joke? Who was this man? What was the deal with the cat? Why was the man *talking* to it? And where did he get off telling Jonah to go home and stay there?

"Look, man," he said, fear and incomprehension blending to form a high-pitched voice most unlike his own, "I don't have a clue what's going on—"

"You do not," interrupted the man. "But you will, son. You will. Heed my warning."

Jonah opened his mouth to retort, but the man disappeared in a swirl of light. The calico gave him one more look of appraisal and then dashed into a nearby alley. Jonah blinked again.

Everything was normal. The deep blue sky was the *only* thing that was that color as the late afternoon gave way to evening. Incoherent chatter, passing cars, and bustling people once again dominated the scene.

Jonah looked around. There was no weird woman, no cat, and no tall, regal-looking man. He blinked again, just to make sure, but nothing had changed. Normalcy was evident in every detail of his environment.

"Um, Jonah," said an annoyed voice, "if you don't mind, some of us actually have lives to live."

Jessica was behind him; he was blocking her path. With a jolt, he realized he was back at the threshold of the office, at the exact spot where the weirdness had begun. How was he back where he started? He had moved at least five feet from the door when the world went blue, yet here he was like nothing had happened at all.

"Jessica," he breathed, "didn't you see that? Didn't you see that blue?"

Jessica rolled her eyes and pushed past him. "I don't know what you've been using, Rowe, but the only thing *blue* out here is my car."

She headed to her car, leaving Jonah bewildered and confused. He had barely even registered her snide comment. The only thing blaring in his mind was one question:

What the hell had just happened?

2

The Danger Zone

The drive home was a blur. Jonah's mind went in twenty different directions, none of which had a suitable or even understandable destination.

The world had gone blue, and it had made absolutely no sense. Then, some woman showed up and asked him for help. Then, the creepy man with the Garfield lookalike came into the picture and told him to go home and stay there.

Had it been a hallucination? Had he finally cracked under the stress of that stupid job? That wouldn't be a surprise. But that occurrence hadn't felt like a hallucination. It hadn't seemed like a figment of his imagination. He had never experienced his vision going blue. He couldn't begin to fathom what it could have meant.

And then that weird lady ... *"You must help us all. You have the power."*

What?

He tried to fit what had happened into some kind of logical compartment of his mind as the elevator opened on his floor. He felt the need to get to his apartment quickly so he could think. He was in such a mental overload that he didn't register the things he normally would have, like the flyer that advertised the biweekly tenant's meeting where they attempted to make the residents more sociable or the crack in the wall that the super always stated was "damaging to the décor," yet he was too cheap to actually fix. He didn't even bother to register the slender and beautiful woman from 7D who walked by him in the hallway. She didn't seem to own any attire beyond form-fitting exercise gear, so the fact that he barely noticed her let him know that his current state of mind was indeed messed up.

He paused, gave her a tiny nod, and then he entered his apartment. The scattered nature of his belongings reflected his cluttered mind.

The only difference was that his mind was not proving as simple to organize as his apartment was.

The couch, television, and kitchen table seemed to cast eerie shadows. One flick of the light switch illuminated the scene. That was the solution to *one* problem, at least.

It had simply been a very vivid, imaginative event, he told himself. It was no secret that he hated his job and dealt with significant stress. He had heard somewhere that going through prolonged periods of stress without adequate rest would have detrimental effects, such as erratic behaviors, nausea, trouble breathing, and in extreme cases, temporary hallucinations. What had happened had to have been that. It would only make sense after that idiot Langton added an hour to work that day. He had been angry. Apparently, angrier than he'd thought.

Besides all that, he always *had* had an overactive imagination. His wild imagination was one of his most prized possessions, one of the reasons why he wanted to be a writer. He had always wanted to be one from the minute he developed the dexterity and strength in his hand to hold a pencil and pen. The problem (or so he had been told back then by well-meaning adults) was that his fascination with "fantastical tales" was unhealthy. In high school, he was told that his brand of writing was known as "grossly imaginative meandering" (he believed that the teacher who'd told him that, Mr. Tann, had invented that classification as he hadn't heard it before or since) and was evidence that he was "incapable of modern writing and was dedicated to imitating the writing styles of authors hundreds of years in the grave.

Despite such criticism, Jonah never truly deviated from his imaginative lore. He continued to write, but the years of unconstructive criticism eventually succeeded in taking the wind out of his sails. Something about it was missing, something that he couldn't put his finger on. He couldn't remember the number of stories and (as he got older) novels that he had begun with reckless abandon only to run out of steam around the midway point. It was infuriating. Perhaps all the stressors he'd experienced came to a head and formed that disturbing occurrence. Yes, that had to be it.

He attempted to distract himself by taking another stab at the writing. At the moment, he had about four unfinished novels on his coffee table. Wait. He rearranged some papers and realized that there was a fifth that he'd forgotten. He shook his head, put on his reading glasses, and picked up the first one. It was an epic tale that had hit a snag at page 217. He put his pen to the page and hoped for an inspiration.

He blinked hard. Right there, in his handwriting, were the words, *"You are wrong. This isn't your imagination."*

And the text was written in black ink. These words, however, were light blue.

The same blue he'd seen earlier.

He closed the half-book and shoved it away. He grabbed another book he'd been working on, not even bothering to process what he'd just seen.

This one was a quick-witted and fast-paced comedy of errors. He went to the last page he was on and realized that he didn't recall the plot. He had discarded this one quite some time ago. Grimacing over the lapse in memory, he flipped some pages back to re-familiarize himself with the story.

Jonah paused on page forty-eight. Right in the middle of a dialogue between his protagonist and a potential romantic interest was a random sentence that was in blue ink: *"I'm not kidding. This is real. Real as it is ever going to get."*

Jonah straightened. He was a completely rational being and perfectly sane. How could he have graduated high school, voluntarily attended school another four years, and then stay on for an additional *two* years if he had been insane?

"I'm not crazy," he told himself. He tossed the comedy aside and grabbed a collection of poems and random thoughts he'd had as a teenager. He looked them over, chuckling at the thoughts he'd had in his head as a teenager. While several poems were corny, some of them were pretty cool. Profound, even. He could alter the world with his work if only someone gave him a chance, and of course, if this cursed writer's block would fade.

He turned to a page dated 7/9/2000, which put him around thirteen years old when he wrote it. He remembered the words on the page, a wonderful brainstorm of his that dealt with a reluctant hero destined to tip the balance in some fictional conflict. He thought about the fertility of his adolescent mind when the notebook felt rather tepid, and then unbearably hot.

Jonah shouted and flung the pages down. They scattered across the floor. As though they were sentient, the pages reconfigured themselves into an organized collection, with one deliberate change. The poem from 2000 was now situated at the top of the pile. The stanza that made up the center of the poem began to steam. Then the black letters burst into flames, which didn't damage the rest of the paper. The words burned for a full thirty seconds, and then the flames extinguished themselves. The page flew from the top and spun toward Jonah's sweaty palm. Reflexively, he caught it. He stared down at the formerly black letters which were now light blue on the paper. The stanza went:

> "*The hero had emotions to master,*
> *Numerous talents to unearth and hone,*
> *For the day was swiftly approaching that*
> *He was heading for a danger zone.*"

A chill went down Jonah's spine.

What the hell *was* this?

He threw the page down and shrank away from it like it was diseased. He went near the window. Maybe the night air would alleviate the fear that riddled his wall of certainty like a hail of bullets. As he looked out of his window, he noticed that this new anxiety that coursed through him was far more pronounced than it had been earlier that day. Not only did this not feel like it would fade anytime soon, it seemed to carry ominous threats and worries.

The silence in the alley behind his building, which he usually lauded if he'd tried to write, was now piercing and eerie as though there were some beast just waiting to let loose a wave of disconcerting sound. The darkness made him uneasy. The shadows outside seemed to hold secrets and dangers that were threats to not only Jonah but to the unsuspecting populace that made up the city nightlife.

Jonah felt a tinge of annoyance amongst his dread. Yes, this had been a weird and disturbing day, but here he was, a grown man, with qualms about the dark. Just how stupid and juvenile was that?

But, a voice in the back of his head reminded him, *these are not random occurrences.* The world, at least in his eyes, turned blue, and no one else seemed aware of it. Then there was the woman that cried for help, the calico, and the man who told him to lock himself down. He had tried to write it off as psychological, but then he experienced the thing with the words on the pages that changed from black to light blue. He headed toward the bathroom for a cold shower. He decided that attempting to rationalize these things might lead to something else.

A shrill sound pierced the night from somewhere outside his window. He darted back to it, afraid that a child hung off of the ledge or something. But when he looked outside, he saw that it hadn't been a child.

The sound had been made by a *cat.*

With a start, Jonah realized that the cat was the same cat he'd seen at the office earlier. It was at the very edge of the terrace and shied away from something he couldn't see. Then Jonah saw a man kneeling in front of the calico. He literally materialized out of thin air. He was so focused on the cat that his features appeared bestial. He was oddly shaded and pale; he resembled a character depiction from a newspaper comic strip, gray and angular with dark circles shaded in on his face, neck, and arms. Jonah looked at him in amazement and horror.

Was he looking at a *spirit*? And why would a spirit want to harm a cat?

Then he remembered something he'd read years ago about how cat's eyes could make out spirits and apparitions that human eyes could not. Although the bit of knowledge was rather intriguing, it did nothing to help this particular situation. It also didn't explain why Jonah could see the spirit. There was nothing feline about *his* eyes.

The spirit crawled toward the cat while the cat tried to shrink away. But Jonah could see that soon, there would be no more room. That cat was running out of space, and if something wasn't done, it would fall into the dark, unseen alleyway. Jonah had to do something, but what?

"Jonah."

It was that man again. He'd just appeared. His sudden appearance startled Jonah so much that he jerked his head upward and slammed into the bottom of the windowsill. Staggered and dazed, he sank to his knees, clasping his head. It felt as though his cranium had been caved in. He slowly turned in the direction of the man, who was visible again once Jonah's jarred senses re-aligned and his eyes came back to focus.

"My sincere apologies for startling you, son," he said. Jonah couldn't help but wonder about his crisp and formal voice, which sounded like he was using diction from an era many years removed. "But yes, that is indeed a spirit you see. He is attempting to kill my herald."

Jonah's head was still smarting, so it took him a bit of time to process this new information. He glanced at the spirit once more. He was about to swipe at the calico, which would have surely knocked it off its perch, but then he realized he wasn't alone. He abandoned the cat completely and headed straight for Jonah.

Then a very strange thing happened.

Time slowed down. Not to a standstill, but to a speed halted enough that Jonah noticed it. The spirit still moved forward, but the time halt made his movements seem slow, deliberate, and dramatic. Jonah also noticed that the spirit, a spectral being, was making audible footsteps on the terrace. The regal-looking man sighed, and Jonah looked back at him.

"I'm sorry about this, but fighting him personally will exert too much of my essence at this time. *You* must do something about it. Consider this a crash course. Again, I apologize."

He looked at Jonah. "You have been endowed," he said. And then he vanished.

Instantly, Jonah felt different. His head didn't throb anymore. The fatigue and fears of the day evaporated like water droplets in heat. He was aware of his surroundings in a manner that was most surreal. He could tell that the alleyway below was lined with six dumpsters that did very little to accommodate the heaps of rotting garbage spilling out of them. He was on the terrace himself now, but he didn't recall when he'd climbed out of the window. He felt as if he had had twenty hours' sleep and then supplemented that rest with caffeine. It felt like a cross between a sugar high and an adrenaline rush.

He hadn't even noticed that the environment had resumed real time. The spirit was quickly approaching, heavy footsteps and all.

Somehow, Jonah was ready. He looked at his television through the apartment window. Strangely aware of what to do, he inhaled deeply and tensed. The television moved slightly, began to tremble, and then a shapeless mass of bluish-white current extracted itself from the set and hovered several feet from it. Somehow, Jonah understood that the current needed transport. He raised his left hand to keep the current in place. The murderous spirit noticed these activities as well, and his eyes widened in shock.

Jonah paid no attention to the spirit's reactions and used his right hand to harness portions of the night air. He hadn't realized it until that moment, but he was able to see the wind gusts and spurts. What was usually an invisible act of nature was now a valuable tool. It made bluish gray outlines against the backdrop of the velvety night sky.

Feeling an adequate portion of wind in his hands, Jonah formed it into a net, which he then guided toward the stationary current. It caught and then headed at the spirit, who gaped at Jonah.

"You ... you're this powerful *already?*" he sputtered, aghast. "But how can that *be?!*"

The current collided with the spirit. He shouted in agony; his form was utterly overwhelmed. Jonah watched in awe as the voltage seemed to be increasing in intensity. The very air smelled of heat...

Then the spirit's form shattered. The remnants caught on the breeze and were scattered into the night. The remaining ones flickered white for a moment and then faded. The calico looked Jonah right in the eye, and Jonah could swear that the look in its amber eyes was one of gratitude. It meowed and hurried off.

Then Jonah nearly collapsed. He certainly would have if he hadn't had the frame of mind to balance himself against the wall. The boundless energy he'd just been in possession of was now completely gone. It had faded as immediately as it had come. He was now so tired he was almost beyond rational thought. His legs felt wobbly and numb, as though he'd run thirty miles at full speed and hadn't bothered to pace himself.

He also noticed that his mind, which had just been so clear and alert, was now back to its normal state. That was not a good thing as the normal state was always muddled. Every trace of clarity he'd had minutes before was gone.

With extreme difficulty, Jonah managed to sling his weight into the open window and drag himself to the couch. He could go no further. This was going to have to do for the night. He knew that if he tried to make it to his bed, he would likely fall down and bang his head against something.

Despite the heavy fatigue, Jonah wondered about the night's occurrences. Had he really seen a spirit? *Two* spirits, if he counted that strange man that had just appeared again? And strangest of all, did he just channel Zeus and summon wind and electricity? Had all that truly happened just now?

The answering machine jarred him out of his sluggish reverie. "Hey, Jonah? This is Jim Ogilvie, your neighbor in 7G. I was wondering if you could fill me in about the tenant's meeting? I can't make it because I've got PTA tonight. I'd almost rather go to the meeting, because at PTA, I'm probably going to sleep like the dead!"

"Not words I want to hear right now," slurred Jonah. He managed to position his body into a comfortable position on his couch and instantly fell asleep.

3

Space and Time

It was the stiffness in his neck that awakened Jonah.

Morning sun rays had cast a glow against the wall of Jonah's living room, which gave him enough light to make out how to maneuver himself. The dream he'd had the evening before had been interesting, albeit disturbing. He'd dreamed that a normal day at work (which was to say, miserable) ended in the world around him being shrouded in blue. Then there was a muddled collage of memories that involved cats on the ledge, spirits with murderous intent, and guys that looked like misplaced nobility who spiked him with some kind of sugar high.

The dream had been so vivid, but that didn't spark his interest. He'd had plenty of wild dreams that involved some literary spark for a book. And those sparks were nothing to brag about. The last thing he needed was another beautiful idea that would fizzle out before he'd even edited or shaped it.

The call of nature forced Jonah off the sofa. Shaking his head again at his literary limitations, he made his way to the bathroom. The sounds of his footsteps were welcome against the silence in his apartment, plus Jonah didn't object to the extra jolt that the noise gave him.

He threw some cold splashes of water on his face to finish the wakeup process, dried his face, and stared at his reflection. He lowered his eyes to his torso, and remembered Mr. Langton's crackpot advice: *"It wouldn't hurt to lose ten pounds or so."*

Jonah had never really cared about his weight. He ate what he wanted but made a point to never gorge. His grandmother had told him that his father had had hypertension, and she hadn't wanted him to eat his way to the same risk. So he never really overdid it. What he noticed in the mirror was neither a six-pack nor a trim waistline. But it was still laughable for Langton, who resembled a bald, badly-tanned Santa, to criticize him.

"Idiot," muttered Jonah to himself, and exited the bathroom. He went into the kitchen for a glass of orange juice when he saw a random page on the floor near his laptop bag.

"How did you get down there?" he said aloud. He picked it up and turned on the kitchen light so he could see it. He dropped it.

On the page, in blue ink, were the words *danger zone.*

All desire for juice was forgotten. He backed away from the page. Last night had *not* been a dream. The blue, the spirits, the power ... it had all been real. Each memory came back into focus, and he found it increasingly more difficult to breathe.

His cell phone vibrated loudly. He yanked it from the counter, thankful for a distraction. *Any* distraction. "Hello? Who is it?"

"Mornin', friend!" It was Nelson. Thank God. If Nelson called, it was validation that he was at least on the right planet if nothing else.

"Good morning," returned Jonah. "What's up?"

"I was just calling to make sure you were all right," said Nelson. Something in his voice made this seem as though it should have been obvious.

"Yeah?" asked Jonah. "Why?"

"Um ... because it's a quarter after ten, and you aren't at work," said Nelson.

Jonah glanced at the microwave clock. Sure enough, Nelson was right. He was officially late for work. He swore loudly.

"Has anyone been running their mouth about it?"

An irritated intake of breath on Nelson's end confirmed his suspicions. "As you know, Jess and Tony made a big stink about it. Langton started his vacation yesterday."

Jonah swore again. Great. Just great.

"Jonah, the big man isn't here, so you know he has his snitches on high alert. Jess and Tony have already been grumbling to anyone who will listen, and they are just the *obvious* snitches. The sooner you get here, the better."

Despite their friendship, there was a trace of sternness in Nelson's voice, which caused Jonah to jump to his own defense. "Nelson, don't you think I know I'm in trouble? I understand what type of situation it is. It is not my fault I'm late. I had a very long night last night and didn't sleep well."

The silence on the opposite end now had an intriguing ring to it. "Long night? Really? And here I was, just thinking you overslept because you hate this place!"

It took a second to figure out what Nelson meant, which further annoyed Jonah. After the freaky occurrences of the previous night, he assumed Jonah had had an escapade? "It was not like that, Nelson," he said through gritted teeth. "My night involved, uh, more serious matters."

"What are you talking about?" asked Nelson, obviously bemused. "Is it something that you want to discuss?"

"No," said Jonah quickly, his hands on his keys and his eyes on that page with the blue ink. "Since it was what made me late, I don't care to think about it. Just run some damage control for me, will you?"

Nelson snorted. "You know I have your back, friend," he said, and they hung up.

Jonah knew that the last thing he needed was a speeding ticket, but he floored the gas until he was within minutes of the office. He slung his bag over his shoulder and broke into a light run. The last time he'd checked his clock, it had been a quarter to eleven. Damn.

He walked in the door, cursing those wretched entrance chimes that betrayed his presence and nullified any hope of sneaking in. Strangely, though, everyone appeared to be settling in themselves.

That was weird. There must have been a fire drill or something.

Inches away from his cubicle, he saw Jessica, who was wearing her usual strategically-buttoned blouse and short skirt. She caught his eye and made to say something, but he decided he didn't want to hear it.

"I already know, okay?" he said, venom in his voice to mask the fatigue he felt. "It happens to the best of us. You're not a perfect employee either, Hale. Just let it go and let me get to my cubicle."

Jessica blushed. "What are you babbling about, Rowe?" she demanded.

Jonah's eyes narrowed. Was she really going to do this? "Jessica," he said slowly, "I know what time it is. I know you were probably chomping at the bit to see me get here so that you could scold me in front of everyone. Well, I've taken your steam. Everyone knows it's eleven a.m., and I showed up just now. That's what you were going to say. You know it, and I know it."

Jessica frowned at him. "I was *going* to ask whether you had your head on straight this morning," she said. "After your 'blue' thing yesterday, I wanted to make sure you were fit to work. But given what you just said, I can only assume not."

A trace of caution dulled his irritation, if only mildly so. He'd forgotten that he'd mentioned the blue to Jessica. "And what is that supposed to mean?"

She glanced over at Anthony, who had snaked over so quickly that Jonah hadn't noticed him. "What it means, Rowe," she said, her voice terse, "is that it is *not* eleven a.m."

She pointed a French-tipped nail at the nearest clock, which read *EIGHT* a.m.

Jonah stared. That couldn't be right. The shift had just started? If that were the case, why had Nelson called him to see what had been going on? Why had his oven clock read 10:15 when Nelson called? Why had the clock in his car read 10:47 before he stepped into the office?

"Is this some sort of joke?" he asked. "I overslept and got up at ten something. Nelson gave me a call and wanted to see if I was sick. I got here just now and was accosted by you. Nelson!"

Thankfully, Nelson had watched the situation unfold and was already on his way over. But his expression didn't look like one of greeting; he looked confused as he walked their way. "Yeah?"

"Tell them you called me this morning," said Jonah.

"Yeah, I did."

Jonah exhaled in relief. "And you called at 10:15, right?"

A truly pronounced look of confusion settled on Nelson's face this time, but he recovered beautifully. "Come on and have a seat, man," he muttered as he steered Jonah away from the piercing eyes of Jessica and the curious ones of Anthony. "Langton's vacation started today, so we can finish our work in peace, at least from him."

Once they had privacy, Nelson said, "You all right, man?"

Jonah's eyes narrowed. "Of course I'm all right. I'm just trying to figure out why all the clocks say eight-something when it's *eleven*-something!"

Nelson, to Jonah's surprise, was beginning to look worried. "Jonah, where did you get that? It's 8:06; the workday just started. We all got here on time."

Jonah couldn't understand why Nelson kept up this pretense, especially after he corroborated the morning call. "Nelson, stop pretending. You called me this morning. You just said so over there."

"Yeah, I did," said Nelson, more quietly because Anthony still watched them. "But I didn't call you about being late. I called you because I was going on a breakfast run this morning, and I wanted to know if you wanted anything."

Jonah blinked. "When was that?"

"About five after seven," said Nelson.

Frowning, Jonah took out his phone and checked the call history. There was a missed call from Nelson that corroborated the early a.m. time. There was no record of a call from 10:15.

Jonah nearly dropped the phone. All these things were too much. First, there were the things that happened yesterday, and today, time jumped back three hours.

"Jonah, are you okay?" repeated Nelson, concerned.

Jonah glanced at the computer screen, which now read 8:12 a.m. "I'm all right, friend," he said, though he wasn't so sure anymore. "Just fine. Rough night of sleep just threw me off. That's all."

* * *

Over the next two weeks, no further strange occurrences happened to Jonah. His senses were on higher alert than usual, but after a few days, he believed that everything was all right. Jonah was normally a curious person and desired to know how things ticked. There had been a time when he would have wondered why such strange things had happened in such rapid succession, but his curiosity was nonexistent this time. He was grateful that his life was once again uneventful. No frightened spirits asked for help, no weird cats were around except the usual strays, and no freakish winds or currents. He decided that that damned job pushed him to the edge. But the weirdness was over now.

That didn't stop the dreams, though.

Under normal circumstances, Jonah's dreams were a muddled collection of ideas and thoughts, riddled with inspirations that needed no further exploration since they would come to naught anyway. His dreams would also be teeming with fractured visions brought on by stressors from work. Many nights, he had either grumbled himself awake about reports or had snapped himself awake talking to Jessica.

But his dreams had changed. While the jumble was as present as ever, some aspects of his mind had a new dimension to them. They now contained various people of all ages, and they seemed to be afraid of something. They were all shackled and fettered and had the physical builds of broken slaves. The shackles would fall away, and their bodies would transform to upright, robust, and strong. Then the chains would return, and their bodies would devolve to the subjugated forms once more. The piteous expressions would return as well, but when he moved to help them, the chains would tighten, and the figures would disappear from sight. These dreams would always be bathed in blue which would immediately change to a dismal gray once the chained individuals were extracted from his line of sight.

Thankfully, Jonah didn't linger on these dreams when he was awake. His mood and mind were assuaged when he looked at his manuscripts and saw that the blue in his dreams had not leaked out of his subconscious and onto the ink of his texts. Life, again, was normal.

Unfortunately, there was a price to pay for that too. With normalcy came all the usual trappings and the usual stress. Once again, being an author was a pipe dream, and his creative stores were as dry as the ink in which he'd recorded his quotes and partial manuscripts. Work was worse than ever. Langton had returned from his vacation more obnoxious, more overbearing, and more rotund than ever. Nelson had confided in Jonah that the day he steered him from Jessica, he had done so in an attempt to deprive her of the ammunition he would surely have provided for her snitching and gossip. While that had been a very kind thing for his friend to do, he needn't have bothered. Not only had Jessica informed Langton of Jonah's "blue" question and the time miscommunication, she'd also, from what Jonah had heard from tidbits at the water cooler, twisted it to make it seem like he spouted weird things like that the entire time Langton had been gone. What followed were two private conversations with Langton where Jonah diligently tried to undo the damage Jessica had caused, but to his frustration, it seemed to sound like further ramblings. Now Langton kept an even closer eye on him, aided by his faithful office spies, most notably Anthony and Jessica. Anthony was easy enough to blow off as he was only present when he wasn't doing some degrading, dignity-sacrificing deed that furthered his status as Jessica's unrequited love slave, but Jessica herself put Jonah in a real bind. If he said something to her, it would immediately be taken to Langton and twisted, but if he ignored her, then he would hear some trash from Langton about him being *eremitic* (Jonah was certain that Langton heard that term on his vacation and had waited for a situation to use it).

"You need to leave this place behind, Jonah," said Nelson seriously one day as they finished lunch. "Yes, I've said it. You should quit."

Jonah took a sip of soda. "And go where?"

"I don't know! Somewhere!" said Nelson unhelpfully. "You don't belong here, Jonah."

Jonah raised his eyebrows indignantly, which prompted Nelson to wave a hand.

"You know what I mean, Jonah. Don't even *try* thinking that way. You have more sense than just about anybody in the office, me included."

"That's not true—" Jonah began, but Nelson chuckled and lifted a hand.

"I'm fine with it. You just could stand to do better. Your writing—"

"Is a work in progress, with a hundred percent work and zero percent progress," interrupted Jonah. "Nelson, I would love to write. Nothing would make me happier than to have people around the world sitting and contemplating the meaning of something I wrote. I don't know why I can't finish my works. I don't know why I keep losing steam. You know, my grandmother used to always say I had a spark. Seems like that spark only has a half-life."

Nelson nodded. Jonah was so appreciative of that. Nelson would never try to diminish or belittle his grievances. It was such a refreshing change from some of the other people he knew.

"Don't think I don't hear you, Nelson," he said. "I appreciate the praise. But my writing isn't working out, and my degree is in this field. I'm not qualified to do anything else. I'm ashamed to say I'm stuck."

Nelson stood, having finished his food. "I disagree," he said. "Your major is not a limitation, and you are not stuck. The door to opportunity is never locked, friend. It might be jammed and warped sometimes, sure, but never locked. You've just got to put some extra force behind your foot when you kick it down."

Jonah raised an eyebrow. "If that's how you feel, then why are *you* here?"

Nelson laughed. "I, unlike you, enjoy this field," he said. "It's the people that mar it for me. If Langton retired, Jessica shut up, and Tony caught a clue, I'd have the greatest job in the world."

Six p.m. took two years to come, as usual, but Jonah had finally made it to his apartment and was excited about the night. It was Friday evening, which meant the next two days were unencumbered by work. He pulled his keys from his pocket at the exact moment the woman from 7D stepped out of her door. This was actually the first time Jonah had ever seen her out of athletic wear, but the snug black dress and high heels that she sported served to accentuate the results of her devotion to fitness. He momentarily forgot his apartment number, wandered past his door, and inadvertently tried to jam his key into 7B. She looked at him curiously, which made him feel even dumber. The last thing he needed to do now was stammer like a dolt.

"You look beautiful," he said, trying for doing damage control. "Got a good night planned?"

To Jonah's relief, she grinned. "Thanks for the compliment," she told him, "but no, I have no plans, per se. I'm calling the night by ear; that's the best way!"

Jonah frowned slightly. "Not to pry or anything, but you get dolled up and go out just to *see* what will happen? And you aren't ever disappointed?"

"Not ever!" she gushed. "It's Friday night! Evening's going to be laced with fun because of that fact alone! I simply go where the night takes me. You never know what wonders you'll find! 'Night!"

Jonah returned the friendly smile and wished her a fun night. While it sounded way too spontaneous for his taste, mentally and financially, his fun night of pizza and Netflix suddenly didn't seem so fun anymore. He stepped into his apartment and flopped onto his sofa, deflated. He wasn't even excited about his pizza coupons anymore. Friday was here, the time to relax. But after the brief interaction he'd just had, his weekend no longer felt like he had been passed a torch. He now felt like he had been passed a wet match.

Why didn't he go out himself? He had never ever been one of the "night-lifers," as he had termed them. He felt like partying and club-hopping only led to trouble, and he wasn't a big fan of drinking as he not only had encountered several recovering alcoholics throughout his life but didn't find the thought of getting smashed all that fun. The notion of waking up one morning and being unable to remember the previous night just didn't appeal.

Jonah thought about sitting there, cooped up and bored out of his mind. Was there any fun to be had in another Friday night of Netflix and pizza? After the shows were watched and the pizza eaten, what would there be to do then?

Jonah glanced at the table and saw those half-finished books. That was enough to cement his decision. He grabbed his keys off of the table and headed out of his front door.

You never know what wonders you'll find. That's what the woman from 7D had said.

Against his better judgment, he decided to see for himself.

Jonah had driven for about ten minutes before he doubted his decision. He didn't know what he'd expected. No magic light popped on in his head, and no magic bells dinged.

Night life made no sense.

How did it work? Sure, he saw dozens upon dozens of people out and about, but he didn't understand the allure. Where was the so-called "fun?" The "hot-spots," as they sometimes referred to it on TV? None of this scene mattered to him. He had no clue how to carry himself. It seemed that most of the party people were more stupid than adventurous. Then he passed one particular club and spotted Jessica. She was all smiles in a dress so tight that it looked like she had painted it on. He could see that she was the nucleus of a little clique of women that had no trouble getting inside. The bouncer flat-out ignored almost a dozen people to let Jessica and her cronies in the door.

Jonah shook his head and made up his mind. Any situation where Jessica Hale was right at home was a situation he wanted no part of.

As he circled the block to double back, he caught a wonderful smell. It was the bakery. Big's Bakery, to be exact. He usually passed it most mornings when he went to work. While he had smelled some wonderful things there, he had to admit he hadn't smelled any scent as wonderful and nostalgic as this one.

It was gingerbread. Almost identical to his grandmother's.

Jonah's grandmother had baked gingerbread for as long as he could remember. While most other people's culinary results were hit and miss, his grandmother's gingerbread tasted the exact same way each time, sometimes even better when she drizzled vanilla icing on it. Gingerbread marked some of the most wonderful memories of his childhood.

Then Nana passed away. No one else's dessert measured up after that.

"You must be saying 'hi,' Nana," he mumbled.

He pulled over. Yeah, it would bring up memories that would probably sadden him, but hey, it would be delicious nonetheless. It certainly smelled as such.

He never got there.

The minute Jonah slammed his car door, lost in thought, time stopped. It literally *stopped.*

Then Jonah got bashed from behind. The force of the blow actually sent him over his car. He crashed into several bags of garbage, which scattered about a dozen stray cats.

Numb with pain and shock, he looked up. A man was gleefully standing over him. He had unkempt hair and an extremely pale face with a bulging, overset jaw. His companion, who matched him in height, had sunken eyes, a large nose, misshapen teeth, and a scruffy, uneven beard. To Jonah, these guys looked like unassuming bums. But there was nothing unassuming about his back pain.

"Yes!" shouted the gray-eyed one. "I'm tangible again! See what loyalty yields? I requested it, and it has been given!"

"Don't get cocky, Walt," said the scruffy one. "The tangibility will wear off. You know that. It is only replenished if we succeed. We still have a job to do."

Walt scoffed. "Killing this miscreant will be easy," he snarled. "Prepare to be tangible for a good long time, Howard."

"I don't know," said the other guy, uncertainty in his voice. "We know about that blue thing; we might need to be careful with this one—"

"Howard, shut up," rasped the one named Walt. "He just did a one-eighty over the car, and that was after just one hit. We've got this one in the bag."

Jonah didn't register half of this conversation as he attempted to sit up. "W-Who are you?" he managed.

"Do your ears work, boy?" snarled the paler man. "I'm Walt, and this is Howard. Our master needed a favor done in return for tangibility. He promised us a year's worth if we took you out!"

"Tan-tangibility?" croaked Jonah.

Walt's gray eyes flashed. "Yes, tangibility. We're spirits."

Shock might have registered in Jonah's body if his back wasn't killing him.

"But you would know all about us," said Howard, "seeing as how you've been vanquishing us with lights and wind."

He turned to Walt. "Are you *sure* it's him?"

Walt's face screwed up in concentration, and Jonah's back pain was offset by a splitting agony at the back of his skull. It hurt with such intensity that he nearly vomited.

"Yeah, it's him," said Walt. "The Mindscope confirmed it. They've been asking for his help through his dreams. The spectral trail is pretty strong."

Howard moved forward. "I get it. He was shielded! After he saved that wretched cat!"

"Yes, he was shielded," said Walt, staring at Jonah as if he was a particularly irksome stain on some surface. "Pretty well too. Don't think we would have found him tonight if he hadn't exhibited such foolhardiness."

Jonah didn't have a moment to prepare before Howard belted him in the gut with his foot. This third point of pain was so strong that Jonah swore again, prompting Walt to smack him across the face.

"Watch your mouth, boy," he scolded. "Do you think that grand-mother that you were just thinking about would approve of such language?"

"H-how did you know—?"

"Walt, this one's an idiot," said Howard. "We will give you some valuable information to take to the grave."

Walt laughed mirthlessly and then turned back to Jonah. "The living haunt the dead, fool," he said. "When a living soul thinks at length about a departed soul, those thoughts trigger links to that person. Thoughts and memories are very powerful things."

Jonah didn't understand any of what he was hearing. Perhaps, if his mind wasn't so clouded by pain, he might have processed some of it.

"We were put on your trail by our master when that spiritess asked you to unblock the path," said Walt, striking Jonah again for good measure. "Then you vanquished Lev with your little theatrics. We would have gone for you then, but that fool shielded you and we lost contact."

"How did you find me now?" groaned Jonah.

For some reason, this earned him another strike to the head. That crazy caffeine rush he'd gotten the other night when he encountered that other spirit would be very welcomed right about now.

"We found you because you are a typical, melodramatic, living being," said Walt. "You living souls can never let folks go. We waited for you to wallow in sad memories about some dearly departed loved one. It was only a matter of time. Your essence is raw, so it was a simple matter. And we were right, weren't we? You went brooding over your grandmother, summoning us to you with your memories. You summoned, and we followed."

Jonah's mind tried working through the pain. There was that thing about "raw essence" again. Thinking of Nana attracted spectral killers? What sense did that make?

"Wouldn't have ever dreamed you would wander out into the night with raw essence," continued Walt. "Didn't the one who shielded you teach you *anything?*"

Jonah managed to rise to his knees. Something told him that if he stood to his feet, he would collapse and worsen his physical state even more.

"I don't know anyone," he told them. "I didn't even know I was ... shielded. I don't know what it means to even *be* shielded."

Howard shrugged indifferently. "Hate to kill such an ignorant one," he said, "but we are simply following orders. Goodbye, boy."

He raised his hand, but something made him freeze. He and Walt both stared at a point behind Jonah and loosed synchronous exclamations. Howard completely forgot about Jonah and lunged somewhere beyond him. A sharp wind swept through the entire area, which made Howard sail high into the air, for which Jonah was grateful. What he was *not* grateful for was the wind blowing the rancid smell of the trash bags.

"NO!" shrieked Walt. He seized Jonah by the throat. Jonah attempted to fight him off, but the spirit would not be denied. If only that man were around to say that *You have been endowed* thing again!

"You can vanquish me! It doesn't matter!" shouted Walt. "But it won't change anything! I will still kill this one!"

Jonah realized the spirit's plan a moment too late. Walt shoved him into the path of an oncoming van.

The seconds seemed eternal. Was this how his miserable life was going to end?

Then, once again, time stopped. The regal-looking man appeared and clutched Jonah tightly.

"It's not your time, Jonah Rowe," he said.

Amidst the haze of movement and sound, Jonah blacked out.

4

The Eleventh Percent

Consciousness suddenly gripped Jonah's body. But he didn't open his eyes. He was leery of what he would see if he did.

His last memory was the ambush by two brutes who claimed to be spirits. But there hadn't been anything ghostly about their hands and feet. He could still feel the proof of that in his upper body. And then there was something about being shielded and finding him when he thought about his grandmother...

Then he got slapped by some wind that had blown one of the spirits away, and then the other spirit had thrown him into the path of a van. Then that weird man appeared and grabbed him. After that, things went black.

Was he dead? Had that guy who'd grabbed him been Death itself, selfishly clamping him into an eternal grasp?

No. That couldn't be. He'd always heard that in death, all pain was taken away. But that wasn't the case, because he still felt dull agony in his back and gut. While he was thankful for that particular fact, it did very little to decrease his anxiety.

If he was still among the living, then what had happened? That van had definitely been coming full speed ahead, yet he was here, not re-calling anything past that point.

Was this some kind of limbo? Some kind of stage between living and dying, where you were departed but pain and feeling were still present?

A meow pierced the silence, finally forcing his eyes open. But before he looked for the cat that made the sound, he took in his surroundings.

He no longer thought he was in a death-like limbo. Because if that were the case, he doubted it would be in a bedroom.

It was spacious and modestly furnished. There seemed to be more of the room than the furniture that occupied it. The walls were a soothing bluish white. An old-fashioned rocking chair was in the corner, which had a dusty, forgotten look about it. A chest of drawers was nearby, and next to his bed were a nightstand and lamp. He could see the morning sun through the lone window.

The windowsill was occupied by the familiar calico, which was perched there like she was standing guard. Though her gaze was penetrating and rather eerie, she made no move at all. She simply meowed again and lowered her head.

The space next to the cat shimmered and darkened. The dark mass quickly formed the silhouette of a tall man, who then gained corporeal form, flesh, and clothing. The visage completed itself, forming the man that Jonah had seen three times now. Even though the man had saved him, Jonah was not very thrilled to see him again. His presence always seemed to precede some sort of trouble.

At first, the man paid Jonah no attention. He took the time to remove a necklace from his pocket and put it on. It was an interesting piece, with what looked to be an intricate figure eight with a line crossing the point where the two rings joined. Once he was finished, he turned his grey eyes to Jonah.

"It's nice to see you awake and largely unscathed, Jonah," he said.

Jonah wasn't about to let what had just occurred go unnoticed. "How did—how did you do that?"

The man looked down at his hands. "A more apt question would be how long can I stay," he said.

When Jonah raised an eyebrow, the man said, "As you have likely surmised by now, Jonah, I am a spirit. As such, forming in the daytime can be very draining. It takes energy, essence, and concentration, and while I am willing, my reserves are greatly spent due to the stunt I was forced to pull last night for you."

Jonah stood. Though the pain in his upper torso was dull, it was still annoying. He was surprised to discover that there were snug bandages under the loose-fitting T-shirt that he was now wearing. The same was true about his left wrist. Even though these discoveries were welcome, he was still focused on the spirit.

By the man's tone, Jonah assumed that he was in for a rebuke for not staying holed up in his apartment like he was instructed to. He was not going to stand there and just take it, either.

"Look, sir—"

"Jonathan," the man interrupted. "My name is Jonathan."

"Okay then, Jonathan," said Jonah with impatience. "Sorry, but I'm not a child to be scolded and controlled. You told me to stay home, but you didn't explain why. If there is one thing you need to know about me, it's that I hate to be told to do something without an explanation of why I need to do it. And I can't just hide in my apartment anyway. I have a job. I have a life. As far as the 'stunt' you pulled last night, I didn't ask you to save me. I'm grateful and everything, but I didn't ask you to."

Jonathan regarded him thoughtfully. "Actually, I *did* tell you why you needed to remain in your home," he said. "I told you that the essence was raw."

"What does that even mean?" demanded Jonah. The man was at least five inches taller, but he wasn't intimidated. He did try for some dignity, however, and drew himself up to his fullest height only to be rewarded for it by aggravating his sore body parts. "You make me sound like—like a piece of uncooked chicken, or something, the essence is raw—"

"What it means, son," interrupted Jonathan in a calm but firm voice, "is that your essence is new to the exposure of the true world. Like a brand new baby who does not yet know how to exercise caution, as an adult does. Or like a young venomous snake that, unlike its mother, has not yet learned to control its stores of poison and will attack you releasing its full sac. Your essence is raw, meaning you were vulnerable in ways you couldn't possibly imagine. As for your job, I wasn't expecting you to hunker down during the day. Spirit activity is limited in the daytime because energy stores are greatly depleted in the presence of UV light. But at night, all bets are off."

"I still don't understand," said Jonah. "What is this all about?"

Jonathan sighed and sat in the ancient rocker. "Yes, you deserve to understand, Jonah," he said. "Do sit down. Rest those injured muscles I'm sure you just aggravated."

Not pausing to wonder how Jonathan knew that, Jonah obliged.

Jonathan took a deep breath. "Tell me, have you ever heard of the notion that humans only use ten percent of their brain?"

Jonah frowned. How was talking about *that* going to lead to explanations? "Yeah, I've heard that. Do you have proof of it or something?"

"It would be a sad world if we only believed in the things that could be proven," said Jonathan, "but in this particular case, the notion *can* be backed by proof."

Jonah looked at Jonathan, confused.

"There are those in the world," Jonathan continued, "that are not constrained by the limitations of only using ten percent of their mind, body, and consciousness. There are those who are wildly perceptive, cannot compartmentalize themselves into what society deems as 'normal,' and are highly intuitive and observant. They are also able to ascertain aspects of spiritual nature, determine connections between various facets of life, and interact with individuals belonging to what has been termed the 'spiritual realm.' This is because they have access to further portions of their minds. They have access to the *eleventh* percent. They are ethereal human beings, or simply put, Eleventh Percenters. I was an Eleventh Percenter when I was of the flesh. And you, Jonah Rowe, are one as well."

Jonah stared at him. He felt like he was on a television sitcom where someone said something ridiculous, and then you heard the laugh track. Only there were no laugh tracks here. Just silence.

"Are you sure I'm who you're looking for?" he asked Jonathan. If this were indeed true, it would make some things in his life make sense, but he certainly wasn't going to latch onto the first explanation that showed itself. "You sure you've got the right guy?"

Jonathan merely smiled. "Jonah, I will answer your question with some questions of my own. Tell me, are you always noticing details others are blind to, yet you have no investigative training to speak of?"

Oh man, Jonah thought. How many times had he seen a downright mistake, and everyone else wrote him off as simply "thinking stupidly?"

Something in his face must have shown confirmation because Jonathan continued. "Have you always been rather inquisitive, asking questions about things that others simply prefer to take as law?"

Jonah nodded slowly. Who was this guy?

"Now answer this one," said Jonathan, who seemed to be enjoying himself. "Are you in the field of mental health or the corporate realm?"

Jonah straightened. "Have you been following my life, or something?"

Jonathan laughed. "Son, I didn't even know you existed until several weeks ago."

Jonah relaxed, if only slightly. "I briefly majored in Social Work in undergrad," he said, "but for reasons I will never understand, switched to accounting."

Jonathan nodded, almost as if he expected Jonah to say something like that. "And how often do your work days feel like you are simply going through the motions?"

Jonah didn't answer. Something told him that he didn't even have to.

"Final question, for now, at least," said Jonathan. "Departed people. Is there something that just refuses to let you believe that they are truly gone? I do not mean the notion that they are 'always with you.'

I mean you just have no doubt whatsoever that they are close? No doubt in your mind at all?"

Abandoning all pretenses, Jonah rose from his sitting position once again, soreness and all, and stepped away from Jonathan. "You're a stalker," he said. "You *have* been following my life."

"Not at all, son," said Jonathan, smiling again. "As I've mentioned, I was unaware of your existence until several weeks ago."

"Then how do you know all these things about me?"

Jonathan's expression became solemn, as if he were about to dole out some bad news. "I know them," he said, "because they are all irrefutable signs that you are one of us. Please sit back down. There is more to explain, and I will likely be forced to fade soon."

Jonah raised an eyebrow. "I thought you said you were done."

"I said I was done with asking you questions. Please sit down."

Jonah heard him say something about fading soon but decided not to mention it. He sat down once more.

"You, Jonah Rowe, are a special case," said Jonathan. "Some Eleventh Percenters have their true abilities permeating their consciousness in some way, shape, or form all of their lives. But yours were buried down deep. You almost resembled a Tenth Percenter."

"Tenth Percenter?"

"It's the term for non-ethereal humans. People that don't have access beyond ten percent of their minds."

"Okay," said Jonah, feeling apprehensive, "if I resembled a regular person, or whatever, what made you think otherwise?"

"Bast," said Jonathan, smiling fondly at the calico as he beckoned her forward. "Spirits and felines have a very close relationship. In many ways, we can help each other endure. Since cats are highly spiritual animals themselves, we can use them as heralds to lead us to Eleventh Percenters."

"How does that apply—" began Jonah, but Jonathan raised a hand. Evidently, he didn't like being interrupted when he was on a roll.

"Bast is my herald," he continued. "One of many heralds. She is clever and resourceful and has been a formidable ally for a very long time. I search for Eleventh Percenters, and she scouts for me, noticing nuances I do not."

"What *nuances* did she notice with me?" asked Jonah.

"She happened across you one day, and was most intrigued by your spirit," explained Jonathan. Seeing Jonah's puzzled expression, he elaborated, "You see, Eleventh Percenters' spirits are sharper and more distinct than Tenths. According to Bast, your spirit was on an almost astronomical level in strength and power. She alerted me, but I must admit that I was not fully convinced until I saw you for myself. So action was necessary, although it was not my intention to startle you. Your essence was so deep that I had to kick start it."

Immediately, Jonah put two and two together. "That was you? *You* were the one that turned the world blue?"

For some reason, Jonathan eyed Jonah appraisingly and then smiled, as if he approved of what he saw. "No," he said. "I had nothing to do with the color that you saw, but I did open the door to the buried aspects of your consciousness. I apologize for the shock this caused, as well as," he made an annoyed face, "Marla."

"Who?"

"The spiritess who appeared to you like a moth to a flame and begged for your help," said Jonathan. "She has been on Earthplane for several decades. Spirits and spiritesses aren't usually so irksome, but she is ready to cross on."

"So why doesn't she?" asked Jonah. "Is 'going into the light' real? The Other Side and all that? Why doesn't she go?"

Jonathan's face darkened, but he recovered quickly. "Other spirits are cautious, but she saw fit to reveal herself," he said, seemingly skirting the question. "In doing so, she put you at a terrible risk. That's why I told you to go on home and stay there. I had to protect you from her blunder because she exposed you."

"Exposed me?" said Jonah. "To what, exactly?"

Jonathan's face darkened again. "A problem. You will learn more about him in time, but I'd rather not bombard you with every bit of information right this second. Anyway, you started trying to rationalize what had happened to you, writing it off as a dream or a random occurrence. I couldn't allow that to happen because what you resist will persist, hundredfold. When an Eleventh Percenter fights their consciousness in raw essence, that is, when they are new to their essence and it is displayed on the Astral Plane, it brings attention. The *worst* kind of attention. It's tantamount to swimming amongst sharks with multiple incisions in your flesh."

Jonah didn't like where this was going. It seemed as though the more of the path that Jonathan illuminated, the more he could figure out on his own. And the path that he was figuring out did not appear to be leading to a likable destination. "You were the one who colored the passages in my stories blue," he said slowly.

Jonathan nodded. "I had to prevent you from denying who you were because, by that time, the enemy was on to you, and their hunting of you would only intensify. But you were stubborn. A minion attempted to attack you that same night, but Bast, who has taken a liking to you, had been watching. Due to her potential exposure of him, he attempted to kill her. You can recall the events of that night as well as I, so there is no need to relive them."

Jonah had the feeling that Jonathan wanted to end this as soon as he could, but his curiosity had not yet been abated.

"What was that all about?" he asked. "How did that work, the whole powers thing? And why did I get so tired?"

"Once again, all will be explained to you later, when there is more time for you to rest and have more mental clarity," said Jonathan. "Back to what I was saying. Your display of power was most impressive, albeit instinctual. But if you weren't exposed before, you *definitely* were then, having just vanquished that spirit. So I shielded you as best I could."

Jonah's eyes narrowed here. He remembered those murderous spirits from the previous night saying he'd been "shielded" well. "So they were right when they said I was shielded. What does that mean?"

"It means you were blanketed with portions of astral light," said Jonathan. "Shielding is equal mixtures of essence for protection and essence to repel. I encased you as heavily as I could. I didn't presume to hide you forever. It was just until your essence matured somewhat. So for a small bit of time, nothing harmful happened."

Jonah thought of that two-week period of quiet that passed. "Back up. The day after I—vanquished, did you say? Vanquished that spirit, I slept like I'd never slept before. I woke up two hours late for work, but then everything went back to 8 a.m. Was that you too?"

Jonathan seemed pleased that Jonah figured that out on his own. "I deemed it necessary to help you. Bast had been watching and informed me of the toxic and uncouth people that surrounded you at your place of employment. As it was my fault you were so fatigued, I assisted you."

"You manipulated *time*?"

"Ah, time," said Jonathan. "So vastly misunderstood and so easily manipulated. One could fill numerous books on how to use and abuse time. But that is another story."

Another story I'd be interested in hearing, thought Jonah, who made a mental note to make further inquiries at a later point.

"I didn't factor in the spirits and spiritesses showing you their plights in your dreams, no doubt prompted by Marla to do so," said Jonathan. "This would not bode well for you in the event of a Mindscope."

"Which is what?"

"Think spiritual fingerprints, and a Mindscope is the tool used to dust for them," said Jonathan. "You left your home last night and thought mournfully about the loss of your grandmother. In so doing, they found you."

That still troubled Jonah. "The spirit last night, Howard, or whoever—said they found me because the 'living haunt the departed' or something—"

Jonathan raised an eyebrow. "He said that? Hmm. I suppose even a broken clock is right twice a day."

"How did thinking of Nana alert them?" persisted Jonah.

"Spiritual bonds, Jonah," replied Jonathan. "We form bonds with family members, romantic lovers, and closest friends. The bonds that are formed do not break, even when a spirit departs from the flesh. If there is positive essence, there is a bond, even if the essence itself has long since ceased. Bonds are strengthened by thoughts. Thoughts, hopes, love, dreams, goals ... these things are not just ideals or perspectives. They are living things. Remember that, Jonah. When a person lingers over a spirit, it sparks and illuminates the bond. Your essence was raw, therefore shielding didn't matter. Once your sad thoughts sparked the bond between you and your grandmother, any spirit bothering to watch only needed to follow the trail."

Jonah let that sink in. He had always heard that grief could lead to harmful situations, but he had no idea...

"Do not misunderstand," said Jonathan as if he'd read Jonah's mind. "By no means does that mean you can never think of your grandmother again. It's just that last night, in the open, in raw essence, your unresolved grief betrayed you, which led to me rescuing you and bringing you here."

"Now that you mention it," said Jonah, looking around, "where *is* here?"

"This is the Grannison-Morris estate," said Jonathan. "It's about three hours from your city. Don't worry; you're still in North Carolina, in a nice little town named Rome. This estate's been on these grounds about two centuries, give or take, and it came into my ownership when I was in the flesh. It serves as a home for Eleventh Percenters."

"I really hope you don't expect me to stay here—" began Jonah, but Jonathan smiled and waved a hand.

"Calm down," he said. "Any Eleventh Percenter wishing to reside here is welcome, but many do not. Some spend summers and winters here, others do not come very often, but we can expect pop-ups on random weekends and holidays. As it stands, not too many people reside here presently. You will see six people here now; everyone else is scattered all over, living their lives. This is a place where Eleventh

Percenters can convene for rest and collect their thoughts. It is also a safe haven in the event of crisis or spiritual upheaval."

Spiritual upheaval ... Jonah didn't understand what that meant. It sounded like a tagline for a church revival or something. "So there are people downstairs?" he asked.

"Oh yes," said Jonathan. "Four residents, plus two young Eleventh Percenters who find the estate much more conveniently positioned than their homes, as they are undergraduates who had no interest in dormitory life."

Jonah nodded, but there was something in Jonathan's voice that seemed evasive, as if a crisis was on the horizon. He silently prayed that it wasn't one of the aforementioned spiritual upheavals.

"We have spoken a great deal, Jonah, but I must go to the Astral Plane to regain my strength," said Jonathan. "I would like you to stay here for the next few days as Monday is Labor Day, and you won't have work."

In light of what had been happening, Jonah had completely forgotten that it was a holiday weekend.

"Get acquainted with your new friends," continued Jonathan, "and I might advise you to put in some time on one of the treadmills on the ground floor."

"Why, exactly, would you advise that?" asked Jonah, who remembered Langton's criticisms and was instantly on guard.

Jonathan moved to the window, where his image began to fade in the sun's rays. "Well," he said in a knowing tone, "I have a feeling that good cardiovascular health will become your best friend."

Jonah pulled another T-shirt over the one he was already wearing (the room carried an odd chill) and exited the bedroom intending to discover just what he'd gotten himself into. He'd never even *heard* of Rome, North Carolina. The moment he stepped outside of the door, however, he was greeted with an interesting sight.

A man, who appeared to be very large and bulky, had propped a chair next to his door. He must have been waiting for a while because he had fallen asleep and was in danger of keeling out of the chair. All Jonah could make out from the bent, slumbering form was cropped brown hair. Thinking of the shock this man would sustain if he toppled out of the rickety-looking chair, Jonah nudged him.

"Um, excuse me? Hello?"

The man started and glared at him with bloodshot eyes for a second, and then his gaze softened.

"Oh yeah," he said, shaking off the remaining drowsiness and standing up. The man looked to be around Jonah's age, was maybe two inches north of six feet, and had a very friendly expression. Now that he was standing, Jonah saw that he was not as huge and bulky as he first thought; the bulk was attributed to the oversized hooded sweatshirt he was wearing.

"I think I saved you from disaster," said Jonah, amused. "You were about to fall out of that chair, and I would hate for you to have been injured during our first meeting."

"Greatly appreciate it," said the man, extending his hand. "I'm Terrence Aldercy."

"Jonah Rowe." Jonah shook his hand. "Did you say Aldercy? I swear that name sounds familiar."

"No, it doesn't," said Terrence, his voice sharp.

Jonah was taken aback, but then Terrence waved a hand.

"It's just one of those names is all."

Jonah was not convinced of that, but seeing as this was the first person he'd met, he wasn't trying for a confrontation. "So I take it you had a reason for camping out next to the door?" he asked.

"Yeah, I did," said Terrence like he was about to reveal some type of earth-shattering secret. He looked in the direction of the oak staircase for a moment, seemed to determine the coast was clear, and then reached into the pocket of his sweatshirt and pulled out a brown bag, blotched with unmistakable grease stains that made the contents within partially visible. "I wanted to save you."

Jonah took the bag, curious. "Save me from what, exactly?"

Terrence extracted his own bag from the opposite pocket, unwrapped a breakfast sandwich, and bit into it. "From the meatless hell of a breakfast you were about to experience."

When Jonah still looked curious, Terrence swallowed and continued. "I'm actually a resident here," he explained. "Many Eleventh Percenters use this estate as a hub or a stopover or stay here for the summer. But I actually reside here long-term. I enjoy it, but I share with a few other permanent residents. One of them, Reena Katoa, is who I'm saving you from."

He indicated a folding chair he'd brought along, and Jonah unfolded it and sat down opposite him.

"You're saving me from this Reena person by giving me," he inspected the contents of the bag more thoroughly, "a sausage biscuit and a side of hash browns?"

"Damn right I am," said Terrence, taking another bite of his own portion. "Don't get me wrong; Reena's awesome. Smart as a whip and paints like Van Gogh. But she is a health nut and a calorie counter in the worst way. If she had her way, she'd probably hogtie us and force feed us lentils three times a day. She is anti-sugar, anti-wheat, anti-fried foods, anti-'processed' snacks, and anti—well, anti-everything in this world that's delicious. I wanted to save you from having to stomach that on your very first day here."

Suddenly, Jonah didn't find Terrence's behavior curious at all. Now he was extremely grateful. As brand new and jarring as all these experiences were, Jonah thought he could think and process more clearly if he had a full stomach. If this Reena woman was as militant as Terrence made her out to be, he didn't want to take the chance of having to get used to new people with a gut full of legumes.

"Thank you," he said to Terrence. "I'm glad you thought enough of me to save me."

"Don't mention it," chuckled Terrence, and the next few minutes passed in silence while they ate the hearty breakfasts.

"You said you are one of the ones who stay here permanently," said Jonah. "Where is your family?"

Some of the mirth faded from Terrence's face. "I was born in New York City—" he began but paused when he saw Jonah's frown. "What?"

"Um, Terrence, no offense," said Jonah, "but listening to you for the past couple minutes ... you have the heaviest drawl I have ever heard in my life. And you're saying you're a New Yorker?"

"I wouldn't have a New York accent, Jonah," said Terrence, "seeing as I wasn't there all that long. I was given up for adoption when I was one. Or two ... I don't really know."

"Really?"

"You think I'd make something like that up?" asked Terrence.

"Nah, I guess not," murmured Jonah. "So you don't know anything about your parents?"

"Just that my mom was black and my dad was Italian," said Terrence with a half-shrug. "But never mind them. They dumped me off, and I was adopted shortly after that. The family that adopted me ... well, they were all Tenth Percenters."

Jonah regarded him. "So when you started experiencing the spirit stuff ... sorry, the *ethereal* stuff—"

"I was told that it was my imagination and that it would stop if I ignored it," grumbled Terrence. "As I got older, of course it didn't stop, and my adoptive parents got really, *really* nasty about it. They started comparing me to their wonderful son. That became their favorite hobby. He was so talented, so well-rounded, so great, so ... normal, if we're calling a spade a spade. He had a knack for football, and they began pushing me to do the same."

Terrence took another bite of his sandwich, took his precious time chewing it, and then continued, "I ain't an athlete, Jonah. I'm a cook. From the minute that I could boil water, cooking is all I've ever wanted to do. I suppose that's where my creativity comes into play; I can cook like nobody's business. I just love it. I enjoy *watching* football and play the occasional backyard game, but I never did more than that. My 'parents' reminded me every day that that was a mistake and how 'unmanly' cooking was. Even when I took up weights, it wasn't enough for them. When I turned thirteen, they decided I wasn't worth their time because I believed in spirits and was nothing like their son, and they kicked me out."

Jonah nearly dropped his food. "Kicked you out? At *thirteen?*"

"Uh-huh," said Terrence with such indifference that Jonah could only surmise that he'd already given it so much emotion over the years that he simply had no more to give. Or had simply buried it. "So there I am, thirteen, homeless, and still confused as hell about why I can talk to spirits and all that. I even got attacked by one or two Spirit Reapers; of course, I didn't know that was what they were at the time, but I guess I did okay ... Well, anyway, my wandering got me here to Rome, near the town square one day. This kid's throwing a football around with his brother. The older one got a little zealous with his pass and the younger one gave chase, not realizing that he'd just run into the street in the path of a bus."

Jonah felt a pang of fear even though Terrence was speaking calmly.

"I ran out in front of that bus and saved that kid," he told Jonah. "He and his brother were so grateful that they took an instant liking to me and convinced me to come home with them."

Jonah was surprised and intrigued. "Huh. That was awfully nice of them to go the extra mile for you. They could've simply thanked you and been done with it."

Terrence nodded. "They took me to their house, to their parents and two older brothers, who were all suspicious of me, which was understandable. Then their father, on a hunch, I guess, asks me if I can see spirits. I asked him how he knew, but instead of answering, he explained the Eleventh Percent to me and revealed that their whole family was just like me."

Jonah raised an eyebrow. "You won these people over that easily?" he asked.

"Hell no, I didn't win them over that easily!" snorted Terrence. "The two kids were Alvin and Bobby, and they were my friends immediately. But their parents and older brothers ... that took some time. Eventually, though, I earned their respect and then their acceptance. Now they call me son."

Jonah looked at his new friend with newfound respect. If he'd taken Terrence at face value, he'd have thought that he'd grown up as a typical jock with nary a care in the world, surrounded by admirers and sycophantic girls. Those who assume...

"So I'm guessing they were how you met Jonathan and wound up being a resident here," he said. "The people that took you in ... did Jonathan help them in the past too?"

"Oh yeah," said Terrence, "and they've all been great to me. Told me not to deny my spiritual encounters as fighting it would only make me more vulnerable. Helped me train so that I didn't see spirits and spiritesses all the time. I lived with them four, five years, then moved here. The kid that I saved, Bobby, lives here too because he didn't want to live in the dorm at his college. Even though I'm a resident here, I go back to that house all the time. I'm one of their sons just like Bobby, Alvin, and the older brothers, Ray and Sterling. On Mother's Day, their mom, Connie, is who I give cards to. I'd do anything for them, and of course, for people here."

Jonah nodded. He'd gotten more than he bargained for by asking Terrence about his family, but that was fine. Now he felt like he'd known him for years, which was always a good sign.

He crumpled the hash brown bag, which was now empty.

"So there are—what, six, seven people here?" Jonah asked, changing the subject. "Jonathan said this was an estate, like one of those huge manors, or something."

"Oh, it is," said Terrence, shaking crumbs from his sweatshirt. "Humongous place. It's just that some Elevenths Percenters don't want to live here all the time. It's not like they're all from N.C. Many don't mind staying here for weeks at a time, but they don't want to be away from family year round. Doesn't faze me either way. I like company sometimes, but I like quiet too."

"So who else is here right now?" asked Jonah.

"You, me, Reena, and Trip," rattled off Terrence. "I already told you about Bobby being here, and there are two other people, Malcolm and

Liz. They're all sleeping in. It's a three-day weekend, so they can all afford some extra Zs."

He stood up. "Now that you are sated, are you ready to meet some folks?"

Jonah was not ready to be a new guy again. That was always the worst part. That was how it was in school, and things hadn't improved when he'd made it to adulthood either. But one thing that slightly dulled his resistance was the fact that there was no way six people could break into several different cliques and talk about people. Not usually, anyway. He stood himself. "Yeah, fine."

Jonah descended the stairs behind Terrence into a huge kitchen with a vast island counter that contained two bowls of fruit underneath a mass of silver and brass pots and pans that gleamed in the room's light. Jonah looked around, mystified. He had never seen a kitchen this size; it looked like it was ready to house a medium-sized athletic team. Only after taking in the entirety of the room did he realize that two other people were there.

A woman was at the sink, chopping vegetables and humming to the tune of whatever song was on her IPod, and a slender black man was at the wide kitchen table.

The lady at the sink was extremely focused as she chopped her vegetables. So *that* was Reena. It almost seemed like there was a maniacal glee in her slightly upturned eyes. Her features had a poised, authoritative look about them. Her black hair, which Jonah was interested to see was liberally streaked with scarlet highlights, was tied behind her head, presumably to keep it out of her face while she worked. Jonah noticed that she was built like a runner, lithe and lean, looking completely at home in baggy sweats and an overlong T-shirt. She took no notice of Jonah or Terrence, but that was likely because she was focused on her music and hadn't heard them enter.

The guy at the table was completely different. His bald head carried headphones as well, but they hung around his neck. His pointed face, unlike Reena's, had turned in Jonah's direction and was contemplating him with sourness and suspicion.

Jonah returned the glare, certainly not inclined to back down, especially when he didn't even know what the guy's problem was. The snide comment forming in his mind was curtailed by the woman, who had suddenly noticed that the kitchen's population had increased by two.

"Morning, man!" she said, giving Jonah a half grin. "I would greet you properly, but I want to finish chopping up these vegetables; I have to make my juice. Besides, I have no doubts Terrence has beaten me to offering you breakfast."

Jonah regarded Reena. Her voice was friendly enough but had sternness in it that Jonah couldn't help but notice. It was clear that she disapproved of Terrence's "rescue," but Jonah chose to ignore it. Since she greeted him warmly and didn't stare at him like he was a landfill by-product (like the guy at the table was), he was willing to give her a chance.

"Jonah, this is Ti—" began Terrence, but the guy cut him off.

"It's Trip." The man's tone was impatient, clipped, and frigid. He returned his attention to his laptop computer before anyone responded.

Jonah's eyes narrowed. "The hell with you too," he muttered. He glanced at Terrence, who seemed to be choking back some evil words of his own.

"Jonathan told us a bit about you last night," said Reena, who was seamlessly conversing and chopping vegetables. "He said to give you some information and fill you in on things somewhat before he had the strength to return."

"Is that right?" asked Jonah, who was not sure he wanted to sit down yet. Sitting down meant sharing the table with that Trip guy, and he wasn't so keen on that, and also, as the new arrival, he had to establish himself accordingly.

But just what the hell was he establishing?

"Don't really know why he said that," said Terrence. "But it's always interesting to have new blood."

Trip sniffed. "I don't see the need to convene just for a new guy," he said. "New Eleventh Percenters pop up all the time. What's the big deal about this one?"

Jonah felt his lip curl. He liked this guy less and less with every word he spoke.

Terrence glanced over at Trip, swallowed, and then switched gears. "So Jonathan had to kick start your aura's essence, huh?"

"Yeah," responded Jonah, still cutting an eye at Trip.

"Well, auras reveal themselves in various colors for Eleventh Percenters," said Terrence. "Each one is unique to them; tells something about their abilities. What was yours?"

Jonah answered him instantly. It was a color he wasn't forgetting anytime soon, after all. "Blue."

Reena dropped her knife. It fell with a clatter into the sink. Terrence blinked a few times as if Jonah had spoken in a foreign language. Even Trip, whose face had seemed to be immoveable from that scowl, showed surprise.

Jonah stared back at them, confused. "What? What did I say?"

No one answered for several seconds. Then Terrence broke the silence.

"Well, Trip, I think we've found your big deal," he said.

5

The Good Look

Jonah had hoped that Terrence, Reena, and Trip would explain their weird reactions, but it didn't happen. He was confused as ever, and it must have been evident on his face.

"Don't concern yourself with it, man," said Terrence with a grin. "I'm sure Jonathan will fill you in when he returns."

Jonah didn't return the smile. Those words didn't sit very well with him. He had had more than enough experience with being noticed for some reason or another. Having grown up in a relatively poor household, he had gotten quite accustomed to hearing mutterings about his clothing (most of which had been made by his grandmother), his generic shoes, and the way he walked with his head down, which had been a feeble attempt to ignore the not-so-subtle comments everyone made. Being the subject of gossip hadn't changed much as an adult either. The faces may have changed, but the behavior remained the same. Jessica and Anthony were merely the latest.

But Terrence and Reena didn't seem like people who were about to do that. Even that waspish fool Trip probably wouldn't be much of a problem. On top of that, Reena had regarded him kindly, and despite the greasy breakfast he'd had, had given him a "heart-healthy" omelet with goat cheese and bell peppers, which definitely made him think twice about any negativity. Why would she and Terrence bother feeding him if they didn't like him?

He sat as far away from Trip as possible and dug in. The goat cheese omelet was definitely an acquired taste, but it wasn't the worst thing he'd ever tasted. Given the events of the previous night, it turned out that even Terrence's breakfast hadn't been enough for him.

"There're still more folks for you to meet, Jonah," said Reena. "Bobby, Malcolm, and Liz will be more than happy to make your acquaintance once they've gotten out of bed."

Jonah glanced at a clock overlooking the stove and frowned. "It's eleven o'clock. Are they sick?"

"Oh not at all," answered Reena, who had seated herself next to him, carrying a bottle of freshly made vegetable juice and an omelet of her own. "Spiritual endowments take a great deal of energy. Once they are extracted, you can get bone-tired, sometimes even pass out. It gets easier the more you do it. They aren't sick, just needed some extra sleep."

She stood up suddenly, pushing her barely touched food to the side. "Come with me."

Jonah rose from the table a little too quickly and grimaced; his back and ribs were still smarting. Reena gave him a rather apologetic look and then beckoned him to follow.

She led him out of the kitchen and into a huge family room, stocked with a few comfortable-looking sofas, a beige throw rug which perfectly matched the recliner on top of it, and a wide-screen television. Unlike the bedroom he woke up in, this place looked much more used and frequented.

"Reena, got a question," he said, noticing this as they descended another set of stairs. "If you, Terrence, Trip, and three other people live here, or crash here often or whatever, why is it that some rooms are dusty? It's like much of this place is unused and haunted."

He was surprised to see Reena laugh. "As you can see just from the little bit that you've noticed, Jonah, this place is very large," she said. "Those of us who reside here year-round certainly don't peruse and inhabit every room. So yes, a bit of dust is present. But it'll be gone in a flash once all our friends are gathered again. While I'm thinking of it, let me apologize for putting you in that dusty bedroom. I prayed you didn't have any allergies, but when Jonathan got you here, it was the closest one, and you needed tending to."

"You taped me up?" asked Jonah, momentarily distracted.

"Yes," said Reena. "Liz—you'll meet her later—is the one who handles most of the medical situations. But seeing as how she was in bed when Jonathan turned up with you, I took care of you. You had some contusions and some hairline fractures but nothing too serious."

"So you were also the one who dressed me too?" asked Jonah, not knowing whether to feel embarrassed or flattered.

Reena paused, registering his meaning. "Don't flatter yourself, Rowe," she murmured. "Men aren't my interest."

"Huh?" said Jonah without thinking.

"You heard me," said Reena, a trace of annoyance in her voice.

Jonah caught the change of tone in her voice and mentally scolded himself. He wasn't trying to offend any of the people he'd just met (with Trip being the exception), let alone the woman who'd treated his injuries.

"Don't misunderstand me," he said hastily, "that's completely cool. I just didn't know, that was all."

Reena didn't respond. Jonah realized that they had reached the bottom of the stairs and entered an expanse of basement space where several elliptical machines, a dozen treadmills, and multiple other home-gym equipment items were located. Unlike the bedroom where he'd slept, these things looked like they were used regularly. But he ignored them for a moment and looked at Reena, whose expression hadn't changed.

"Sorry if I offended you," he told her.

"You didn't."

"Truly, I just didn't know."

"Well, now you do," said Reena, coolness in her tone. "Any other questions?"

"Yeah," said Jonah, keen on changing the subject before he grated any further nerves. "Why did you bring me down here?"

"Oh, yeah," Reena's annoyed expression faded, making Jonah thoroughly relieved. "Jonathan told us about your display of power the night you rescued Bast. It sounded pretty impressive, by the way. But then he said that afterward, you slept for nearly sixteen hours. Your cardio health must be shot."

"Oh." Jonah shifted his feet uncomfortably. Fitness had always been a sore spot for him. He had never been morbidly obese or anything, but he'd always had to deal with plumpness and a slightly sagging midsection. He had never considered it that big of a deal, though he managed to, almost unthinkingly, come to own a large amount of darker, oversized clothes to hide it. And Mr. Langton's most recent comments about his weight were still rattling around in his head.

"That isn't a problem, and don't feel bad about it," said Reena. "You know how many people have issues with cardio health? But as an Eleventh Percenter, it would benefit you to have a strong heart, stamina, and endurance. Spiritual endowments can be very draining in that regard, so you have to build up your energy."

Jonah eyed the treadmill curiously. "So you want me to start looking like you and Terrence?" he asked.

Reena laughed, and Jonah was glad to see her smiling. "Terrence was blessed with a mesomorphic body type, so he always looks strapping, despite eating so much crap," she said. "I'm a runner, so it just so happened to work in my favor when I found out I was an Eleventh Percenter."

"Really?" said Jonah, stepping onto the treadmill and putting the setting at a manageable pace, keeping his ribs in mind. "When did you find that out?"

Reena sat down on a weight bench near Jonah's treadmill. "About ten years ago. I was fourteen. I've been able to see spirits and sense their presence all of my life, though at that time, I had no clue what it meant. My family frowned upon it, told me if I knew what was good for me, I'd put my imaginary friends away. When my uncle passed, I wondered why I *didn't* see him like I'd seen all the other spirits. But I didn't dare ask. My family was already less than pleased with me because I was such an 'abnormal' girl..." She closed her eyes and took a deep, calming breath before continuing. "It was Jonathan who told me the reason why I didn't see my uncle."

"And why was that?" asked Jonah.

"Because we Eleventh Percenters can't see the spirits of our own loved ones," said Reena quietly. Clearly, this troubled her. "Nor can we see the spirits of other Eleventh Percenters once they've passed."

Jonah was in motion due to the treadmill, but looked closely at Reena. "Did you try to share that information with your family?" he asked. "They Eleventh Percenters too?"

"No idea," said Reena tersely. "Didn't get the chance to ask."

Jonah knew there was more to that story but chose to respect her. After all, it wasn't like *he* was planning on volunteering his life story anytime soon.

"You've got a bunch to learn, Jonah," said Reena, standing up, "but you have help, and you aren't alone. Besides, I think that over the next few days, Jonathan and the rest of us will have your head spinning."

Jonah wasn't sure he enjoyed the sound of that, but he nodded at her. "I've always liked learning new things."

Reena smiled at him, bade him goodbye, and went back upstairs, leaving Jonah to allow his thoughts to wander.

So he was an Eleventh Percenter. He still didn't really understand what that meant. Jonathan's explanation, though slightly helpful, only raised more questions.

Was anyone else in his family an Eleventh Percenter? Had his grandmother had the ability to see spirits too? And what did the "raw essence" mean? Was he supposed to hide at night from now on?

He wondered if his parents were Eleventh Percenters, but that was impossible to know. He had never known them. His grandmother never talked about them much, but he had managed to wheedle some information out of her nonetheless. His father had taken off before he was born. Jonah didn't even know his name. His mother, Sylvia, had been his grandmother's daughter and hadn't been a much of a bargain either. She'd given birth to him and then pawned him off onto Nana.

From what bit that his grandmother had told him, Jonah's father had been significantly older than his mother and they hadn't been married, so distancing themselves from Jonah, the result of their tryst, would "protect their reputations." Upon hearing that story, Jonah couldn't help but feel like an accident. An unwanted inconvenience. His grandmother had insisted that this was not the case and that she was grateful that his mother had given him over to her because she hadn't been, in Nana's words, "parent material." And now Nana was gone, and to this day, he didn't know whether or not either of his parents was still alive. It was what it was; he couldn't miss people he'd never known.

Jonah pushed those less-than-pleasant thoughts aside and racked his brain, perusing some of his earliest memories. If he had been born an Eleventh Percenter, there had to have been *something* in his past that would have indicated it.

As a child, he had had a wild imagination. All too often, he would envision mystical battles with mythical creatures and played them out in the sandbox or the front porch of his childhood home. He could always come up with some interesting position in which to put his action figures and then come up with wildly outrageous epic tales to explain why they were positioned so. Oh, if he had only bothered writing down some of the tales that flew around his mind then! He knew words, and exactly how to use them, before he'd even read them. The words would just flow as if they had a mind of their own. Could *that* have been something? Could those wonderful insights that shone so brightly in his youth have possibly been spiritually inclined inspirations?

He thought about the ghost stories his grandmother used to tell him. He also remembered that, while other kids had found them very frightening, he found them fascinating, almost as much as the tales he'd conjured in his young imagination. They always interested him; he would actively ask his grandmother to tell more ghost stories while thinking about how to mold his own.

He thought about how the ghost stories were the ones that excited him the most—the stories that involved the mythical beings, the tallest of tall tales, the ones that always involved suspending one's disbelief. That had to have meant something. Was that some sign of who he truly was?

The treadmill beeped loudly, alerting him that the half hour was up. As it slowed to a stop, so too did his musings.

Doubt, the same old doubt that had always been present, settled into his mind once more. Minions, otherworldly spirits, whatever, were after him to the point where he'd been warned he wouldn't be safe at night for a while. Yet, spirits supposedly *needed* him. That was made evident by the weird spiritess, Marla. Jonah also hadn't forgotten those dreams—the people, all those people, fettered and emaciated. The shackles fell away, and they appeared fresh and strong. Then, the chains returned, and the invigoration ceased. Jonathan had mentioned an enemy, but he hadn't elaborated. Jonah had powers that he had no clue how to actually use. He was now around people that were like him, who had been practicing how to use said powers, but he also didn't even know what to *use*. The brief thing with the wind and the electricity, was that it?

It was all too much. It was *still* too much. And on top of it all, he still didn't know what it was he was supposed to be doing.

He caught a glimpse of himself in the shiny, plastic surface of the treadmill screen. "Well, Jonah," he muttered to himself, "what now? You still don't know who you are, and yet again, you are in another situation where you know less than everyone else."

He stepped off of the treadmill and found himself grateful for the warm exertion that coursed through his muscles. Reena was right. It did help him out.

Ascending the stairs, Jonah quickly found his way back to the family room and crossed it to go back to the kitchen. It was when he heard his name that he paused.

"—Blue Aura? He's got to be remarkable!" came Terrence's excited voice.

"Has to be," said Reena's voice. "The essence surrounding him is one of the most powerful I've ever sensed. No wonder Bast took to him so quickly."

"You think he will—you know—do what a Blue Aura supposedly does?" whispered Terrence.

"Calm down before you piss yourself, Terrence," said the cold voice of Trip. "So he vanquished a minion with some cheap parlor tricks. Doesn't mean he is anyone's savior."

Jonah felt a flicker of anger. What was it with this guy?

"Trip, shut up," snapped Reena. "Your policy of not trusting new people will get you nowhere."

"It's a wise policy, however unpopular it might be," said Trip. "So some new guy experiences beginner's luck, and suddenly he is supposed to be the damned Second Coming? He could be a Spirit Reaper."

"I said *shut up,* Trip," repeated Reena. "He is not a Spirit Reaper. He couldn't be. Why would Walt and Howard have tried so hard to kill him if that had been the case? From what Bast intimated to Jonathan, they were beyond bloodthirsty."

"Downright ferocious," said Terrence. "They know. They have to."

Jonah heard a chair skid across the floor, indicating that Trip had stood up from the kitchen table.

"Forgive me if I'm not impressed," said Trip. "I'll believe he's worth something when I see it, and not a second sooner."

"As an Eleventh Percenter, Trip, that's a closed-minded thing to say," said Terrence sharply. "Besides, your thoughts on it are irrelevant. You heard him. He is a Blue Aura."

"Exactly," said Reena. "Problem is, *they* know that too, especially now. I hope, for Jonah's sake, that his essence matures quickly. The longer it remains raw will determine how long he remains in danger."

Jonah fidgeted a little, causing the door to creak. The conversation within immediately ceased, but Jonah readied himself by darting back about ten feet or so. When Reena, followed closely by Terrence, pushed open the door, he bounded forward so as to give off the impression that he'd just come up the stairs from the workout room.

"What's going on?" he said, hoping to sound offhand.

Terrence sighed with relief, but Reena said, "Glad you got some exercise. Hope you aren't too tired because you and I are about to leave."

Jonah frowned. "Where are we going now?" he asked.

"Just to give you a good look at the real world," said Reena.

She had a set of keys already in hand and was heading for the front door. Jonah followed, wondering about what he had just heard.

Why was he in danger? And what, or who, posed a threat? Was it this "enemy" everyone had mentioned or, thought Jonah wildly, was it these three people who'd just been talking about him in secret?

Upon exiting the estate, Jonah was immediately distracted. He found himself marveling at how grand the place was. It was entirely made of brick; he thought it resembled a mixture of a colonial-style home and haunted mansion, though the whole Eleventh Percent thing made the haunted notion rather moot. There were numerous windows, which made Jonah wonder just how many rooms were within. This place had to be owned by someone well connected or influential. Seeing the size of it from the outside made him understand what Reena had meant when she'd told him that they couldn't possibly inhabit the whole of the place. The grounds were what really got him. They were lush, vast, and ringed by forest. Just through an opening of cedars lay a wooden bridge arching over a very large pond, which led to a wooden gazebo with stone steps.

Jonah wasn't one for plants, but the grounds and its gardens brought back memories. Nana truly would have loved this place.

Wait, a pessimistic voice had reared itself in the back of his mind. *Wallowing in sad memories is what almost got you killed in the first place. Put those to the side now.*

He hadn't noticed that Reena had been watching him the whole time with an expression that looked like ... suspicion?

"Wonderful, isn't it?" she asked.

"Yeah, it is," said Jonah, feeling slightly nostalgic and not fully registering her expression. "Takes me back."

She beckoned him to her car. "To what?" she asked.

"Nothing I can share, I suppose," said Jonah. "As it was my emotional thoughts that almost led to me getting killed, I'd rather not say it and run the risk of putting you in danger."

She nodded, understanding. "Raw essence can be a pain, especially when it comes to stuff like loss. Don't think you have to disconnect for the rest of your life. Your essence will mature, and your emotions will no longer betray you. Now, how much of our conversation did you hear?"

"Huh?" asked Jonah, taken aback.

Reena grinned and shook her head. "Men," she muttered. "You may have fooled Terrence, Jonah, but I know better. The treadmill was only set for thirty minutes; I watched you do it. If you were at a normal pace, you could have bounded up those stairs in two minutes at most. And then you nudged the door and tried to act like you'd just come back up. And besides," she made a rather sharp turn, and suddenly they were rolling through a neat suburb, "you betrayed your own self with that damned, 'Huh?' That's the second time you've done it today."

Jonah grimaced, feeling idiotic and annoyed. "I heard you talking about me doing 'what blue auras do,' whatever that means," he admitted. "Terrence thinks I have some great potential, and that fool Trip thinks I'm a flash in the pan."

Reena's suspicious expression relaxed, turning collected and serene. "Trip's out of line," she said. "He has no right to be a jerk like that. He's had it pretty rough, so I suppose it is *minutely* justified."

"We all have things in our past that trouble us, but it doesn't mean we make everyone else pay for those mistakes," said Jonah dismissively.

"You are new to your awareness of being an Eleventh Percenter," reminded Reena.

"Maybe," said Jonah, "But I'm no stranger to stressors."

Reena was silent for a moment. "I'll give you that," she said, "but being an Eleventh Percenter sometimes takes a toll."

"I don't doubt it, but you and Terrence aren't dicks," countered Jonah.

Reena laughed. "Yeah, that would be a succinct way to describe Trip."

"So what were you guys talking about?" asked Jonah. They could debate about Trip all day, but it would never change the first impression. The first impression was always the one that lasted. Langton, Jessica, and Anthony were perfect examples of that.

Reena halted at a red light and sighed. "There is so much that I don't know, Jonah," she said. "According to Jonathan, upheaval is on the horizon. He sensed it. Now, upheaval can be good, even great, or it could be very bad. He is very tightlipped about it, and prefers to reveal most of it to you himself. That will probably happen tonight."

Jonah shook his head. To call that information unhelpful would be an understatement. "Why you all were in awe when I said my aura was blue, then?" he asked. "Speaking of which, I need to point out something. My aura can't be *exclusively* blue. The colors of people's auras change all the time, every single day. Maybe it was just blue that day or something. It's probably an entirely different shade now."

Reena nodded, as if that were a fair statement. "That is true, amongst *regular* human beings, you know, the Tenths," she said. "But with Elevenths, that's not the case. The color of our auras, no matter our mood or emotion, is always in compliance with the *root* of our personalities. It never changes."

Jonah let that sink in. It was no weirder than anything else he was learning after all. "Yeah, okay. So why is it such a big deal that my aura is blue?"

Reena's shock still hadn't worn off from that. It was still evident on her face. "Do you know what a Blue Aura signifies?"

"No."

The light turned green, and they were off. They had driven almost five miles and had parallel parked on a tree lined street before Reena answered. "There are several opinions and variations, but there is one that seems to withstand the test of time," she said carefully. "A person with an aura displaying blue represents balance, or the coming of a more balanced existence: sustaining life, transmitting powerful essence. A Blue-Aura individual is a born survivor. Blue Auras are very powerful people even amongst those without our powers, but for an *Eleventh* Percenter..." she hesitated. "When it comes to the blue aura, many normal people, that is to say, Tenth Percenters, exhibit it commonly. Blue is very common for them, but rare for an Eleventh. Quite rare."

"You say that as if it's a bad thing," said Jonah.

"No, no," she said, "it's not a bad thing, just ... Jonah, would you like to know how many Blue-Aura Eleventh Percenters there have been? Eight."

"Eight this century, you mean?" asked Jonah.

"No," said Reena. "Eight *period.*"

Jonah couldn't help but feel a faint surge of anxiety down his spine. "Let me guess," he ventured, "I'm the eighth, and the seven before me were all a big deal in some way. A *huge* deal. You mentioned upheaval. Am I to take it that Blue-Aura Eleventh Percenters were around during times when shit was about to hit the fan?"

Reena regarded him cautiously, and then nodded. "Yes. You can *definitely* take it that way."

Jonah's brain was still processing the information Reena shared when they parked at a cozy little park area near the town square. Reena pointed out a bench for him to sit on, left to get a soy dog, and returned with a mineral water for him. Jonah had no idea what they were doing there, but while Reena ate, he had more time to think.

So he was a Blue Aura. The eighth of only eight in history. He was supposedly a big deal, a big deal that was destined to bring about some type of upheaval. Swell.

It only made sense. Jonah's luck had been rotten for as long as he could remember. He was used to that. But *never* had his shortcomings caused ripples that would result in some type of massive upheaval. And he still didn't know who the "enemy" was. He wished that people would cease with the cryptic crap and be helpful.

"What are we doing here, Reena?" he asked. His mind was teeming with questions, but it didn't seem that anyone was going to yield any answers until they were good and ready.

"I brought you here to the town square because I wanted to know how well you would do with something," said Reena. "Now, look around."

Jonah stared at the town of Rome's citizenry. It was a small yet bustling populace. Mothers moved about with children, elderly people conversed with each other, and adolescents meandered on corners. It was a setting in which Jonah was very familiar. He had grown up in a small town and left at eighteen.

"It's just small-town people going about their everyday lives," he observed, shrugging. "No biggie. The town that I grew up in, Radner, was even smaller than this one."

"I figured that," said Reena. "You didn't strike me as a city guy. But anyway," she finished her food and tossed the wrapper in a nearby trash can, "your essence was kick-started, so this might be interesting. Now close your eyes, take a very deep breath, and *really* look at them."

Feeling foolish, Jonah closed his eyes and inhaled deeply. When he opened his eyes, he started so violently that if Reena hadn't been sitting there, he'd have upended the bench.

The townsfolk were still bustling about with one profound addition.

Every citizen he saw from this vantage point in the town square was now accompanied by spirits.

Jonah stared. He couldn't believe his eyes. There were spirits that showed all demeanors: joyful, expectant, tense, parental. Everywhere he looked, they were with someone. A young child had a few elderly spirits that shuffled alongside him. A female senior citizen was impatiently moving from aisle to aisle in the grocery store while a male spirit that appeared to be of similar age placed a calming palm on her shoulder. Jonah wondered if she felt anything there.

A stranger sight was a man in his early thirties who sat not far from them in the city square. He looked so sad and withdrawn that Jonah couldn't understand why he'd bothered to come out amongst people.

Next to him, a woman about the same age spoke to him affection-ately as though she were trying to explain a difficult subject. The man wasn't looking at her. Jonah couldn't help it when his eyes stung. He didn't have to be a brain surgeon to figure out the situation.

"A recent loss, then?" he said to Reena, his voice crisp and formal so as to prevent it from cracking. "His wife must be trying to assist him in letting her go, but he can't. How could he?"

"We never want to let go of the ones we've lost," said Reena. "What he needs to do is integrate it into his life and learn to live with it. Clinging to his grief is counterproductive to him."

"What? How?"

"I can also get a read off of his essence," she said. "I guess I forgot to tell you I could do that. He is not only sad but scared. Terrified. He has at least three children, daughters, I think, and he never imagined having to raise them alone. He doesn't even know how to."

Jonah felt such pity for the man. He would never be as bold as to say he completely understood how he felt, but he knew all too well the feelings of isolation, fear, and anger.

"Pitying the bereaved doesn't help them," said Reena, who had cor-rectly interpreted Jonah's expression. "Trust me when I say that you will go insane if you attempt to shoulder others' grievances."

Jonah shot up and got in Reena's face. The anger had erupted in him so suddenly it was jarring. How could she be so indifferent? "You make it sound so easy!" he snapped. "When you go through it, you understand that it is not as easy as 'showing no pity.' The man's wife is gone from him forever. He is a single father now and has to ad-just to transitions so quickly that he'll probably need therapy in a few months. I know what the man is going through. I can't tell you how alone I was when I lost my grandmother. She was the only one who would listen to my stories, who fostered my imagination, who let me believe that I even mattered in the world. Clearly, it was wrong of me to expect you to understand."

Reena's eyes flashed. "Excuse me?" she whispered. "Not expect *me* to understand? You don't know a thing about me, Jonah Rowe. Not one damned thing. You think you own the franchise on knowing what it's like to feel alone? Why? Because you have been dealt a shit hand because people bullied you in school and gossip about you at work?

"Try having *my* life. Try being the unwanted result of a fling your mother had with a local innkeeper. Try watching your mother marry and have three other daughters that she favors more than you because they were full white and not half Samoan. Try being interested in girls when all the other girls your age were boy-crazy. Try coming out to your parents and having them instantly turn on you and label you an 'abomination.' Try having your mother uproot you and your family from your home in Hawaii and go all the way to Virginia, hoping that being around her relatives will 'cure' you. Try having most of those relatives dislike you because you are not only lesbian but biracial.

"Try having an uncle who was the *only* one in the family who loved and accepted you. Try having to live with that uncle after your mother threw you out, saying you would 'corrupt' her other daughters. Try having that uncle get killed in a car accident because some idiot who was dialing on a cell phone ran a stop sign. And on top of *all that*," she made a circular, all-encompassing motion with her hand, "try also having the ability to see and interact with the spirit world. Try all that, and then tell me if you alone understand isolation."

Even through Jonah's frustration, he could see that he put his foot in his mouth yet again. Though the shock of Reena's words crashed over him, the defiance engendered by the grief kept his resolve steeled. But it was difficult to remain angry after hearing such experiences. No amount of stubbornness could change that.

"I didn't know what you'd been through, Reena," began Jonah, his voice much calmer. "I'm sorry. But it doesn't change the fact that your experiences greatly affected you in *your* life a certain way, and my experiences affected me differently in mine. But like I said, I am sorry."

Reena sat back down on the bench, inhaling and exhaling rapidly. "Give me a few minutes, and I'll forgive you."

Jonah nodded, understanding. "Fair enough."

In the awkward silence that followed, Jonah began to notice some things about the spirits that he hadn't before. Some of the spirits that were moving about with the people were slightly translucent; he could see through them as though they were veils that concealed nothing. Others, however, were shockingly opaque, solid, and almost indistinguishable from people that were in the flesh.

"Why is it that some spirits are more defined?" he asked.

Reena, still irritated, barely looked up. "The more defined a spirit is, the more they are still being mourned," she said. "The more transparent ones indicate how far their living counterparts have progressed on the path to acceptance. When a person has fully accepted a loved one's passing, that spirit will vanish entirely, and people will appear completely alone."

Jonah looked here and there. "But *no one* is completely alone."

"Exactly," said Reena.

Jonah thought on that. Acceptance took a strength and perseverance that precious few people possessed. He knew for a fact that *he* didn't have it. And from the look of it, no one in this town did either. It made him wonder if gaining the strength to fully put a loss behind you was even attainable at all.

A thought fell into his mind, but Reena said almost instantly, "You won't see her, Jonah."

Jonah stiffened. "Do you read minds or something?"

At that, Reena actually laughed. "Not even," she said. "Essence reading and mind reading are *very* dissimilar. I can't see a person's thoughts. It's more like I can glean what they are thinking by the emotions they show, which alter the composition of their essence. Most people wear their emotions on their sleeves and are, therefore, very easy to figure out."

Jonah rejoined Reena on the bench. He supposed it had been kind of obvious what he'd been feeling. "Okay then, why won't I see her?"

Reena looked Jonah in the eye, and he was thankful to no longer see anger there. "I told you. We can't see the spirits of the ones we've lost or the spirits of other Eleventh Percenters. That's the dilemma."

"Why? Why can we see spirits of these Tenth Percenters but not Elevenths?"

"Tenths don't have the spiritual attunement we do, so they can choose to be in spirit when they leave the physical. But for us, when we go, we're just gone," said Reena quietly.

"Then why can we see Jonathan?" asked Jonah. "Isn't he a spirit? An Eleventh Percenter spirit?"

Reena returned her gaze to the ground. "Jonathan is a Protector Guide. Different rules apply there. Don't ask me about them," she added quickly as Jonah was about to do just that. "I am still of the flesh just like you. I wouldn't know."

Jonah stared off into the people. That bit of information stung. It was as if Reena had just said, "*You have this power to interact with a whole bunch of spirits except for the one that you want to see.*" It just seemed unfair. And wrong.

Jonah was distracted by yet another thing he hadn't yet noticed. The spirits carried a range of emotions. Some of the spirits seemed joyful and upbeat. Others seemed more solemn, or even sad. But there were others who seemed … detached. They carried woebegone, fractured expressions, almost as if they didn't want to be there. He was just about to make an inquiry of Reena about this when he noticed a brown-haired woman standing mere feet away from him. He recognized her instantly but noticed that her features were now more distinct. His mental depiction hadn't been wrong that day; her eyes were a clear brown, her skin fair. Her hollow cheeks were not stretched out in fright, but she looked anxious and determined nonetheless.

Marla fixed Jonah with a pleading expression, which was made more disconcerting with those shockingly clear brown eyes. "Help us," she whispered. Even the whisper was faraway and indistinct. "Do you see the sadder ones? The beaten ones? I am one as well. Creyton has chained us. He has blocked us. Free us; the afterlife was not meant to be a prison!"

She backed away, completely passing through a bench as though she didn't notice it.

"Help us," she repeated, then vanished.

"Um, Reena," began Jonah, but he hesitated when he noticed that she, too, had noticed the weaker, disengaged spirits. Apparently, she hadn't registered Marla, so he wasn't so inclined to bring her up at that moment. "Why do some of the spirits look like they don't belong?" he asked instead. "Some of them are content enough. Happy, even. But others just seem, I don't know, out of place."

Reena made a wry face. "They *don't* belong here," she said. "But I think we better go now, essence feels as though it's changing."

"But—"

"Allow me to show you how to disconnect," interrupted Reena. "It's much like the volume of a radio. You can make it loud, soft, or turn it off completely. It all depends on your breathing."

"Why is that?"

"The more oxygen your brain has, the more concentration you have," she explained. "Now, implement the breathing you used to see the spirits. Close your eyes, and then concentrate on willing whatever you see to close."

"Whatever I see?" asked Jonah.

"Our brains interpret opening and closing our ability differently," said Reena.

Jonah closed his eyes and took a very deep breath. Reflecting on what Reena had just told him, he focused, and an image came clearly in his mind, almost as though it had been waiting to be summoned. It was a stage of actors, all finished with a performance and taking a bow. In his mind's eye, he willed the curtain to close in front of them, officially ending the show. He opened his eyes to see that the spirits were no longer visible. Once again, it was simply the serene scene of people going about their Saturday-morning routine.

"Well done," said Reena, looking genuinely impressed. "You achieved it so quickly!"

Jonah frowned. "How did you know I couldn't see anything any-more?" he asked her.

"Your essence," replied Reena. "When you were watching the spirits, it was buzzing, almost electric. Now that your sight is back to normal, so too is your essence. That process went a lot more quickly and more smoothly than I thought it would. Let's head back."

She strode off toward the car. Jonah followed, unable to deny the fact that the questions Reena answered had only lead to even more complicated questions.

6

A Fighting Chance

The trip back to the Grannison-Morris estate was mainly silent and uneventful. Though Reena was still rather cool toward him since their argument, Jonah could tell that her mood had improved since he had succeeded with seeing the spirits, which Reena referred to as "Spectral Sight." According to her, it was mystifying that he'd achieved it so quickly. While Jonah found the achievement fascinating, it made him apprehensive as well.

First and foremost, seeing those spirits in such large numbers like that was unnerving. It was similar to being told for years that there was no such thing as aliens and then one day seeing an armada of extraterrestrial ships in the sky. To have illusions torn asunder so quickly and utterly would have been frightening for anyone, and it wasn't exactly reassuring to know that if he wanted to see them *again*, he actually could. To categorize that as "odd" would be the understatement of the century.

Despite that, however, it made several things make sense. The existence of spirits on Earthplane, as Reena had called it, solidified the fact that he wasn't just some weird guy. These past couple of days where he felt he had been losing his mind had been frightening; it just felt so emasculating and demoralizing, trying to get a firm grip, but then learning that there was nothing *to* grip. His fascination with spirits had to have had some base or root in the fact that he was an Eleventh Percenter. But why hadn't he ever gotten an inkling of who he truly was before now?

Or had he?

Now that he thought about it, there *had* been some questionable occurrences in his childhood. He distinctly remembered going to church with his grandmother and recalled seeing a sweet older lady waving at him from the cemetery. He'd happily waved back, only to have people ask him who he'd waved to.

An even earlier occurrence unearthed itself from the recesses of his memory bank. As a second grader, he had been bullied incessantly for various things, each new one more foolish and sillier than the last. That particular time, their newest reason had been because his shoes weren't new like everyone else's. They'd even come up with a song to commemorate the moment. Although he'd long since forgotten the song, he hadn't forgotten his classmates reminding him all day long that his shoes were old and cracked. It became too much, and tears of shame and anger clouded his vision. In an attempt to escape that stupid little song they'd created, he ran away from them, far enough for the teacher to lose sight of him. Head down in frustration, he hadn't noticed that he'd reached the road.

Suddenly, a man in a dark brown suit was there. Jonah stared at him, puzzled. The man had shaken his head vigorously and pointed a finger toward the school. Jonah hadn't thought much of it, assuming at the time that it was just some random adult who had been passing by and noticed a little boy who wasn't where he was supposed to be. But in the twenty-twenty perspective that hindsight provided, Jonah recalled a bit more. Not even five seconds after the man had re-directed him from the road, two transfer trucks had barreled by, each going in opposite directions. By that time, Jonah's teacher had realized that he was missing, discovered him, and scolded him for wandering away from the rest of the class. But when Jonah had pointed out the man that motioned to him to return to the class, he saw that there was no man to point out. The only thing at the road was the flurry of traffic that came after the trucks.

Why hadn't he remembered those things until today?

Then, another forgotten memory arose; one that he hadn't forgotten so much as written off as an emotional response.

When his grandmother had died, his brain had become so saturated with anger and grief that no messages of any kind were able to penetrate at all. In fact, each attempt to improve his mood, cheer him up, or calm him down had had the opposite effect; he'd only gotten angrier and his grief only intensified. Why couldn't they all realize that hearing that Nana was "at peace" or "in a better place" or "soaring with the angels" brought him no joy whatsoever? Why couldn't they see that none of their condolences were helpful? They probably would have helped him more if they had actually just shut up and let him grieve.

The funeral was a nightmare. That white casket would be etched into his memory for the rest of his days. He'd wept unabashedly; he hadn't given a damn what anyone did or said. Then came time for the viewing. For the several days preceding that hellish day, he'd been dead-set against viewing her. "What's in that box is not Nana," he'd snarled at everyone. "I don't know what it is, but it's not her. I don't want to remember her like that. I don't want to remember her ... *dead.*"

It had been his cousin Joanie, one of those random relatives that may as well have been strangers, who had convinced him otherwise. "The closure will do you good," she'd said. "You will regret it forever if you don't get closure." Like a fool, he'd listened.

Nana, the indomitable woman she was, whose presence he had gotten so accustomed to, who had only been sick twice in her entire life, was lying before him, finally finished after over nine decades of living. She'd appeared to be asleep, which had only made matters worse. He'd tried to place a hand on her shoulder, but it was impossible. It felt like an invisible force was restraining him. *Figures,* he'd thought angrily. *I can write all over paper, no problem, but this same hand can't move three inches.* Steeling himself as best he could, he'd said quietly, "Bye, Nana. Goodbye."

And then his brain had gone silent. Quieter than it had been in days. There was no jumble of thought, no irritation, and no anger. Just ... silence.

Then, as plain as day, he'd heard some pleasant female voice say, "It's not goodbye, Jonah. Not goodbye at all."

It was so sudden it hadn't really registered. But when he saw the presiding minister standing there, face set, arms outstretched, he dissolved into a new wave of tears and didn't give the incident a second thought.

Until today.

His thoughts were interrupted by a handkerchief obstructing his vision. Reena, apparently, had long since parked. He hadn't even realized they were back. She had allowed him to have his moment and now held a handkerchief out to him, asking no questions, but looking as though she understood.

"Experiencing Spectral Sight can really throw our memories into new relief," she said quietly. "I need no explanations and will ask no questions. Your experiences are your own until you are ready to share them."

Jonah noticed the copious tears that had fallen down his face onto his shirt. He took the handkerchief from Reena without comment, dried his face, and composed himself. "I'm sorry."

"No need to be," said Reena. "I am sorry myself for being so cold."

"It's fine," said Jonah. "We both needed to understand. What is Terrence doing?"

He noticed that Terrence seemed to be doing some type of frenzied ballet in the yard.

Noticing his puzzlement, Reena laughed. "It's Capoeira. A type of dance fighting."

Jonah climbed out of the car. "I've heard of that. It's Brazilian, right?"

"Yes," said Reena. "Terrence is pretty good at it. Good thing too. He needs more focus."

"Really?" asked Jonah. "That's cool. He told me that he liked to cook but wasn't an athlete. Is he a chef? Or does he teach people Capoeira for a living?"

Reena burst out laughing. "You should tell him you thought that. Terrence is a janitor that goes back and forth between the two high schools in Rome."

"What! *Why?*"

"The same reason why I do clerical work when my passion is painting. The same reason why you're an accountant when your desire is to be a writer. Working our way into our respective niches is a struggle."

Jonah stared at her. Could they possibly have the same struggles he did?

"Trip?"

"He is a jazz musician. Saxophonist, actually. He has gigs here and there, but he currently works as a substitute teacher."

"Nothing wrong with substitute teaching," said Jonah, shrugging. "But depending on the schools, it just might contribute to why he's such a douche."

Reena snorted. It was clear that she was no fan of Trip either.

At that moment, three complete strangers exited the estate, either to join Terrence in exercise or go about some other routine. Jonah figured they must be Malcolm, Bobby, and Liz.

"Morning, finally!" Reena called to them. They looked to her, then at Jonah, and came in their direction instead. "Jonah, meet Malcolm Mercer, Bobby Decessio, and Elizabeth Manville."

Malcolm was a tall black man of medium build with a military style buzz-cut atop a slender face, long nose, and brown eyes. He shook Jonah's hand with a sly smile.

"The newest greenhorn," he said. "But if Terrence says it right, you might come along pretty well."

There was kindness in his voice, but Jonah could tell by his tone that he didn't use it too much, so he must be a quiet man by nature.

Malcolm looked over at Reena. "How long did it take him to achieve Spectral Sight?" he asked.

"Got it on the first attempt," said Reena.

The boy, whom by process of elimination was Bobby, looked at Jonah as though he was the strangest thing he'd ever seen. In regard to height, Bobby was a runt; Jonah doubted he was five feet eight inches wearing shoes. His hair was a bit shaggy but didn't quite reach his eyes. Jonah estimated that his frame was probably meant to sustain maybe a hundred eighty pounds, but Bobby had somehow packed at least two hundred forty pounds of muscle into it. He hoped that Bobby didn't have small-man complex, because if that were the case, he could easily see him having a mean streak a mile wide. Then again, Jonah also remembered Terrence's story about Bobby. If he was considerate enough to bring a homeless kid home, maybe he didn't have a mean streak. He had continued to appraise Jonah all that time. "First time? I wonder if your powers are as attuned as your Sight."

"Couldn't tell you," said Jonah. "I've only had to use them once."

Bobby looked at Jonah almost sympathetically. "If you are who Terrence says you are, that's going to change *real* soon."

"But don't worry, though," reassured Malcolm. "We'll all help you along."

Jonah's face burned slightly. One of the banes of being a new individual was that undeniable feeling of being a step or two behind everyone else.

"If you get bruised up in the process," chimed in Reena, "I can patch you up. Or better yet, Liz will. Right, Liz?"

Jonah looked at Liz, who laughed at the statement. She looked to be either a few months before or a few months after eighteen. Her dazzling jade-green eyes would have made her seem very intense, but this notion was offset by the sheer warmth in her features, which made her look very likeable and pleasant.

"Yeah," she said, shaking his hand with both of hers, "I can fix you up wonderfully."

Jonah frowned. "Not to sound contentious, but why are you so confident?"

Liz grinned. "My aura's Green, just like my eyes. Healing comes naturally to me. And I'm strengthening that gift through research and education; I'm a biology pre-med major. I love making people feel better."

Jonah was pleased with her answer. Just being around this inordinately happy girl was a welcome distraction to the sadness and tension he'd had earlier.

"You will heal just fine, so long as you exercise along with it," Liz continued. Her tone, though authoritative, was still playful. "Did you sleep well last night?"

"Pretty decently, yeah," said Jonah.

"You'll sleep more tonight, that's a promise," said Bobby, his tone so matter of fact that Jonah regarded him curiously.

"Why?"

Terrence had joined them by that time and chuckled, having heard the last bit of conversation. Malcolm, Liz, and Bobby looked at each other, looking rather amused themselves. Even Reena, who had been relaxing against the car during most of the conversation, was smiling.

"What's funny?" he asked her. "Am I going to get some kind of spectral hazing or something?"

The group laughed aloud at that. "No hazing, just friendly fun," said Bobby. "Now, let's get some rest. Jonathan will have us busy tonight."

They left Jonah to sit on the porch. The ache in his back, while still present, had receded considerably, and the discomfort in his ribs was manageable. As he watched his new friends going about different activities, he wondered with slight anxiety what they had planned for him, but he'd go along gladly. The new guy had to establish a reputation quickly, and any distractions from revisiting thoughts of mourning would be welcome ones.

As the sky gave way to a deeper shade of blue, the other residents led Jonah down a dimly lit path behind the Grannison-Morris estate. The path seemed almost unending, which prompted Jonah to ask, "Does this all belong to one person?"

"Yeah," said Terrence. "Well, technically, to all Eleventh Percenters who want to call it home. So I suppose all this land belongs to us."

"And *you*, Jonah," added Reena.

"Where exactly are we going?" asked Jonah.

"The Glade," said Reena. "It's our training grounds. Jonathan told us to meet him there."

Almost as soon as she'd finished speaking, the path gave way to an expanse of land that preceded a cemetery. Some of the headstones were large enough that Jonah could see the engravings on them from where he stood. He scanned them, frowning. He didn't know what to make of it. All of the names, Beechum, Hunter, Maxton, Cobb ... few of them seemed to have the same name.

"Um, who exactly is interred here?" he asked.

"Eleventh Percenters," said Bobby. "A great deal of people have called this place home. Of course, not all of them are buried here but many are. There are Tenth Percenters here too."

His counterparts all stood apart from each other but seemed to be in a planned, circular formation. A formation, Jonah noticed, that placed him in the center. It was quite foreboding to be the center of attention in such an eerie place.

"Rather morbid, this place," he commented.

"Why do you say that?" said an intrigued voice.

Jonah turned to his left, the direction from where the voice came. Jonathan stood there, and Jonah was certain that he had not been there moments before.

"Why do you say that?" Jonathan repeated. Now it was seven pairs of eyes on him, but none of them (with the exception of Trip's) were accusatory or cold.

"Because it's depressing!" exclaimed Jonah. "Convening near a graveyard?"

Jonathan's intrigued expression didn't change. "And who said that it was depressing?"

Jonah looked at him. "Um, everyone!"

"I see," said Jonathan, looking pensive. He moved closer to Jonah, beckoning the others to move closer as well. "Tell me, Jonah, what is the thought that comes to your mind when I mention, say, ice cream?"

Jonah raised an eyebrow. Was this a trick question? "Uh ... I don't know, something to savor, an enjoyable treat that's delicious?"

"That's good," said Jonathan "Now, bearing that in mind, what would the thought be about ice cream if you were, let's say, lactose intolerant?"

Jonah blinked. Trip gave him a look of scorn.

"Exactly," said Jonathan. "The tables would be turned. Just like a porterhouse steak is heavenly to a great many people but not a vegetarian. Or driving is a wonderful experience to a driver, but to someone who was traumatized in a car accident and has no interest in learning to drive as a result, the meaning is very different. So, too, is this cemetery. And passing. They only have the meaning of depression and morbidity because everyone has assessed them as such."

Jonah was bewildered. "A nice thought, Confucius, but loss is sad. Anyone who's been through it will tell you—"

"Loss can be sad, but not because it's *supposed* to be," interrupted Jonathan. "Nor does it have to be morbid or depressing, as you put it. The term that would be most accurate would likely be 'misunderstood.' I'm willing to give you that. It is misunderstood. No one talks about it; they simply hide within themselves and allow their sanity and resolve to wither and break down without ever trying to understand exactly what passing is. Since it is not comprehended, the label of 'morbid' is slapped upon it and treated as law. Very limited train of thought, wouldn't you say?"

Something was building up in Jonah. Was it annoyance? Anger? "You make it sound like an ideal or something," he said.

"Ideals are invaluable to every facet of learning," said Jonathan. "There is very little that is known about what happens after passing. Wouldn't extending people's knowledge be advantageous to understanding a spirit's situation?"

"Situation?" said Jonah. "You make it sound like ... like they're still alive or something."

Jonathan looked pensive again. "And you disagree?"

Jonah's eyes narrowed. Was this guy serious? "Hell yes, I disagree! Their suffering is over!"

"And why do you say that?" asked Jonathan in a musingly calm tone that was beginning to irritate Jonah.

"Because they're *dead,* Jonathan!" spat Jonah.

Jonathan looked pleased, as if they had reached some sort of understanding. "No, son," he said. "They are not."

Now Jonah was angry. New guy or not, he would not be played for a fool. He didn't need it from a spirit; he had plenty *living* people in his life that did it already. "Jonathan? Do you not see these graves—?"

"They are not dead," repeated Jonathan. "The flesh and organs ceased to operate, of course, but that is not death."

"What are you talking about?"

"There is no such thing as death," said Jonathan. "To be frank, there is no such thing as birth either. There is only life. Life is all there is."

Jonah stared at him for a few seconds and then looked at everyone else. He hoped that one of them would dismiss all this as folly. But that didn't happen. They all continued to look at him with pity and resignation, as if they all remembered being where he was now.

"That's really deep, sir," said Jonah, "but it's nonsense."

"Oh, great day in the morning," snapped Trip. "This idiot can't be the Blue Aura, Jonathan. He is too goddamn stupid."

Jonah moved toward Trip, assault on his mind, but Terrence and Reena, the nearest to him, darted forward and restrained him. Jonah noticed that Reena had a remarkably strong grip for someone built like a runner. He expected speed from her but not strength.

"Calm down," she whispered. "Don't let Trip get to you. If you give him an inch, he will take *two* miles."

"He is doing a good job of taking miles already," snarled Jonah.

"It's fine," assured Terrence. "Watch this."

Jonah remained stationary, and they returned to their places. Jonathan fixed a firm, reproachful look on Trip.

"Titus Rivers III," he said, "rudeness and tactlessness are unnecessary. Learning paths vary no matter where we are in our lives. If your comments are not productive to growth and further learning, kindly hold your tongue."

Jonah didn't know what had Trip more nettled; the fact that he'd just been rebuked, or the fact that Jonathan had used his given name. Whatever the case may have been, Trip eyed him even more frostily, though he complied and fell silent.

"Life doesn't ever end, Jonah," continued Jonathan as though there had been no interruption. "Living cannot cease. That is something that man cannot alter, in any way, shape, or form. You have been endowed."

Jonah braced himself, expecting the surge he'd had the last time Jonathan had uttered those words but none came. He noticed that the ones around him were now the ones possessing the vitality.

"There is the spiritual essence before it enters the flesh," said Jonathan, and Terrence pointed a finger into the air, leaving a brightly gleaming white dot where his finger had been, "the sojourn into flesh through new life, which has been termed as 'birth,'" Reena dotted the air, "young life," Trip jabbed a finger upward, "mid-life," Bobby inclined a finger, "elderly life," Malcolm raised his finger, "and the time when the spiritual essence detaches itself from the flesh, which is termed 'after-life.'" Liz held up two fingers. Jonathan waved his own hand, and Jonah finally understood their odd formation. The white dots that had been placed there by the others were now joined by illuminated bands, also white, like a type of spectral connect-the-dots. The last empty space filled and formed a dazzling ivory circle, which spun gracefully in midair.

"As you can see," said Jonathan, who looked amused at the shock on Jonah's face, "a circle is formed. And circles have no origin, and they *certainly* have no end. Therefore, no 'birth' and no 'death.' Only the circle that is life."

Jonah stood frozen. If the theatrics were supposed to alarm him, they had succeeded. It was a powerful thing, a shocking revelation. As he was attempting to process it, he remembered that he had a voice.

"That's um, uh, interesting," he sputtered.

Jonathan chuckled, as did some of the others. Of course, Trip's mouth remained resolutely twisted. No one seemed to care.

"You took that well," said Jonathan, nodding approvingly. "I have seen other Eleventh Percenters faint when they saw that."

Jonah didn't think he was going to faint, but he could see how someone might have.

"You pointed out these graves here, Jonah," continued Jonathan. "They are indeed representations of people that have made their sojourns from the flesh. But when their physical forms ceased to function, they did not die. Their life changed form. In this case, they returned to spirit."

"Back up," said Jonah. He decided to avoid Trip's gaze as the scornful expressions would surely tick him off again. Instead, he glanced at Terrence, who gave him a sort of half-grin and nod. The nonverbal communication signified that yes, this *was* a mindboggling matter, and it was best to ask as many questions as possible. "Are you telling me that all those things they've been saying for centuries, the 'death is inevitable' stuff, the 'man must surely die' stuff ... all of that is a downright lie?"

"Well now," said Jonathan, "to write it all off as a 'falsehood' would be slightly harsh. Time, word of mouth, and history have an interesting way of twisting what's accurate. There have been innumerable instances of glossing over wrongdoing and tampering and shaping what's fact so as to meet whatever the popular notion is at the particular moment. To simply view it as people being insincere is flawed as well, because that is not always the case either. Therefore, we won't say 'lie.' I would prefer to say that it was more like spreading a rumor, which consequently caught fire."

Yeah, thought Jonah, *a damn near eternal fire.* "Okay," he said. "Say that it is a rumor that caught fire. Fine. So is there any truth to the rumor?"

"A wonderful question, Jonah," said Jonathan, nodding with approval. "When a person's body physically ceases, something does indeed end. But it's not their *lives.*"

"So what occurs if people don't actually pass on, then?" asked Jonah.

"But they *do,* Jonah," said Jonathan. "People pass on. That's not just a nice little sentiment; people literally *pass* into Spirit. Pass on to the next phase of their lives. If you've ever heard the phrase that people 'pass from this life into the next,' you've got the idea."

"Uh-huh," said Jonah. "So basically, you are saying that physical life is a hindrance? So if someone is terminally ill or killed in an accident or murdered, that a kindness has been performed? So if I get hit by a truck tomorrow, the reckless driver is doing me a favor because I'm just *passing on* to some other realm of existence?"

"No," said Jonathan, his voice stern. "Do not think along those lines at all. Murder, as in wrenching one from their physical existence, willfully killing with absolutely no cause, is *not* what I mean. Fatal accidents, terminal diseases, and the like are extremely unfortunate when they occur. But the 'finality' piece of it exists only in the physical realm, or Earthplane. Spirits live on, as you see with me, with Marla—" he paused, mouth twisting, "and Howard and Walt, as well as the Spectral Sight experiment conducted earlier today by Reena."

He inclined his head in her direction.

"Okay," said Jonah, feeling as though he had been lifting weights with his mind. "This is deep, and I won't pretend that I've gotten it all, but I'll bite. Lord knows I've experienced enough weird stuff lately to believe that what you say holds some weight. Now the million-dollar question: where do *I* come in?"

Jonathan didn't answer but looked kindly to Reena.

"You, like us, are an Eleventh Percenter," she said. "That is a huge deal. We can see and sense the presence of spirits and spiritesses, but it doesn't stop there. We have access to the Eleventh Percent, the portion of our mind that allows spiritual interaction. Therefore, we can affect the physical *and* spiritual worlds."

"Yeah?" said Jonah. "How?"

Jonathan chimed in once more. "There are spirits who voluntarily walk the earth who sometimes need access to the Astral Plane. There are also those who feel they 'died' wrongly, and are so full of rage and fear that they need to be purged, or cleansed. And then, in some cases, there are evil spirits who use their spiritual essence to adversely affect the physical and spiritual world as well as the workings of the peaceful spirits."

"So you fight them?" asked Jonah, looking around to them all. "You fight *spirits?*"

"Well, it isn't a situation where we sit around and wait for evil spirits to rear their ugly heads," said Terrence. "We aren't like some type of police that monitor dark spirit activities—"

"We can't be the ones that get *that* job, no," mumbled Bobby, which won him his very own scowl from Trip.

"We do not battle spirits like ethereal soldiers or anything," Jonathan continued, "but even so, battling sometimes does occur. Is fighting spirits so far-fetched, Jonah? You have already done that very thing."

"Oh yeah..." muttered Jonah. He remembered the electric show he'd performed with that spirit who'd attempted to harm Bast. "So why do some spirits fight? What is there to be gained?"

Jonathan's expression darkened. Apparently, this was a touchy subject. "They have been promised ... rewards," he said, seeming to weigh the words in his mind. "Not all spirits (and the warring, rebellious ones are referred to as minions) desire to traverse between the physical and the Astral Plane or simply transition peacefully to the Other Side. Some become prideful and greedy when they experience the liberties that spectral existence provides. Some are desperate, frightened even. Fear and worry are powerful motivators, so some of them offer their services and become minions. In return, they are given increased range over spiritual power, temporary tangibility, and free rein to cause mayhem, natural or otherwise."

"Let me see if I'm getting this," said Jonah. Weird and unreal as it all was, he was determined not to be behind. "So there are spirits who actually don't care to cross over, cross on, or whatever. They stay behind to screw things up. They enjoy being on Earthplane even though they don't belong here?"

Jonathan was giving Jonah that meaningful look again. "There are, as I am sure you are aware, people that fear passing into Spirit," he began. "Remember that fear is a powerful motivator. As spectral beings, spirits' perspectives and mentalities change somewhat so as to accommodate the new phase of living they are experiencing. Imagine having a spiritual perspective combined with a mental state that is still influenced by your human personality."

Thinking of corrupt individuals that were still physically alive was bad enough, but to imagine the existence of corrupt *spirits* was more than a little scary.

"I'm ... not sure that I want to," Jonah told Jonathan.

Jonathan nodded. "It is indeed a frightening notion. Some people fear crossing on. They don't know what awaits them on the Other Side. None of us do. So they choose not to bother with it. They stay and offer their services."

"Reminds me of the Asphodel Fields in Greek mythology," said Jonah. It gave him a sense of grounding knowing that he could correlate the current matters to things he already knew. "People who'd led questionable lives were afraid of harsh judgment and punishment, so they chose a state of eternal neutrality in the Asphodel Fields."

Malcolm nodded thoughtfully. "I read mythology too," he said. "I recall the stories about those fields. It would be nice if these minions had chosen eternal neutrality, but alas..."

"And I believe that I can thank dear old Trip here—" Trip was so surprised by Jonah mentioning his name that he actually flinched then stared in arctic curiosity, "—for supplying the name of those whom those spiritual minions serve." He looked to Jonathan. "They're called Spirit Reapers, right?"

Jonathan glanced at Trip, who in turn was giving him a look of stubborn defiance. There was no doubt in Jonah's mind that Jonathan had correctly surmised Trip's earlier accusations. "Yes, they are called Spirit Reapers," he responded. "Rogue Eleventh Percenters who have chosen to use their spiritual gifts for dark purposes."

"And the main one, the *worst* one, is named Creyton, right?" asked Jonah. "He was the one who sent Howard and Walt after me that night outside the bakery, when I was thinking about Nana."

The mention of Creyton's name caused everyone, even Trip, to snap undivided attention to Jonathan. Jonathan leaned in slightly.

"How do you know of Creyton?"

"That spiritess Marla," replied Jonah. "She mentioned something about Creyton blocking some path and that—uh—they needed some help."

He did not want to sound egotistical and say that she specifically said *his* help, especially since he didn't know how to even go about doing that.

"Wait, wait, wait," said Liz, a trace of fear in her voice that Jonah hadn't yet heard there. "Hold up a second. Did you just say that that touchy-feely spiritess Marla said Creyton blocked the path?"

She, Malcolm, and Bobby looked at Jonathan and Trip. It suddenly occurred to Jonah that this group didn't have all the information. Jonathan closed his eyes. Reena looked at Jonathan curiously, and Terrence seemed at a loss for words. It was Trip, of all people, who broke the silence that had suddenly befallen the group.

"Yes," he said, casting a glare at Jonah, as though to say, *Thanks, idiot.* It was becoming clearer and clearer by the second to Jonah that he and Trip were just simply going to be enemies. Jonah had had experiences with guys like Trip, who would take an instant disliking to people with no concrete reason. He was the enemy simply because he was the new element. It was such an ignorant standpoint to take, and it just served to elevate the enmity between them by a few more notches. "Dear Mr. Rowe here found a jarring way to say it, but yes, Creyton has blocked the path."

Jonah resigned himself to the fact that he was once again behind. "What path?" he asked rather pointedly.

It was best that someone he liked answer the question; if Trip passed any more accusatory glares or snide comments, they'd come to blows. Jonah didn't want that at all, seeing as they were in a cemetery. He was certain that fighting would only achieve the opposite of the departed one's "resting in peace."

Jonathan sighed, glanced daggers through Trip again, and muttered, "The Path to the Other Side."

Liz gasped, Bobby tensed, and Malcolm and Terrence just gaped. Reena looked as though Jonathan had just spoken in another language.

"And you two knew about this all along?" she demanded.

"Hey, it wasn't your concern—" began Trip with venom in his tone, but Jonathan raised a hand to stop him.

Jonah wouldn't be denied that easily, though. Before Jonathan began another of his long-winded explanations, he needed to know a couple of things. "You speak of the next world, or Other Side, or whatever it's called, like it's different from the Astral Plane," he said. "They are one and the same, aren't they?"

"No, they are not," said Jonathan. "The Astral Plane is a spectral place, but beings can travel between there and Earthplane. The Astral Plane is a plane of existence with its unique beings, purposes, and functions, just like Earthplane. The Other Side is where the spirits and spiritesses go when they are … done. Or they desire to no longer stay on Earthplane or the Astral Plane. They are ready to move on to whatever is next. Spirits that are defeated in Spectral battle, good or evil, go there as well. Once a spirit or spiritess goes to the Other Side, they do not return."

"The Astral Plane is *not* the Other Side?" asked Jonah, floored. "What is the Other Side, then?"

"I cannot answer, Jonah," said Jonathan. "I stayed behind. As I said, spirits and spiritesses do not return from the Other Side. That place is a different realm of existence entirely."

"So this Creyton guy has actually blocked *death*?" demanded Jonah. "An Eleventh Percenter can do that?"

Liz slowly raised a hand to her mouth, Bobby and Malcolm stared as if just struck dumb. Terrence looked highly discomfited, Reena looked nervous, and Trip angry. Jonah, however, barely registered these reactions as his own shock and incredulity took the lion's share of his attention.

"Remember what you've just learned, Jonah," said Jonathan. "Life never ends. It simply changes form. No 'death.' But he has prevented spirits and spiritesses on Earthplane from crossing on. There are some who choose to stay on Earthplane, aiding and guiding their living counterparts, but there are others who desire to cross on to the Other Side. Because of Creyton, this isn't happening."

"But … why?" asked Jonah.

"Power," Jonathan said. "He's found a way to keep spirits and spiritesses wishing to cross over imprisoned on Earthplane to usurp their essence and corrupt their powers."

Jonah thought of the spirits he'd seen in his dreams, the ones that had been fettered and bound then free and whole. They were verbalizing their plight and desires through action. "I've understood something," he said, and they all looked at him. "When you shielded me, I started having regular dreams about spirits chained up. They never spoke, but they changed forms. They wanted me to know what was going on, but they didn't tell me because I'd think about it. And they changed form often so I wouldn't inadvertently call them mentally and be tracked."

"And yet that happened anyway," hissed Trip.

"Will you *shut up,* Trip?" snapped Reena.

"How did he do it?" asked Jonah, ignoring them both.

Jonathan looked away from Jonah, his grey eyes like newly cooled steel. "I don't know. All I can tell you is that he's gained strength through morphing pure spiritual essence into nefarious tools. And he has found a way to block the path with those tools. It is truly the damnedest thing I have ever seen."

"Who *is* Creyton?" inquired Jonah. "What do we know about him?"

"We'd be here for the next several weeks giving biographical information," said Jonathan, his voice grave. "But what you need to know most is that he was an Eleventh Percenter. Well, still *is*. But the thrill of power and his influence on the facets entailed by life corrupted him. He wanted to keep spirits on Earthplane to learn from them. Steal from them. Figure out how the aspects of spiritual life could be transformed into gains here in the physical life. He wanted me to help him. He wanted all of our friends to help him. He was refused as keeping spirits subjugated is against nature. And he didn't take kindly to that."

It was clear to Jonah that everyone in the circle had already heard this story, but from the absolute silence it invoked, they were still appalled, much like Jonah was now.

"He disappeared for a few years, and no one had any idea what had happened to him," continued Jonathan. "Then, out of nowhere, he returned, a full-fledged Spirit Reaper. He had also discovered a way to grant spirits tangibility and had amassed a faction of allies: Spectral beings, Spirit Reapers, and others."

Jonathan closed his eyes and sighed. "We were … tragically unprepared. We were decimated. I myself was killed fighting him. Many of the remaining Eleventh Percenters scattered, horrified at his newly developed ethereality. The Eleventh Percenters who were cut down in battle met an even worse fate upon passing into Spirit. Their essences were usurped by Creyton. It made him that much more powerful. For reasons unknown to me, Creyton didn't attempt to usurp my spirit. But I wasn't crossing on and leaving the ethereal world to his mercy. I stayed behind, became a Protector Guide, and began the task of mentoring new Eleventh Percenters, as well as doing what I could to protect innocent people from him."

Everyone remained silent, occupied with their own thoughts. Delicately, Jonah broke it. "When did this happen?"

"The Decimation occurred in 1943. But the blocked path has occurred within the past ten months."

"*Ten months?*" shrieked Reena and Liz in unison. Bobby was speechless, but he paled at the news. "You've been keeping this—"

"Silence!" said Jonathan, but it wasn't sharp or angry. It was more resigned and strained than anything else. "You guys have your own lives and don't hear everything that goes on."

"We stay here often enough with school and all—" began Bobby, but Jonathan interrupted him.

"The blocked path also coincided with Creyton beginning a rather strategic killing spree of Eleventh Percenters," he confessed.

Jonah saw that everyone else was just as shocked as he was.

"Any of our—" Reena began, but Jonathan quelled her with a sharp shake of his head.

"I don't know," he said.

Jonah glanced over at Trip and frowned. Was he imagining it, or did Trip look just a bit uncomfortable when Jonathan said that? He caught Jonah's eyes on him, and his expression hardened once more. The suspicious thoughts that began forming in his mind almost prevented him from registering that Jonathan was still talking.

"Not every Eleventh Percenter resides at this estate, as you all know," he was saying. "Some live on their own, others spent years here and then moved on, and some are just here seasonally. I monitor many of them, if possible; I am a Protector Guide, after all. But several, through lack of caution or simply being in the wrong place, have been experiencing some questionable demises. Tenth Percenter medical professionals are completely baffled, which almost certainly means dark ethereality. Therefore, this knowledge was concealed from so many of you. I did not wish for you to be Mindscoped and therefore at risk of being harmed."

"So why tell them—us," said Jonah, "why tell us now?"

"Because you are here, Jonah," said Jonathan. "The Blue Aura. Creyton knows you're here, which may prompt him to elevate dark ethereal activity, particularly against you. And I'd like our friends here to assist me in training you."

"Wait, wait, wait," said Jonah. "You knew there was a Blue Aura out there?"

"I had my suspicions," said Jonathan. "Or, should I say, my hopes."

"So that means *I* am his biggest target?" demanded Jonah. "I don't know anything about being an Eleventh Percenter! I'm practically a sitting duck for a hardened Spirit Reaper who is already on a killing spree!"

"You are not," said Jonathan. "You are in our midst and will receive training. Because of this, you—all of us—will have a fighting chance."

7

Embarrassing Clarity

Jonah stared at Jonathan and the others. He didn't know what was about to happen, but he had an idea that he was about to get a crash course of some sort. He was not thrilled about that; he did *not* do well when he was thrust into the limelight. He always embarrassed himself or had experienced people acting as if his mistakes were so irreversible that he shouldn't have even bothered trying. Those experiences were bad enough dealing with people he knew. And now he was supposed to be embarrassed in front of strangers?

Bobby looked at him with an expression of renewed determination. It was clear to Jonah that the guy was still not pleased with information being withheld from him, but he seemed focused now that he had something to do. Liz appeared to be biting her tongue, but chose to put her mind on the task at hand. For the moment, her blaring silence seemed similar to Trip's. Malcolm's expression was inscrutable.

"You've been planning these things for a while, haven't you?" Jonah asked Jonathan.

Jonathan's expression was set. "I prefer to create solutions rather than ruminate about problems. Now, onto the meat of the evening, I suppose?"

He looked at Jonah with eagerness in his features. "Jonah, you can't learn everything in a night, of course, but defense is always a good start."

"Huh?" said Jonah.

"Defense," repeated Jonathan. "As I said, we aren't warriors, but you need to know how to defend yourself should the need arise. Your vanquishing of that Minion was magnificent, but I must admit that I will be truly impressed when you can do those things based on your skill, not involuntary reaction."

Jonah noticed that everyone else seemed to be girding themselves for something. Not a good sign.

"I'm not even sure I can claim that," he said, now starting to feel overdressed in jeans and a thermal top. "You gave me that endowment and practically told me what to do."

"Nah," piped up Reena, a gleam in her eye. "Jonathan provided the *endowment*, but the *expression* of it was all you."

"Are you serious? I couldn't do that if you paid me—"

"We are capable of anything," said Jonathan. "You'd be amazed the feats that are possible when there is no confusion, doubt, or fear through which to plow. However, I must admit that I probably should not have endowed you so heavily. I didn't wish you to be harmed, nor did I wish any misfortune to befall Bast."

"Are you saying that I can achieve that mental clarity on my own?" asked Jonah, not even bothering to hide his skepticism.

"No," said Jonathan. "Only Spiritual endowments bring about mental clarity because the Spiritual Plane is not confined by the limitations of the three-dimensional mindset. The whole 'I can't do it' mentality doesn't exist."

Jonah blinked. "Sorry?"

"Invoke a spiritual entity to provide you with endowment," assisted Bobby.

Jonah stared at the headstones, feeling awkward. He moved to the nearest one (some WWII veteran) and muttered, "Um, can you endow me, please? I kind of need some help here."

He waited. Nothing happened.

"You can't do it like that," snapped Trip.

"Okay, Mr. High-and-Mighty," retorted Jonah. "What the hell am I *supposed* to do, then?"

"It's an easy mistake to make, Jonah," said Reena, who seemed to want to attack Trip as much as Jonah did. "You have to ask respectfully with clear intent. And he's no good—he's crossed on."

"Reena," said Jonah, his face screwed up in confusion, "how am I supposed to know who is—I don't know—*available* to help me?"

"Calm down," said Reena, placing a hand on his shoulder. "Breathe. Remember what I helped you with concerning Spectral Sight."

Jonah turned back to the headstones. They were, at the moment, completely unremarkable. Nothing stuck out or did a funny "calling out" to him. There was just the quiet of the evening, supplemented by the chirping of the birds and crickets. He centered his breathing, closed his eyes, and once again visualized the stage curtain fully lowered. *Open*, he willed it. *It's show time.* Obediently, the curtain raised in his mind. His Spectral Sight was active. He opened his eyes.

Things were almost as they were before he'd closed them, but now some of the headstones had changed. Some remained utterly unremarkable, but several dozen now shone with a pearlish gleam. The gleam was faint but noticeable and seemed to illuminate certain stones with an otherworldly glow. Jonah knew somewhere in the back of his mind that if this had occurred to him only a week ago, he would have likely suffered a breakdown. Now, though, he had to admit that he found it kind of cool.

He moved to one of the illuminated stones. This one happened to be another WWII veteran.

Clear intent, Jonah thought. *Respectful.* He was a writer. Words were his life. He could do this. "Brave soldier," he said in a clear, strong voice, "you did this nation a matchless and precious service by laying down your physical life in combat. Now, I humbly ask you to do me the honor of endowing me with spiritual strength."

Reena looked at him, impressed. So, too, did Terrence and Malcolm.

"I've always had a way with words," said Jonah, shrugging.

The gleam that cascaded the tombstone suddenly elongated and solidified, taking the form of a soldier in his forties with a weather-beaten face, determined eyes, and a heavy jaw. He was quite a strapping form with an elegantly creased uniform and high-ranking insignia. His form remained transparent, but his presence was still imposing. It filled Jonah with respect and gratitude. If anyone deserved peace, it was this guy.

"You honor me with your words, Eleventh Percenter," said the spirit. "I would consider it an honor to aid you. You have been endowed."

Immediately, Jonah's every particle surged with energy. The aches of his stomach and back were now almost nonexistent, and though his doubts and trepidation had not yet faded, there was definitely a focus in his mind that had not been present before.

"Excellent," said Terrence. "Let's get started!"

Terrence moved forward with a swiftness Jonah wouldn't have thought possible of such a tall, large frame and blindsided him with a shoulder tackle. He hadn't expected it at all. It was concussive force, most likely from the endowment Terrence possessed. He collapsed on the ground, dazed.

"For future reference," said Terrence, sounding apologetic, "when someone charges, crouch low and use their momentum against them. Awareness of your surroundings is crucial."

"Yeah?" gasped Jonah. "Why?"

He shouldn't have asked. His legs were cut out from underneath him with unerring speed. The blow was so swift and impactful that Jonah did a full back flip and momentarily landed back on his feet before keeling over again.

Scrambling to his knees, he quickly saw who the culprit had been—Reena.

"That's why," she said. "Spirits move at preternatural speed. Some ethereal humans can as well. Awareness of surroundings can help you use the endowment in your favor."

Note to self, thought Jonah, *when turbo-Reena barrels through, jump like a 'roided kangaroo.*

"Remember, it's only defense right now, man," said Terrence, "and don't get aggravated. It's your very first night."

Jonah barely had time to register that fact when it felt like a cobra grasped him from the rear. Gasping harshly, he heard Bobby's voice say to him, "If you have to block something, it's got to be by instinct. Sometimes you will have two minutes, at other times, only two seconds, like now."

Still clamping Jonah in that unyielding grasp, he whipped Jonah around. It was only then that Jonah heard the rapid steps.

Trip was bounding forward, a look of savage glee on his face. No doubt he had been waiting for them to begin training Jonah, as it would provide him with the perfect excuse for a cheap shot. That smug look infuriated Jonah. He didn't know how much time elapsed, but a single thought, clear as the night sky overhead, sprang fully formed in his mind. *That idiot won't hit me. I won't give him the satisfaction. He* won't *hit me.*

He shut his eyes.

BAM.

Expecting to feel the ground once more, he'd braced himself. No ground. He was still upright. He hadn't even been knocked backward. Stunned, he opened his eyes and saw Trip on the ground, dazed and cursing. The others stared at Jonah in shock.

In front of him was a wall of vapor, morphed to the front of his body so it looked like a second skin that had detached itself and moved a few feet forward. Despite hovering about two feet in front of him, it mirrored every move he made.

"Do you see that?" exclaimed Liz. "He took the vapor in front of him and solidified it! Made it into a shield!"

Jonah's mind was turning. He decided he didn't want to be hit, and so it didn't happen? Was that how it worked?

Malcolm extended his hand to Trip, but Trip raised himself without the assistance, flashing Jonah a look of the purest loathing. Jonah shrugged.

"Hey, it's about blocking, right?" he grumbled. "That's what you're teaching me, isn't it? Well, it happened. Deal with it."

"What I want to know," said Reena slowly, "is *how* it happened. Jonah, how did you do that?"

The minute Jonah thought about it, the shield of vapor dissipated. "I have no idea, Reena," he told her. "I just thought in my mind that I didn't want to be hit." Which was true as far as it went; he didn't see the need to mention that he specifically did not want to be hit by Trip. "And then that shield thing was there."

Reena stared. "How about you try it again?"

The second they resumed, however, Jonah knew that trying another burst like that was hopeless. Maybe it only worked on people he hated, like Trip. He actually liked the others.

The grueling exercise took another hour and a half. Jonah would have loved to have experienced some breakthrough halfway through, have his senses open up, and suddenly repel every move that occurred. But that simply didn't happen. As a matter of fact, he was thankful for the soldier's spiritual endowment because he was so roughed up that he was willing to bet that he'd have been sorer than he already was when Jonathan stepped forward and called a halt for the evening. Terrence extended an arm to Jonah, who took it glumly.

"We are going to work on that shield," he said quietly. "I ain't ever seen nothing like it."

Jonah didn't see what the big deal was. It didn't appear very remarkable, and when he actually put some thought into how he did it, it dissipated back into the air. The moment had been over so quickly it had almost felt accidental.

Malcolm, Liz, and Bobby, who had been especially irritated about being kept in the dark about Creyton's recent deeds, had now resumed their usual personalities. Jonah figured that while Bobby was performing physical activity, which he clearly loved, the world could be ending the next day, and he wouldn't care. If he was so excited about roughhousing, Jonah shuddered at thinking just how long it would take to be on par with them all. Reena eyed him with interest, and it was obvious that she was eager to experiment with that shield, just like Terrence. For some bizarre reason, he felt as though it would be cool to impress her. He couldn't understand why he wanted to do such a thing, seeing as how Reena wasn't going to actually fall for him. It just felt like something he had to do. Weird.

"All right, my friends," said Jonathan clearly. "You know the routine."

In unison, everyone around Jonah fell to their knees like they were about to pray. But then Jonathan narrowed his eyes, and they all shuddered slightly and looked fatigued as if they'd run a triathlon. Trip and Bobby actually fell forward, panting, only having prevented full face plants by throwing their arms out in front of them.

"You might want to kneel, Jonah," warned Jonathan. "I estimate you have about twenty more seconds."

"Twenty seconds?" said Jonah blankly. "Before wh—?"

And then it happened. Jonah felt as if he crashed off a sugar rush with no grace period beforehand. His legs were like jelly as he crumpled to his knees, grimacing at the discomfort he felt there. The pains that he hadn't registered while endowed with the soldier's essence were now thrown in full effect. He swore softly as his arms, lower back, and torso were screaming with pain.

"That's why you kneel," said Reena, recovering her strength. "It can be draining when spiritual endowments are relinquished. That's why cardio fitness is imperative. You simply don't know what kind of injuries can be sustained falling from full height, so we kneel. Much less force and momentum."

"Thanks for that," gasped Jonah, who was being helped to his feet by a fatigued Malcolm.

"Don't worry. You will get used to it, and I am not just saying that either," he said in his quiet voice.

"Yeah? And how are you doing with that?" asked Jonah.

"A steady work in progress," replied Malcolm with a grin.

Jonah looked forward to the day when it would no longer feel like he was being clocked by sledgehammers when endowments were taken. Terrence offered him an old-school canteen, which he took gratefully and gulped nearly half of it down in two swallows. Even though the water was tepid, with the level of fatigue Jonah felt, it tasted like the nectar of God.

"Why so glum?" asked Terrence.

Jonah guessed he wasn't doing a good job of hiding his disappointment. "I don't know, man," he replied. "I have now seen, with embarrassing clarity, just how out of shape I am. I'm not cut out for this, Terrence."

"What were you expecting on day one of training, Jonah?" scoffed Terrence. "To be flawless? Be some paragon of perfection?"

Jonah eyed him seriously. "No," he said. "Just to be better than I was."

"Expected some magic spark to fire off in your mind?" said Reena's voice, and Jonah turned to see that she, Bobby, and Liz had joined them. "It doesn't work like that. What happened tonight was exactly what was supposed to happen."

"Let me let you in on something," said Terrence, who glanced over at Trip who was conversing with Jonathan. "When Trip had his first training session, so I heard, he was on his back for almost the whole hour. When he lost his endowment, he slept for seventy-two hours afterward."

That lightened Jonah's mood considerably. " 'So you heard?' " he asked. "You weren't here when Trip first got here?"

"Nope," said Terrence. "Trip started hanging around a bunch of years before we got here. He's some years older than us. Year shy of thirty."

They joined Jonathan and Trip, who were heading back to the estate.

The trip had definitely not felt this long when they were heading to the Glade, thought Jonah. He had to improve his cardiovascular health, and quick. For the past few minutes, he'd been thinking how, up to this point, his weight-management issues hadn't ever mattered. But now, judging by the soreness, fatigue, and lack of coordination, he was now acutely aware of all of his physical limitations.

Reena hung back a few steps to catch up with him. "Don't judge yourself so harshly," she said, clapping him on the back. "You were bound to be humbled on the first day. Works wonders on your focus, though."

Jonah frowned at her. "Is one of your gifts clairvoyance or something?" he asked.

She laughed. "Clairvoyance? No, just reading people's essences. Not sure I'd even want to read their minds! People's minds can be dark places ... that I know from my own experiences."

"Then how did you know what I was thinking?" asked Jonah.

"I told you before that men are obvious," Reena replied. "Besides, you wear your opinion of yourself on your sleeve for the entire world to see. And you don't have anything to be ashamed of. We will help you get up to scratch. It will come, don't worry."

Jonah felt good about having friends who would assist him and wished his professional colleagues were as helpful. Then, with a jolt, he realized that for the first time since he'd begun working at Essa, Langton, and Bane, Inc., he had gone almost a full day without thinking about the place. He had always known that he was better off without that job and that he didn't belong there. It was just that, up to that point, he had always wondered if the problem had been him. Was he not competent enough to do his job? Did he lack, as Jessica had wondered aloud once or twice (and Langton had agreed, though he wasn't aware that Jonah knew), the "E.L.B. Inc. mindset" that they always mentioned?

It had made his desire for his writing to succeed that much greater. If *only* he could get past the damned writer's block.

"Reena," he said.

"Yes?" responded Reena. They'd made it back to the estate and had just started up the steps.

"I would like to see some of your paintings, if you don't mind."

Immediately, she looked on guard. "Why?"

Jonah was taken aback by her expression. "Because you said it was your passion. I would like to see what your other talents are besides athletic attunement and making heart-healthy food."

Her face relaxed. "Fine. But you need to eat something first. A small salad, maybe. Then I will show you my studio."

Jonah, grateful that she'd taken that stance, gave a quick nod.

"Nice save, Jonah," muttered Terrence from behind him. Jonah supposed that he wasn't the only one who noticed Reena's sharp expression. "Just do yourself a favor and be honest. If you don't like something, just say it. Remember, your essence changes when you lie."

"Wha—?" said Jonah, but then he remembered Reena's ability. "Right. Gotcha. Thanks, Terrence."

At the kitchen table, everyone ate in silence, broken only by random conversation. It was obvious that despite the hard training, they were still occupied with the information that they'd learned. Trip scarfed down a sandwich with alarming speed, mumbled something about a musical insight he'd just had, and left the table without another word. Jonah watched him leave with a scowl.

"Okay," he said, "what is Trip's deal? Is he always this cheerful? Tell me now, so I can at least have a valid reason to hate him."

Everyone at the table chuckled, as if they all felt the same way, yet Jonah felt that it was a touchy subject nonetheless. Jonah wasn't moved by that either. Everyone suffered hardships and misfortunes. For God's sake, if Jonah's personality reflected the crap he'd experienced in his life, he would have been the biggest asshole on earth.

"Trip isn't very trusting," said Terrence. "Guess he's been burned a lot in his life. He's not warm with anyone. He has cast-iron armor on and doesn't let people in. At *all*. Maybe with time..." his voice trailed off.

"I don't see why I should accommodate him like that," grumbled Jonah. "He doesn't know me."

"Exactly," said Bobby, though Trip's behavior seemed to have angered him as well. "He doesn't. I suppose some people are just like that. Some folks are just either hot or cold. Strangers get rode hard before they earn respect. Until that time, shields are up and active."

"Speaking of shields," said Malcolm, "that was a work of art, Jonah! And you have no idea how you managed it?"

The question actually distracted Jonah. He had still been wondering if Trip had skeletons in his closet. If he did, Jonah was willing to be patient. Given time, skeletons always managed to rattle when least expected to.

"I really don't, Malcolm," he told him, "but I plan to find out. When I set my mind to something, I'm determined to do it."

Except for the writing, a small voice reminded him. He ignored it.

"I just saw Trip coming," he continued, "and said in my mind, 'I won't take a hit from him.' That was the result. But when I thought about it, the shield faded."

"Well, that was your first mistake," said Liz, who'd been silent up to this point.

"Huh?" said Jonah.

"Thoughts can sometimes prove detrimental," she said. "Not all the time, of course, but in times of defense and offense, thinking, or at least too much of it, can hurt you."

"Why?" Jonah understood the fallacy of over-analysis, but he couldn't see why thinking would, or could, hurt anyone. It went against just about everything he'd been taught.

"Brains, while an asset, are not the only thing you need," said Reena. "That's why we're helping you get up to scratch, with reflexes and everything. It builds the mind."

"Wait a minute," said Jonah. "You just said thinking was bad—"

"No, she did not," said Jonathan, who had just materialized near the kitchen door. The cat-flap flew open, revealing Bast. She bounded forward underneath the table, rubbing legs and ankles affectionately. Jonah, who had finished his salad, beckoned to her absently, and she leapt to his lap and settled there. "She said that too much thinking is not good for anyone. And your *brain* is just in your head. Your *mind* encompasses your whole body."

Without warning, Bobby flung the salt shaker at Jonah. Jonah yelped and threw up a hand to deflect it. The others looked unsurprised at this, and Jonathan's regal features pulled into a grin.

"There is a reason why they are called *unthinking* reflexes, Jonah," he said. "Remember that."

Jonah grimaced. Oh, *how* thankful he'd be when he was no longer the newbie. He didn't care much for information that was new to him being obvious to everyone else. At the very least, when he had gotten some time and skill under his belt, he wouldn't have saltshakers thrown at him.

"I'm headed to bed," said Bobby, and he started up the stairs, stopping to glance at Jonah. "Get some rest, Jonah," he said, a devilish gleam in his eye, "'cuz tomorrow, you're beginning weights." He grinned, which Jonah returned halfheartedly. This was shaping up to be a painful weekend.

"Going to be involved in more defense lessons tomorrow night?" Malcolm asked him.

"Of course," said Jonah, showing eagerness he wasn't entirely feeling at the moment. "Only way the embarrassment will fade, right?"

"How right you are," said Malcolm. He left, Liz behind him, with a kind smile and a quick wave.

"I believe I promised you that I'd show you my art," said Reena. "You are welcome to come, Terrence. Won't take long."

There was a sort of bitter finality in her voice that Jonah had come to associate with his own annoyance when a literary spark fizzled out in his mind.

They went through the kitchen and down some stairs, which led to a room almost as spacious as the workout room. The moment Reena flicked the lights on, Jonah's jaw dropped.

Her paintings, in his opinion, were some of the best works he had ever seen. It was obvious that Reena had been painting for years as some of her art looked more aged than others. He wandered from canvas to canvas, attempting to understand this beautiful world that was completely foreign to him.

Some of Reena's art was obvious, such as her own renditions of the *Vitruvian Man* and her own personal (and quite accurate) stab at the *Mona Lisa*, but others were her own creations. She had done a painting of a brilliant highway that reached a fork of vibrant red and then split, the left road a lovely shade of white, and the right one a dazzling gold. It was quite captivating.

"Can you explain this one to me, please?" Jonah asked her.

"I refer to it as *The Roads of Desire*," said Reena, her voice mechanical. "The plain road is the road that the majority of people take, the one they know. They dream at length of a road of peace," she indicated the pure white road, "which is free of attack, woe, strife, and stress. But they also think of the road of riches," she motioned to the golden one, "fame, prosperity, fortune. People desire peace, yet at the same time, desire wealth and glory. They are unaware of how to have both, so they stay on the ordinary road. It's more of the same old thing, but it's safe and familiar, so they keep taking it."

Jonah was fascinated. In his own experiences, he had never known athletic people to be philosophical. Simply put, most of them had just been idiots. It was quite an interesting thing to behold. In spite of himself, he began to feel that the isolation that he had unconsciously accepted might possibly fade among his new friends. He was about to ask her more about *The Roads of Desire* when his eyes fell upon another painting. It appeared to be an abstract heart with various pumps that seemed to be overworking it. It appeared to be of different colors, which seemed to be the result of some kind of bruising or attack. He contemplated it pensively.

"What's the name of this one?" he asked.

She looked at him impatiently. "It's right there. Don't you see it?"

"Not without my reading glasses, no," said Jonah.

Reena sighed. "It's *The Impressionable Heart*," she said.

Terrence, who had been quiet up to this point due to his own preoccupation with various paintings, had joined them. "Reena, you don't have to explain it. It's fine. Jonah, let's look at her fruit portraits—"

"No, Terrence, it's all right," said Reena, sighing again. "Jonah, I painted this when I was in the midst of angst-ridden adolescence, before I'd gotten over my mother disowning me. There are four quadrants to this heart. The greenish one," she pointed out, "is the me that I had been told I should be; the one that would be successful if she focused only on school, got married, and bore a nice, healthy litter. The reddish one is the me that I saw at the time. Angry, worthless, 'abnormal', and cynical. Or so everyone told me. The blackish one is the result of trying to accommodate everyone's fantasies of me. Trying to be a good little girl, who, as my mom put it, 'didn't rock the boat.' There were so many colors in it, influencing it, eroding it, that it went to black. The bluish white one," she pointed at it almost wistfully, "is the me I want to be. Successful, fit, at peace, having finally found my soulmate, who is just as at peace with herself as I am. But these four parts don't mesh, because they are all impressionable. Too damned impressionable."

Terrence looked at Reena with a somber expression. Jonah was silent for a few minutes after she was done. In that moment, he understood, at least partially, what Reena meant when she said life could be hard for an Eleventh Percenter. On top of the issues you dealt with just being who you were, there was this extra part. How to incorporate them all into who you were would be enough to stress anyone.

"Reena, this is all brilliant," he ventured. "You are really talented! These things shouldn't be hiding in a dark basement! You should do something with it!"

Reena shook her head. "No."

"What? Why??" said Jonah. "You have a wonderful gift!"

"As I'm sure you do with your writing," muttered Reena.

"Woman, please," scoffed Jonah. "My writing is garbage compared to this."

"After what you said to the soldier's spirit out there tonight, I highly doubt that," piped up Terrence.

Jonah glanced at him in a "You're not helping" sort of way, to which Terrence stubbornly replied, "Your writing ain't garbage. I know that for sure, and I've never even read your stuff."

"Jonah, I can't display my art for the entire world to see," said Reena. "It would almost be a crime. When I paint, I can be who I want to be. Paint what I want to paint. To show my happiness in art form when it doesn't match what I feel inside would be demoralizing. So it stays here. Good night."

She turned and left then without another word, leaving Terrence looking resigned and Jonah looking flabbergasted.

2 a.m.

Despite what the clock said, Jonah still couldn't find it in himself to be tired, let alone sleep. The soreness had not passed, but it was easy enough to ignore. There was too much on his mind to focus on pain. So much to know, so much to understand. To learn that so many truths that he had held for all those years simply weren't true was jarring enough. But then he saw Reena's superb art and heard her caustic words about it. How could she be so dead-set against showcasing a gift that she so plainly possessed? She had said displaying her art would be criminal. What was *criminal* was the fact that that treasure trove of art was rotting away in a basement.

But then he remembered Nelson's impassioned pleas to him to keep up with his writing, which he had treated, and was still treating, with the same disregard as Reena had for her painting. He would reach a snag and just quit. He'd quit writing so many times in his life he'd lost count. And here he was, telling Reena to show the world her gift while he was trying so hard to deny a literary trait that simply wouldn't leave.

Plus this new discovery. He was an Eleventh Percenter. He couldn't deny *that* any more than he could deny that he was a writer.

"Thorn in your side, Jonah?" said a familiar voice. Jonah started, and Jonathan laughed.

"My apologies," he said, sitting in the chair opposite Jonah's bed. "Bast intimated to me that your essence was in disarray, and I wanted to lend a hand if I could."

Jonah swung his legs off of the bed and stood, staring mutinously at the calico.

"Thanks a lot," he grumbled.

Ironically, Bast leapt onto the bed and curled. Jonah turned to Jonathan.

"It's just a lot," he said quietly. "I have learned a lot, yet I have a lot to learn. It is fascinating stuff; don't get me wrong. But a lot of it is also unsettling. And once you know the truth, you can't, you know, *un*-know it. It's just a bunch to take in."

"It is," agreed Jonathan, "but truth can benefit you in ways you can't yet imagine. Up until today, you thought you were going insane. If the truth hadn't been revealed, you very well could have."

Jonah's insides went cold at those words. As a writer, he valued his mind and imagination. The mere thought of it ever being unstable was almost too much to bear.

"And here I am, destined to cause some kind of upheaval," he muttered. "I have a great deal to learn, and am facing someone who has been terrorizing people since forever and is killing off Eleventh Percenters now. Kind of lopsided, wouldn't you say?"

"Not at all," said Jonathan. "You think experience is the most dangerous weapon there is? Experience is indeed invaluable, Jonah, but it also has its flaws and consequences. I'm sure you have heard older people say, 'I've forgotten more than you will ever know.' Well, Creyton has forgotten a great deal. Experience can make one deadly but also woefully complacent."

Jonah looked into Jonathan's eyes, which were remarkably aged despite his young visage. In that moment, he felt that he could trust him with any information. This entire time, two things had been tugging uncomfortably at the back of his mind.

"Jonathan, you chose to stay here," he said. "As a Spirit Guide or something—"

"Protector Guide," corrected Jonathan. "The Spirit Guides are a little higher up on the totem pole."

"Yeah, that," said Jonah, "Protector Guide. But you have free rein to jump between Earthplane and Astral Plane, right?"

Jonathan surveyed him. "Yes."

In a tone that he hoped was offhand, Jonah asked, "In your travels, have you seen a thickset woman, black hair with streaks of gray, and old-school, rather thick-framed glasses?"

Jonathan was not fooled at all. "Your grandmother crossed on, Jonah," he said softly. "She bypassed the Astral Plane and did not stay behind. After such a long physical life, she deserved the peace."

"Good," said Jonah, his voice flat because he didn't trust it otherwise. While he was grateful that his grandmother was not among the spirits and spiritesses being usurped and pilfered by Creyton, he couldn't avoid the stabbing pang of hurt that he felt upon hearing that she was irreversibly gone.

"She hasn't truly left you, Jonah," said Jonathan. "Your grandmother can be on the Other Side, freely expanding her knowledge in the next phase of her spiritual life, and right with you," he pointed two fingers at Jonah's heart, "lending you her love and support in the times that you most need them. Remember, though it was a most unfortunate circumstance, that you called her memory to you when you were saddened? She is there for you always. She lives in you."

Jonah nodded slowly. The information about Nana he could handle. Probably. But there was another question that nagged him.

"Is God real?" he asked. "Have you met God?"

A grave yet sympathetic look took over Jonathan's face. "That is a matter that your physical mind would not comprehend."

Jonah's eyes narrowed. "So that's a 'no.' "

Wide-eyed, Jonathan shook his head. "That is not what I meant at all."

Jonah grimaced. In the past, he'd had conversations with older people, veritable stores of knowledge (so-called), who preferred not to breach a subject because his "young mind would not understand." Now here was a spirit, a being who had been beyond Earthplane, telling him his "physical" mind would not understand God. His grandmother had raised him to be religious, but he'd dispensed with religion when she'd passed. But it was still disheartening to hear Jonathan's response.

"It's a simple question," he said. "Is there a God and have you met him. Yes or no. Simple."

"That is where you are wrong, Jonah," said Jonathan. Once again, his expression was sympathetic. He truly looked like he was holding back emotions of his own. "The inquiry you are making is not a simple one. No doubt you were taught ideals which stemmed from religious doctrine. It would not be my place to endorse, or shatter, anything you hold dear. Spiritual path is something that is beautiful and enlightening, but most importantly, *personal*. Private. Your own interpretations. So if I were to answer your question concerning a Supreme Being, it would yield no benefit to you."

"Really," said Jonah, unconvinced. "Why's that?"

"The reason for that, my friend, actually *is* simple," said Jonathan, looking relieved at this fact. "Let me give you an example. Say I asked someone what they thought of a particular animal. A rat, for example. Person A could say something to the effect of 'I enjoy those animals. Harmless foragers. Hardworking.' Person B could say 'Rats are disgusting! They carry diseases!' Person C could say 'I have had bad experiences with rats, and for that reason, I don't think they are safe.' Further still, Person D could say 'I have never seen a rat before. I wouldn't know.' Those were four different answers to ONE question. However, all the answers were true in the interpretations of the persons asked. So *my* answer to your question may not be *your* answer to your question. Therefore, your physical mind would do well to continue forging and establishing truths on your own."

Jonah stared at him. "Um—did you make fortune cookies or something when you were alive?"

Jonathan laughed at that. "As I have already explained to you, Jonah, I am *still* alive, just not physically so. Now, get some sleep. You need it."

He disappeared, leaving Jonah thinking that the embarrassing clarity he'd experienced during his first training session wasn't the only clarity he'd be gaining from now on.

8

Concern and Chaos

Jonah felt like he had barely warmed the sheets when Bobby came bustling in wide awake at 5:50 a.m., telling him that it was time to hit weights. Jonah guessed that arguing with him would be useless, so he got up, pulled on a tank top, and grinned as much as his exhaustion would allow. He was surprised to see Terrence at the stairs, ready to join them.

Bobby looked at him curiously. "What are you doing up, Ter?" he asked.

"Do I need permission to lift weights?" asked Terrence. When Bobby shrugged and led the way, Terrence fell in step with Jonah and said in an undertone, "I'm here because Bobby gets very focused and intense when he works out. It wouldn't be good for you to like him and then come to hate him in such a short period of time."

Jonah could see that that was a very serious concern for Terrence, and within the first ten minutes of weightlifting, he was thankful for his presence. Bobby was a magnificent physical specimen for such a vertically challenged guy, but his entire demeanor changed the minute he picked up a dumbbell. He was such an intense, focused, and competitive workout partner that it was daunting. His tenacity in that gym was in such a raw state that it was almost primal. The circuit that Bobby put Jonah through, even at the level of a beginner (or what Bobby said was beginner) was one of the most brutal things that he had ever experienced. If it hadn't been for Terrence's encouraging words and rationalizing, "cut him some slack, Jonah, he's had it hard because of his stature," he would likely have branded Bobby a psychopath and abandoned the workout altogether. As it was, he was barely able to lift his hands above his elbows when he was done. Since the nearest bathtub to his bedroom was back through the kitchen, he ran into Reena there, who quaked with mirth when she saw his discomfort.

"Take a bath in some water that is as hot as you can bear it," she advised. "And toss some of this in there."

She tossed a can of salt at him, which he grabbed out of the air, though his arm felt like it had complied only grudgingly.

"What do I need the salt for?"

"Salt baths soothe your muscles," said Reena, again with that unmistakable tone that the information should have been obvious. While that annoyed Jonah greatly, he was very much relieved that their awkward encounter mere hours before appeared to be forgotten. She was as sprightly and alert as Terrence and Bobby had been, which puzzled Jonah. How could they be so alert after four and a half hours of sleep?

"What are you about to do?" asked Jonah, still eyeing the salt with skepticism.

She spread her hands, indicating her athletic wear. "Run, of course!"

Jonah frowned. "Reena, there are six treadmill machines downstairs."

She scoffed. "I find that exercising in the open is the most beneficial. See you!"

She was out of the door before Jonah could make any further inquiries. Terrence, who had followed Jonah into the kitchen, grinned at him before filling a glass with water.

"She is a fanatic," muttered Jonah.

"Eh, I suppose it's a mania with Reena," agreed Terrence. "But what's the alternative? Bobby?"

Jonah's eyes bulged, and Terrence laughed. "You better get in a bath, man," he said. "Your body's going to turn on you and become your enemy if you don't."

Twenty minutes later, Jonah lay prone in a bath of brine and nearly scalding water. Reena turned out to be right yet again, as the salty water provided remedy for the aches from the previous nights that were now warring with the fresh ones after Bobby's psycho workout. It was calming, but it also gave him time to think.

When Jonah first prepared himself for the bath, he'd accidentally caught a glimpse of himself in the mirror and sighed. The hazel eyes that stared back at him were those of a very confused individual. So much had happened in such a short period of time. He possessed a Blue Aura and apparently was capable of massive upheaval. That thought was not a reassuring one as in his own experiences, upheaval hadn't been the greatest of things. Just two days ago, *two* days, he thought he was just another statistical dot in the population. Now, he knew that he was not just a statistic. He stuck out conspicuously, had a mortal enemy, and was supposedly on the path to be some sort of savior. Was that supposed to be a good thing? Was that supposed to be a great feeling?

As he thought on the undesirable gut and utterly mundane profile that made up who he'd become in twenty-three years, he could only disagree.

He dried. His muscles still ached but were far more cooperative than they had been before the bath. He went back to the dusty bedroom in which he was bunking and pulled on some jeans and a polo shirt. He went outside and wandered to the gazebo. The place was so serene and quiet. There weren't any places like this near his apartment back in the city. On a hunch, he closed his eyes took a deep breath and willed the stage curtain to open.

There were no spirits or spiritesses in his line of sight, but that was fine. He activated Spectral Sight for a specific one.

"Marla?" he said to open air. "You would benefit me greatly by show-ing yourself."

Focusing as hard as he could, he thought of the woman that had given him such a drastic shock not so long ago. Ten seconds later, a bright spot in the morning sunlight seemed to shimmer, and she emerged with a look of pleasant interest on her face.

"This is a surprise," she said. "To what do I owe the pleasure, Jonah?"

"I wanted to shake things up, for once," he told her. "I wanted to speak with you when I wasn't in a state of shock."

"And would it be safe to ask why?" inquired Marla. There was a bit of a drawl in her voice, but she spoke as though she had taught herself to suppress it when she was physically alive.

"Because I wanted to know some things about you," said Jonah. "First and foremost, when in the forties did you d—I mean, pass into Spirit?"

She looked, if possible, more surprised. "How did you know that?"

"Well, you have the forties hairstyle and getup. And the string of pearls that were so commonplace then. I know all that because I read a lot. Seen a bunch of pictures."

Marla sat down opposite Jonah. The seat creaked, showing its age. She seemed rather wistful as she went back in her mind. "It was in 1941. December 7th, of all days. Nobody remembered poor Marla, as that's the day that 'lives in infamy,'" she said.

Jonah looked at her. "I'm sorry about that. You passed on the day that Pearl Harbor got attacked. So I'm guessing it felt like it was secondary."

"Something along those lines," responded Marla.

"So what happened?" asked Jonah.

The sadness on Marla's face became more pronounced. "Creyton killed my husband."

"What?"

"Yes." She lowered her head.

"Was your husband an Eleventh Percenter?" asked Jonah, stunned.

"No, Tenth Percenter, just like me," Marla said, her tone soft. "He was a big-time owner of many things, but his bread and butter were the mills. He was gone a lot. It made me suspect things, and I heard a lot of rumors, but he was still my husband, and I loved him. One day, and I'll never forget it," she closed her eyes, "he needed to travel to

Shreveport. Said he was working on a career deal that 'would change our lives' or something. I knew better, but I didn't dare say anything. The next day, the sheriff tells me that my husband lost control of his car and ran off a bridge."

Jonah winced. That was a horrible story, but there was something weird about it.

"Not to sound callous or anything, but—" he began, but Marla stopped him with a wistful smile.

"How can I sound so matter of fact?" she supplied. "I've had several decades to practice acceptance, Jonah."

Not knowing how to reply to that, Jonah simply plunged. "How did you know that it was Creyton?"

Marla slowly transferred her gaze to the grounds. "Of course I didn't know it was him at the time," she said. "I assumed that it was an enemy that my husband had made. He was not a kindly man. Be that as it may, I was never the same without him. I didn't leave our home for eight months. But one day, I did. I must admit that I have gone over the decision two million times since then. I drove to the site of my husband's accident."

Jonah stared at her, surprised. "What were you hoping to achieve by doing that?"

Marla smiled that wistful smile again. "Your guess is as good as mine, Jonah. Closure. Finality. Any feeling other than the emptiness that had engulfed me for so many months. Anyway, I left the car, found a steady perch at the embankment and just stood there. I was so overcome with emotion. I don't know what I expected to happen. Maybe get a glimpse of him? Would he be haunting me if I actually desired to see him? But nothing happened. Not a single thing. I was heartbroken. Tears flowed. Fatal tears, I'm sad to say."

Jonah frowned. "Fatal tears?"

"I was crying, that was why I—why it happened," whispered Marla. "I couldn't stem the tears. They just flowed and flowed, and I was half-blinded. I turned to step down from my perch, but my vision was so blurred I lost my footing, and a strong gust of wind was all my momentum needed to take me over."

Jonah looked at Marla, horror-struck. He was instantly sympathetic as he was reminded of his own near miss due to being blinded by tears in his childhood. Marla saw his face and shook her head.

"Ancient history, darling," she said, her voice almost achieving humor. "But I remember the air ripping at me, and the water feeling similar to soggy dirt. I felt pain for the slightest of moments, and then I was numb. Felt absolutely nothing. And it was at *that* moment that he showed himself."

"You mean Creyton?" asked Jonah.

"Yes, Creyton," said Marla, closing her eyes. "I will never forget it. That inhuman expression and those vile dark eyes. I had no idea what he was doing there. But when he saw me, he said, 'Your spirit will be a welcome addition to the fold.' Then, I fled. I don't know how I got away, so please do not bother asking. But I met Jonathan, who explained to me that I *hadn't* escaped the water. Can you believe it? I hadn't even realized that I was ... was..." Her voice trailed off into teary-eyed silence.

Jonah moved nearer to the spiritess, concerned. "But you're not d—I mean gone, Marla," he said. How could his friends judge this spiritess so harshly? How could they be annoyed with her? How could Jonathan talk of her so contemptuously as if she were some sort of irksome gnat or something?

"My life is gone, Rowe," said Marla. "I get that I am still alive and all that. But what good is living if I can't feel as though I am alive? I'm in this—this limbo, no longer knowing companionship, no longer knowing love. To add insult to injury, pardon the pun—they never even found my body. The current took it out to—somewhere—hours before anyone even realized something was amiss."

Jonah couldn't think of a time he felt more pity for anyone, even if the pity was futile. "Did you at least re-unite with your husband? Had he stayed behind in spirit form, like you did?"

Strangely, the question made her stop crying. Her bated breathing abruptly ceased; it was as if all her emotions had instantaneously shut down. "No," she told him. "He crossed to the Other Side. Lucky bastard. But by the time my physical life was over, Creyton was keeping tabs, was blocking all the stops. I learned of the Eleventh Percenters, and began going to them for help. Sadly..." she sighed, and Jonah understood. Revealing her presence made them all vulnerable. A spirit's presence couldn't be forced upon an Eleventh Percenter; it was tantamount to sending up a flare.

"I apologize for showing myself to you, Jonah," said Marla. "I suppose I never learn. I am sincerely apologetic. I am ... well, not just me, there are many of us. We just desperately want to continue our journey, even if it is an imitation of physical life. That's why I asked for your help."

Jonah didn't know what to think. Marla's presence had frightened him out of his mind that day, but she needed help and had jumped the gun. She hadn't been zealous; even if she didn't reunite with her husband, she desired freedom. How could he be angered by that?

"We'll help you, Marla," he said. "I admit that I don't have the strongest grasp on everything that's happening yet, but we'll make everything clear for you. You will be able to go to the Other Side ... or *wherever*. Who knows? The Other Side just might bring you the joy you lost all that time ago."

She smiled in spite of herself, tears of gratitude on her face. Jonah looked away. "Do you—do you cry with every emotion?" he asked.

Marla laughed. "I do not, Jonah Rowe. It's just pleasantly refreshing to see that wonderful men still exist. You want to aid a distressed woman. It's so gallant, sweet and kind, and a reminder of romantic days long since passed."

Her words made Jonah feel a little awkward. He didn't see it the way that Marla did. He only wanted to help the spiritess find a little peace. He didn't see how that translated into him being a gallant crusader. "Uh, thanks," he managed.

With a parting smile, Marla vanished. Jonah continued staring in silence until Liz showed up out of nowhere, a straw hat atop her head and a watering pot in tow, and asked him if he was interested in assisting her with the gardening.

As luck would have it, that Sunday was littered with distractions strong enough that Jonah was almost jarred out of his thoughts about Marla. Reena had prepared an enormous salad for everyone, which was flavorful enough with her dressing, which consisted of lemon juice and olive oil. He found it entertaining to listen to her and Malcolm debate about whether or not the fat content in ranch dressing, which was his favorite, would be enough to nullify the nutritional content of the salad. Evidently, Liz had just about forgotten about how information had been withheld from her, because she was as joyous as a kid when she left the garden. Bobby had gone back to the downstairs gym for another weight training session, which both Jonah and Terrence politely declined. When Terrence told Jonah the best ways to make salad delicious was to add everything that Reena did not, Jonah tentatively asked why he didn't go further with his culinary aspirations. Terrence's smile faded somewhat, but he jocularly replied that such things "weren't in his financial realm." Not desiring to have a repeat of what had occurred with Reena, Jonah decided to let it go.

Jonah had a pleasurable time of things with them all, from conversing with Terrence to perusing more of Reena's art (Jonah decided to look silently this time, though the intricacy and beauty resulted in him biting his tongue almost to bleeding in refrain), and before he knew it, evening had overtaken all, and it was time for another training session. Jonah was more prepared this time, wearing borrowed trainers, sweats, and an over-stretched T-shirt, but he only felt confusion when he saw that his counterparts all wore thermals.

"Malcolm," said Jonah as they walked the trek to the Glade, "the evening temperatures haven't dipped enough for you guys to wear thermal."

Malcolm just grinned and shrugged. Though Malcolm was a quiet guy, his grin still put Jonah on his guard.

Jonah was prepared to seek endowment from the soldier again, but he was encouraged to alternate (Jonathan explained that different endowments made one aware of their versatility), so this time, he chose the essence of an elderly spiritess. He was much more gentlemanly in his approach, which he knew would earn more respect with Liz. He hoped that this session would be easier on him, given the fact that he was still feeling effects from the weights.

Wrong. It was, if anything, *more* intense.

They'd circled him again, though in the absence of Trip (who'd been seething because Jonah's shield had caused him significant contusions and a few loosened teeth), the ring was tighter. Reena explained the circular approach by telling Jonah that a panoramic view would improve his reflexes and better prepare him for the unseen dangers. He still got humbled, but he was pleased to discover that his senses were opening up to some slightly higher degree than the first night. He could turn more readily, be more cognizant of his surroundings, and began to feel a weak prickling sensation when someone neared the back of him. This must have meant that he was beginning to sense attacks. A little bit, anyway.

It was with this dawning realization that he successfully blocked a strike from Malcolm and shoved him off. They were both so shocked at the block that Jonah missed an opportunity to actually *counter* the strike, and Malcolm promptly resumed offense.

He'd just turned away from Malcolm and faced Bobby, who made to grab him with those cobra-like arms. Surprisingly, Jonah side-stepped and used Bobby's momentum to send him staggering forward. Jonah lost his own footing for just a moment but avoided falling. He was excited by his moment of prowess, and it cost him. The prickle at his back prompted him to turn, and it was Reena that he faced now. She didn't strike or even do another one of those speed attacks. She widely drew her hands apart and clapped them together with more than mortal force.

Instantly, the night froze. The comfortable dusk air suddenly plummeted to what felt like sixty degrees below. Jonah swore and trembled violently as a stinging, all-encompassing cold overwhelmed him. It felt as if someone had taken a hundred daggers, let them sit overnight in subzero temperatures, and then stabbed him with them.

He lay on the ground shivering and eyed everyone sharply. "I t-t-take it that's w-w-why you g-g-guys are w-wearing those thermals?" he chattered.

Everyone grinned, and Reena said, "It was necessary that you learn that rogue spirits and spiritesses, as well as Spirit Reapers, don't always just hit and kick."

She clapped her hands again, sounding a lot less prominent this time, and the arctic conditions dissipated, leaving the air tepid once more.

"Reena, what in the *hell* was that?" demanded Jonah the second he reached his feet.

Reena looked devilish, which given the recent spell of frigidity, Jonah found ironic. "Have you ever heard that spirits can cause cold spots? Well, that's just a little gift of mine that I've been perfecting for several years. I can dip the temperatures for a matter of minutes, but after about five or ten, I have to desist because it saps more energy from me when the endowment has passed."

Pins and needles were now informing Jonah that his blood was moving warmly in his veins again. "Can we all do that?"

"Don't think so," said Reena, retying her hair, which had come loose during training. "Eleventh Percenters have unique talents, just like everyone else. There are a couple of things exclusive to each of us."

"How does that work if endowments can enhance all of us with spiritual essence?" asked Jonah.

"We all have basic powers that spirits and spiritesses have," said Terrence, "but we each have specialties. Reena's strong spots are cold spots, speed, and essence reading. As you probably know from this morning," he grinned and flexed a quick muscle, which prompted the powerfully built Bobby to snort derisively, "mine is strength-based."

Jonah's eyes bulged. "I didn't know spirit essence could make you stronger."

As if he could no longer hold back, Bobby chimed in. "Spirits have transcended physical life, and therefore are no longer bound by limitations," he said. "At least not physical ones, anyway. So whenever a situation calls for ethereality, we can use those abilities to our advantage, tempering and honing what we can. But everyone has their signatures."

"Like that awesome shield you conjured," said Terrence with admiration. "And that thing that Jonathan said you did with the winds and the electricity. I was psyched about hearing that one. Sounded amazing."

"I thought so, too, Terrence," muttered Jonah, "and I was the one who did it."

At once, everyone knelt and relinquished their endowments. After the usual mastering of brief fatigue, they made their journey back to the estate.

Jonah thought of Jonathan's remarks on the fluidity of time, because before he knew it, it was Monday afternoon, and Terrence surmised that since he lived three and half hours away, it was best if he returned almost immediately.

Malcolm was a carpenter, and it seemed that he was the only one of Jonah's new friends that actually found contentment in what he did. Even though he had the day off, he disappeared to his wood shop out back.

Liz and Bobby decided to take a day trip to Boone since they had no school.

Reena's clerical job called near noon, saying they needed her for some reason. Seeing as it was a holiday, Reena was more than a little annoyed. Trip certainly wasn't going to assist Jonah with so much as a stick of chewing gum, let alone a ride home, so that meant the task of shuttling Jonah back to the city (his car having been left there) fell to Terrence, who was more than willing.

"I actually enjoy driving," Terrence explained. "Seeing open road is therapeutic for me."

Jonah had to admit to himself that he was not anxious to leave the Grannison-Morris estate. He had only been there about two and a half days, sure, but he'd enjoyed it. He had never had such a stretch of simply living since being on his own. He had the grueling weight session with Bobby, though Terrence, bless him, had remained along to see to it that Bobby appeared sane and rational. The couple of trainings with the endowments were about the same, plus Reena's half-freezing him had pointedly reminded him that he still had a long, long way to go (and that wasn't a pleasant thought either. It made him feel more behind than ever). But that was one of the reasons why he was reluctant to leave. He loved learning. However brief the Labor Day weekend was, he'd enjoyed every aching, knowledgeable, frozen moment of it. He understood that there was a lot left to learn, strengths to test, and training to do, because as his own manuscript had told him, he was embarking into a danger zone. Bearing all that in mind, he did not think it a good thing that his progress had to be halted because he had to return to Essa, Langton, and Bane. In the grand scheme of things, billing reports just didn't seem important. Far from looking forward to that damned cubicle, he was quite bummed out. The images of Mr. Langton's, Jessica's, and Anthony's faces in his head brought about such annoyance that he sort of hoped that Trip had made another waspish remark. Retaliation would have provided *such* a wonderful outlet.

"Cheer up, Jonah," said Terrence. "Is your job that bad?"

"Yes," replied Jonah, "it is."

"It can't be any worse than cleaning toilet stalls and being called to a scene where someone saw fit to show the world their lunch," said Terrence.

"You know what, Terrence?" grumbled Jonah, "I don't know. I swear I might ask you to switch jobs with me. At least the contents of a toilet, vomit, and bags of trash can't snitch on you and make your life a living hell."

"That's true," nodded Terrence, "but in your situation, at least the snitches smell good and can properly manage their fluids."

In spite of Jonah's mood, he laughed at that.

"And besides, Jonah," said Terrence after the mirth had faded, "the estate isn't going anywhere, and we aren't either. You are coming back this Friday, aren't you?"

Jonah stared at Terrence. "Is this a question?"

Terrence laughed again. "Well, there you go. Perhaps this week will pass quickly as you have something to look forward to."

"You've no idea," said Jonah. "After a week of looking at Langton, Jessica, and Anthony, even Trip's worst comment would sound like the nicest thing ever."

Terrence shook his head, and they set out.

"Say, where is Jonathan?" asked Jonah as he settled into the car and buckled himself in.

"Eh, most likely on the Astral Plane somewhere," said Terrence, shrugging. "He'll come by and tutor and mentor us, do the trainings and whatnot, and then he will go off to the Astral Plane for stretches at a time."

"Stretches?" asked Jonah. "What was the longest?"

"Oh, three weeks, give or take."

"What! What could he possibly be doing on the Astral Plane for *three weeks?*"

Terrence smirked at Jonah's incredulity. "Remember, man, time on Earthplane, or physical plane, or whatever you want to call it, isn't the same as time for spirit or astral beings. Those three weeks we experienced might have been, I don't know, forty-five minutes to Jonathan. Spirits and spiritesses think of time as a bad joke. Most of them have fun playing with it. Physical time is actually the slowest time there is. Ironic, since Tenth Percenters refer to it as *real* time."

Jonah thought on that for a moment. "Are there any Eleventh Percenters that can manipulate time? Has that ever happened?"

A troubled look crossed Terrence's face, and some of the warmth went out of his eyes. He didn't answer Jonah until they'd accelerated onto the highway. "That's really, really dangerous," he finally managed. "I'm only aware of it happening once, and it was a disaster. A tragic disaster, so I heard."

"Why?"

"Long story."

Jonah had expected that. His new friends seemed to think that they were doing him a kindness by not frontloading him with information. Why didn't they understand that he wanted to learn as much as possible? The can had already been kicked open, so there was no point in holding anything back.

"I wonder if Jonathan knows Marla's whole story," he said, deciding to switch gears. So time manipulation was another story for another day? Fine. Whatever.

"Why do you wonder that?" said Terrence.

"Apparently, that's one of the reasons why she is stuck." He told Terrence of the conversation he'd had with the spiritess in the gazebo.

Terrence's brow furrowed. "Can't say I ever heard that story," he said. "When Marla hounds us, she never goes any further than screaming our names or crying out '*Help!*' We've just come to ignore her; she does it so often."

Jonah felt a pang of annoyance. "Why doesn't someone just help her?"

"Because, Jonah, it ain't that simple," said Terrence. "The blocked path affects a bunch of spirits and spiritesses. I don't think even Jonathan knows how Creyton managed to block it. To help her, it's necessary to help all of them. You ever see them in your dreams?"

"Yeah," said Jonah. "Chained and weak. It's quite disturbing."

"Yeah, it is," said Terrence. "But that's who we are trying to assist. Marla is one of many. But no one even knows how Creyton caused this mess to start with."

Something stirred in Jonah's memory about what Marla had said about the path, but before he could voice it, he was distracted by vivid red dots of light that seemed to blink erratically off the highway. He looked curiously and saw that these lights all seemed to be congregated in the midst of an uncompleted housing complex that, from the looks of the torso-high-looking grass, metals that were only discernible in the thick growth because the parts that weren't rusty gleamed halfheartedly in the sun, and the brownish and yellowish tinge of the once-white vinyl sidings had long since been abandoned.

"Um, Terrence," said Jonah, uncertainty in his tone, "what's the deal with the red pin pricks of light over there?"

Terrence barely glanced at them. "That's the Mandy, or I should say, was *going* to be the Mandy," he said.

"Wait, Mandy?" said Jonah. "The Mandy Housing Development? *The* Mandy? I know about that place. The story, I mean."

"Do you?" said Terrence, and there was something ominous in his voice.

"'Course I do, it was all over the news back when I was in the fourth or fifth grade," said Jonah. "The Mandy Housing Development. Some guys from ... New Jersey, I think it was, bought up a bunch of land and were building up some high-end, restricted community or something. But there was some scandal because the real estate firm was siphoning money off of the project and then forcing it back into activity before people realized it was gone. Their brilliant scheme failed, but no charges were filed. People got bought off, right?"

Terrence's eyes narrowed as he switched to the fast lane. "Nope."

"That was what was all over the news," said Jonah.

"Of course it was," said Terrence, "and they really *were* pilfering people. But that was just half, well, less than half of the story. If the whole truth got out, there would have been a crap storm, and everyone would have been labeled insane."

"I don't follow," said Jonah.

Terrence was silent for a moment and then began to speak. "The Mandy Housing Complex was being constructed on top of Tilford Cemetery, which was a part of one of the local Southern Baptist churches some forty, fifty miles from the Grannison-Morris estate. The upper pecking order in the real estate firm figured that since the church had been demolished some seventy years prior, no one would register the cemetery there. So they dug out the remaining headstones and nothing else."

"*What?!*"

"Yep," said Terrence with a dark tone. "Moved what was left of the tombstones and that was it. Went straight to work."

"But ... but..." sputtered Jonah, "They just got away with it?"

"Well, from a *legal* standpoint, yeah," said Terrence.

"Leg—" began Jonah, but then horrific comprehension settled upon him. "The spirits of the people buried there—they fought back?"

"Something like that," said Terrence. "You know that thing they put on tombstones about 'resting in peace?' An Eleventh Percenter came up with that. That's not just respectful. It was a code to ward people off from disturbing the deceased because disturbing the departed's resting place can have bad consequences. The owners of the Mandy, along with their crooked lawyers, learned that too late."

"What happened to them?" asked Jonah, slightly uneasy about the answer.

"None of us really know," said Terrence. "It all happened before I was at the estate, and not even Jonathan knows the whole story. All that is known is that by the time that it was discovered that there were bodies underneath that development, no charges could be filed because the guilty parties were in no state to go to jail."

"Why was that?" asked Jonah.

"Well, the CEO—he passed into Spirit under mysterious circum-stances," said Terrence, his voice hesitant and deliberate, like he was telling a ghost story. Which now that Jonah thought on it was exactly what it was. "The others involved suddenly all went frickin' crazy."

Jonah tensed, a gesture made very uncomfortable because of the tight, ill-fitting seat belt. "The angry spirits ... *ran the owners crazy?* Is that what you're telling me?"

"No idea how they did it," said Terrence, "but yeah. All those sharp suits wound up in a nuthouse. The whole thing was hushed up, and the financial scandal story spread like hell. People just put up a bunch of 'Keep Out' signs, and the complex was abandoned. Those spirits are psycho."

"How can you be a psychotic spirit?" asked Jonah, disconcerted.

"Remember that all Earthplane-dwelling spirits, the ones that didn't cross on, still carry their human personalities," said Terrence. "Now, bearing that in mind, imagine you are a spirit, angry, frustrated, feeling disrespected because your burial place lay decayed and forgotten. Then some real estate bigwigs come and disrupt said forgotten ground by building goddamned houses on top of you. You'd be a little pissed off, right?"

Jonah said nothing for several miles. That whole thing sounded terrible. A situation that had had detrimental consequences for all souls involved, living *and* departed. Jonah realized that it was still going to take some time for him to wrap his mind around the fact that the departed souls were still very much alive, and therefore could still be adversely affected through various means. Or adversely affect others.

"So what happened to the spirits?" he asked.

"We don't know how to help them or even what they'd need," said Terrence. "They are so angry, chaotic, and vicious. Messing with them is like messing with time: dangerous."

"Has anyone ever tried an endowment?"

"Yes," said Terrence, "and the guy was killed."

"What?"

"Eleventh Percenter named Aaron Miles," said Terrence. "He lived at the estate some years before I moved there. Trip would remember him, I think, but talking to Trip ... Well, anyway, from what I've heard, he was a decent guy and everything. Was a writer, actually, just like you, and an Orange Aura."

Jonah raised his eyebrows and prompted Terrence to continue with a rolling of his hand.

"Unfortunately, one of his downsides was the fact that he was prone to impulsivity," said Terrence. "Mind you, I wasn't there; this is what Jonathan and some of the older Eleventh Percenters told me. He was always pulling reckless stunts, tried to find Spirit Reapers to fight—you name it. Then apparently, he decided that he would endow himself with a Mandy spirit, just to prove he could."

Jonah could not see where Terrence was going with the story, but from the tone of his voice felt fear in spite of himself. "And?"

"He went to that construction site, bragged about being able to handle them, and they responded by endowing him," said Terrence, shaking his head. "The volatility of the spirits tore him up, so I heard. I'm not being dramatic; they said it literally *ripped* him apart. His body practically combusted. It was like sharks devouring minnows in the water. His spirit crossed on. I bet you that even in the afterlife, he was traumatized by it."

Jonah stared ahead. "So Mandy spirits ... bad. Got it. Why the red dots then?"

"Extreme aggression," explained Terrence. "They are so freakin' chaotic that we can see traces of their essence without even going into Spectral Sight. Best to leave them be."

"I don't doubt it," said Jonah, still unnerved.

"You wonder about my cooking aspirations," said Terrence, who seemed rattled by his own narration and was anxious to change the subject. "May I ask about your writing?"

"Oh." Now it was Jonah's turn to adopt the glum, pessimistic expression that Reena, Terrence, and Trip had all previously worn. "Isn't much to it, really," he said at last. "I've been writing since I was strong enough to hold something to write with. The words just pour out of me; I just love it. And then—I hate what happens next."

"Which is what?" asked Terrence.

Jonah sighed. He glanced up at a highway sign, half hoping that the city loomed near, but he saw, irritatingly, that they were still about forty-five miles out. There was no way he could evade the story. "I won't go into grave detail," he muttered.

"Fair enough," said Terrence.

"Words come out in reckless abandon, and then, they just stop," said Jonah. "It's like I'm on the path to the rising action, or even to the climax, and the fire, the motivation, just dies. Not even embers are left;

the idea goes ice cold. It's like I have, I don't know, selective writer's block or something."

Terrence nodded, and Jonah was grateful that he didn't try to diminish his anguish or rationalize it with some cockamamie explanation. "Maybe we all might be able to help each other," Terrence told him. "Perhaps we can all bounce ideas off of one another or something like that. Maybe outside sources could be helpful, you know?"

It was such a simple and unexpected gesture that Jonah readily accepted. "I should warn you, I don't know anything about half the stuff you guys are interested in."

"And I don't know a damned thing about writing a book," countered Terrence. "And that just might be what we need to help us."

After sharing a laugh, the two of them continued the rest of the trip in silence. Jonah took in the sights while Terrence perused the radio stations, which became increasingly trickier as they moved into highway stretches that contained densely forested areas. They were in the city in record time, a fact that Jonah didn't think was something to be overjoyed about.

Terrence noticed Jonah's mood and clapped him on the shoulder. "Look at it this way," he told him, "it's only a four-day work week. If I can go through the motions with the mops and broom and what have you, you certainly can slog through four days of eight hours of work. Then it's back to the estate."

"Nine hours," grumbled Jonah. "I probably should have mentioned that my boss increased the workday by an hour so as to 'boost productivity.' So that means on Friday I won't be on the road until at least quarter till seven."

Terrence shrugged, unabashed. "Hey, that means you'll get to the estate just in time for training."

Realizing that there was no deterring Terrence from the bright side in this situation, Jonah just decided to smile and murmur agreement. The elevator ascended to the seventh floor almost instantly; Jonah was beginning to wonder if some nameless spirit was playing with his senses as some kind of joke. The doors opened smoothly and revealed the hallway, which was as welcoming to Jonah as having a root canal with a rusty spoon.

"Seems kind of tight-packed in here, no?" said Terrence, eyeing the narrow hallway with mild distaste.

"Yes, indeed, but we all can't have the luxury of living in an expansive estate, oh Spoiled One," said Jonah with mock scorn.

At that moment, the woman from 7D exited her apartment in her usual form-fitting athletic wear, water bottle in tow. She froze, eyeing Terrence with a keen interest.

"Hey, Jonah," she said brightly without even looking at him. "Aren't you going to introduce me to your friend?"

Before Jonah could utter a single syllable, she thrust out an athletic-taped hand to Terrence.

"Leta Sytch."

As Terrence took her hand with a grin, Jonah blinked with indignation. He'd passed this woman in the hallway for almost two years, and he'd been lucky to have exchanged twenty words. But Terrence, a complete stranger, shows up with him, and learns her name in seconds?

"Nice to meet you, Leta," said Terrence. "Name's Terrence Aldercy."

"Aldercy?" said Leta with interest. "I think I've heard that before."

"Doubt it," said Terrence hastily, "it's not like it's a common name."

"It's a nice one, though," persisted Leta, prompting Jonah to force himself not to sneer. "What's its origin?"

"It's Latin," said Terrence without skipping a beat. "Well, Latin-rooted, anyway. Means 'leader' or 'chief.' "

"Really?" said Leta. "Self-fulfilling, I hope."

Oh, dear God, Jonah thought to himself, but aloud he said, in what he thought was a polite voice, "Leta, please don't allow my friend and me to interrupt your workout." And in an undertone to Terrence, "Get in here, playboy."

Terrence smirked and bade Leta goodbye, who continued to the elevator rather reluctantly.

"Jealous much?" joked Terrence.

"Shut up," murmured Jonah.

"What?" said Terrence. "Woman was *fine!*"

"Oh, calm yourself," said Jonah, trying and failing to hide annoyance with humor. All traces of the attempt faded entirely when he smacked the light switch, which illuminated his junky apartment. Jonah was thankful he'd at least loaded the dishwasher before he'd gone out that Friday night.

"I know you have a trip ahead of you, and work in the morning on top of that, so I won't keep you, man. Here you go."

Jonah passed over gas money and some of his partial manuscripts.

"Appreciate it man!" said Terrence. "And I'm truly looking forward to reading some of this."

He waved the manuscript.

"Enjoy it, at least until it's done," said Jonah. "I will be back to the estate on the first thing smoking come Friday."

He said it jokingly, but suddenly, Terrence looked serious.

"Take care of yourself, Jonah," he said. "And if anything happens, anything at all, give us a ring."

Terrence's abrupt change was odd, but then Jonah remembered the first attack, though foiled, had occurred right on the fire escape outside his window.

"I will, Terrence," he said. "You have my word."

Terrence's expression cleared once Jonah said that. "Want me to come back up here Friday?" he asked in a much lighter tone.

"Oh no, that's cool," said Jonah. "I want to master that trip myself."

"No problem." Terrence gave him an informal salute and left. Jonah latched the door and surveyed his living room, reluctantly taking in all the reminders of his work and life.

"Four days to go," he grumbled to himself, sincerely hoping that Tuesday, Wednesday, and Thursday would not prove to be unbearable.

9

Reaper and Minion

Jonah's mind was so cluttered as he wondered who actually controlled the flow of time. Tuesday and Wednesday dragged by with about the same speed as an injured tortoise trudging through mud. It was obvious that Jessica had been hissing about him behind his back again as he had to endure another absurd staff meeting Tuesday afternoon where they were once again reminded of how "commitment to the company" was paramount. Jonah couldn't help but notice that every time Jessica spoke, she always seemed to linger an accusatory gaze upon him. Anthony would do the same once he'd surmised that he had Jessica's unwritten and unspoken permission to do so. He had long since quit attempting to figure out how Jessica and her manservant had such a hold on Langton, or was it Jessica who had a hold on Langton *and* Anthony simultaneously? Whatever the case was, it was tiresome and irritating.

Jonah would have drifted into a welcome slumber in the cubicle had he not occasionally stolen glances at pictures of the estate, which he'd taken before he'd left.

Around the seventh time he'd done this, Nelson gave him a slight frown.

"What do you keep staring at on your phone?" he asked jokingly. "Did you have an interesting weekend that you desired immortalizing?"

Not the interesting that you're *insinuating,* thought Jonah. "Just ... road tripped this weekend. To the country. There was a place in this town, an estate, which brought back memories."

Nelson straightened, interested. Jonah had already confided in him the idiocy and foolishness he'd dealt with throughout his childhood, so it was no surprise when he said, "Good memories from your past? Just from seeing a house in the countryside? Man, maybe I ought to spend more time down there."

Jonah grinned and made general small talk about it but didn't elaborate. He felt that talking too much would raise awkward questions, not to mention possibly slow the progression of time even more.

Eating was entertaining, but even that process was slow. But that had nothing to do with Langton or Jessica. Though Reena had been at work when Jonah left with Terrence, she had still made her presence felt before she headed out. Once he'd shown the *slightest* interest in getting in better shape, she'd passionately pounced on the opportunity to help him, though he hadn't actually asked for her assistance. She'd told him to put in at least two walks a day on a treadmill, which was manageable enough, but then she'd given him a damned eating plan, which he'd eyed appallingly.

"It's only a touchy subject because it's new to you, and you've probably never gotten health advice from a woman," she'd told him. Jonah had looked at her, wide-eyed, while Terrence had shaken his head warningly; apparently once Reena got into her vein about fitness, she would not be denied.

"Now if you're hoping for instant gratification, you can cancel that now," she'd continued. "But you will get positive results if you eat food in the right combinations. So don't mix carbohydrates with meat—"

"What?"

Reena had been undeterred. "Don't mix fruit with grains—" she'd paused when Jonah gave her another incredulous look. He had always preferred fruit toppings to syrup on his pancakes, so that one was a sharp blow.

"You've got to be joking," he'd told her.

"No, I'm not. Combinations of fruit and grains cause irregularity. And you'd do well to eat fruit for breakfast and not any more pork or other fried meat."

Jonah had been thunderstruck. Bacon and eggs, something that was a staple most of his mornings, had to be halted?

"What?" Reena had said with marked impatience.

"Reena," Jonah had said to her desperately, "I grew up on these foods. I can't let them go, just like that. For God's sakes, I'm a country boy—"

"Well you'll be a *screwed* boy, in more ways than one, if you don't listen to me," she'd replied, completely unmoved.

With that conversation still in his mind, here he was, snacking on carrots and celery instead of his usual chips or Reese's. Even if Reena had had the right idea, it was going to take a minute, or two, or five, to get used to an influx of rabbit food having more prevalence on the daily menu. He watched every single French fry that went into Nelson's mouth.

He slogged through two days and reached Thursday, which he'd begun to doubt would ever arrive. Six p.m. had arrived in all its mane and majesty, and he was gratefully buckling himself into the car when he noticed a vaguely familiar mane of unkempt, oily hair and lifeless eyes. Jonah stared, all relief vanishing on the spot. It was Walt, one of the minions who'd tried to kill him. Even without his crony, Howard, Walt looked menacing.

Jonah's eyes shot left and right. There weren't any spirits to endow him around this place, and even if there were, he doubted that his ability to fight was up to scratch after two trainings.

While anxious thoughts raced in his mind, Walt reached into his trench coat and pulled out something that gleamed in the late afternoon sun. Jonah made out what it was instantly. It was a tire iron.

Walt looked at Jonah with a sinister smile and brandished the tire iron for him to see. Then he spoke. Although it was a whisper, Jonah could hear him perfectly, even over the traffic and the chatter on the street that separated them. They were two simple words:

"Tangible again."

A particularly large service truck loudly hurtled by, and when it passed completely, Walt had vanished.

Jonah stared at where the spirit had been for several more seconds and then steadied himself. He made to crank his car, but with a jolt, hesitated.

Realization occurred to him. It dawned alongside a wave of fresh panic. The tire iron, Walt's proclamation that he was once again tangible, meaning that he could touch and feel once more...

Had he done something to the car?

Immediately, Jonah jumped out of the car and shrank away from it as though it were diseased. He had no idea what Walt could have done. He inspected the tires first, obviously, but there didn't appear to be any sign that anything had been tampered with. Besides, it wasn't like Jonah was a mechanic; Walt could have easily been parading that tire iron around to simply imply that he'd tampered with *something*...

"Jonah?" said a curious voice, causing Jonah to jump.

"What?"

It was Nelson. He had advanced quietly and looked puzzled. "I saw you backing up from the car. Something wrong? You broken down? Need a jump?"

It took Jonah a few seconds to register the offered aid. "Yeah," he said absently. "I mean no, Nelson. I don't think it's the battery. Something is amiss though."

"Do you have Triple A?" asked Nelson.

"Of course I do," responded Jonah in a more steady voice than he'd had previously, "but I'll call them tomorrow. Listen, Nelson, can you give me a lift home?"

"Sure, that's no problem," said Nelson, and Jonah was thankful that he did not linger or ask awkward questions. Gratefully, he made to stride past Nelson, who didn't budge.

"Jonah? You'll need your wallet and laptop, won't you?"

"What?" asked Jonah again, and then it registered. "Oh. Right. Yeah."

Apprehensively, he approached the car, not knowing at all what to expect. When nothing happened, he grabbed the needed items, ignored the dirty look from a passing Jessica, and allowed Nelson to lead the way to his car.

Later that evening, Jonah gave the incident hard thought after picking through one of Reena's health-conscious meals. He grudgingly accepted that he *did* think more clearly when his gut wasn't weighed down with the usual TV dinner, carryout, or greasy burgers he'd usually have after work.

He stared at his cell phone, not entirely certain why he wasn't doing what he promised with calling his friends at the estate the minute something had gone wrong.

But nothing *had* gone wrong. He did not have a single shred of proof that that lunatic spirit had done anything to his car. He hadn't even bothered to start it. Was it even worth calling and saying, "Terrence, you and Reena better get down here. Walt showed me a tire iron, and I assumed he damaged my car?"

He frowned in disgust. Given how far-fetched the words were in his mind, he didn't even want to know how they'd sound spoken.

He slumped on his sofa, closed his eyes, and willed the curtain on the stage to open. Breathing diaphragmatically, he opened his eyes.

To find his apartment empty.

He hadn't known what to expect, but there was no movement whatsoever in his home. He was alone.

Only now being alone didn't feel so great. Why was it suddenly uncomfortable?

He sighed.

"Nana," said Jonah clearly. It was a desperate card and long shot after what Reena had told him, but he plunged regardless. "Nana, I don't even know if you can hear me. But if Jonathan was right, even those who have crossed to the Other Side are still with us."

The silence continued, almost defiantly so.

"Listen, Nana." Why was he persisting? "I need your help. I kind of find myself wishing I was in middle school again, when my biggest concern was why girls never talked to me and how to best dodge the comments about my clothes. But this is so much bigger than that. Nana, I never knew I had this … thing. The Eleventh Percent. The power to work with Spirits, and whatever else. But now that I know, I'm not sure I can handle it. I'm not cut out for this, Nana. I can't even fight. Yeah, I know, I've only done two trainings, but why can't it come naturally? Why can't *anything* come naturally for me? I'm a wreck. I'm jumpy; I feel like I'm being followed, for God's sakes. I'm running from parked cars. If you can give me just one sign that I can get through this, I'd greatly appreciate it."

He stared, listened, and hoped, but the silence was almost as tangible as Walt had claimed he was.

Had it been childish to hope she'd respond? Stupid? Hadn't someone, *something,* volunteered the information that his grandmother's passing was not the end? He hadn't been crazy; that had actually happened. But now, nothing like that occurred.

He shut his eyes angrily, practically demanding the curtain to close. He reopened his eyes, impatiently registering that his blurred vision wasn't entirely attributed to the fact that he'd closed them so tightly.

"I don't blame you," said Jonah, wiping his face with added force to assuage his feelings of weakness. "If I were you, I wouldn't want to talk to me either."

He grabbed his cell phone, opened the photo gallery, and scrolled to a picture of the estate.

"One day to go," he muttered.

Friday arrived, and though Jonah had looked forward to it all week long, the events of the previous day had had such an effect on him that he woke up feeling that there was no need for a ticker-tape parade.

Remembering Reena, he consumed a breakfast of yogurt full of strawberries and honey. This breakfast began to feel less than adequate rather quickly when Nelson, who had agreed to give him a ride to work that morning, took a longer, more scenic route that included two McDonald's, an IHOP, a Waffle House, and a hole-in-the-wall diner that they could smell from the street. The place didn't look like much at all, but the smell alone made it intriguing. Twice he bit back the impulse to tell Nelson to stop but then heard Reena's voice in his mind, talking of "phantom hunger," and declaring that the food was "only appealing and enticing because you know it is there."

However much he missed Reena, there were brief periods where his thoughts of her were none too positive.

His mood was not improved forty-five minutes later, when they'd arrived at the office and the Triple A representative had coldly informed Jonah that there was absolutely nothing wrong with his vehicle. Everything had checked out fine. His irritation was exacerbated by the fact that Jessica had told Langton that Jonah's car had sat there all night in front of the office, conveniently forgetting to mention that there might have been trouble with it. He was then subjected to another meeting with Langton that the company property was not an outpost of his apartment complex's parking lot, and if it occurred again, it would be towed. This was made worse by the fact that Langton had used an irritatingly jovial voice the whole time. Idiot.

Jonah already hoped that Friday would be over soon, and it was barely nine thirty.

Attempting to put the previous night's irritation out of his mind, he closed his eyes, willed the stage to open, and took the calming breath. Several of his colleagues had an assorted mixture of people around them. A few even had Spectral pets at their heels. Mrs. Souther, the kind-natured older lady who did the filing and never forgot anyone's birthday, had a formidable-looking but kind-faced man by her side. His serious expression and professional gait gave Jonah the impression that he had been a hard-nosed businessman in his physical life, but his warm brown eyes, barely wrinkled face, and creases about his eyelids showed him as a truly caring, loving individual who had probably smiled a lot. As he hovered near Mrs. Souther, Jonah could tell with no doubt in his mind that the man's love for her, despite his being in Spirit, had not diminished at all. In spite of his recent negativity, Jonah smiled.

Nelson had several other beings around him too. They appeared to be of the slightest substance, as though the faintest touch would make them scatter like ash, but they stayed near him as though they wanted to shield him from harm.

Jonah noticed that although there were many people in the office in addition to the physical beings, they all fit comfortably within the space. He remembered what he'd learned about spirits and spiritesses manipulating space as easily as time. There were enough people in this office to make the New Year's crowd at Times Square jealous, yet they all moved about with such an undisturbed grace that they may as well have been alone. It seemed as if, on the spirit plane, there was a wealth of space and time for everyone, and no one had to stress about not having their own piece of it. It was a very intriguing thought, and it made Jonah think of the fact that maybe people wouldn't act so waspish and snide to one another if they were afforded the same luxury on Earthplane. But a rather disturbing thing jarred Jonah out of his thoughts.

Not every spirit and spiritess was pleased to be present. Although they did not appear as morose as those ones he'd seen in the town square of Rome, there was an anxiety about them … or was it fear?

Frowning, he also realized that many of them seemed to be shackled. There were no chains, just clamps that were fit tightly about their hands and feet. They seemed to be made of some smoky vapor with a bluish black hue, but they looked rather frail. Jonah's curiosity got the better of him. Surreptitiously, he beckoned to the shackled spirit of a portly man with black, curly hair, brown eyes, and a rather brooding expression.

The gesture was not missed; Jonah was sure he saw the man's beady eyes widen for a fraction of a second and then narrow.

Jonah beckoned again, this time with stronger intent. "I know you noticed me," he muttered under his breath. "If you would only face me so I could ask you some questions!"

What you're doing is dangerous.

Jonah froze. A deep, croaky voice had just spoken into his mind. His other thoughts had gone quiet. It was just like at his grandmother's funeral.

Um, thought Jonah uncertainly. He had never communicated mentally. Hadn't people always said that hearing voices meant you were crazy? *The spirit that I just tried to talk to—is this you?* he thought in his mind, hoping to make a proper connection.

No voice came, but Jonah swore that the man nodded infinitesimally, confirming the question. *I repeat, what you are doing is dangerous.*

What exactly is it that I am doing?

Bringing your attention to me! said the man's voice in Jonah's mind. *You are one of the Eleventh Percenters; it's obvious. Are you aware of Mindscopes?*

Jonah recalled the spirit Howard saying something about that some time back. Jonathan hadn't really explained them beyond calling them a way to dust for spiritual fingerprints. *What exactly is a 'Mindscope?'* he thought at the spirit.

The portly spirit's eyes darted, as if he suspected people in black suits to come and get him or something. *It's the ethereal act of delving into another's mind to decipher thoughts,* he said in Jonah's mind, *and also the tool used to manipulate one's desires, fears, and emotions. You need to cease this now! You are making us both vulnerable to Mindscopes!*

Calm down, Jonah thought. He recalled something Jonathan had told him. *The last time a Mindscope was used against me, it was because I was thinking of a loved one. You're a complete stranger to me.*

No! the man's voice shrieked furiously. *We're not strangers now! That changed the minute you beckoned to me! It appears your essence is raw. Maturing, but very much raw!*

Jonah felt aggravation creep up inside him. There was that damn "raw essence" again. Would someone bother to speak to him in layman's terms? The raw essence that the spirit said was "maturing?" He didn't appreciate sounding like some wine or cheese or something.

I'll cut to the chase then, Jonah thought. *The shackles ... why don't you take them off? They look lighter than air.*

The man looked at his wrist bitterly. *He keeps us chained for our essence,* he said. *The clamps keep us from getting too far away. That way, he can rein us back in.*

Jonah straightened. Just how many prisoners were there? Just how many people had Creyton blocked?

Look—

I can't tell you anymore; I will be punished badly enough as it is, the man said in Jonah's mind. *You are the one who can remove these binds, but you must make haste before they find you. Please leave me be; I have caused enough damage and aroused far too much attention. They will come for you. You will need help. You have been endowed.*

Jonah felt the vigor and energy course through his body, but his anxiety and puzzlement prevented him from appreciating it.

How could he be in danger? He thought of the endowment forced upon him by Jonathan that very first night all this mess began. He had been in a fair amount of danger that night as well, seeing as the Minion had been right outside his window. And here was another endowment, thrust upon him.

What fresh hell would there be this time?

And why had that spirit been so afraid of achieving contact? Why had he reminded him of the Mindscopes? It wasn't like when he thought of his grandmother. He loved her and missed her terribly. That was different. It had to be, seeing as he didn't know that man from Adam and had no feelings toward him whatsoever. What could that link achieve? That spirit had been so scared. Marla just happened out of nowhere begging for help, and she'd been uninvited. So what was the deal with that guy?

Jonah was so deep in thought that he hadn't realized his Spectral Sight had passed, though he hadn't willed the curtain to close. Out of all that had just occurred, that was what struck him as odd. It was as if his mind had willed itself to clear for an oncoming attack.

He rose from the cubicle (it wasn't like he was doing any work anyway) and made for the door. If the portly, petrified spirit was correct and something was about to happen, he wasn't about to get accosted in the office. Nelson was around, Mrs. Souther ... hell, he didn't even want Jessica or Anthony to get hurt. Now, *that* was something.

He stepped outside. The fresh air had a calming effect on him, but the only thing out of the ordinary was a familiar pair of amber eyes on him.

"Bast!" exclaimed Jonah. "What are you—?"

His voice trailed off. The poor cat looked spent. There was a haggard, ruffled consistency to her fur, the very soles of her paws looked inflamed from overuse, and her gaze, penetrating and sharp at the best of times, had an underlying look of plea in them. It was as if she had been traveling for days.

"Hang on," said Jonah. "Don't move. Well, yes, *do* move, to the alley. But do it in about five minutes, okay?"

He went back to his cubicle and extracted a can of tuna and bottled water. They were remnants of a care package he and Nelson had stashed away in the event that they had to evade any more of Mrs. Souther's mystery meat casserole that she always brought to the break room. Sweet lady though she was, her cooking was questionable.

"And just what are you doing?" came the unpleasantness that was Jessica's voice.

"Getting a bite for my housecat," replied Jonah. He jerked his chin in that direction. Thankfully, Bast had remained stationary. He was willing to bet anything that she was aware of the prying eyes.

"Housecat," repeated Jessica. "Well, why is it not, I don't know, *in your house?*"

"Because—because she's a socialite," gambled Jonah. "Four walls can be confining to anyone ... or any animal."

Jessica's eyes narrowed. She glanced at Bast again. Jonah didn't wait for her to leave, completely indifferent to her at the moment. Within the next two minutes, he had unearthed a cereal bowl out of the trunk of his car and beckoned Bast into the alleyway.

"Here," he muttered to her, placing the now-open can of tuna and cereal bowl of water under Bast's nose. With a meow of gratitude, Bast dug in to each of them. A glance at his watch told him that it was eight minutes past noon.

"Bast, look," said Jonah. He was pleased to see that something about her was changing. He assumed being sated would have that kind of effect. "It's my lunch break now, but I have to get back into the office before I go, or Jessica will say that I coaxed a cat to work in order to leave early or something. I can't ask you to stay for six hours, but when you're done eating and everything, find Jonathan—uh, however you find him. Tell him that something really strange is happening. I've just been spiritually endowed, and I have no idea why. I think the spirit who did it was trying to prepare me for another attack."

The cat dipped her head into a nod. Jonah still found it strange that she understood what he was saying. With a quick nod himself and swift stroke of her ears, he re-entered the office, pleased with the knowledge that he was spiritually endowed against whatever might happen, as well as pleased that an ally was present, even if that ally was a presently malnourished calico.

Jonah was at his apartment in less than twenty minutes, a feat only made possible because he wasn't really registering the consequences of speeding. He'd officially showed his face so as to avoid Jessica's snitching or story twists, and was now home, wolfing down another of Reena's recipes of chicken salad flavored with sea salt instead of table salt. Being that such a small portion was made, he'd eaten it in another ten, searched *The Daily Rap* for anything useful (of course there wasn't, save for the continuing upswing in crime), and sat anxiously at his computer researching spirits.

Sadly, or perhaps maddeningly, the majority of the search engines yielded little to nothing about spirits, save the sensationalized Hollywood garbage he already knew. It seemed that no hint of information that even faintly concerned Eleventh Percenters existed. Jonah swore in frustration. How could Eleventh Percenters exist throughout time and no one say anything, however stupid or insane it sounded?

A yowl caused him to nearly jump out of his seat. He turned his attention to his fire escape, stepped out, and looked down.

Bast was standing below his window alongside three other cats. Apparently, they chorused a loud, synchronized meow to get his attention. He descended the fire escape without a moment's hesitation.

"Bast, have you contacted Jonathan?" he asked the calico, and then mentally rebuked himself for actually expecting an answer.

Bast's counterparts didn't move, nor did they make a sound. Bast hadn't moved herself, but her eyes had. They had locked onto Jonah with an almost unearthly intensity.

Jonah stared right back, not embarrassed to admit that he was completely oblivious. "Is that your way to communicate? Because I'm not getting it."

Bast still hadn't moved an inch, remaining stock-still with her eyes transfixed.

"Look," said Jonah, eyes narrowed, "you called me for something. You didn't think your sound would carry alone, so you got your buddies here to help. Got that. But I'm not getting anything else. What's up?"

Bast's statuary stance remained unchanged. Her eyes were as still as her body.

"Look, cat," said Jonah, impatient, "tell me what Jonathan said; otherwise, I need to get back to—"

Then something frightening happened. His mind began to teem with erratic emotions, impulses, and panic that were completely opposite of what he had just been feeling. There was no voice, but a sentence, clear and distinct, splashed across his brain:

"Danger! Look behind you, now!"

Jonah whipped around so suddenly that it might have resembled a dance step if a bystander happened to see. He turned just in time but barely had time to register the tire iron heading for his face, formerly heading for the back of his head.

Jonah darted his weight left and allowed Walt's momentum to carry him through. The spirit had crept up to him with absolutely no sound. It was like his tangibility existed only in his upper body and hadn't reached his feet. He stumbled forward but recovered immediately.

"You stupid idiot," Walt rasped. "I never said that I was going to use the tire iron on your *car.*"

He swiped again, but somehow, Jonah had expected it. The point of that spirit's out-of-nowhere endowment made perfect sense now. He backed out of the path of the swing, grabbed the nearest thing at hand, and flung a particularly heavy and foul-smelling bag of garbage at the spirit. Walt probably didn't cherish his newly given tangibility at this moment, because he caught a pile of someone's long-discarded meals full in the face.

The endowment provided Jonah with options, but he knew that he was still inexperienced. Merely attempting to keep the tire iron far away from his head, he took advantage of Walt's temporary disorientation and charged him with as much force as possible. The force sent both of them backward into more mounds of trash, and Jonah realized too late that he was at a disadvantage. Walt was a spirit, but Jonah was a physical being. He wouldn't be able to breathe underneath cascades of plastic, sludge, and who knew whatever else. He scrambled to his feet and saw that Walt was already wresting himself free of the mess, a livid expression on his face. With all the garbage smeared across his visage, he would have looked like a fool had it not been for the tire iron and the murderous gaze.

With a snarl, he lunged, and Jonah tensed. *That shield would be nice right about now,* he thought to himself, but ten seconds later, the only thing in front of his face was Walt, tire iron in tow. Jonah only narrowly missed the swipe this time.

"What do you want from me?" he demanded. "I'm not who you're looking for! I'm no threat to anyone! I'm—"

Jonah lost his balance in the treacherous terrain of bags and fell hard. His head banged against some tough substance. He had enough of his mental faculties to register that the head injury would be a great deal worse if it hadn't been for the endowment, but white dots still obscured his vision. It cleared just in time for him to see Walt, rife with filth and anger, holding the slightly edged butt of the tire iron over his heart.

"Asinine fighting skills, if we could even label this a fight," he said, his voice contemptuous. "Normally, I kill for the essence to imbue me, but I'll simply do this one for enjoyment."

He made to jab the weapon home, but the silence was pierced by Bast's feral hiss. Strangely, Walt collapsed, writhing in agony. He dropped the tire iron and didn't seem to notice; whatever pain he felt seemed to be all-encompassing. Not sure how to vanquish him (as he didn't think any electric tricks were possible at the moment), Jonah lifted the tire iron himself, intending to take advantage of his attacker's weakened state. The second he drew back, however, he found that he couldn't bring himself to do it. He *physically* could not bring himself to do it.

His arm paused when he began to draw it back. He was at an awkward stance as he hadn't yet regained full control of his posture. He wanted to dart his eyes around to see what was happening, but then realized that he couldn't move them either.

It was as if all substance was sucked out of the air and life stopped. He was frozen.

"That is enough entertainment," said a hoarse, grating voice that made Jonah's insides as frozen and useless as his outside.

He couldn't turn to see the owner of the voice, but he had a mind-numbing suspicion from the moment time stopped. This time wasn't like when Jonathan tinkered with time, which had simply felt confusing. There was something negative, eerie, and just *wrong* about this. It seemed constricting, forced, almost like time was reluctant in stopping but got ruthlessly coerced into doing so. The air prickled with a sinister edge. Who else could it be?

"You can stop your attempts to break free as they are futile," said the voice, but now the figure to which it belonged sidled into Jonah's frozen line of sight.

The man was impressive in stature, easily four or five inches over six feet, but his height wasn't what Jonah noticed most. His skin was pale, like he spent his formative years in a dark, windowless room. This was a stark contrast to the dark clothing and hair. His eyes, which were a dark grayish color similar to an overcast sky, had no trace of humanity in them, which only added to the foreboding Jonah felt in his immobile body. The five-o'clock-shadowed face was angular and presently contorted into an expression of hate. Jonah could only marvel at how young he looked, despite supposedly being around for decades on end. His thin, but by no means frail, form cast an unnerving, fearful profile, which was only accentuated by the black staff he gripped in his right hand that was tipped with an intricate crow figurine.

"So you are the Blue Aura?" said Creyton, eyes narrowed. "Fitting that you are soiled with refuse and muck the first time I see you. Because if you're fighting was any indication, I'd say that is exactly what *you* are."

Even frozen in time, anger surfaced inside Jonah's body. This freak had known him for two minutes and was already ragging on him?

"Surely, you aren't surprised by these occurrences?" said Creyton, moving at a smooth pace despite the scattered garbage. "I pray that Jonathan has informed you that time is merely a plaything. But even if he had, I would not be surprised if you didn't comprehend it. Your stupidity is etched in every detail of your face."

There was condescension in every syllable Creyton uttered. It seemed like he thought it a disservice not to explain to Jonah just how worthless he thought he was. Jonah's apprehension continued to build.

"I could continue this forever," murmured Creyton, "but it is beneath me. Know that I could kill you and reap your worthless soul at any time, Jonah James Anderson Rowe."

Jonah's eyes would have widened if he had been capable of movement. He had not used his full name for years and had all but discarded his middle names since high school. How did this man know them? His shock almost prevented him from catching what Creyton said next.

"I have plans to attend to and do not wish for Jonathan's meddling. It would only muddy the waters. You will survive this, Rowe, because I have two messages for you. First, you will go back to Rome and tell Jonathan that if he thinks my plans can be stopped, he is sadly mistaken. Second, I want you to understand that you are *not* equipped for this, boy. Do yourself a favor and walk away. You are no threat. Your existence continues only because I've allowed it. You have been warned. I will not do so again."

He tilted the crow-tipped staff to the left, and time resumed with explosive force, like it had been building pressure while Creyton had been halting it. Jonah was blasted backward and knocked out cold. He was brought back to consciousness only after the insistent prodding of Bast's paws.

10

The State of Things

"What the *hell* happened to you?"

Jonah returned to his apartment and grabbed his duffel bag, Bast on his tail. He hadn't given any thought to the fact that his workday was not yet over. He'd thrown his belongings into his car while Bast jumped into the passenger seat. His mind swirled like a sandstorm that had no plans of stopping. Driving was purely muscle memory. It didn't register to him that he followed the directions, made the turns and changed lanes, and took Exit 81 to the estate without a second thought. It didn't register to him that Bast repeatedly maneuvered from the front seat to the back as if she had decided to keep a watch on what occurred on the road.

Least of all, it hadn't registered to him that he was filthy and gave off the rancid odor of soiled pampers, cigarettes, and foul vestiges of substances that were at one time food but had since devolved into something else entirely while it languished in the dumpsters.

It was this shocking and appalling appearance that met the horrified eyes of Reena, who had just stepped out of her own car, Liz, who had just returned from her bio lab and planned to rest before gardening, and Terrence, who, though he was a janitor and probably had more experience with nastiness than all of them combined, looked as if even he'd never seen anything so foul in all of his life.

The question was asked, but beyond that, no sound or movement had been made.

"What happened to me?" managed Jonah at last. "I got into a fight, got time-slapped, and feel like I ran three miles, played a basketball game that went on for four overtimes, and then whitewater rafted upstream."

Although Jonah had been in a mental haze while driving, he had maintained the wherewithal to say inwardly to the spirit, "*Look, I appreciate you giving me the endowment. I'm making a three-hour trip, and I can't lose the endowment on the road.*"

Apparently, the message got through, because the spirit had complied. When Jonah left the car and began to walk to the estate, however, the endowment evaporated. He somehow managed to ignore the fatigue and the impaired breathing long enough to settle cross-legged on the porch.

"Jonah, what happened to you?" repeated Reena. "And could your information be a little more distinctive this time, please?"

"Reena, I think he *might* need to soak in the tub for a couple weeks first," said Terrence. "Then he can tell us everything. Jonah, it's obvious you were just released from an endowment, so it'd probably help you to drink some water too. You up to that?"

Jonah gave a half-shrug. He hadn't even realized that Liz had disappeared and returned until she knelt in front of him.

"Liz, you might want to move downwind," he warned. "I'm not at my best right now."

Liz hadn't even wrinkled her nose. "You don't smell any worse than the stuff I just handled in my bio lab," she told him. "Now sit still, and let me concentrate."

She splayed her fingers in his face, and the tips began to glow jade green. Jonah's eyes widened.

"What the—?"

"I'm checking for injuries," she explained, moving her green fingertips around his upper body. "The green at my fingertips indicates that my endowment is hard at work gauging whatever malady you may have. Now please be quiet."

She continued for another couple of minutes and then stood. The bright green at her fingertips faded.

"Head injury, but it is surface level and largely negligible," she said. "Some mild bruises, but you'll be all right. Now come on in so we can get you cleaned up."

Jonah stood and walked inside, Reena and Bast behind him. Reena carried Jonah's bag and, despite Liz's words, still eyed him with concern. Jonah took a few sips of water just to say that he had done so, and then went upstairs, peeled off the soiled clothes, and lay in the tub.

Even though his thoughts swirled far less vigorously now that he'd wound down, they were no less jumbled. Walt had showed up again, more bloodthirsty than the first time. Then Creyton, the Alpha Dog himself, showed up, frozen Jonah in time, berated him for merely existing, and then left him in a sprawled heap. He had no idea what to make of any of it, and though his brain fired on more cylinders than usual, his form was as still as the hot water that engulfed him and dulled his aches.

After maybe forty-five minutes, he left the tub, dried, and dressed in some spare clothes from the chest of drawers in the room he'd had the previous weekend. He came downstairs, well aware that everyone had been talking about the incident the whole time he'd been cleaning off. He wasn't up to talking just yet and accepted Reena's salad without complaint.

"Now are you going to tell us what happened?" said Terrence, a trace of impatience in his voice.

Jonah did not answer. He chose to weigh words in his mind as he swallowed a particularly large portion of lettuce. "How do you contact Jonathan?" he asked Reena.

"Oftentimes, we use one of the heralds, but on occasion, all we have to do is meditate on it a second or two, then ask him to show," responded Reena, taken aback. "Why?"

"Hang on," said Jonah. He didn't know what prompted him to know this; perhaps it was the subtle prickling on the back of his neck. Slowly, he scanned the room.

"Jonathan is already around here somewhere."

"Very good, Jonah," came the approving tone of Jonathan's voice. Seeing the surprise on Terrence's and Reena's faces from his sudden appearance, he simply smiled.

"Elizabeth sent one of the heralds to summon me from my traverses," he explained. "I have been monitoring Minion activity, and now the heralds are shoring up our recent fortifications."

"Recent fortifications?" said Liz, puzzled. "I just called you five minutes ago, sir—"

"Elizabeth, you are well aware that time on the Astral Plane does not work the same as it does on the Earthplane," said Jonathan, with another fatherly smile. He turned to Jonah. "What has happened, son?"

Feeling more confident now that Jonathan was around, Jonah launched into the story. He covered everything from the experimenting with Spectral Sight to being time-frozen amongst the dumpsters.

"If it hadn't been for Bast, I would have been finished," said Jonah. "It was like she slapped the warning into my mind through her eyes or something."

"Yes, that would be exactly right," said Jonathan. "Felines lack the capacity to voice their feelings, but the heralds have the ability to intimate thoughts that take the form of written words when your mind translates them."

When Jonathan stopped speaking, Trip, who had come into the kitchen and appeared to have recovered from his bruising, murmured, "Well, I can tell you one mistake you made, Rowe."

Very slowly, Jonah turned his face to Trip. "And what might that have been, *Titus?*" he asked.

Trip's eyes narrowed maliciously, which prompted Jonathan to raise his hand. Clearly, he had no interest in the conversation potentially going on a violent tangent.

"You spoke to a spirit that was shackled," the Protector Guide told Jonah. There was an authoritative note in his voice that let Jonah know that his and Trip's snipes would have to be quelled. "The chained spirits and spiritesses are the one who are usually used as unwilling subjects. Their essences are usurped regularly, and they are clamped so that Creyton can reel them in at any moment."

Jonah frowned. "Those clamps looked about as transparent as windowpanes," he said. "Why couldn't they just break them?"

"Christ alive," sneered Trip. "Do you know anything at all? The chains are made of ethereal materials. Ethereal materials don't need to look strong to *be* strong. If they were that easily broken, do you think spirits and spiritesses would ask for help?"

"The flaw in speaking to one of Creyton's spirit prisoners," chimed in Terrence, "is that they are bound to the Reaper who controls them. Monitored, I guess you'd say. That Reaper hears what they hear and sees what they see."

Jonah thought of the dreams he'd had with the fettered spirits looking sickly and frail and then being unchained and whole. While their movements were desperate, they had never actually made sounds.

"So is that why he chose to speak in my mind?"

"Yes," said Jonathan. "Mental communication is extremely difficult to detect. Gave you a little breathing room."

"But you told me that traceable links could only be made through emotional bonds or something," said Jonah. "This man was a stranger—"

"A stranger that you actively sought out and then communicated with," Jonathan reminded him. "Curiosity, impatience, frustration ... these were undoubtedly present in your mind when you beckoned him. Your mood alone was enough to provide strength to any link."

"So I can't even ask what's wrong?" demanded Jonah. "They can ask for help, but we can't ask what's wrong?"

"Seeking out spirits is a risky business, particularly one that is enslaved and shackled, Jonah," said Reena. "We have to allow *them* into our consciousness, and even then, it's only safe to communicate for small periods at a time."

Jonah felt that faint pang concerning the dreams once more.

"What is it that Creyton told you again?" asked Jonathan.

Jonah reminded them all of Creyton's proclamations concerning being unstoppable. "His plans were underway and wouldn't be derailed, and we were only alive due to his mercy," he concluded.

Terrence leaned forward after the brief silence that followed these words. "You said Creyton froze you in time. What did that feel like?"

Jonah thought about it carefully. "Have you ever had one of those experiences where you are on the fringe of being awake, but your body is still kind of asleep?" he asked Terrence. "Like your mind is awake, eyes open and moving, but your body is immobile? That's the closest thing I can think of to describe it. *Scary.* I've never felt anything like that. He kept going on and on about how he could have easily taken me out."

They all fell silent once more as if they wanted such a frightening feeling. Jonah was almost inclined to tell them not to as it was almost bad enough seeing them imagining it as it was to recall experiencing it.

"Jonathan," he said, which jarred all of them back to themselves, "why did it feel like there was an explosion when Creyton put things back to real time?"

Jonathan's face darkened. It left Jonah strangely unnerved, as those hardened features looked almost as dangerous as Creyton's. "Because Creyton wasn't manipulating time, he was forcing time to go against itself," he told him. "It is beyond dangerous."

"What?" said Jonah. "Why? He said time was a plaything. You even said yourself that time was easily displaced and meddled with. Remember what you did for me?"

"Of course I do," said Jonathan. "But I don't do those things regularly, nor do I force them. When I tinkered with time, they were absolute last resorts to assist you in getting out of hazardous situations. He froze you in time merely to posture and gloat. I believe you can see the difference."

Jonah lowered his head. "Yeah, I can see it," he said, almost reluctantly. These things did not make him feel like he could hang with any of them, and certainly not like a credible threat to Creyton and his psycho minions.

"These are the reasons why Creyton is dangerous," said Jonathan. "His prideful actions, reckless manipulation of time, blocking spiritual paths … it is detrimental to nature. His deeds have had disastrous consequences and will lead to more."

"Okay," said Jonah, "do you have any idea what he has planned?"

"Just suspicions," murmured Jonathan. "But unfounded suspicions are not helpful to anyone and serve no purpose if voiced because they engender assumptions that are then misused and twisted to fit said suspicion."

Jonah lowered his head, resting the bridge of his nose between his thumb and forefinger. He had *really* grown tired of the hazy riddles. "All right, Mr. Sage," he said, and Terrence snorted, "maybe I ought to ask you something more to the point. Where does that put us? What does it all mean? What is the, uh, state of things?"

"It means," said Reena, nodding to Jonathan, "that you need to take off the polo shirt and get a tank top. We are getting back to your training."

They were out at the Glade almost immediately, but Reena had insisted that Jonah have some protein first, and as he had spent his lunchtime in a struggle for his physical life, he gladly accepted a tuna sandwich on rice bread. Though it did not entirely wipe away the fatigue he felt, being sated did work wonders for his mental state.

So Creyton did not view him as a threat. At all.

But he was the Blue Aura, and that had to mean that, at the very *least*, he wouldn't go quietly into the night. Bearing this in mind, the training and having some semblance of purpose whittled away some of the misgivings in his mind.

That was, at least, before the actual training started.

Jonathan was present again, though he engaged in very little dialogue, trusting the actual legwork to the rest of them. Bobby, upon hearing of the recent attack on Jonah, abandoned his plan of one more workout and going to bed early. Jonah wondered about his previous thoughts of Bobby having a mean streak. He had been wrong about that, and he was happy for it, but he did show the aptitude for those behaviors when he was engaged in physical activity.

Jonah had just pulled himself up from another of Reena's damned speed attacks, having forgotten to sidestep her. Only this time, he'd had no time to recuperate. Malcolm instantly clamped him from some point behind his back. Jonah couldn't help but note such a strong clamp from such a thin man.

"Expect any and everything," advised Malcolm, and positioned him in front of Terrence, who charged at them full force. Instantly, Jonah understood that Malcolm intended to hold him there until Terrence gored him like some rage-filled rhinoceros.

He would *not* endure that.

The memory of being trapped by Creyton imbued him with a fuel that he instantly knew how to employ.

Terrence was near … nearer now…

Jonah made up in his mind that Terrence's attack wouldn't connect. He closed his eyes.

A strange thing happened. Terrence was mere inches away, yet the very second that Jonah decided that this attack wouldn't work, he felt a strange sensation at his shoulder, waist, and knees. It felt as though both he and Malcolm had been yanked to the right. A grunt of discomfort prompted Jonah to open his eyes, and he saw Terrence sprawled on the ground, stunned.

Jonah pulled free of Malcolm, and turned to see that the stunned look on Terrence's face was mirrored on everyone else's face as well. Not Jonathan's, though. He stood near a birch tree, where he looked at Jonah with something that looked like approval.

"Did you see that?" Liz whispered to Bobby, but Jonathan cleared his throat loudly.

"Shocking things often occur in these situations," he said. "Training provides the framework for capabilities not previously thought possible. Don't pause, my friends. Please proceed."

Jonah barely had time to register his achievement, or whatever it was that had just happened; it simply felt like someone had grabbed him and pulled him out of Terrence's way. But he also had a suspicion that this was the way Jonathan preferred it to be. That way, he couldn't have time to believe his own hype.

When training recommenced, Jonah found himself paired up with Liz, which he assumed would be a lopsided thing (Liz was two inches shorter than Bobby). When he attempted offense, however, he immediately realized that he'd made a very bad assumption. Liz was not as fast as Reena, but she was still able to sidestep him. Despite this, Jonah caught a small break and had Trip to thank for it. From the moment Jonah arrived at the estate, Trip had made no secret that he loathed the ground that Jonah walked on. So if he had access to a cheap shot, he would take it without a second thought. But Jonah had gleaned from the very first training (had he really begun to think this way in such a short amount of time?) that Trip preferred to capitalize off of the momentum, not actually initiate an attack. He also knew that Trip enjoyed it when Jonah was on the receiving end of particularly impactful attacks. So it was no surprise to Jonah when Trip's eyes flashed with glee when he glanced over Jonah's shoulder.

Jonah about-faced and hunched, seeing Bobby there much like Terrence had been minutes before. He managed to use Bobby's momentum against him and flipped him over his head. To Jonah's amusement, it just so happened that Bobby collided with Trip, which knocked them both over.

Feeling quite pleased with that particular turn of events, he turned around to be brutally greeted with a fist to the gut from Liz. It didn't have the force of Terrence's or even Bobby's, but it was agonizing. He crumpled to a knee with his eyes shut tight and a venomous swear word fighting to escape his mouth.

Liz's green eyes gleamed with triumph and then concern as she helped Jonah back to his feet and promptly whirled him around, where Malcolm grasped him while they were still face to face. Malcolm gave him no time to think. As quickly as he had clutched him, he'd released him and pushed him left, just in time for Reena to jar his sensations with a thunderous clap of her hands.

The temperature dipped to an ungodly level once again, and Jonah hugged himself tightly, though he avoided falling to his knees a second time.

Reena clapped again, and the temperature elevated to its normal level. "Overconfidence can get you gravely injured, Jonah," she told him. "I watched and read your every move. After your offense kicked in, you got a little too happy about what you'd done. I know the male ego is fragile and requires regular stoking, but hubris is an attribute that will bring you absolute disaster in a real fight."

Jonah straightened with a grimace because his midsection was still smarting from Liz's punch. "One, why is it so wrong to be pleased with myself? I've been a whipping boy all this time. Two, could you please, for the love of God, use other moves than your inborn freeze ray? Three, who the hell says *hubris?*"

Reena laughed. "Artists do." She noticed him still favoring his stomach. "A little break, I think."

They all settled to seated positions, Terrence and Malcolm very complimentary of Jonah's bursts, but Trip coolly commented that it would be impressive when it wasn't accidental. Jonah made an incomprehensible grunt and turned to Reena and Liz. Jonathan came nearer to Jonah.

"Be kind to yourself, Jonah," he said at once. "Honing is the best part. It allows accidental triumphs to become instinctive, and random moments become harmonious and integrated. Possibilities are infinite, much like life."

He smiled. Jonah didn't. "I'm glad *you've* chosen to see it that way," he muttered. "I haven't perfected anything. And Creyton—"

"Is a ruthless killer with extensive power," finished Jonathan. "But he wasn't born onto Earthplane knowing those things."

With a great deal of effort, Jonah didn't retort. Apparently, it was simply Jonathan's way to give advice such as this. Jonah didn't need any more experience with being told that he could change the world. He still hadn't yet gotten the memo.

His writer's block hadn't yet gotten the memo either. He pushed that annoyance back and turned to Liz.

"What exactly did you do when you hit me?" he asked her. "That hurt like hell."

Liz surveyed her tiny fists and shrugged. "I'm not a strong girl. Not the fastest either. I'm a healer, so I wouldn't fight much anyway. If I have no other choice, though, I have to rely on points of weakness. If I can't put force behind a hit, then it's a matter of knowing *where* to hit you. I've found that you don't need power if you simply know the best point."

"Well, I'll give you an A-plus there," said Jonah.

Liz moved nearer to him and placed her fingers at the smarting area. With a firm press, the pain ceased.

"There you go," she said.

Jonah thanked her, and she beamed. He began to feel protective of Liz. The girl was too young, chipper, and bubbly to have to deal with dark spirits.

"So I've got to ask," he said to Reena, "what was the big deal earlier? Why did everyone want to stop and stare?"

Reena frowned. "You aren't aware of what happened?" she asked.

Jonah's puzzled look was enough to confirm this.

"Terrence missed you," said Reena, still eyeing him with interest. "It was like something invisible pulled you clear."

"It was a very interesting thing you achieved there, Jonah," said Jonathan. "If you don't mind my asking, what were you thinking at that time?"

"I don't know," said Jonah, who felt on the spot again. "Malcolm had me clamped; guy's got pincer's for a grip—" he thought he saw

Malcolm give a half-smirk, "—but when I saw Terrence charging, I just knew that I wasn't getting hit again."

Jonathan was silent for a second, looking pleased. "See how thoughts are living things? You decided that you would not be touched, and it was so. Extraordinary, Rowe. Extraordinary."

Jonah wasn't quite sure how to respond to that, so he simply continued drinking his water.

The training ended shortly thereafter, and even though Jonah experienced no other monumental breakthroughs, he felt like he could finally return to the estate without feeling like an amateur who'd spent several hours making a fool of himself.

Despite the faint feeling of achievement, Jonah was still disheartened by the fact that his grandmother had not responded to him when he was in Spectral Sight the previous night. A word. A sign. A pick up in the wind. Any one of those would have sufficed. And also, he was more shaken than he'd let on by the experience with Creyton. This man was a menace to the natural order of ethereality and had been since before Jonah was even born. Despite his years, he looked maybe ten years older than Jonah due to usurping the essences of spirits. Jonah also wondered just what kind of influence this dark Eleventh Percenter had that enabled him to twist and warp people's views so much so that they were willing to lay down their own physical lives just because it guaranteed them some sort of power.

Nothing about it felt right. And Jonah was supposed to be a big deal too? It seemed hilarious. So far, being the Blue Aura didn't even make him equal to his friends, let alone Creyton.

But at least he had people to support him. It would have been a different monster entirely if he had been forced to fly blind. That realization served to assuage his hurts and concerns.

"Don't know what frame of mind you were in when you drove here," said Terrence, which brought Jonah back to reality, "but I'm sure that you would agree that you can't drive your car back to the city like that, right?"

Jonah didn't register what Terrence meant at first, but then he noticed his car and grimaced. The interior was an absolute mess. He looked at his driver's seat, which was so stained it wasn't even funny. He could smell it from the crack in the window. "Did I smell like that when I got here?"

"No," said Reena, applying an ice pack to her forearm, "you smelled worse."

Jonah sighed. Another thing to deal with.

When they'd almost reached the steps to the estate, they saw Bobby and Liz conversing. Bobby broke away from the conversation long enough to give them his attention.

"I noticed you looking at that mess in your car," he said.

Jonah shrugged. He didn't want to talk about it. He saw Liz's eyes flicker with pity, which really didn't help matters.

"Don't worry about it, man," said Bobby. "Terrence and I will get it taken care of for you."

"What?" said Jonah. "Seriously?"

"Oh yeah," said Bobby, but he didn't seem too keen on further explanations as he'd resumed his conversation with Liz. Jonah looked at Terrence, but he didn't elaborate either.

"Brace yourself, man," he advised.

The endowments evaporated seconds later, leaving them all winded. Jonah was sure that Bobby, Liz, and Malcolm would drag themselves upstairs soon, but he stayed where he was and closed his eyes for a moment.

"Jonah," said Reena.

He opened his eyes. "Yes, Reena?"

"Let's talk before you go to sleep," she said, "but not here. Too many distractions."

She rose and looked over at Terrence, whose head had tilted over while he dozed. "Terrence."

He didn't stir.

"*Terrence!*" she snapped, and he jerked awake so violently he almost fell off of the couch.

"What? What is it?"

"Come with us," she muttered and headed off.

Sharing a questionable look with Terrence, Jonah followed suit. They went through the kitchen, through the workout room (Jonah was thankful for that), and they came to rest in Reena's art studio. Jonah wondered why they came all the way down here. Reena almost felt like she was about to initiate him into some secret society. He noticed Terrence was looking confused as well.

"Jonah," said Reena without preamble, "first off, your writing is amazing."

Jonah blinked; he hadn't expected that at all, so it didn't even compute for a few moments. "Oh. Oh, thanks. Thanks a lot actually. But you brought us all the way down here to tell me that?"

"Of course I did," she said. "Your writing is probably very precious to you at this stage, so I didn't want to talk about it around Bobby, Liz, and Malcolm."

Jonah thought for a moment, realizing that he was grateful for her consideration, but then he frowned.

"Wait, I gave that piece of manuscript to T—" he began, but Reena waved a hand.

"He let me read it too," she said, "and I thought what you had so far was great."

Jonah noticed his half-book on one of Reena's tables and saw that it was the epic he'd been writing. He was suddenly annoyed; that was a book he had such *high* hopes for, the one that he'd hoped would be his ticket out of Essa, Langton, and Bane. But it, like the rest of them, had fallen flat.

"I'm glad that you think so," he told her, trying with all the strength he had left to grin. The second he did it, he regretted it. He didn't know how sharp Terrence was, and he probably wasn't too observant right now due to the fact that he was fighting sleep, but Reena possessed eyes and a sense of observation that almost nothing could escape.

"What's the issue?" she asked.

Jonah plopped down, the familiar bile of inadequacy finding its way back. "It's difficult to explain. A very long story, plain and simple."

Reena raised her eyebrows. "It's not like you're going anywhere," she said.

The look on her face was intractable. He shook his head resignedly. Maybe he could put it in a nutshell.

"Terrence already knows this, more or less," he began, "but I love to write. It's the one thing that no one could ever refute about me. When I was a kid, I wrote every day and loved it. Still do. But as I got older, something happened. I have developed this … block. I couldn't explain it even if I tried. I have some truly excellent ideas," he motioned to the yellowish pages of the manuscript, "but then I can't finish them. You have no idea how maddening it is."

"Yes, I do," said Reena. She looked at Jonah with understanding.

"*We* do," amended Terrence. "Why do you think I don't brag about my cooking?"

"And you know a bit about my painting," said Reena. "But Jonah, your writing just might outstrip us both."

Dear Lord, thought Jonah wearily, *isn't it bad enough hearing this from Nelson? Don't they realize these compliments only make it more annoying?* "It isn't all that great," he mumbled. "I'm not that great. If I were, I would be able to finish it."

"We aren't going to let you be hard on yourself, Jonah," said Terrence, indignation in his tone. "You made me a believer just with those 217 pages right there."

"You wouldn't allow me to hear any flack about my paintings," added Reena. "You think I'm going to allow you to downplay that?"

She pointed at the pages. Jonah shook his head, almost managing a laugh.

"Look at it like this," said Terrence, "like I told you on the highway, we can all work on our snags together."

Jonah didn't say anything. It was actually a very considerate thing Terrence suggested. He settled on a short nod, flashed a cold glance at the uncompleted novel, and changed the subject. "Not to sound suspicious or anything," he said, "but my writing can't be the only reason you brought me down here."

Terrence was looking at Reena as curiously as Jonah was, but Reena just smiled. "You might be an essence reader yourself."

"Oh no, just familiar with the 'private meeting' setting," replied Jonah. "So what's up?"

"I was wondering if you would be averse to Terrence and me helping you develop your skills away from prying eyes. If Terrence agrees, of course."

Terrence's puzzled look faded. "I'm all for that!"

Jonah didn't share this enthusiasm and straightened in alarm. "You think there is a spy—"

"No," said Reena, waving a dismissive hand. "God, no. I just thought you didn't want to be put on the spot in front of everyone for once."

"Now that would be a welcome change," said Jonah. "Let me guess—you want to get me up to snuff?"

"Undoubtedly," said Reena.

"You had to ask that, man?" said Terrence.

Jonah raised an eyebrow at Terrence, who wasn't even aware of Reena's plan until a few seconds ago. "I've got to know," he persisted, "why are you so gung-ho about it, Reena? And you, Terrence? What's the purpose of giving me the extra help?"

Reena looked at Terrence, who seemed completely onboard by now. Jonah felt as if something he didn't like was coming. "First of all, Creyton is a psychotic Spirit Reaper skilled in treachery, murder, and pilfering spirits and spiritesses. At the current time, you are trained to do billing reports and write stories. Not an equal match on any level."

"Gee, thanks," grumbled Jonah. Did she have to be so blunt when she stated the obvious?

"Another thing," said Terrence, flashing an annoyed look at Reena, "if you are anything like me, you don't like skating behind everybody else."

Jonah didn't answer. He knew he didn't have to.

"Besides all that," said Reena more kindly, "Creyton and those minions have begun wiping out Eleventh Percenters with renewed vigor, according to Jonathan. Some of them may have even been associates of ours, even if they haven't lived at the estate for several years. They had no warning and paid the price. But you are here with us now, and you are our friend. And I'll be damned if I lose a friend."

"*We'll* be damned," added Terrence.

Jonah looked at them. Terrence and Reena were two people that he barely knew. Yet they wanted to do whatever they could to survive, as well as see to it that he survived along with them. Their expressions were so certain that Jonah thought that maybe, just maybe, things might work out well.

Might being the operative word.

"I'm in," he told them.

11

Dream Street

Jonah had no idea what he'd just volunteered for nor did he know what Reena had in store for him. The first unpleasant surprise he encountered occurred right after he'd agreed to Reena's plan.

"So when is this going to begin?" he asked.

Reena stood, giving him that sharp, introspective look. "Now."

Terrence gaped at her. "Seriously? But we just dropped our endowments! You really want to start now?"

"Yes," said Reena, tightening her black and scarlet hair back into a ponytail. "*Right* now, actually."

Before Jonah knew it, they were back in the Glade and choosing new endowments.

Jonah opted for an endowment from the spirit of an older-looking man who looked like he'd been a laborer of some kind in his physical life. As Jonah gave thanks and felt the endowment surge through his body, he found himself strangely ready for new challenges. It also helped that the endowment seemed to assist him in compartmentalizing his feelings of doubt and inadequacy.

For the moment, anyway.

"Ready to roll," said Reena, all business. After hearing the change in her voice, Jonah began to suspect that, in many ways, Reena could be just as intense as Bobby. "Jonah, remember this: whether you are on defense or offense, the key is not to think."

Jonah frowned. "You've got to be kidding. Don't think?"

"I think what Reena means is not to think so hard," said Terrence. "Strategy and thinking things ahead are all well and good, but it's not always possible to do that in the thick of things."

"Not always possible?" repeated Jonah. "Are you actually advocating *not* having a plan?"

Reena looked Jonah dead in the eye. "Did you have a plan when Creyton suspended you in time?" she asked.

Jonah's face fell. Even if he had had a plan, there was no possible way he could have implemented it while he was a frozen sitting duck. Satisfied at the affirming expression on Jonah's face, Reena continued.

"Although I do enjoy planning, I will concede that sometimes a great deal of it can throw you off. What good is having twenty plans if you can't pick one? This is where the mind comes in."

Jonah raised an eyebrow. "Um, Reena … you just said not to think."

"Not to think *painstakingly*," amended Reena. "And besides, that has to do with your brain. I said *mind*."

Jonah didn't know what made him do it, but he glanced at Terrence, who flung a rock at him.

He blinked and dodged it, and with a jolt, remembered the similar occurrence with the saltshaker. "Unthinking reflexes," he recalled. "The brain inhabits the head and the mind inhabits the entire body."

"Very good, Jonah," said Reena, nodding. "By the time your brain would have registered that, the rock would have already bashed your nose. You simply acted and see what happened. Just like before, you didn't think about that shield, you thought about not getting hit. And the results worked in your favor."

"And you only knew that you didn't want me to hit you," chimed in Terrence, who seemed to be warming to this idea more and more, "and just like that, you were out of the way."

"Which is where we are now," said Reena, and with no further words, lunged at him.

Jonah knew he should have been ready, but he hesitated too long, trying to process it all. Trying to *think*. He feebly attempted to salvage the situation by sidestepping Reena, but he was too late. He found himself on the ground, grumbling self-deprecating swear words under his breath.

"That might have worked if you hadn't wasted the extra time thinking so hard," rebuked Reena. "Stop erring on the side of caution and allow your mind to take over."

As silent as the dark that surrounded them, Terrence had locked Jonah into a full nelson hold. Reena watched intently.

Don't think, he told himself, though this was hard to achieve because Terrence's vise hurt something fierce, *Break it, you weak son of a—*

Jonah didn't know how it happened, but Terrence exclaimed in surprise and freed him. Reena had vanished from his line of sight.

It was eerily quiet. He didn't even hear Terrence. But something in his mind warned him to turn around. He couldn't tell what direction the threat was, he just had to expect it.

Then, without rational thought, he whipped around so smoothly, it was as if the earth had moved him and not his own feet. Reena had maneuvered behind him but not to grasp him. She was about to employ that cold-spot trick of hers.

Hell no. That was Jonah's only thought. He grabbed Reena's wrists and focused all of his strength on preventing her hands from connecting. That was a feat all by itself. Jonah was larger than Reena, but she was deceptively stronger.

Reena looked surprised for only a second but then recovered and struggled against him. It seemed like they were locked into some kind of inverted arm wrestling match. Jonah hoped that Reena would give something away in her expression, but Reena's eyes were unreadable.

Jonah was about to attempt something else when a prickle of warning put all of his senses on edge. He didn't even hesitate. Surprisingly.

Willing himself out of the way, he felt tugs at his torso and shoulder once more. He had no idea how it would happen, he just knew that he wouldn't be in harm's way. As an added bonus, he had moved far enough away to brace himself.

It happened quickly. Reena's hands connected, no longer fighting Jonah's restriction. But the person that now faced her was Terrence, who had been behind Jonah. Jonah closed his eyes tightly and flung his arms around himself, but the cold wasn't quite as bad. Maybe it was only impactful when he was directly in Reena's line of fire. Or line of cold, rather.

Terrence trembled violently and would certainly have sworn if his teeth weren't chattering. Reena looked over at Jonah, looking pleasantly surprised.

"Not bad at all, Jonah," she said. "A start, but a very good one."

Jonah was pleased, but then remembered how he'd gotten humbled the last time he'd preened. He acknowledged the compliment with a nod.

"Reena," croaked Terrence.

"Oh, right," she muttered. She clapped once more, and both Jonah and Terrence could once again appreciate the subtle blessings of warmth and comfort.

"Some of it felt easier that time," said Jonah. "And by the way," he turned to Terrence with a look of irritation, "getting accosted from behind has gotten tired."

Terrence, no longer freezing, looked at Jonah and smirked. "Sorry," he said, "best way to get people to react."

Jonah gave him a dark look and turned back to Reena. "It felt like I almost knew what I was doing there," he remarked. "I didn't know that blindly reacting could yield such results."

"It wasn't blind," said Reena. "Your mind and body already know what to do. It's time that your brain got the memo. Now kneel. I don't want you to sustain a head injury when the endowment departs."

They didn't speak much as they returned to the estate. Reena bade Jonah and Terrence good night, and Terrence went to the kitchen for dietary sustenance. Jonah went upstairs, settled on his bed, and immediately dozed off.

The dream started off normally enough. He was sitting at a table, feeling very pleased with himself. A woman approached, looking apprehensive and hopeful.

"Here you are," she said, with a reverence in her voice that Jonah had never heard in his life. "You have no idea how long I've been waiting for this!"

Her voice was quite sycophantic, but Jonah didn't mind it much. It was at that moment he realized that he was in a palatial bookstore. He was sharply dressed but didn't mind it. Something told him that he had dressed this way for himself, not because he had to go to the office. There were books as far as the eye could see, but the majority of people weren't there for them. They were in the most informal, disjointed line he'd ever seen, but it only added to his glee.

They were here for *him*.

The line was comprised of doctors, blue-collar heroes, businessmen, teenagers, everyone. Each and every face showed admiration, awe, and joy. A glossy hardcover novel was snugly clamped in every trembling hand. The adoring smiles only became more pronounced when he strung the calligraphic letters together and formed his name within the covers (when had he learned to write like that?). It seemed that for every book he signed, there were dozens more awaiting the same treatment. He could not make out the title of the book, but he could see that all of them were written by J.J.A. Rowe, the pen name his grandmother suggested for him when he was in the fifth grade writer's club.

He was a success. At long last.

The fandom didn't die down either. The atmosphere was euphoric. Jonah signed book after book, his grin wider than a game show host's. And why shouldn't it be? He'd made it.

Left to right his hand went, fatigue being the most laughable idea on earth. He simply didn't want it to end.

"Been waiting a bit for this, haven't you, Rowe?" said a voice.

Jonah looked up. The man in front of him was extremely tall and cloaked in an ash-colored duster. His eyes cast an appraising look at Jonah, but it wasn't one of adoration like the rabid fans he'd previously been entertaining. He surveyed Jonah's puzzled face with doubt. Or was it skepticism?

Jonah didn't know what to make of this strange man, but he wanted him gone. He was the only one not smiling, the only one who wasn't treating Jonah with deference. It didn't take a brain surgeon to figure out that this guy was the polar opposite of the buzzing, prosperous setting represented in this bookstore. The man seemed apart from it somehow. Detached.

"Sir," said Jonah, the nagging feeling increasing, "I'm glad you appreciate my literature. But I'm pretty busy here, so I hope you understand if—"

The man laughed. It wasn't the excited laughter of everyone else. It was a cold, hard, cackling sequence that made Jonah's hair stand on end. "I'm not here for a book, boy," said the man with derision. "I've come to see if you can handle the coming storm."

"Coming—?" began Jonah, but the man quelled him with a look and pointed at the bustling crowd outside of the store.

Jonah stood, removing his reading glasses as he did. There wasn't anything odd that he could see, but then he heard a *CAW* that was audible over the din in the bookstore.

A black crow circled the crowd and then nosedived.

Jonah moved toward the windows, oblivious to the fountain pen still clutched in his hand. After the crow's abrupt descent into the crowd, he'd expected someone to start, jump, or make some cry of surprise, but that didn't occur. Instead, someone innocently bumped into another man, a mistake that was almost invisible. The man turned, however, and began viciously attacking the person who bumped into him, causing a raucous disturbance within the throng of puzzled folks.

Jonah flinched at the violent reaction and turned to some of the security. "You might need to call someone—"

His voice was drowned out by another *CAW*, this time from another area. Another crow swooped into the crowd, and more altercations began, far more intense than the first. Two more crows arrived from nowhere and simply descended. Now the crowd was in a full uproar. A gunshot rang in the air, and Jonah's blood ran cold.

At the sound of the gun, the patrons in the bookstore dissolved into chaos, which mirrored the hell outside. Jonah was in near hysterics and had no idea what to do, his shouts for calm falling on deaf ears.

The outside crowd was in a panic as two more shots pierced the air. Now people were being trampled underfoot. The crowd inside the bookstore began bearing weight on the glass, not even bothering to try the front door. To make matters worse, the outside crowd appeared to be doing the same thing, taking no notice that the people inside the doors were pressing with equal force.

Jonah attempted to shout again, but his voice didn't work. As he attempted to escape, he noticed that some faces in the crowd were familiar. The memories were vague in his mind, but still familiar: A lithe woman, whose dark and scarlet hair was askew as she looked for an opening in the crowd. A slender man looked terrified as the over-whelming numbers crushed him. Jonah also watched as three other people he recognized were trampled. He stared outside, then back in the bookstore, never feeling as hopeless and useless as he did at this moment.

Then a ringing sound pierced his ears, and he came to a realization so fierce that it just about stopped his heart. He turned his head, ignor-ing the dreadful screams, crashes, and slams, to see yet another crow, this one larger and more menacing than the others, swooping its over-bearing wings over the crowd with such force that Jonah could have sworn they created a breeze.

The ash-cloaked man's gaze had never left Jonah. He stood his ground during this whole debacle, completely undeterred.

"My God," was all that Jonah could manage.

"Instead of talking," the man sneered, "you ought to master your fear and stop this."

The large crow spread its wings and descended. Jonah's horrified shout was not heard by the frenzied masses, but by Terrence, Reena, and Bobby, who were shaking him awake.

"Jonah! JONAH! Wake up!"

Going from fretful sleep to instant consciousness like that was jarring. Jonah felt as if his spirit had been extracted and then slammed back into his body. He shot upright in the bed and barely missed headbutting Bobby. Terrence looked at him, worried and confused.

"What happened?" he demanded. "Are you okay?"

Jonah didn't answer. He simply stared at his friends. They were safe. But he wasn't satisfied. He rose and hurried from the room, barely aware of three sets of feet chasing him.

"Jonah! What's going on?" Reena demanded.

Jonah didn't answer. He couldn't talk, couldn't risk the distraction. He had to know, had to be sure, had to have confirmation with his own eyes—

He leapt the last four stairs and landed in the kitchen, which was empty. Jonah barely broke stride as he ran through the room, burst through the kitchen door, and ceased.

Malcolm and Liz were there, conversing quietly, while Trip was off to himself, headphones on and a notebook in his hand. Malcolm and Liz's conversation stopped when they saw Jonah. Trip gave him a dirty look.

Jonah just stood there and took all of them in. The footsteps had ceased behind him, and he wrenched his eyes away from the individuals in front of him and looked at the ones that had chased him from the bedroom.

"Jonah?" said Reena, looking concerned, but Jonah ignored her.

"Safe," he whispered. Even the whisper seemed laborious; the screaming left his throat raw and his voice weak. "You're all safe. All intact. *Safe.*"

Terrence stared at him. "Jonah, is there any reason why we *wouldn't* be safe?"

Jonah slumped over to the sofa. "I had a horrible dream," he told the room at large, closing his eyes so as to prevent the dream from draining from his mind.

"You're worked up over a damn nightmare—" began Trip, but Jonah had anticipated his snide comment, and responded, "Shut up, Trip. I'm trying to remember it all."

His eyes were closed, but he could tell his words had left a trace of frigidity in the silence. It didn't matter.

"Okay," he announced. "Okay, I got it."

He told them everything. Obviously, he didn't see their reactions because he kept his eyes closed, but the random intakes of breath let him know that his recounting of the dream had the same effect on them as it had on him. When he reached the imposing, long-haired figure, he heard someone grumble. He chanced opening his eyes, and with a start, saw that Jonathan had appeared at some point during his recollection.

"How long have you been here, Jonathan?" he asked.

Jonathan eyed Jonah carefully. "From the moment you began recounting your dream," he said. "Please describe the tall figure again."

Jonah did. Those cruel eyes and brutal features would not exit his memory anytime soon.

Jonathan nodded at the end of Jonah's description, a very solemn expression on his face. "And what did he say?"

"He mentioned something about a coming storm, and then he said something about getting over my fear and stopping it," Jonah told him. "I think it was probably the worst dream I've ever had."

Jonah noticed Trip and Jonathan glance at one another, which was odd.

"It was only a dream, right, Jonathan?" asked Jonah.

Jonathan stood up and eyed Jonah once more. "Possibly, it was," he said at last. "Let's get back to our routines, people. I will be back this evening. Rowe, be prepared for your training, okay?"

He vanished. Malcolm and Liz stood, still looking at Jonah with worry.

"You're sure you're all right, Jonah?" Liz asked.

"Yeah, I'm good," said Jonah, his voice full of a confidence he didn't feel.

Jonathan had simply appeared to listen to him and then vanished just as quickly. Why would he have appeared to hear him out if it were "possibly just a dream?"

"I'm good," he repeated.

He turned and beckoned to Terrence and Reena to follow him. The minute they were out of earshot of the others, Terrence opened his mouth to say something, but Jonah waved a hand to silence him.

"What is Jonathan not telling me?" he demanded.

Reena sighed. "I don't know what he's not telling you," she said, "but I know the fact that you had that dream is a bit, um, weird."

"Why is it weird?" asked Terrence, and Jonah was thankful that the question came from someone other than him as he wasn't entirely sure he wanted to know the answer.

"Because Creyton is planning something, that's no mystery," said Reena. "I still can't believe Creyton had the power to block the path to the Other Side, and on top of that, his minions are suddenly acting bolder and more vicious. When Jonathan told us that Eleventh Percenters were being killed off, it seemed almost random. But now there appears to be another piece to it."

"Which is what?" asked Jonah.

"Creyton and his followers have always liked killing," said Reena. "But just blind carnage that could bring unwanted attention? Why would he want all eyes on him if he is supposedly planning something so huge? But look what's happened. Creyton blocks the path and starts killing off Eleventh Percenters, sends two minions out after you, and then you dream about some type of 'coming storm.' They might be connected."

Terrence sniffed. "Are you suggesting that Creyton is using excess spirits and spiritesses to clog the path? That makes no sense at all. The path to the Other Side is not a pipe somebody can stop up. We already know that he stays young because he usurps spirits and spiritesses, but he can't possibly have the strength to use those endowments to empower himself, maintain the army of minions, and keep the path blocked. He'd drain himself to hell."

"Wait, what?" said Jonah.

"Think about it, Jonah," said Terrence. "When we lose our endowments, we get very tired. The scope of power that we use had to be light, because the drain always occurs. Creyton might be a *hell* of a threat, but he is still an Eleventh Percenter. Take his endowments away, and he'd be slogged just like the rest of us would be."

Jonah thought on that. "He must have figured out a way to keep himself endowed then."

Reena shook her head. "Impossible. Endowments are not permanent; they work like adrenaline. Bursts are good, but your body can't sustain it long-term. Your heart couldn't take it."

"That might be true, Reena," said Jonah. "I have no doubts that you know your stuff. But I don't think that that man spends any time in a normal state of being. Wouldn't he be *aging* if he didn't have spirits endowing him?"

"There is no way for him to be in permanent endowment," Reena insisted, but now she didn't sound so sure.

"So far as we know," said Terrence. "We got Creyton's powers, Tenths and Eleventh Percenters passing into Spirit mysteriously, and Jonah's dream."

He looked at Jonah. "I think you're asking Reena the wrong question, man."

Jonah looked Terrence in the eye, and then met eyes with Reena. An understanding passed between the three of them.

"It's not what Jonathan is not telling us," said Jonah. "It's what he might not even know himself."

12

Caws of Change

Their conversation weighed on Jonah's mind as he ate Reena's breakfast, which consisted of fruit salad and grapefruit juice. He could think of almost nothing else, which was irritating, seeing as how he could think and focus more clearly since he'd been on Reena's eating plan. And considering the fact that he was currently focusing on Creyton, he wasn't sure that clearer mental faculties were a good thing.

After cardio, Reena painted for about two hours, while the others went about their own routines. Jonah surmised that Reena painted to clear her head and process things, but he had no such luck. After all, he had no easel and no knowledge of painting. But he did have one outlet.

Provided that said outlet didn't cause him more stress.

With a sigh, he went upstairs to his room and pulled out a pen and pad. He went about the normal routine and prepared to stare at the page for several minutes.

One's anguish can be as resolute as bars on the cell in which they imprison themselves.

Jonah blinked. Did he just write that?

Mind clearer than it had been in a long time, he wrote on:

The misconception of mankind is that prisons are extraneous. This is not the case, as extraneous factors can be altered or erased with laughable simplicity. That which lies in the internal is made of stronger material by far as it is unseen, ever evolving, and limitless.

The truest and most beneficial course of action, then, is to morph and transform the prisons we create in our own minds, for as they are opened, so too are the ones that were physically manifested.

Jonah sat back. He lifted the paper and stared at it like a rare jewel or a winning Powerball ticket. The words came out of him as if they'd always been there, and with gathering excitement, he found that he wasn't done yet.

He wrote with fervor, speaking at length in the same vein that he'd begun. It came so readily that he didn't know where to stop. He hadn't had a literary inspiration in so long. The feeling was just all-consuming, like waking from a deep sleep or a dormant muscle suddenly being stimulated through exercise. He was so focused that he hadn't even registered Bast's presence on the bed next to him. Her meowing hadn't mattered. As far as he was concerned, it was familiar, a simple extension of sounds that were associated with the estate. The chirping birds, the sounds of the insects, Bast's meows … they all came with the territory.

A sound that did not fit those criteria, however, met his ears and jarred him out of his writing. The sound was unfamiliar. Alien.

Frowning, he stood up and walked to the window. From his bedroom, he scanned the scene that made up the side view of the land. Judging by its length, the grass had been freshly cut. The gazebo was superbly placed; it seemed to serve as the centerpiece of that portion of land. Jonah could not appreciate this at the moment, though, as the sound that he'd heard had no place amongst such serenity. It was a sound foreign to what he was accustomed to hearing here. What was it?

Just then, Bobby bounded into the room, his eyes alight with a determination almost as bright as the smile.

"Hey Jonah! How are you doing?"

"Doing all right, Bobby," said Jonah, still staring outside. "What's up?"

"Figured you would like a healthy distraction from funky dreams with a nice stiff workout," he said.

Normally, Bobby's excitement would send Jonah in the opposite direction as Terrence was otherwise occupied and couldn't accompany them. At the moment, however, he welcomed a tough distraction. It just might purge his mind of what he desperately wanted to deny he'd heard.

"Sure, Bobby," he heard himself say.

"Great!" Bobby clapped Jonah round the back so hard he almost forgot the sound right then and there.

Sixty-five grueling minutes later, Jonah tried very hard to thank Bobby for the training session but settled for a pained nod of the head when he realized he didn't have the strength to speak. He headed to the bathroom and ran water that was as hot as he could bear it. He prepared to throw table salt in the water when he heard Trip's voice in the hall.

"Mess is worse than I thought."

Jonah paused in the act of salting his water and listened. Trip continued to ramble incoherently.

"Messing up plans, bumbling fools ... Blue Aura dumb fuck ... need to end that quick..."

Jonah yowled as scalding hot water burned his fingers. He was perched on the edge of the tub, and Trip's grumbling caused him to forget to turn off the hot water. He swore, turned it off, and prevented most of the excess water from sloshing onto the floor. Even so, he had caused a bit of a mess.

After the racket he'd made, he wasn't surprised that he didn't hear anything else. Frustrated and forgetting that his upper body was sore as hell, he went back downstairs to ask whoever he saw for the nearest mop, which happened to be Terrence.

"Hey, Jonah," he said. "The interior of your car looks good as new!"

"Really?" said Jonah, distracted. "Thanks!"

Terrence frowned when he saw that something occupied Jonah's mind. "What's wrong?"

Jonah confided in Terrence the brief mutterings he'd overheard from Trip. Terrence rolled his eyes.

"Jonah, Trip hates everyone," he said. "He is one of the most anti-social people I know."

"Then what was the mess he was talking about? And what, pray tell, do you imagine 'has to end quick?' "

Terrence shrugged. "Could've been anything, man. I don't know."

Jonah took a deep breath. "I think he wants *me* out of the way for some reason," he told Terrence.

Terrence met Jonah's eyes with incredulity. "Wants you out of the way? Jonah, I doubt Trip wants to kill you. He ain't the nicest person; he's a sour little shit. But a murderer? Nah."

Jonah allowed himself to be cautiously relieved. Slightly. "Any other thoughts about what's going on, then?"

Terrence sighed. "Not a single thing, man. And Jonathan's off-plane right now, so we can't ask him."

"Why does he spend so much time on the Astral Plane?" asked Jonah.

For some odd reason, Terrence glanced over Jonah's shoulder and then beckoned him outside where they settled next to Jonah's newly cleaned car. Instantly, Jonah figured out why they were out here. Terrence relaxed his back against the car and pulled out a pack of jelly beans and a bottle of fruit punch from his pocket. After giving the front yard another quick scan, he started speaking.

"Jonathan ain't what you would term human, obviously," he said. "He chose to stay behind and become a Protector Guide, which was weird because he is brilliant and good enough in ethereality to be a full-fledged Spirit Guide, but he chose Protector."

Jonah raised an eyebrow. "There is a difference?"

"Oh yeah," said Terrence as he savored the fruit punch. "Spirit Guides are higher up in the pecking order, more range of power for ethereality, access to further understanding of the Planes, can't be usurped ... that kind of thing. Protectors are spirits that want to stay close to their friends and family, monitor the spirits that didn't choose to cross on, shore up spiritual defense on Earth and the Astral Plane, stuff like that. And *they* can be vanquished. But Jonathan opted for that instead of advancing. He wanted to keep training and mentoring, have a more hands-on approach, I guess. And guessing is the only thing I *can* do seeing as how he made those choices years and years before any of us were born."

He scanned the yard again (Jonah snorted) and then continued. "But to answer your question, Earthplane has its limits and reminders. I think that he goes to the Astral Plane to remind himself every so often that there is more than just teaching us."

"More?" asked Jonah, intrigued. "More as in...?"

"As in more than the usual negative stuff he protects the estate from, I think," said Terrence. "More than the usual hustle and bustle. Spirits and the Astral Plane ain't bound to anything three-dimensional. He knows all that, of course, seeing as he stayed behind, but he likes to remind himself every now and again."

Jonah thought on that. It was a concept that he could almost understand. Sometimes it was refreshing to go into one's self and detach from all things stressful. It was what he did when he was writing. Still.

"What does a spirit have to stress about?" he asked, puzzled. "I mean, he's d—uh, in Spirit. Aren't like, all life's questions answered after you pass away, or something like that? The Other Side is perfect!"

Terrence tossed some more jelly beans in his mouth and washed them down with punch. "You probably should be talking to Reena about all this, but I do know some stuff," he said. "The Astral Plane and the Other Side are two different places, remember? You only go to the Other Side if you choose to cross on. But the Astral Plane is like a hub. Where spirits and spiritesses have access to if they still walk the Earthplane. Where you can find the Spirit Guides, other spirits and spiritesses, other Protector Guides, guardians, or whatever."

Jonah frowned. "So even though he's a spirit, he doesn't know *anything* about the Other Side?"

"Nope," said Terrence. "No one does. That place is beyond all of us, even the Spirit Guides."

Jonah wondered how that might feel. But he remembered that Jonathan made a conscious choice to stay behind. Jonah was grateful to have the guidance, but he wondered how being limited to just Earthplane and Astral Plane would feel. The whole thing was a little too deep for him to deal with at the moment, but his musings were interrupted by Bast, who jumped on his lap, stretched, and settled herself. Jonah scratched her ears.

Terrence laughed. "I think you have a brand new soulmate, Jonah."

"I don't mind," said Jonah. "She's saved my physical life twice now."

"That's what we are all here for, man," said Terrence, sobering. "We take care of each other."

He stood abruptly. "Take a look at your car, man. Let me ditch this stuff and find Reena. I might get a workout in. Hopefully, I'll still be loose by the time we have to train tonight."

Bast tensed, and Jonah made to warn Terrence, but it was too late. Reena was there. She'd snuck on them so quietly that Jonah could have sworn she'd materialized like a spiritess. Terrence's hands still full of sugary treats, and he looked so stunned and guilty that Jonah could only laugh.

"Terrence, do you know what sugar and Red 40 mixed together can do to your system?" asked Reena.

"Aw, come on, Reena," said Jonah, allowing Bast to stand and scamper off. "Live a little! Couple snacks never hurt anyone."

"I'd rather live a lot, thank you very much," snapped Reena, "and a couple of snacks *will* hurt you. Particularly ones with high fructose corn syrup and disgusting confectioner's glaze."

"Can you guys come up to my room? Got new material I want you to see," said Jonah, successfully curtailing Terrence's retort and piquing Reena's interest. They were up there in minutes, and Jonah put the papers in her hand.

Reena hadn't read the entire page before she'd exclaimed, "Jonah, this is incredible!"

Jonah couldn't help but feel pleased with himself as he passed the pages to Terrence, who read with his eyebrows raised.

"You sure you didn't come up with that opening quote from an English lit book or something?" he asked.

Jonah narrowed his eyes. "That's all me, Terrence, no book. I have a knack for writing. I just can't follow through."

"Yet," Reena corrected him. "Jonah, you truly have a gift."

"Nah, darling," said Jonah. "*You* have a gift. Can we see your new—?"

Jonah's voice trailed off as something outside the window caught his eye. Trip was moving near the outer edge of the forest.

"What's Captain Ass doing?" he said to Terrence and Reena. "I didn't peg him as the yoga type."

Reena frowned as they watched Trip move his hands slowly through the air as if he were practicing Tai Chi. If that was indeed what he was doing, thought Jonah, it didn't look like it was working very well. With each movement, Trip's scowl became more pronounced.

"Weird," said Reena. "He's usually making music during this time."

"Unless there are stray musical notes in the afternoon air, Trip is up to something else," said Jonah.

"Jonah," said Terrence, looking only slightly bemused, "there is probably a logical explanation for him to be doing ... whatever it is he is doing."

"Terrence, he looks like he is trying to slap an invisible face," snapped Jonah.

"Let me go ask him," said Reena. "I truly want to know what the hell he's doing."

"Now will you believe my suspicion from earlier is valid?" Jonah asked Terrence.

Terrence shuffled his weight, but Reena turned toward Jonah, curious.

"Suspicion?"

"Oh, yeah, I didn't tell you..." Jonah recounted Trip's mutterings from earlier. Terrence still didn't look convinced, but Reena had that troubled look on her face again.

"Let me go talk to him," she repeated. "Be ready to eat again in about forty-five minutes, Jonah, and if you value your digestive system, Terrence, you will trash those jelly beans."

Terrence scowled as Reena exited the room. "Can't wait for training this evening," he grumped. "I'm gonna tell Jonathan we need to spar, and I'm picking Reena. Bad enough I have to eat that rabbit food three times a day…"

Still grumbling, he left as well, but Jonah barely registered either of them leaving. He only had eyes for Trip, who now held a vial and seemed to be capturing empty air within it.

* * *

Whether or not Reena got the chance to speak to Trip was anyone's guess as Reena wasn't able to tell him or Terrence anything. Trip was on all of them like a shadow, but Jonah couldn't figure out whether or not that was intentional. It had him so occupied with thought that he hadn't even bothered to return the sneers that Trip gave him in passing.

He wondered about what Trip's supposed "mess" could be. Just what was it that Trip wanted to end quickly? And exactly what plan was he convinced that Jonah was messing up?

When Jonah attempted to approach Reena, she shook her head and darted her eyes at Trip, who was listening to his music. When Jonah mouthed, "*He's got headphones on, Reena,*" she mouthed back, "*I will talk to you later.*"

Jonah decided to retreat to the gazebo again, this time carrying his notebook. He was surprised to find that despite his frustration, the words still came freely. He blazed through a dozen pages of writing before he even remembered Trip's suspicious behaviors again.

Jonah felt great after writing. He thought the serenity of his surroundings may have contributed to it. Despite the positivity, he had that nagging suspicion that the spark would fade again. It also happened at that very moment that his ideas became muddled and clotted once again. Out just like a light.

"Shit," he grumbled. "Snuffed out quicker than I thought."

He closed his eyes and attempted to stifle the frustration. When he opened his eyes, he saw a collection of spirits and spiritesses on the grounds.

He frowned. How had he gone into Spectral Sight? He hadn't willed the mental curtain to open.

Marla was present again and gave him a melancholy smile. Jonah grimaced. First frustration, now guilt and pity.

"We'll help you, Marla," he murmured. "I don't know how, but we will help you all."

She flashed him a hopeful smile and then disappeared.

Jonah surveyed the other spirits and attempted to figure out why he'd gone into Spectral Sight. He also did it to take his mind off of Marla. All he could offer her at the moment were kind words, which made him feel ashamed. He had no idea how to help her, no idea how to fight Creyton, no idea what to do. Just like his writing. Just like that stupid job at Essa, Langton, and Bane.

He was startled from these thoughts when Bast showed up beside of him.

"Come looking for me, Bast?" he said. "Not getting any attention back at the estate?"

Bast came forward and allowed Jonah to scratch her ears. He noticed that a few of the spirits made eye contact with the two of them. He also noticed that the ones doing this were chained, like the ones he'd encountered at the office. He remembered what happened that time, and immediately dropped his gaze. He didn't have any interest in repeat performances that might involve crowbars.

He closed his eyes and visualized the curtain closing, figuring the best way to avoid disaster was to be done with Spectral Sight. *Close,* he thought to himself. *I'm not communicating with them. I know what will happen.*

Bast leapt to his lap, but he didn't register it, because when he'd opened his eyes, the spirits were still visible. Not a single thing had changed. They were still there, as corporeal as ever, and some stared at him even more intently than before.

Jonah had no clue what was going on. How had the curtain opened when he hadn't willed it to and stayed that way?

Had he accidentally left that part of his brain open? He could already feel anxiety rising. Seeing spirits everywhere was *not* something he wanted to experience twenty-four-seven.

It took him a few seconds to realize that Bast was nudging his hand.

"Not now, Bast," said Jonah. "Can't you see I have a problem right now?"

Bast swiped his arm with her claws.

"OUCH! Damn it, what do you want?"

Bast nudged Jonah's pen and pad to him. He scowled. "I'm not thinking about writing, Bast," said Jonah (he regretted how coldly he spoke to her, but that cut hurt something fierce). "Inspiration's faded again."

Bast wasn't deterred in the slightest. Her nudging became slightly more insistent.

Jonah grabbed it, utterly perplexed. "All right! What is it?"

Suddenly, a curious sensation filled Jonah's right hand, spreading the length of his arm to his shoulder. The back of his skull tingled; it was similar to the feeling in his arm.

On its own, Jonah's hand wrote, *Calm yourself, Jonah Rowe. You are not going insane, and you are not locked in Spectral Sight.*

If Jonah had been in control of his hand at the time, he'd have likely dropped the pen. As it was, he felt some degree of control over his arm once more and was reassured by the presence of Bast, who didn't look tense or frightened.

He wrote back, *What is this? Who is this?*

The sensation coursed through his hand once again. *This is automatic writing. We are using a spiritual linkage to communicate to you non-verbally. This is the safest way to communicate with you. Do not lift your head! Stay focused on the paper. You will fire a link to Creyton if you make eye contact and invite us in your mind any further.*

It dawned on Jonah who this must be. They were the spirits he had seen, speaking as a collective. It was a wild idea, a crazy idea, but with all that had happened to him, was anything wild anymore?

A sudden thought occurred to Jonah, instantly filling him with fear. *I've looked at you already!* he wrote. *Earlier! I saw you in chains and everything!*

Jonah's hand shuddered and wrote, *Collect your emotions. All is well. We weren't communicating then. That is why it is imperative that you keep your head down and not look at us. You went into Spectral Sight because we wish to give you a warning.*

Warn me about what? wrote Jonah.

The opponent, the snake in the grass, is among you. Among us.

A chill went down Jonah's body that had nothing to do with the sensation in his arm. *The opponent? Like a spy?*

A very dangerous spy, his hand wrote independently.

Jonah wrote back almost immediately. *Is it Titus Rivers?* he wrote. *The sour-tempered guy everyone calls 'Trip?'*

Goosebumps popped up on Jonah's arm, as though the entities that communicated through it were frightened. *We cannot disclose names,* his hand wrote. *It could make you vulnerable to Mindscopes. You have our apologies.*

Jonah's eyes narrowed. If there was one thing Nana had taught him, it was that the easiest way to answer a question was by not directly answering it. *I'll respect that,* he wrote. *But I need some type of validation. Evidence. Is there anything you can say?*

Jonah's arm shuddered again, but this time it appeared to be hesitation, as if some of the collective were afraid to answer, while others were desperate to try. All parties present must have reached a compromise, however, because his hand wrote: *The woods. The evidence you seek lay in the woods opposite the estate's front. You must make haste!*

Jonah left the gazebo immediately. He didn't even realize that the spirits had finally disappeared nor did he register that his arm was once more in his control. He hurried as fast as he could and almost collided with Malcolm, whose arms were full of groceries.

"Wow," he said, looking impressed. "A crazy workout this morning and now you're running? Bobby and Reena are rubbing off on you, man."

"Yeah, w-well that's me," said Jonah, attempting to catch his breath. "I want to improve as soon as possible!"

Malcolm chuckled and went inside, leaving Jonah with a hitched grin that quickly faded. Jonah hadn't ever bothered to pay much attention to these woods. The cedar and pine trees were extremely tall and curled into an elaborate U-shape, like the trees were forming a natural cul-de-sac or something. It was at that moment that Jonah appreciated just how naturally insulated the Grannison-Morris estate was.

But that information was immaterial right now. He had no idea where to look. The spirit's message hadn't even been cryptic. It had simply been vague.

Swearing softly, he made to return to gazebo and grill the spirits more when a twig snapped. His head snapped in the direction of the sound, and he moved toward it. He had made it maybe twenty paces when a figure came into view, who clearly desired to be hidden. Jonah dipped behind a large cedar and glanced around.

It was Trip. His thin figure stiffened as if he sensed that someone was near him. He looked around, frowning, but Jonah didn't move an inch. He tried not to even breathe.

He was relieved to see that Trip turned and continued further into the woods. Jonah stared at him. Why was he trying so hard to be hidden? The yard was empty. Jonah hadn't seen anyone but Malcolm, who was inside now. What was Trip doing?

He made a split-second decision and followed.

Jonah snapped a twig of his own, darted behind a tree, and checked to see whether Trip glanced back. The hesitation cost him, because it made him lose sight of Trip. Swearing again, he started moving, hoping that Trip hadn't gotten too far ahead of him. After about fifteen more feet, Trip's voice broke the silence.

"Why are you doing it? Huh?" he demanded.

"Why am I doing what, exactly, Titus?" said a woman's voice, which Jonah recognized as Marla's.

"You've got to be kidding," snapped Trip. "You assume I will sit here and explain what you are doing? You're convoluting everything, you stupid spiritess bitch."

"Titus, I don't know what you're talking about," said Marla, desperation in her voice. "Why did you summon me here? Was this meeting supposed to be a secret?"

"No, it's not supposed to be a damn secret," snarled Trip. "You know I do my sound experiments out here. I summoned you because I knew you were around. You were guaranteed to be moping around here somewhere."

Tears fell down Marla's pale face. "Titus, I only want help," she said. "I've been deadlocked on Earthplane for far too long. I wish for peace—"

"Spare me," snapped Trip. "You will stop showing yourself to us and throwing everything off. Stop volunteering information to every Eleventh Percenter you see. And most of all, you will stop revealing yourself to Rowe. If you don't comply, I *will* find out, and you will regret it. Do not force my hand."

Marla looked like she had been slapped. "Titus—"

"Get out of my sight," snapped Trip. "And *don't* call me Titus."

Eyes full of tears, Marla vanished, and Trip stalked off. He didn't even pause or look to his right where he would have seen Jonah frozen behind a cedar.

Jonah walked to the small clearing once he no longer heard Trip's footsteps.

What was that all about?

Jonah jumped again. What he had heard that morning had just pierced the air again. When Jonah followed the sound, he experienced yet another icy chill.

In the direction Trip had just gone, Jonah saw the source of what had broken his creative writing vein that morning. It was the same sound he'd heard in that awful dream.

The sound was the caw of a black crow perched in the branch of another low-lying tree. It met Jonah's gaze for several moments then took flight, heading in the direction of the estate.

13

Blip on the Radar

Jonah didn't know how long he stood there. The crow was on the grounds, cawing like it owned the place, and had flown toward the estate. God in heaven, if it was like those crows in the dream...

He felt like he had a spiritual endowment as he ran, because he experienced no fatigue, no cramping, and no stitches in his side. He found Reena first; it was almost like he'd willed her to him. She was on her laptop in the family room, searching for vegetable-heavy recipes. She looked up at him with an expression of greeting, but the words she must have been planning to say must have faded in her throat when she saw the look on Jonah's face.

"Jonah? What—?"

Jonah shook his head, grabbed her wrist, and tugged her behind him to her art studio. He completely ignored her questions but was thankful that they didn't stop her from shuffling behind him. Jonah didn't know why, but he was not surprised to see Terrence there. Apparently, he'd found a nice spot behind Reena's easels to finish his junk food. He hopped to attention the second he saw them and threw a bag to the side. "Reena! I thought you'd be—"

Then he noticed Jonah's vice grip on Reena's wrist and frowned. "Um, what's going on?"

Reena was so confused that she hadn't even noticed Terrence's sugary snacks. "Jonah, are you okay?"

"Not really," said Jonah. "Trip is foul."

Terrence rolled his eyes. "Jonah, if you are on that thing again—"

"Look at these," said Jonah, irritated. He showed them the papers he'd done through the automatic writing. "I didn't write that myself. You've seen my handwriting. You can even see the differences on the page!"

"Okay," said Reena, looking over the pages again. "I'll go with it. But what does this have to do with Trip? What did you *find* in the woods?"

Jonah told them the brief encounter he'd seen. He recalled every word. It was as if he could still see Marla's expression of hurt and fear and Trip's look of loathing.

When he finished, Jonah saw, with satisfaction, that they looked alarmed.

"Reena, what did Trip say he was doing this morning?" asked Terrence.

"He said he was trying to capture something," said Reena. "Something about the sound being off in the air."

"Reena, you're telling me you *bought* that crap?" said Jonah, incredulous.

Despite the moment, Reena's eyes narrowed. "Jonah, Trip works with sound. I imagined he might know a bit more about the subject than I would."

"That could very well be," said Jonah, "but I assure you that the only sound that was off in the air was the sound Trip made when he lied through his teeth. Plus that damned crow was there. They work for Creyton. I *know* they do. I'll bet the hand I don't write with that Trip is passing information to him through the crows."

Terrence looked at Jonah blankly. "Passing information through birds, Jonah?"

Jonah met Terrence's eyes, completely unabashed. "Terrence, we use cats as heralds and scouts. Cut me some slack here."

Terrence's face fell. "Point."

Reena hadn't yet stopped staring at the lines on the paper. "*The snake in the grass is among you ... among us...* What are you doing, Trip?"

"I've got no idea," said Jonah. "But the question now is what we can do to stop him."

"Jonah, what are we stopping?" said Reena. "We don't actually know what the man is doing! And where does Marla fit in?"

"There you go!" said Terrence. "Summon her and ask her! That spiritess volunteers everything!"

Jonah shut his eyes to will her to them, but then he opened them and punched the nearby wall. "That *bastard*," he growled. "We can't ask Marla."

"Um, why not?" asked Terrence.

"Those Mindscopes," said Jonah. "Trip's already scared her to hell. If we ask her, that will cause links to fire to Trip, and he'll tell Creyton."

Terrence and Reena looked deflated, which mirrored how Jonah actually felt. The spirits had written to him that the answer he sought lay in the woods. Yet that "answer" only created new questions. If Trip was indeed involved in a plot against them, that knowledge was neither helpful nor informative because they didn't know *what* he had done. Jonah felt like there was a missing piece that should be right in his face. It nagged him; it was almost like having a word on the tip of his tongue that he'd know if he hadn't been talking about it.

"We need to inform Jonathan," said Jonah.

"Inform him of what?" said Reena, her old authoritativeness in her voice. " 'Hey Jonathan, Jonah was hijacked by a collection of spirits who warned him of a spy, which we think is Trip, but we can't check because he saw Trip telling Marla not to contact us.' Too full of holes, Jonah. Besides, it holds no weight, Trip telling Marla to leave us be. Marla is inordinately clingy. She has wanted help forever."

Jonah scowled. When Reena put it like that, it *did* sound like the hollowest thing in the world. And the feeling that there was a piece they were all missing still lingered in his head. But there was one piece that no one could deny.

"Trip is doing something," he repeated. "And we have to find out what it is. Creyton is behind all of it, I'm sure. It's just us three. We can't tell Malcolm and Liz because they'll feel snubbed again, with good reason. And Bobby—oh God, Bobby will grab Trip by his throat and demand to know what's going on. We've got to figure it all out. No more Eleventh Percenters can be killed because of this."

The reminder of those Eleventh Percenters seemed to remove any doubts that remained in Terrence's and Reena's minds. Jonah hadn't known any of those people, but if they'd perished because of Trip, he hated him all the more.

"I'm with you, Jonah," said Reena.

"Of course I'm there too," said Terrence. "But how are we supposed to face Trip now? What do we do when we have trainings? This is gonna make things really awkward."

"No, it won't," said Jonah as he surveyed a blood-red painting of Reena's that featured a broken sword, which he found strangely apt. "Trip is plotting against us. Now we have an excuse to thrash him without repercussion."

The remainder of the day passed in a kind of haze. Jonah spent it wondering what Trip was doing with Creyton. It made him sick with concern, doubt, and anger. Terrence and Reena seemed to steel themselves when he suggested investigating, but that was only after they'd been reminded of the Eleventh Percenters who had been murdered by Creyton and his minions. They were still reluctant to believe the worst of Trip, and felt that there was more to the story than they knew. Jonah was willing to give them that. They had known Trip longer, and probably thought they knew what he was capable of. He thought that that might compromise their judgment and make them blind to the notion that Trip could be capable of betrayal.

This was the first time in Jonah's life that he was happy to be the new guy. It had its limitations, but it also had its benefits, because he hadn't yet become so emotionally enmeshed with everything that he was blind to a serpent in the grass.

Besides all that, he'd had enough experiences with false people. They could rope you in with any combination of charm, kindness, wit, and other honorable traits. But that was what made Jonah so confused. Trip didn't *have* any of those traits.

Dinner was an uneventful affair, as Liz chatted animatedly about her bio lab while Bobby mused at length about fresh ways he could challenge himself with weights. Reena seemed to pass the entirety of the meal in contemplative silence, which she effectively pawned off as attentiveness to Liz. Jonah pushed his suspicions as far down as they would go and distracted himself with conversation with Malcolm and Terrence.

"Is the trireme coming along nicely, Malcolm?" Terrence asked.

Malcolm nodded, half indifferently, half bitterly. "Having trouble bringing it in. Can't get the angles the way I want them. Hardest thing."

"Malcolm is a sculptor and a carpenter," explained Terrence, seeing Jonah's puzzled expression. "Makes some of the greatest stuff I've ever seen, like that gazebo you keep wandering off to."

That made Jonah sit forward. "*You* made that gazebo, Malcolm?"

Malcolm glanced over at Terrence in what was plainly an irritated expression, but his expression cleared somewhat when he began to speak. "And the wooden clock in the family room, the swan in the hall, and the breadbox there." He nodded toward the counter.

Jonah had never noticed the bread box, but now that he did, he noticed that the craftsmanship was nothing short of amazing. "That is awesome, man."

Malcolm shrugged. "Eh, it's all right."

"*What!*" said Jonah. "Why do you say it like that?"

"It could have been better," mumbled Malcolm.

"Could've been—?"

"I'm really critical of my work," said Malcolm. "Let me talk, let me train, let me do—*anything*. I can do it with no problem. But when it comes to crafting, that takes every fiber of my being."

"Why is that?" asked Jonah, now scrutinizing the breadbox as best he could but finding that his only criticism was that the bread within that blocked the interior carpentry from view. "That is great!"

"We tried to tell him that," said Bobby, who put aside his fitness magazine and shook his head. "That breadbox you're admiring? Malcolm re-did it sixteen times."

"Seventeen," corrected Malcolm, a trace of sullenness in his voice. "I'm throwing *that* one out too."

"What?" said Jonah again, but this time, he noticed that the same disbelieving word was intoned around the entire table. "It's perfect!"

Malcolm stood up so abruptly that Jonah half expected him to attack him, but he only moved past him to grab the bread box. "The *fleur-di-lis* designs on the sides are uneven. The door doesn't snap shut; you have to work it a little. Plus, the lacquer is cracked on the side. Not perfect."

Terrence, Reena, and Liz stared at the box sadly. Bobby had the same expression, but it was directed at Malcolm.

"Malcolm, I can't understand why you don't see the greatness of this!" persisted Jonah. "How could you say this isn't perfect?"

"Can you not relate, Jonah?" said Malcolm quietly. "Can you not think of a time when you wrote one of your stories only to deem it weak and cast it aside? And does that fear not carry over to your next project? And the next?"

Jonah blinked. Malcolm had described it almost like he'd been there.

Malcolm nodded, correctly judging Jonah's silence. "On to the next one, like I said."

Jonah meant to reply, but Trip walked in. For a moment, Jonah felt something he couldn't place. Was it fear? Anticipation? The urge to punch him in the face?

A glance to his left revealed that Terrence and Reena had experienced something similar, but neither of them made a sound.

Trip's eyes narrowed when he saw Jonah looking in his direction. "May I have my face back, please, Rowe?" he grumbled.

Jonah felt his own eyes narrow but was denied the chance to retort when Trip said to the room at large, "Jonathan wants an extra hour of training tonight."

Reena raised an eyebrow. "Why is that?"

"Said it would benefit *him*." Trip pointed in Jonah's direction without looking at him.

Jonah felt anger and irritation well up inside him. "I have a name, Cue Ball," he growled.

Trip gave him that infuriating appraisal yet again. "Just one name? I can think of several."

"So Jonathan will be helping us out, then?" said Malcolm before Jonah could respond to (or throttle) Trip. "He's back on this plane?"

"Long enough for this," said Trip, apparently pleased that Jonah had to settle for silent stewing. "Then he is returning to the Astral Plane."

Jonah couldn't understand why Jonathan spent so much time on the Astral Plane. But then again, Jonathan was one of the most mysterious beings (he couldn't say *people*, could he?) he'd ever met. But he had very little time to think on that. He looked at Terrence and Reena, and an understanding passed between them. No words until they had proof. Or at least something more substantial than spiritual gossip. They all headed to the Glade.

The training was enjoyable for Jonah, who found that he could release his frustrations there. He'd endowed himself with the spiritess of a woman who'd been a medic of some kind, or so she said. His skills were indeed coming along. He also thought it best to keep that analysis to himself for the time being. Being egotistical would probably get him drilled in the worst way, yet it brought him satisfaction when he sidestepped Bobby's bull-like charge and then prevented Liz's nerve tweak. It only took *ten* seconds to get back to his feet when Reena used her gift of speed to bowl him over.

As they took turns pairing up (Jonah enjoyed being in the shuffle as opposed to being the piece of meat), he found himself paired up with Trip.

Both Terrence and Malcolm volunteered to switch, but Jonathan waved them away. No words were exchanged, but Jonah thought he understood. It was a naïve hope to think that one could only ever work with people they liked.

Trip moved forward with a strike, made much more powerful by his endowment, but Jonah managed to block it. Jonah attempted one of his own but missed by a mile. Quick as a shadow, Jonah felt a blow soften his back. He was on the ground seconds later, taking in an unwanted inhale of freshly mown grass.

The back of his shirt was grabbed rather roughly. "This is why your skull was almost caved in by the crowbar, Blue One," said Trip.

The anger that had laced Jonah's insides when Trip gave his appraisal back at the kitchen hadn't subsided after all. He didn't realize he had gotten up; he just knew that he wanted Trip out of his face. One punch ought to do it, just long enough for Trip the spy to shut up—

"Spy" must have been the trigger, because the next thing Jonah knew, Trip was flying backward, like someone had hooked his shirt from behind and pulled. He collided with Terrence, who had just parried a strike from Bobby. The both of them took a rather sloppy spill in the ground.

"You—!" snarled Trip, but he couldn't immediately retaliate because he was tangled with Terrence. The inconvenience gave Bobby enough time to lift and restrain Trip, but it was almost like he was on autopilot. He, along with everyone else, was too busy staring at Jonah.

"Jonah—" began Reena, but Jonah shook his head.

"He deserved it," he growled. "I'm trying to learn how to defend myself, not listen to snarky com—"

"No, no!" Reena interrupted. "Your hand!"

Jonah looked down. What he saw not only diminished his anger (most of it, anyway) but puzzled him. He hadn't realized that his right fist was still clenched, but it wasn't his fist that had grabbed everyone's attention. His fist appeared to be swaddled in semi-transparent vapor, encasing it as though it were a protective glove an inch or so above his flesh. He unclenched his fist, but the clouded glove remained, slowly swirling about his hand and wrist like it was attempting to escape.

"You—you took a handful of fog from the air," said Liz, breathless. "Encased your fist with it..."

"Like brass knuckles," said Bobby, "but foggy."

Even through Terrence's amazement, he snorted. "So, foggy knuckles? Please, Bobby, don't tell anyone else that."

"Very good, Jonah," said Jonathan quietly. "Return it."

Jonah didn't really have to think about it. The minute he imagined it gone, the fog unwrapped his hand like the layers of an onion and returned to the other clouded mist that surrounded everyone's feet.

"Very productive, my friends!" said Jonathan in a rather boisterous voice that Jonah could swear was forced. "Rest, relax your muscles. Jonah, may I have a word?"

Everyone knelt and returned their endowments, but it didn't seem that anyone was drained enough to sway this time. Even through his fatigue, Trip's look of loathing was absolute. In the evening light, his angry eyes were as dark as the bruise that now shone on the side of his face. The look of contempt mirrored the face of that tall man whose hardened face invaded Jonah's dream...

With a jolt, Jonah had some idea of what might be happening. He thought of the dream, which had fallen back into his head when he thought of the tall, weird man.

Okay, he thought to himself, *that much I can tell Jonathan.*

He went toward the spirit, who beckoned him to walk with him. Jonathan led Jonah down a path that was shrouded in misty fog not unlike the clearing they'd just left. Jonah stared at it apprehensively. In the night's gathering darkness, it seemed like a void.

"What's on your mind, Rowe?" asked Jonathan.

Oh man, Jonah thought, *the million-dollar question.* "I was thinking about my dream a minute ago," he answered, "but then we came over here, and I got to thinking that ... this dark path looks creepy."

Jonathan laughed. "Dark paths only have the meaning attributed to them," he said.

"That may be true," said Jonah, "but it's a centuries-old attribution, and it's almost always valid."

"Indeed," said Jonathan. "But notice that you said 'almost.' It's much better to interpret your own meanings rather than the ones that are inherited."

Jonah frowned. Apparently, Jonathan reveled in his moments of depth, but *he* didn't. If Jonathan weren't a spirit, Jonah would have suggested that he start his own horoscope column. Then he could regale everyone with his so-called philosophy. "You wanted a word," he said. "What's up?"

"Ah," said Jonathan in a thoughtful tone, though Jonah was certain that his grey eyes had suddenly sharpened in focus. "First, I would like to tell you that I believe you are coming along well. You are a great deal more responsive."

"I don't think training can take all the credit for that," muttered Jonah. "Reena's rabbit food has a hand in it too."

Jonathan smiled. "Reena helps in more ways than one," he said. "She's great at instructing but is also willing to be educated herself. Those are the makings of a great Eleventh Percenter, which she already is."

"She doesn't view herself as great," said Jonah. "That art she has down in the basement is practically *rotting*. And Malcolm! Superb carpentry that he repeatedly replicates trying to get it perfect—"

"And you are a talented writer who loses steam at every critical juncture," said Jonathan shrewdly.

Jonah froze. "How did you know that?"

"All Eleventh Percenters are artistic in some way," said Jonathan. "Having access to further depths of our brains than Tenth Percenters, we experience thoughts that cannot possibly be placed into words, so our expression is veined through creativity. Your writing, Reena's art, and Malcolm's woodwork—all expressions of a sharply cognizant brain."

"Hang on," said Jonah, distracted. "We are all like that? Then why doesn't it work out?"

"Who says it never works out?" asked Jonathan.

Jonah kept the annoyance out of his voice. "You know what I mean, Jonathan. Why do I get blocked? Why can't Reena see the beauty of her art? Why is—?"

"All valid questions, Jonah," said Jonathan, "but I cannot answer. Doubts, blockades, perfectionism—those are self-imposed. The harmony must be achieved from within. That's one thing I cannot teach you."

Oh great, thought Jonah. *Someone who calls himself an instructor then says lessons must be learned on their own. What kind of instruction was that?* "Anything you can tell me about my dream?" he wondered aloud.

Jonathan didn't answer immediately, and Jonah wondered whether or not he was trying to figure out what to conceal. "Jonah, some things are better if personally surmised," he said. "That said, what have you surmised?"

Fighting the urge to swear out of irritation, Jonah thought on it. "I don't know. Those stupid crows flew into the crowd, and things got worse wherever they landed. It was like people didn't realize that the conflict was external. They just seemed to be focused on surviving. In the dream, I tried to stop them, or at least decrease the panic. It all failed. Then that guy told me to stop panicking and fix it. But I didn't know how. It was like some unseen force was making people's resolve weaken, and they were softening their own selves up so something bigger could attack almost completely unopposed. The discord was a painful distraction, that's true, but … I think it was a prelude to something worse."

Jonah thought of that larger crow, the one that had been in the bookstore. If that one had entered the crowd, God only knows what would have happened. The thought still made him shudder.

He glanced at Jonathan, who looked satisfied about something. If Jonah thought he'd share, he was soon disappointed. Jonathan didn't ask any further questions.

"I can't figure any more than that," said Jonah. "Those crows created havoc."

Jonathan placed his hands behind his back. "Creation is a powerful thing," he said. "It's not something to be taken lightly. You have no idea the opportunities brought about by those who use their creativity as a tool and not as a crutch."

Jonah didn't quite know what any of that meant, but he had to mention something that troubled him. "Jonathan, creativity isn't always a tool. I haven't forgotten what Reena said. Blue Auras show up in times of upheaval. I don't want to create upheaval. I don't want to make bad things happen."

"Bad?" said Jonathan. "Why would you say that? Cold is upheaval to someone who is experiencing heat exhaustion. Warmth is upheaval to someone with hypothermia. Both are overhauls, but they are *welcome* overhauls. Upheaval doesn't always have to be negative. As I've already said," he gestured toward the darkened path on which they were walking, "it comes down to the meaning that you personally create, not the one that's inherited."

Jonah just stared. The guy was on a roll, wasn't he? He thought about telling Jonathan his suspicions of Trip but hesitated. He had no concrete proof, and when he thought about it, he still didn't really understand what he'd heard and seen. He found himself almost buying into what Jonathan was saying about not fully understanding the meaning of it all.

"Rest well, Jonah," said Jonathan rather abruptly. "I must return to the Astral Plane. Remember what I've said."

Jonah shook his head. "Jonathan, wait. You said you wanted a word with me. But we got off on a tangent, and you must not have gotten to it. We actually didn't talk about anything."

Jonathan smiled. His eyes were alight with an incredulous gleam. "Didn't talk about anything? I wouldn't go that far. I wish you a peaceful evening."

"But—"

Jonathan vanished, though Jonah hadn't blinked or turned his head. He had disappeared, leaving, as usual, more questions than answers.

Even after Jonah had rejoined the group, showered, and settled into bed, sleep found him slowly. He had no idea how much time he spent mentally chewing on things when he finally dozed off.

He was walking down a dark hallway. It was dank, musty, and gave off the feeling of something that had been vastly neglected for a long while. Jonah could make nothing out on the walls; it appeared that they were laced with a deliberate layer of darkness. He glanced behind him, but he could not see where he had started walking. Strangely, though, it didn't appear to be aimless wandering. He continued toward the only source of light there was, which was at the very end of the corridor. Strangely, that seemed deliberate too. Jonah walked for another few minutes but paused when he heard his own name.

"Rowe is hysterical," an oddly distorted voice said.

Jonah squinted. He could make out nothing as the darkness veiled his vision the minute he exited the corridor. He assumed that he was in some type of study but couldn't make out anything beyond that. Every detail was sufficiently shrouded from his eyes.

The oddly tampered voice continued. "If you have seen him fight once, you've seen all he has."

"So all is still on schedule then?" Though Jonah's eyes gave him neither clues nor confirmation, there was no mistaking the cold, cruel voice of Creyton.

"All is in accordance with your wishes, Master," said the voice.

"Have the seeds been planted as well?" asked Creyton.

"Certainly," said the voice in what had to be a gleeful tone, but it was hard for Jonah to tell through the distortion. "The Eleventh Percenters doubt. They keep secrets among themselves. They train distractedly. They talk about *breadboxes and paintings.* It is amusing to behold."

"Remain steadfast in your duties," said Creyton, his tone showing no trace of pleasure or satisfaction from what he'd heard. "You are not there for comedy or leisure."

"Of course not, Master," said the voice hastily. "I was merely remarking on the simplicity of this threat."

"Good," said Creyton. "I will need sharp—"

His voice faltered. Jonah heard a very faint noise as if someone had brushed up against a table.

"Master?"

"A very minor irritant," said Creyton, anguished. Jonah cursed his lack of vision. What had happened? "When everything has come to fruition, this will no longer occur."

"But Master," said the voice, and even through the distortion, Jonah could hear concern. "Rowe could possibly benefit from luck or chance. We have seen that time and again. Perhaps—"

"Luck or chance?" Creyton's voice was malicious again. "Jonah Rowe is not a big enough blip on the radar to even warrant uncertainty."

14

The Halfway Decent Gesture

Jonah had gotten back to his apartment complex in record time that Sunday evening, which annoyed him greatly. He truly wished he could stay at the estate until the last possible second, like Liz and Bobby did, but no such luck. He had to show himself at the office bright and early the next morning.

The elevator finally opened to reveal the shabby hallway, a sight so unwelcome to Jonah that it may as well have been that darkened path he'd walked with Jonathan. He had come to associate this place with his stressors. It represented nothing more than just the small gaps he stayed there before going to the office. All he did there was eat and sleep.

The jangling of his keys must have gotten the attention of a few other tenants, but it was an unexpected voice that said, "Jonah!"

Jonah turned to see the girl from 7D. Oh, wait. He knew her name now … Leta. She had dropped her name so readily in the presence of Terrence, and *he* had never seen her before. Add another two pounds to his irritation.

"Where is your friend?" she asked, trying and failing to keep the eagerness out of her voice.

Uh-huh, thought Jonah. *So my existence only matters because you want to know about Terrence?* "I don't know. Home, I suppose."

"Really?" said Leta. "Does he live in the city?"

"No," said Jonah. He was well aware that she wanted details, but he wasn't giving her anything. He'd be damned if he was going to be the vessel of information for her attempt at a love connection.

"Oh." The disappointment in her voice was so obvious that Jonah was almost overcome by nausea. "Well, I'm glad I caught you anyway."

"Oh?"

She produced a package in blood-red paper that was so meticulously wrapped that Jonah was put in mind of a pricey present or some corny limited edition trinket. "This was left at your door when you were gone."

Jonah frowned. "What are *you* doing with it? How come it wasn't left at the desk?"

"Good question," said Leta, who looked as puzzled as Jonah felt. "But someone just put it by your door yesterday afternoon. It looked so nice and expensive that I put it in here with me so no one would take it."

The gesture was rather considerate, and Jonah felt a little guilty for being short with her. "I appreciate that, Leta. It's just rare these days for people to do things like that."

He took it from her and felt his guilt fade faster than water down a newly unclogged drain. There was a folded piece of paper tucked in the wrapping which contained Leta's phone number. Jonah wasn't stupid enough to think that it was there for *him.*

"Considerate gesture, my ass," he grumbled, but his voice didn't sound as irritated as it could have. He had other things on his mind.

Jonah had not had the chance to confide to Reena and Terrence what he had seen in his dream. Trip had been near them all morning; he hadn't shut himself in his room like usual. Jonah had already figured out that Trip was nosing around, probably in an attempt to glean new pearls of wisdom to take to Creyton. It angered him to no end Trip spied on them like that—who else would know about his fighting? Who else would have known about Malcolm's breadbox? And who else would have called his actions "luck and chance?" Jonah had already made up his mind that if Trip showed his bruised face in another training, he'd practice wrapping fog vapors around his fist again so as to give him a fresh one on the opposite side. Perhaps if his mouth was in pain, he couldn't run it so much. He'd written down the dream and convinced Terrence and Reena to come visit that week (there was no fooling Reena as he'd volunteered to assist her in preparation of veggie burgers and tofu fries earlier that day in order to get some privacy, and she'd instantly called him on it) to talk about it. So with his friends coming on Tuesday, he had at least one thing to look forward to that week.

And now this package...

Jonah lifted it and weighed it carefully in his hands. It couldn't have been a bomb or anything. But what would he know about bombs?

Jonah cursed himself. When had he become so dramatic? There was no way in hell this was a damned bomb. But what was it, then?

He almost regretted ripping off the intricately wrapped paper but felt some savage pleasure when he saw that he'd accidently ripped Leta's number along with it. The cold smile quickly slipped off of his face, however, when he saw what lay within. There were six manila folders bound by lace with a leafy-looking page on top of them. Frowning, he put on his reading glasses and read:

Blue Aura,

Time is short. Shorter than you can fathom. Your continued existence is a blessing, but it has greatly riled the enemy. His spy is lurking amongst you and is just waiting for you to completely lower your guard.

Prevent this. Mindscopes mandate that I assist you in this rudimentary manner, but I pray that this is enough. I believe that you have brought about the final straw. Prevent the worst from happening.

Jonah stared at the parchment. What the hell did that mean?

He could be sure of one thing, or at least partially sure: the final straw had to be crowning Trip in the face. Did he view Jonah as a threat, then? That made no sense. If his worth was so scant in Trip's eyes, why was his continued existence "riling" anybody? After all, Creyton had already said that Jonah wasn't a "big enough blip" on his radar, hadn't he?

Jonah tossed the leafy paper aside. He'd run himself insane if he deliberated over that stuff. As irritating as it was, it would have to wait until he could discuss things with Terrence and Reena. If they had any lingering doubts in their minds about Trip's duplicity, he was certain this would clear it all away.

"What are the folders?" Jonah asked himself. He carefully opened the first one, and a series of photographs fell out. They were in black and white and had been taken from a clandestine vantage, like they'd been done by a private investigator or a cop on stakeout.

Jonah looked them over. There was nothing remarkable about the people in them. Then he noticed that there were other figures in the photographs as well that were not quite distinguishable from the shadows. He could see that the physical subjects looked windswept, like the days when the pictures were taken were gusty. Jonah inspected them and discovered that there were spirits in the pictures.

"That's no shocker," murmured Jonah aloud. He had expected the photos to reveal something groundbreaking. This was a letdown.

Wait—

He picked up a photograph that had previously been obscured. It featured a kind-faced woman with hair that could have been red. Jonah couldn't tell for sure as it was black and white. There was a slightly tightened look on her face while she sat at some café reading a book. This particular action was unremarkable, too, because there were other patrons that were equally entranced in their own activities. What caught Jonah's attention was a figure hidden in the shadows. Jonah recognized the malicious gaze, unkempt appearance, and pointed features at once. It was Jonah's old friend and one of Creyton's minions, Walt.

Tension forming in his gut, he dropped the picture and fished through the others, now searching with a purpose.

"Where there is one," he said to himself, "there has got to be the other…"

And sure enough, in another picture of the same woman was Walt's bearded, pockmarked buddy, Howard. Jonah looked at every single picture in that folder, and it was the same, Howard or Walt together, separate, or with comrades that Jonah hadn't yet had the displeasure of meeting, watching this lady at different spots: an office that must have been her job, at equestrian stables, at a grocery store ... Jonah had a sick feeling that he just might know who she was, though he never saw a name on the file. He also felt that he knew why she had been watched.

The glacial feeling in his gut intensified. With every ounce of resolution he had, he placed the pictures back into the folder and willed himself not to touch the remaining five.

Wait for Terrence and Reena, he thought to himself. As good an idea as that was, he didn't think he could keep it all to himself. He distracted himself by reaching for a snack so full of calories that Reena would've spontaneously combusted if she'd known he was eating it. But it didn't matter. If his suspicion was correct, their problems with Trip spying were not nearly as bad as they were going to become.

Monday and the initial part of Tuesday passed rather quickly. He simply could not focus on those stupid billing reports and was pleasantly surprised to discover that when he stopped lying to himself about finishing them, the time passed all the more quickly. Jonah figured that whoever it was that handled time must have decided to do him a kindness because before he knew it, Terrence and Reena were at his door. Reena hadn't even bothered to change from work.

"Good to see you again," said Jonah. While he was thankful to see his friends much sooner than the weekend, he was more eager to finally get his suspicions off of his chest. "Terrence, you just missed your admirer."

"Actually, no," chuckled Terrence. "Just met her in the hall. She just about wet herself."

"Oh," said Jonah, a grumpy note creeping into his voice. "So tell me Reena, what did you think of that woman? She's been fawning over Terrence from the moment she met him."

Reena's eyes scanned Jonah's apartment. Not with disdain, he could tell, but for what would be the most accessible escape route. That didn't reassure him. "She was cute," she said at last, apparently satisfied with her scanning. "Complete and utter ditz but cute."

Terrence shook his head. "It is not a prerequisite for all women to be headstrong and bossy, Reena," he said.

"Keep telling yourself that," Reena replied. "I'll remind you of it when you tire of beautiful fools. Where is your bathroom, Jonah?"

She showed him a gym bag.

Jonah bit back a laugh. He wondered if Reena felt as uncomfortable as she looked in her professional wear. "It's right through there."

Reena left to change. Once she was gone, Terrence lowered his voice. "What did you have to tell us, Jonah? You seemed like you were going to have a coronary if you couldn't talk soon."

Jonah shook his head. "I got a bunch to tell you, man," he muttered, "but I'd prefer to tell you both. Maybe you two can help me make hide and hair of some things I've recently found out."

Terrence raised an eyebrow, but didn't press further until Reena returned from the bathroom, looking much more comfortable and loose in jeans and a polo shirt.

"Alright," said Jonah, "first and foremost, I can tell you about Saturday night."

He told them about his conversation with Jonathan, and the dream he'd had when he'd finally got off to sleep.

Terrence looked tense, Reena uncertain. "What did the voice sound like?"

"That's what I'm saying," said Jonah. "It was completely off, sounded like they were talking through an outdated intercom or something."

"I must say, Jonah," said Reena, "you don't have any way of—"

"Knowing that it was Trip?" finished Jonah. "Reena, who else would have known about the lucky shots I got in during training? Who else knew about the breadbox conversation with Malcolm?"

Reena couldn't answer, and Jonah couldn't help but feel a slight sense of triumph.

"What was Creyton's 'minor irritant,' I wonder?" said Terrence in Reena's silence. "What seeds have been planted? And what is his plan?"

"Terrence, you told me in Reena's studio that Creyton had to be in endowments twenty-four-seven or something, or he'd drain and show his true age, right? What if hijacking all these spirits and blocking the paths has adversely affected him? Maybe that's the irritant."

Reena looked apprehensive. "He can't be in permanent endowment," she insisted. "If he were to ever relinquish them, it would likely kill him."

"Reena, you talk about this guy like he's human," chided Terrence. "He's not. Hell, I'm not even sure he ever *had* any humanity to begin with. There is no way he'd still look thirty-something if he were using endowments and regularly releasing them. And how did he block the path?"

Reena was silent again, looking clearly troubled. Jonah had no idea what to tell her. As if they didn't deal with enough odd things almost daily, whatever Creyton had done, or was currently doing, seemed to push further than even that.

"Guys," said Jonah. "There is more. When I got back home on Sunday, a surprise was here for me."

"Surprise?" said Terrence. "Who did that?"

"No clue, but the messenger was your damn admirer." He told them about how Leta had hidden it due to the package being delivered straight to his doorstep. At that, Reena sat up straighter and quickly scanned the apartment again.

"So somebody involved in this knows where you live," she said.

"Not cool," muttered Terrence.

Jonah felt a surge of gratitude toward his friends for caring about his welfare as it wasn't often that he had someone treat him as though he mattered. Even so, he waved a dismissive hand. "I appreciate your concern," he told them, "but I truly think I'm good."

Reena raised a skeptical eyebrow, but Jonah handed over the paper that had lain across the folders. Terrence and Reena read it through, each of their expressions looking more confused.

"Felt the same way, trust me," said Jonah, "but if they said my 'continued existence is a blessing,' I don't think whoever left this is a threat."

"Good point," said Terrence, "but what is this 'final straw?' "

"I have no idea," shrugged Jonah. "Ticking Trip off too many times?"

"What's in the folders, anyway?" asked Reena.

Jonah felt that icy knot in his stomach again. He hoped more than anything that his suspicion was wrong. "That's what I need your help with," he said, hoping to sound offhand.

He handed them the first file he'd looked through on Sunday. Reena opened it curiously and lifted up the picture that showed the kind-faced lady at the coffee shop. She dropped the photograph, which Terrence picked up with some puzzlement.

"Reena, what's wrong?" he asked then glanced at the picture. His eyes widened.

Jonah could barely contain his gut feeling now. Part of him still clung to some last desperate hope that he was wrong. "Reena? Terrence? Who's—?"

But Reena shook her head and snatched the entire package out of Jonah's lap, tossing two of the folders to Terrence. She anxiously opened one of them and pulled out a photo.

"God, no—"she whispered. "No—"

Jonah was frightened to see that Terrence wasn't doing much better. He'd opened both folders at the same time. He looked in a state of shock as he released a quiet swear.

"Where did these come from?" asked Reena faintly.

The hope to which Jonah clung to was now slipping. "They were delivered anonymously," he said. "I told you that."

"There has to be some type—" Reena rifled through the photographs, "—some trace—" she grabbed the package and turned it inside out, "—of identification—"

"But there wasn't any," said Jonah, flabbergasted. "It was like they were sent by a spirit."

Reena and Terrence looked at him, and he realized what he'd said. Though he accepted being an Eleventh Percenter, it was still jarring to know that he lived in a world where a spirit delivering a message was actually possible.

"Who are those people? In these pictures?" he repeated.

Terrence lowered the picture he held, which featured a thin guy whose skin looked grayish in the black and white setting. His hair and eye color could have been anyone's guess. "Those three, we don't know," he answered, pointing to three piles of pictures. "But this boy," he showed Jonah the thin guy, "—was named Abel Ford."

He picked up a picture of a girl who looked maybe Reena's age, and shook his head. "Her name is … *was* Rebecca Cayce."

"This one," said Reena, lifting the picture she'd dropped earlier, "was named Lillian Darby."

The subarctic bomb in Jonah's gut exploded and filled every trace of his insides with numbing, debilitating cold. His worst fear was confirmed. "These are those Eleventh Percenters who were murdered by Creyton," he said numbly. "Three were strangers … and three … used to live at the estate?"

"I can see you suspected that already," said Reena, wiping a tear from her eye. "I *knew* we might know some of them, but I didn't want to believe it. We weren't particularly close to Abel; he only showed up sometimes on holidays, but we hadn't seen him in about three years; we just assumed he'd moved on for good. Rebecca lived with us at the estate until her dad was stationed in California, but she always called to see how everyone was doing. And … and Lillian…" her voice trailed off.

"I think I got it," said Jonah. "You and she were together at one time?"

"No," said Reena. "We could have been, but she was too much of a loner. She moved into the estate the same day I did. Was there almost four years and then joined the Peace Corps. I remember Liz wanting to re-establish ties with her; she was just talking about it last month. We didn't actually know she was one of the ones that had been killed."

Terrence clutched the arm of the chair tightly. "They were being watched? All of their habits were monitored? The minions knew when they would be alone?"

Reena looked at Lillian's picture again. "*And* vulnerable," she added.

Jonah looked at both of them, still unnerved but now feeling pity for his friends. He was, after all, no stranger to grief. "I'm sorry," he muttered, not knowing what else to say. "But how could Jonathan not know who they were?"

"Jonathan doesn't know everything, Jonah," said Reena. "He is a powerful Protector Guide but still a *Protector* Guide. Besides, many Eleventh Percenters have come through the Grannison-Morris estate. He wouldn't remember every single one. And it's not like he could communicate with them once they'd passed. You know we can't—"

"Yeah, I remember," interrupted Jonah. He didn't need reminding that Eleventh Percenters couldn't see the spirits of other Eleventh Percenters. "When did this happen? Their passing, I mean."

"I'm guessing within the past several months," mumbled Terrence. "Liz and Bobby only met Lillian and Rebecca a handful of times; they moved out years ago. That was one of the reasons Liz wanted to re-establish ties. Abel just fell off the face of the earth. But then again, he was always in his own world, so we didn't think much of it." He hung his head. "They had their whole lives ahead of them, and then Creyton just killed them. Took their lives like they were nothing."

"But life never ends," said Reena, but Jonah could tell that she was simply trying to reassure herself.

Terrence put his head down out of respect. Though Jonah was one of them, he felt like he was intruding on a private moment. He pushed a box of Kleenex in Reena's direction just to do something helpful. He had hung his own head but jerked it up again so violently that he popped his neck. His sudden movement jarred Terrence and Reena out of their silence.

"Jonah?"

He stood up. "Life never ends..." he said slowly. "Flesh and organs cease to operate but spirit continues. Spirits can either cross on, stay behind, or have some other influence."

"Um, Jonah?" said Reena. "No offense, but why are you spouting the obvious? We already know all that."

"Of course you do," said Jonah, "but Creyton does too!"

"Jonah, what are you getting at?" asked Terrence.

"Your friends, along with the three strangers, were killed within the past several months," said Jonah.

"Yes, we already said—"

"Jonathan said the paths to the next world have been blocked for around ten months, right?"

"Yeah..." said Reena, but Jonah thought he could see comprehension on her face. Terrence's too.

"That first night I trained with you all, Jonathan told us that spirits can choose to stay behind and help people if they wish," said Jonah. "But spirits that choose to cross on turn into essence before they move on to the Other Side. He said essence meant for the Other Side has no place here and can be manipulated to dark uses. Creyton has got to be using the essence he usurped from the Eleventh Percenters he killed. I'm willing to bet that *that* is a material powerful enough to block the path to the Other Side!"

Reena and Terrence looked at one another, and they, like Jonah, found this startling revelation both illuminating and disturbing.

"My God, Jonah," said Terrence, "you might be on to something."

"He *is*," said Reena. "The spirits of Tenth Percenters are powerful. Even more so when they are no longer constrained by limits most regular humans impose upon themselves. But even *that* wouldn't be sufficient enough to block the path."

"No," said Jonah. "But the essence that's trapped here as a result of the blocked paths turns bad, right?"

"Yeah," said Terrence. "It ain't meant to be here. No place for it."

Jonah looked at Reena. "So what effect would spiritual essence meant for the Other Side have on Earthplane?"

Reena placed her hands at her temples. "It would be just like a human body," she said. "When a body properly eliminates waste, everything is regulated and healthy. But when it's blocked and eliminations aren't happening as they should, the excess that is stuck in the body becomes toxic, like bile. It simply shouldn't be there. So since it *is* there, bad things can happen."

"And how would that translate on Earthplane?" asked Jonah.

"I'll tell you how," said Terrence with a grimace. "Unexplained behaviors. Violence. Increased anger and emotional instability. Civil unrest, I think it's called."

Jonah's thoughts took a dark turn. Crime waves. The city where he lived had seen a spike in crime that the papers had been dramatizing to no end. Increased fights. People suddenly being violent when they hadn't shown those capabilities before in their lives. A state of worry, fear, and anxiety. "All the things that have been happening for the past several months," he murmured. "It's like a bird swooped down and—and—"

He slammed an open palm on his coffee table. "Those crows!" he shouted, and Terrence and Reena jumped. "In my dream! Wherever they landed, things went straight to hell! It's just like *that!* My dream was showing me the real world."

"You better hope that's not true," said Reena.

"Yeah, that sucks, I know," said Jonah, "but we can't deny—"

"No, you're not getting me," said Reena, her voice grim. "You said in that dream, the largest crow never landed. If your dream represents real life, the biggest thing hasn't happened yet."

On that happy note, they all resumed silence. Jonah broke it.

"Trip is keeping Creyton informed of the worry this is causing," he said. " '*In our midst?*' Got that right. Told Creyton we were no threat at all. And those Eleventh Percenters that were killed … the strangers, your three friends…" he looked at the photographs scattered across his table. "Please don't tell me that in addition to his substitute teaching and music gigs, Trip also does freelance photography."

Terrence and Reena looked at each other. "No," they said in unison.

"Good," said Jonah, relieved, but he noticed their grim faces. "What?"

Reena sighed. "No, it's not freelance."

Jonah felt like these new revelations made him smaller. He felt like the world was growing larger all around him. "That's probably it, then," he said. "The biggest crow? That's Creyton's plan." He thought of his dream being mirrored in the real world. If that were true, that meant seeing his friends trampled ... He didn't want to think about it.

"I need some food," said Terrence suddenly. "You mind...?"

"Help yourself," muttered Jonah. Terrence got up and went to the kitchen. In a matter of minutes, he came back with a large box of chocolate chip brownies. Reena glared at Jonah coldly, but Jonah raised a quelling hand.

"Task at hand, Reena," he said quietly. "Please just focus on the task at hand."

Reena's expression softened, and she said nothing. She joined Jonah in staring at Terrence's absent scarfing of brownies. Jonah knew that they, like him, wondered what was about to happen.

15

Kodak Moments

Terrence and Reena crashed at Jonah's apartment that night. Neither felt up to driving. Reena had also hypothesized that Terrence, who was so full of fudge brownies that even Jonah wondered where he had put them all, was incapable of driving over a three-hour period.

Sleeping arrangements were hastily made, and Jonah offered his bed to Reena, which she promptly shot down ("Are you trying for gallantry? No thanks."). She opted for Jonah's sofa bed, which came free rather reluctantly due to infrequent use of it. Terrence took up residence on Jonah's writing recliner, which lately served no other purpose than being a rather unsightly clothesline.

They prepared to leave early the next morning, yet Jonah envied them. Not only would they return to the estate, but both of them had the day off from work. Before they left, Reena decided to take the photographs (Jonah assumed that it was for sentimental reasons). She took the pictures of the three strangers as well because she felt that they should receive respect too. Jonah had no problem with that; the pictures represented a frightening notion to him, and he was relieved to be done with them. He noticed something interesting as he assisted Reena with putting the photographs back in their proper folders. A photo of Abel Ford had fallen, and as Jonah retrieved it, he saw a thinly written number in the right hand corner. He looked at the others.

"There are some pictures missing," he said, frowning. "They aren't sequential. See? Some jump from photo nine to photo sixteen..." His voice trailed off when he noticed Reena's downcast eyes. It was obvious that the "life never ends" truth didn't deter from the loss, no matter how strong the ideals were. He locked eyes with Terrence and let the matter drop. No one would care about numbers on a photograph.

"Let me come back with you guys," he suggested. "You'll need help with Trip. I know that Malcolm, Liz, and Bobby can't know all of it because of Mindscopes, but won't that make them vulnerable?"

"It might," said Reena quietly, "but how can we inform them now? They would go from being slightly vulnerable to being in definite danger."

"I want to help you," persisted Jonah. It was frightening, yes, and he didn't know *how* helpful he would actually be, but sitting on the sidelines just didn't feel right.

"Jonah, go to work," said Terrence. "You said you had your evaluation today. Given what you said about that job, you shouldn't risk any flack."

Frustration settled on Jonah like a heavy coat. He felt absolutely useless, like he was allowing his friends to walk into a snake pit or something. He was still so new to it all—what could he do? Being a Blue Aura meant he was a big deal? Right. He didn't feel capable of saving anything.

Then Terrence had to remind him of that damned evaluation. He knew that Jessica and Anthony were on the warpath, especially since that unauthorized half-day he'd taken. Monday and Tuesday had been a blur, that was true, but through that blur, he recalled the cold and satisfied glances from Jessica, as if his fate had already been sealed. He also remembered the piteous looks of Anthony. He resigned himself to the second invisible coat that had draped over his shoulders.

"Cheer up, man," said Terrence. "That evaluation will be a cinch. And don't worry; we'll update you. You make it seem like cell phones don't exist." He brandished his own with a laugh that Jonah could tell was forced. "We'll keep an eye on Trip. You'll be back on Friday, won't you? Trip won't end the world in seventy-two hours."

Jonah noticed that even Terrence seemed like he was reassuring himself. That gave him no comfort at all. "Fine," he said. "But you will fill me in on every single thing until I'm back there. Take care of Malcolm, Liz, and, well I'm sure Bobby can crush about anything, but take care of him too. And yourselves."

"We've been at this for a while, Jonah," said Reena with a small smile.

"So were your friends there," countered Jonah. It might have been a little too honest, and a little too soon, but he didn't care. He didn't want any of them to get hurt or killed. Reena's eyes narrowed slightly, but Jonah didn't drop his gaze or apologize. Reena was intelligent; surely she knew the point he was trying to make.

"We've got one ace left," said Terrence. "We aren't in the dark. We know what's going on, remember? We can't be caught off-guard."

That didn't reassure Jonah, but he knew better than to force the issue. "You're right," he said grudgingly. "Knowledge is power, right?"

Though his tone was quiet, his mind still raged. He was well aware that they could take care of themselves; he'd seen examples of it when they'd trained. Reena could never be caught by most attacks. Terrence wasn't as powerful as Bobby, but he seemed able to hold his own well enough. Good stuff there as well.

So *why* did he feel like they were in such danger? Why did he feel like Trip had yet to play his worst, most dangerous card against them?

Man, if he could only talk to Marla. The one time he actually wanted the spiritess's company, it was impossible. Typical.

"Safe driving," said Jonah.

"You know it, man," said Terrence, clapping him on the back.

"Until Friday, friend," said Reena warmly.

"Of course."

They left Jonah, who wished that there was more he could do or say.

Essa, Langton, and Bane was rife with anxiety. Business was still down despite the extra hour, and people feared the inevitable layoffs. People went about their usual routines, but tension overrode everything. Jonah even overheard Mrs. Souther whispering The Lord's Prayer.

"No offense, Jonah," said Nelson, tone full of concern, "but you look like hell. Have you been eating?"

An interesting question, when taking Reena's eating plan into account, thought Jonah. "All is well there, Nels," he told him. "Just tired. I've got a lot of stuff on my mind."

"Oh, really?" said Nelson, an odd look of excitement in his eyes. "Working on an unfolding story?"

"Wha—? Oh, um, yeah. You could say that," responded Jonah.

"Yes!" Nelson rapped the cubicle wall in delight. "I'm really glad to hear that! We both know you don't belong in here with your talents languishing. Stories are what you know."

Jonah couldn't tell Nelson what really swirled in his head, but oddly enough, it felt good to unload some information. "Nelson," he said carefully, "that's the thing. I don't know how this—story—will play out. There are some, uh, characters in the situation that are rather iffy. I don't know—how to work out the climax."

Nelson waved his hand dismissively. "If anyone can hash out a tough story, it's you, Jonah. Stuff always works out when people bother to see it through. At least you and I," he dipped his head and lowered his tone, "are channeling stress constructively. You know Clyde from HR mugged someone last night?"

"What?" said Jonah, incredulous. Clyde was by far one of the meekest, mild-mannered people Jonah had ever met. He was always decent to everyone and always had kind words. "Clyde *Brennon*? Mugged somebody?"

"Yeah," said Nelson. "We were all freaked out by it. Can't imagine what he was thinking, though. Claimed he 'had an urge,' or so I heard. Not like he needed money."

But Jonah didn't bother with hypotheses about monetary gain. The fact that Clyde Brennon, the nicest guy on the planet, would mug someone because of an "urge" made Terrence's words ring in his mind.

Crime. Civil unrest. People acting in ways they wouldn't usually act.

The dark essence. It was screwing with people's minds.

"Nelson," said Jonah quietly, "have you seen people around here acting weirdly? Like, abrupt changes in their personalities or something like that? You know I try not to pay attention to folks around here."

"Hmm," said Nelson. "Couldn't tell you really, Jonah. With this crime wave, I suppose everyone's acting strange. Anthony did something nice, and there was no benefit for him personally. That's a first."

Jonah was disappointed but nodded. "Yeah, it is."

"Scratch that, there *were* probably some personal benefits for him somewhere." Nelson frowned. "He's been hanging around Jessica too long ... Now he is suddenly photogenic."

"How do you figure?" asked Jonah, who'd lost interest in the whole thing because it involved Ant and Jessica.

"Jonah, were you on another planet the past two days?" chuckled Nelson.

"Yes," said Jonah. "Why?"

"Some guy was here taking a bunch of pictures."

Jonah shot up in his seat and overturned so much paperwork that it hit the ground with a thud. "Pictures?"

Nelson started at Jonah's dramatic reaction and straightened, looking curious. "Yeah, pictures. It's not a big deal; he said they were for the paper."

Who would suddenly come in and start photographing the office for the paper? "Didn't that seem a little bit odd to anyone, Nelson?"

"Of course it was odd," said Nelson, who looked alarmed at Jonah's behavior. "But since when has Langton done anything that makes sense around here?"

"How does Anthony come into this?" asked Jonah.

"No idea," replied Nelson. "What's it matter?"

"A lot," mumbled Jonah. He turned his back on Nelson and searched for Anthony. He wouldn't be hard at work, unless you counted sucking up—

"Anthony," said Jonah. He found him at Jessica's desk, where he'd placed a few lilies. It was the first and last time he'd be happy to see Anthony Noble.

"Rowe! Can I help you with something?" said Ant, uncertain. He clearly didn't know what to make of this because Jonah had always done his best to avoid him. Jonah knew Anthony thought he had an ulterior motive.

"You hired a photographer to take pics in here?" asked Jonah in a would-be-casual voice.

"Uh, no," said Anthony, whose eyes narrowed. "He approached me at the coffeehouse down the street. Apparently, he'd been waiting for a good long time."

"To what?"

"To talk without being overbearing," responded Anthony. "He must have known I'm a pretty big deal here."

Jonah disregarded that last part and plowed on. "So he just said he wanted to take pictures of people in the office? What else did he say?"

"He said..." Anthony glanced over Jonah's shoulder; it was plain that he wanted to surprise Jessica with the flowers, and Jonah was disrupting his grand gesture. "He said that *the Daily Rap* was just looking for shots of office life. Why? Are you looking for a bit of limelight? You needn't worry. He seemed particularly interested in your section—"

Jonah must have paled. He felt his face go cold. "What did he look like?" he whispered.

"And why would you want to know that, Rowe?" asked Anthony suspiciously.

"Answer the question, and I'll leave you to your flattery," said Jonah.

Jonah was pleased to see Anthony's smile. "Uh ... an African-American guy with no hair," he said. "Looked to be in his early thirties, I guess—Rowe?"

Jonah abruptly turned his back on Anthony and headed for his cubicle. How did Trip find his job? How did he happen to know that Ant was the simplest-minded one and therefore the right one to approach?

He shut his eyes tightly and willed the curtain to open as widely as possible in his mind. If they were watching him...

The spirits were there again, and Jonah paused by the water cooler near his cubicle to do a scan. There wasn't anything out of the ordinary; there were the moderately opaque spirits and the slightly more transparent ones. Fascinating though the phenomenon was it did nothing to assist Jonah at the moment. He rolled his eyes in frustration.

"You all right, Jonah?" asked a colleague. Jonah looked at the guy and remembered that his name was Fredrick Park.

"Doing well, Fredrick," said Jonah. He grabbed a disposable cup and took some water. It might look a little suspicious if he was at the water cooler and not drinking any water. "Say, did you notice the guy taking pictures here the past two days? I must have been in a completely different world."

"Guess I can relate," snorted Fredrick. "It's easy to trail off when you're on edge about the possible layoffs."

"Right," said Jonah.

"But to answer your question," Fredrick caught more water in his cup, "that guy who was taking the picture for *the Daily Rap?* He wasn't noticeable really. He faded to black so nicely you wouldn't have known he was there. Suppose it had something to do with seeing the natural work environment, which probably would have been when everyone's *not* biting their nails to the elbows worrying about their jobs."

"Right," said Jonah again. He hadn't put it past Trip to be devious, but how could he have not noticed him taking pictures? Work was boring, but there was no way he could have tuned him out entirely. Surely not.

Fredrick was still talking. It took Jonah a few moments to realize it. "—but Photo Guy was friendly enough. He took that job seriously. Must be fun not to worry about job security, you know? I wonder how they train them to fade in the background like that. Almost like a ghost."

Fredrick laughed softly, but now he had Jonah's full attention. "What did you say?"

"Oh, about job security? Anyone's fair game except maybe Jessica, which I'm sure is another story—"

"No, no, no," said Jonah impatiently. "The gho— I mean, spirits."

Fredrick raised an eyebrow. A woman near them turned her head at his mention of spirits, but Jonah ignored her.

"I wasn't..." Unsurprisingly, Fredrick looked confused. Why, after all, would anyone have latched on to a word describing something that didn't exist? "I wasn't talking about ghosts, per se. You know the cute little stories that parents tell kids? You can only see a ghost if they *want* you to see them? I meant that the photographer was efficient like that. Came in and faded into the background like a ghost that didn't want to be seen."

Movement caught Jonah's eyes at a point beyond Fredrick's shoulder. Another colleague of his had an elderly spiritess behind him with understanding eyes and a face that showed more wisdom than age. Jonah was certain that the spiritess made eye contact with him for a moment but then turned to Jonah's colleague's back. But Jonah looked at her and noticed that she was one of the more opaque spirits. He was thankful for this because if she had been more transparent, the gesture would have been too faint for him to notice.

She gave him a sharp nod. He paused but then understood.

"Thanks, Fredrick," said Jonah.

"For what?" said Fredrick, confused.

"For talking," muttered Jonah. He was back at his cubicle in such a short period of time he might have flown. He dialed Terrence's number, and Terrence answered almost immediately.

"Hey, Jonah. What's up?"

"Terrence, I got a question about Trip. All Eleventh Percenters have some specialty, right? Something that is like a trademark for them?"

"Yeah, that's right," said Terrence. "What do you need to know about Trip?"

"Is one of Trip's signature things a fade out? Like—like willing himself not to be seen?"

There was silence on Terrence's end for several seconds. Jonah was almost concerned that Terrence's phone had dropped the call. Then, Terrence finally spoke. "Jonah, how did you know that?"

Jonah gritted his teeth. He was *never* always right; why was it happening now? "Trip has been taking pictures of me, just like the ones we saw," he said shortly. "He spent two days at my job, telling whoever saw him that he was a photographer for *the Daily Rap.* I never noticed him *myself* because he was doing that fade-out thing I just described."

"What? Hang on—"

He put Jonah on hold to share the information with Reena. Then he was surprised to hear Reena's voice on the receiver. "Jonah, Terrence just told me what you said. That doesn't make any sense! Did anyone check their facts? Anyone ask for his credentials? Did anyone even talk to a representative from *the Daily Rap?*"

The moment was tense, but Jonah still managed to laugh. "This office doesn't have the most competent staff, Reena. If Langton knew, he'd probably eat it up as some recognition from the city. Besides, Trip probably knew his way around a bit anyway. He knew enough to approach Anthony, who is the company idiot. The minions are probably watching *me* now."

More silence. Jonah hoped that they weren't going to swap the phone again.

"You need us to come back?" asked Reena.

"No," said Jonah, his voice firm. "You need to get home and put the others on guard. Trip is probably counting on us being divided up in different places. We'll be too easy to pick off if we're split up."

Reena didn't answer, which, to Jonah, was almost as bad as confirming what he'd just said.

"Reena, Jonathan told me there are bunches of other Eleventh Percenters who spend time at the estate," he said. "Can any of them be called for extra backup?"

Reena gave a sigh that couldn't mean anything well. "That would be a good idea in many cases, Jonah, but I don't think it would work. If Trip is the spy—"

"*Since* Trip is the spy," corrected Jonah with heat in his tone.

"Right, right," said Reena, but Jonah could tell that she still had trouble with it. "Since Trip is the spy, he is among us and that makes us vulnerable to the Minion's Mindscopes. Larger numbers might mean more victims."

Jonah was thankful that Reena couldn't see him over the phone as he'd made a very wry face. Just because she was right didn't mean he had to like it. "Then I'm coming there."

"Jonah, are you crazy?" demanded Reena. "What about your job? You said everyone is on tenterhooks about layoffs and terminations, so—"

"I don't care," snapped Jonah, and he was surprised to realize that he actually meant it. "You think I will sit here and let you all sit there with that bastard spy because I don't want to lose my job? Forget it. Six Eleventh Percenters have been killed in the past year, Reena. Three of them were people you guys knew. I know they aren't really dead or whatever, but it doesn't take away from the fact that they were taken from this life *before* their time! You just said backup is out, so you will need what available hands there are! I don't know how Creyton plans to use the information that Trip's giving him, but it will *not* result in any more killing. And I will be damned if you guys get blindsided while I rot in this cubicle, scared of a stupid boss and his shameless snitches."

Jonah's words left a ringing silence.

"All right, Jonah," said Reena finally. "Just be mindful of—"

The phone was snatched from his grasp. Jonah whirled around to see the culprit and saw that it was in the French-tipped clasp of Jessica Hale.

Jonah's blood began to boil. He shut his eyes tightly, willing the curtain to close. *I need the curtain to close,* he said wordlessly. *I don't need a physical and spiritual audience.*

"That's *quite* enough flapping your gums on the job," she said, her voice waspish. "My God, Rowe, if you worked as hard on billing reports as you worked your mouth, you might not be so low on the totem pole!"

Nelson took a sharp intake of breath. Jonah's other co-workers froze as well. Jonah took no notice as an acid-laced fury rose inside him. It was so all-consuming that it extinguished all rational thought. "Jessica," he said, using whatever resolve he could scrounge to keep his voice level, "give me back my phone *now*."

Jessica looked amused. "Have I invoked a reaction? Well, pay close attention, Rowe. You know full well that cell phone use is prohibited in this office. Mr. Langton made it clear that if we wanted to turn things around, focus was imperative. Did you miss that memo, or could you not be bothered with office etiquette because you spend your days pining for your literary pipe dream?"

No one spoke, but Jonah caught Nelson's widened eyes. The silence spiraled horribly before Jonah said, in a voice barely above a whisper, "Jessica, I am asking you nicely. *Give. Me. Back. My. Phone.*"

"You're getting angry?" said Jessica in surprise. She really felt secure in her role as boss's pet; it was written all over her face as she took a few brazen steps closer. "You're mad at me for upholding rules? You're angry that your friends are only willing to talk to you via phone because they don't want to be seen with you? No wonder you're alone, Rowe. No wonder Mr. Langton questions your relevance to this company. Your lackluster performance must be attributed to the fact that you lie to yourself about being an author and spend your time cuddling nasty stray felines—"

"SHUT THE FUCK UP, BITCH!" roared Jonah, and everybody jumped. Jonah thought he felt energy release itself from him, and he could have sworn the office lights flickered. But it didn't matter. Jessica's eyes widened in shock, and her skin turned a nasty blotchy color.

"You think that because Langton's wife looks like a starved horse and the bright spot of his day is staring at you that you can lord yourself over us like you own the place?" Jonah went on. "You are an employee, just like the rest of us. Make no mistake about it. Just because Langton can't see that face value is the only value you have doesn't mean *I* will sit here and kowtow to you as well."

Nelson let out a low whistle. Fredrick wore a look of such alarm that it appeared his face was stuck that way. Jessica remained statuary. Her eyes were absolutely frigid.

"I've got you pegged," continued Jonah, vaguely aware that his clock and pencil sharpener were both buzzing. "Your outfits are in blatant disregard to the etiquette you claim to uphold. But I get it. Your plunging necklines, perfect makeup, and streetwalker skirts don't fool me. Behind it all, you're just a weak little slut who hides your inadequacies behind a C-cup and attempts to divert attention from your fallacies by seducing your little slave, Anthony."

As sudden as the wind, everyone turned around to look at Anthony, who made a choking sound and slopped water down his front. Jonah ignored him.

"You want to talk about work ethic, Jessica?" he snarled. "Try grasping this. Maybe people would respect you if you actually *did* some work. Perhaps if you worked something besides your hips and your mouth, you'd get a promotion the right way. But this day, this minute, right now, I am done with you. I find peace in telling you just three more things: Quit your damn chiding, catch a clue, and *fuck off.*"

Jonah yanked his phone from her grasp with no protest. She remained stock-still and white as chalk. Jonah now registered the reactions of others. Nelson was in tears from his attempts to suppress his mirth, Anthony opened and closed his mouth wordlessly, and several other people said nothing, but their faces showed full agreement.

But none of it mattered. He had bigger problems.

"Mrs. Souther," he said, his voice restored to politeness, "please tell Mr. Langton that I'm taking a personal day and will be invoking some vacation days for the rest of the week."

"My pleasure, darling," said Mrs. Souther warmly. She was trying hard to keep her face impassive, but it was clear that she had enjoyed the exchange. Then someone snapped a picture of Jessica's face with their phone. The flash jarred Jonah back to reality, and he left the office.

16

In the Cold of the Night

"I would have paid money to see that," said Terrence.

He and Bobby laughed hysterically when Jonah recounted the story to them at the kitchen table at the estate. After three hours of uneventful driving, Jonah's anger had abated somewhat, and he could appreciate the humor of his excoriation of Jessica. The levity was only a light boon, though. The tension and anxiety smarted in his mind. They were akin to a tack embedded in someone's foot.

"Jonah," said Liz, uncertainty in her voice, "what about your job, though? I get why you did what you did, but it sounds like Jessica is better to have as a friend than as an enemy."

"She was already his enemy," said Reena. It was obvious to Jonah that she had no love for women who used aesthetic means to advance themselves. "Served her right. Kudos, Jonah."

"I appreciate that, Reena," said Jonah. "Say, what were you going to warn me about over the phone?"

Reena stood, still nettled over such a superficial woman. Jonah made a mental note never to set her up on a blind date with a beautiful idiot. "I was planning to tell you to make sure that no minions screwed with your car."

That hadn't occurred to Jonah. Even though he'd safely made it to the estate, a slight chill went through his body as he thought of what might have happened.

Terrence had sobered. He looked at Jonah, who looked at Reena, and the nonverbal communication was taken accurately in all three of the gazes.

"Malcolm, Liz, Bobby," said Reena, and they turned their attention to her. Jonah had no problem with Reena telling them their suspicions; he felt that if it came from him, it would sound spiteful and full of bias. "We need to tell you something. I will apologize because it's not a great deal of information. But the more you know, the more vulnerable you'll be to the Minion's Mindscopes." She took a deep breath. "We believe Trip is a spy for Creyton, and he was the one who betrayed Eleventh Percenters to him."

Liz gasped. Malcolm and Bobby just stared. While Jonah's heart went out to them, his dislike for Trip increased.

"Proof?" murmured Malcolm.

"These." Reena dumped the photographs that had been delivered to Jonah's door onto the table. Malcolm, Liz, and Bobby looked at them.

"I don't know these people," said Bobby, pointing to the strangers, "but I seem to recall this guy—Abel? Abel Ford, right?"

"Right," said Reena. "He hasn't been around for a while, but that's him."

"And these two," said Liz, pulling two photographs nearer, "Rebecca and Lillian, right?"

"Yeah, that's right," said Terrence. "The others—I think they were in the wrong place at the wrong time."

"Like hell they were," snapped Jonah. "All they were doing, all *any* of them were doing, was living their lives. And Trip handed them to Creyton."

Liz looked at him, doubt and confusion in her eyes. "What are you saying?"

"He'd been studying their habits, trying to figure out where they were the most vulnerable," said Jonah. "As you can see, Howard, Walt, and other minions are around them in each picture. They're spirits, after all. They have nothing but time. They waited like vultures, readying themselves for when the carcasses were still."

Tears welled in Liz's eyes, and Bobby placed a hand on her shoulder. Jonah almost didn't have the strength to add to the drama. "Trip has also been taking pictures of me," he revealed. "He was at my job the past two days, taking pictures of my section of the office."

"I don't understand why you didn't do anything," muttered Bobby.

"I didn't see him," grumbled Jonah.

"He was at your job for two days, and you didn't notice?" said Malcolm.

"Nope, I didn't. He made sure I didn't see him."

"But—" Malcolm's confused face cleared. "He did that fade-out thing. The-willing-you-to-focus-elsewhere thing, right?"

Jonah nodded. The silence that fell between them after this action made him very uneasy. It felt like a pit. The more they deliberated in silence, the more probable solutions escaped their grasps and fell into the gaping chasm.

"Jonah, this is not the time to be rash," said Reena suddenly.

Jonah looked at her, shocked, and then grimaced. "I'm going to need you to give me advanced warning when you read my essence," he muttered.

She smiled in spite of herself.

"Why, exactly," said Malcolm, "is Creyton using Trip to get us?"

Reena's smile slid off of her face. Jonah helped her.

"Creyton is using the essence of the Eleventh Percenters that were killed to block the path to the Other Side," he said. "The blocked path is causing ethereal essence not meant to be on Earthplane to become dark and venomous. I'm guessing he has promised Trip more power through the dark essences."

There was more silence, only broken by Bast and several of her feline friends walking in through the cat flap. She had an urgent look in her eyes, which told Jonah that they were of the same mind. Circular talking would lead them nowhere.

"I've got an idea," he said, and everyone looked at him. "I didn't see anyone watching me when I went into Spectral Sight. Spirits cannot hide from us, at least not when we're in Spectral Sight. I think we all need to go into the Sight and keep watch. I'm sure you all would know who is malevolent and who is simply moving about."

"What about Trip?" said Bobby. It was clear that he wanted to take action … action that was as violent as possible.

"Well," said Jonah, "where is Trip now?"

"He had a gig tonight, about two hours from here," said Terrence.

"We'll keep watch around the estate, then" said Jonah. "Trip'll have to come back eventually. We can request endowments and accost him the minute he sets foot on the grounds. He will tell us everything he passed to Creyton, and we'll use it against him when we present it to Jonathan. Reena, you can read essence, so you will know if he lies."

Reena gave Jonah a piteous look. "It doesn't work like that, Jonah," she said. "Essence and truth are two very different things."

"You just read me a second ago—"

"I read that you were *impatient*," said Reena. "The rest was deductive. It's common sense that impatient people do rash things. I'm not capable of delving into your brain or anything."

Jonah didn't have anything to say. Brainy people making perfect sense could be so annoying at times. He had no further suggestions, so he went over to Malcolm's breadbox, grabbed slices at random, and crammed them into his mouth. Apparently, the action prompted ideas to come to Malcolm, who piped up at that moment.

"Hang on, Reena," he said. "You can't read minds, but you can tell how Trip would *feel* if he lied. We may have a weapon there."

"That just might work," said Terrence.

Reena thought it over and nodded. "Worth a shot if it will save us," she said.

Jonah nodded quickly, and then shut his eyes and willed the curtain to open. When he opened them, several spirits were on the grounds beyond the windows, but none looked like they posed a threat. Good signs, for the moment at least.

Everyone left the table, and Jonah could tell that they were in Spectral Sight as well.

"I must ask you guys," said Liz suddenly, "if being aware of these things makes us vulnerable, why fill us in now? What makes this different from when info was held back about the paths being blocked?"

She didn't sound accusatory, but there was a faint edge in her voice.

"I can answer that," said Jonah, sparing Reena. "If we are to stop Trip, we have to trust each other. It might make us all vulnerable, but we are no longer at risk of being solitarily slaughtered. We are a team and not a band of individuals, after all."

Liz's face relaxed. Bobby gave a quick nod, and Malcolm smirked. Reena looked impressed yet again (why was she so surprised?), and Terrence mouthed, "*Way with words, huh?*" Jonah just shrugged. He couldn't be clouded by ego once Trip returned, after all.

But Trip did not return to the Grannison-Morris estate that night. Nor the next day. Nothing out of the ordinary occurred during that time either. Spirits and spiritesses were present as always, moving about or conversing, but nothing even remotely threatening happened. Jonah and the others hadn't left the estate; they didn't want to be absent when their presence was most needed. But after forty-eight hours of inactivity...

The lapse in time proved, at least in Jonah's opinion, to be both gift and curse; gift because some of the fear, worry, and tension had faded, and curse because the two days, no matter how vast the estate might be, made them edgy, frustrated, and all the other telltale signs of cabin fever.

"But where is he?" persisted Jonah. "Has Trip ever just vanished like this before?"

"No," admitted Reena, who yawned and stretched as she, Terrence, and Jonah were about to finish their watch. They took it in threes and also enlisted the help of Bast, her other herald friends, and several spirits and spiritesses. Those that weren't on patrol either trained or slept. Jonah hadn't had practice with sleepless nights since cramming for exams in grad school.

Prolonged Spectral Sight had weird effects on his eyes too. After staring around at spirits and spiritesses for a few hours, his eyes had the same sensitivity they had when he'd first gotten them dilated for his reading glasses.

Reena had tightened her eyes and exhaled; she had just come out of the Sight as well. "This behavior is most unlike Trip," she commented. "He usually comes back from work, and then proceeds to music or pic—" her voice caught, and Terrence shook his head.

"Just out of curiosity, what do you see when you go into Spectral Sight?" Jonah asked, hoping to distract from the sad moment.

Reena half-smiled. "I see a message inside a particularly difficult painting being ascertained," she said. "You?"

"A stage. The curtain rises for an acting troupe's performance."

"You know what I see?" said Terrence. "I see muddy water clearing somehow. You guys' brains process profound crap and all that, but that's what I get. Stupid muddy water."

Reena smirked. "Terrence, you drool when you sleep, did you know that?" she said.

Terrence flushed. "How long was—?"

"Long enough for her to make a pencil sketch," laughed Jonah.

Reena lifted an uncannily accurate lead-drawn illustration of a slumbering Terrence, which caused him to flush even further.

"Excellent watchfulness, by the way," said Jonah in mock admiration.

Terrence's eyes narrowed. "Have your moment," he retorted, "but we will see just how much joy you feel after you have Reena's glorious meal of celery sticks and tofu."

Reena laughed. Jonah didn't.

They had the "meal" shortly thereafter. Jonah was sated (or about as sated as one could be after a meal of celery sticks and tofu) and decided to pass some of the evening by taking another stab of writing. Malcolm, Liz, and Bobby were on watch now. Although it was almost nine at night, Jonah looked forward to another watch. It would take his mind off of what he viewed as a sad writing effort:

The mind perceives danger as a monstrous, ever-changing beast, but the power lies in the perception alone rather than the threats, abilities, or capabilities of the beast itself. Beasts are contently shrouded behind the foreboding veils or lore, tradition, and painstaking superstition, when in reality, the monster can be the equivalent of a harmless marsupial, such as a tree sloth, or a lazy animal who yields no threat at all, such as a frog. Rarely does this tend to matter in most cases as fear does the monster's task for them. So when true danger rears itself, it is not surprising to see that the enemy you sought was not the enemy at all. The power is perception, and perception only.

"Great," mumbled Jonah. "But I'm trying to write an epic, not write out a textbook."

The front door opened, and Malcolm, Liz, and Bobby filed inside, blurry-eyed and slightly fatigued from having just relinquished endowments.

"All yours," muttered Bobby. "Man, Jonah, I swear, if Trip is visiting his favorite aunt or something..."

Jonah didn't even dignify that with a response. Hell, judging by his writing, he'd better keep his words to himself, lest he bore them all into sleep.

Jonah was back in Spectral Sight and ready for another watch. He just needed to find a spirit to endow him. He stood and tossed the papers aside at the same moment Bobby turned on an oscillating fan. Jonah hadn't bound his composition, and as a result, it flew around the room in a matter of seconds.

"Dammit," he snapped. He lunged for them, but all that did was make a fresh gust of air, propelling the pages even further. With a grunt of frustration, he chased them. When he ran past the window, he saw a terrified spiritess out of the corner of his eye. He skidded to a halt and took a second look. The petrified face vanished as suddenly as it had appeared, but another face was brought into full relief after the clouds shifted and freed the moonlight.

"Wha—?"

Then a painful, icy surge ran the length of Jonah's veins. The moon had cast silvery light on a face that Jonah had only seen once but recognized instantly. How could he ever forget that inhuman face, black hair, dark eyes, and angular jaw? Creyton was standing in front of the estate with a dozen or so minions with him.

Jonah's eyes widened, and out of the corner of his eye, he saw Terrence pick up his composition.

"Wow, you've done it again, Jonah!" he marveled. "Great writing!"

He reached the door, already turning the knob.

"Terrence, don't," Jonah sputtered. He saw Creyton lift his crow-tipped staff so the face of the murderous-looking bird aimed at the front door.

"Will you stop being so modest?" said Terrence. "I said that it was great! Can't you see that?"

"No! STOP!"

Jonah made to shove Terrence from the door, but in the second that elapsed, time stopped. For the briefest moment, he saw Terrence's puzzled face, which might have been comical in the still moment—

Then time resumed with concussive force. The room exploded, and in seconds, what once was a cozy family room was a mess of flying projectiles. Wood, metal, and glass cascaded upon the scene like a precarious rain.

Jonah was blasted backward; he didn't have a clue where his friends were. On the edge of consciousness, he thought he heard Creyton and his minions laughing as they crossed the now non-existent threshold.

17

Illuminated

Jonah felt several painful sensations at once.

There had been some kind of explosion, but there was no heat. The blast had been as cold as the grave. He recalled flying through the air for a small period of time, and then everything was a haze of sound and pain, followed by silence.

He had no idea what had happened. Had he been killed? Did he not survive that blast? Had it ended, after all? He felt pain, which should've meant that this wasn't the case, but he wasn't reassured by that. If life never ended, did that mean that *pain* never ended either?

Jonah opened his eyes when completely unfamiliar voices met his ears. For the faintest of moments, he thought they were his friends, but after what had happened, they wouldn't sound that gleeful and excited.

"What happened in here?"

"Ain't got a clue, but I don't think nobody's here to notice."

"You think it was firebombed?"

"Fool, if it was firebombed, then where is the *fire*?"

"Oh yeah…"

Jonah tried hard to gauge where he was, but only patchy dust met his gaze. He was sprawled on something hard and oddly shaped. It was positioned underneath his back. Something heavy was on his chest and left shoulder, and a huge dark wedge had gotten lodged over that.

He seemed to be in the remains of furniture, but he was saved from being crushed by—

Huh. That was interesting. He was underneath a haphazard pyramid-shaped shelter, which must have been made when the widescreen got blown off the wall and lodged against a book shelf. That meant that the things on top of him were books.

Jonah sighed. One way or another, words were going to kill him.

"Man!" one of the gleeful voices screeched. "Look at this breadbox! Did you know they still made these?"

"They don't," said another voice. "Might be worth a fortune! Look at the designs!"

Blood roared in Jonah's ears and he shot bolt upright, sending wood, shrapnel, and books flying. "Put that damn breadbox down," he growled, though his voice wasn't that impressive. He was much too weak for that.

The screeching voice belonged to a squat lump of a man with disheveled brownish hair. His beady eyes showed very little intelligence, and his massive girth showed that he was a seasoned pro at stuffing his face. The second voice was obviously the brains of the two, which, judging by his filthy clothing, didn't mean much. He had an unshaven face, matted, uncut hair, and muddy brown eyes. By the looks of them, they were attempting to loot any spoils they could salvage from the wreckage of the family room and kitchen, which were now open and visible due to the gaping hole in the front of the estate.

The two pillagers made rude exclamations and fled, though Jonah couldn't understand why. He was completely alone and, in this state, not much of a threat. Maybe they were frightened because there was another live person in the place. The taller one bolted at breakneck speed, not even waiting for the squat one, who squealed yet again and waddled so fast that he nearly lost his ill-fitting jeans in the process.

"Put it ... down," repeated Jonah weakly to the backs of the retreating looters. "It's perfect ... perfect."

His momentary surge of adrenaline cost him dearly. He was so drained that it felt as if his very spirit clamored to escape his flesh.

He staggered into what remained of the widescreen, slid down, and faded out of consciousness yet again.

An insistent nudging at his left hand roused him again. Heralds pawed at him. Bast succeeded in waking him when a stray claw pierced his left wrist.

"Ow … Ow, stop that," snapped Jonah feebly. "I'm awake."

Bast meowed at one of her cat friends; it was like she gave some kind of command. The tabby darted out of the hole that used to be the front of the estate.

Jonah was no stranger to cuts and bruises, but this was nothing like that. It felt like there was acid in his ankle and shoulder. The latter had been dislocated and the former was either broken or severely sprained. He probably had a concussion as well, if the dizziness was any indication.

He took them, he thought weakly. *They're gone, and I let it happen.*

Bast pawed his arm again. He looked straight into her eyes, and Jonah instantly saw a message intimated into his mind. Bast wanted him to go into Spectral Sight.

Jonah closed his eyes and willed the curtain to open. It took a few tries because his head throbbed so badly, but he finally succeeded. In front of him stood a familiar figure with a weather-beaten face, knowing eyes, and a strong jaw. It was the spirit of the military veteran who usually aided him in training.

"Looks like you've been through a war of your own, son," he said in an authoritative voice. "But let's not trouble your already injured head with falsehoods. Your friends have not been killed. We would know if that happened."

Jonah hardly dared believe it, yet relief and hope filled him. "Where are they, then?"

The veteran shook his head. "You ask me something that I cannot answer. Now, please, son, ask me the right question."

Jonah looked at the spirit's pleading expression, and figured out what he meant. His head throbbed in protest as he focused. "Soldier," he croaked, "will you aid me in rebuilding my strength?"

The soldier didn't smile, but he gave Jonah an expression of approval. "Thank you, son. *That* is the right question."

"I can't help anyone," grumbled Jonah. "I'm broken. By the time I heal, it'll be too late."

The veteran looked at him, suddenly austere. "Do yourself a service, son," he murmured. "Climb out of the future, and think only of this moment. Realize the outcomes of the future are created out of decisions made in the present moments. You have been endowed."

The soldier vanished, and his endowment surged through Jonah's body. Bast jumped into his lap and curled there, settling so resolutely that Jonah felt like she would not move for several years.

"All right, cat, move," said Jonah quietly, but Bast didn't budge. He made to move her physically, but hesitated when he felt sensations in his injured limbs. The acidity in the lower half of his right leg dulled to nothing. His shoulder gently re-positioned itself, and the coppery taste in his mouth no longer had a source. He was mending, and Bast had relaxed on his lap to ensure that he remained still. With a feeling of gratitude, he complied and didn't move a muscle.

The disorientation cleared from his head and was replaced by an anger that he had never felt before in his life, not even with Jessica.

This wasn't his fault. It was *Trip's* fault.

The minute his ankle could take his weight, Jonah did a quick inventory of the damage. There was the hole in the wall, and the family room and kitchen lay in ruins, but other than that, he didn't see any other damage. It appeared that Creyton's blast was contained only to those two rooms. He knew where they were and how to hit them. They couldn't have been any threat to him or his minions; they had all just released their endowments and were practically powerless. Trip had been conveniently absent. Had he briefed Creyton on that too?

Jonah tucked Malcolm's breadbox under his arm like a football and descended the stairs to Reena's art studio. Thankfully, nothing there was damaged. The dull ache in Jonah's shoulder faded as the healing finished. The war veteran's endowment was highly beneficial. It made Jonah feel like nothing had even happened to him.

Physically, anyway.

Jonah didn't remember anything, but he could piece together what had happened: Terrence hadn't heeded his warning and probably got knocked out cold by the blast. Reena had probably been taken by surprise, Liz too. Jonah was sure that Bobby tried to put up a fight, but he would've been no match for them without an endowment. Malcolm had likely been blindsided. Trip was conveniently out of the game. He was undoubtedly tucked away somewhere, satisfied that his part in the scheme was complete. But this couldn't have been the full scheme if they'd been taken while still physically alive. That's what the spirit had told him, after all. Did Creyton want to take them and *then* kill them? Did Trip want to watch or something? They hadn't shown such restraint in the past, so why would they do so now?

Jonah's blood boiled. He turned his back on Reena's paintings and paused.

A door off the stairs was ajar. The explosion must have rocked the walls so forcefully that it had damaged the bolt and opened the door.

"What're you guys hiding in here?" said Jonah to himself. "Got anything, Bast?"

The calico simply stared and did nothing. Jonah opened the door all the way and felt his mouth fall open.

The room was full of weapons.

Jonah blinked to make sure that his eyes didn't deceive him. He'd known these guys for several weeks now, and not a single one of them had mentioned anything about weapons.

He meant to step forward and staggered; the veteran's endowment had been released. He felt the fatigue set in, but it was manageable. Jonah asked no questions. That endowment had been a means to an end. Every injury he had from the explosion had been righted.

"Thanks, old friend," he said to open air and focused on the room.

The walls and tables were laden with all types of weapons. Jonah recognized some, but there were others he'd never seen in his life. He wondered what would happen to his friends if anyone saw *this* stockpile. Then he realized that that was probably the reason why the door had been bolted.

There were short daggers, metallic clubs, maces, war hammers (Jonah *thought* that was what they were at least), and—spears? *Spears?* Even amongst this medieval-looking stuff, those things seemed particularly archaic. Archaic but still *deadly.* The tips on the ends were so frighteningly thin that they could have been honed with a laser.

Jonah moved further into the room, wondering which of these weapons would work best on Trip. Or should he be thinking about Creyton? He scanned everything but didn't mentally mesh with any of them. Daggers? He wasn't fond of blades. The clubs and maces were a little too ostentatious. And the spears? Yeah, right.

Jonah's vision became more obscured the further he walked into the room, so he flicked the light switch. Nothing happened. Creyton must have smashed the circuit breaker. Swell. He swore to himself, thinking just how beneficial light would be to him at this moment when the solitary bulb in the armory flickered.

His head shot up. The light bulb swung there, dark and inactive as ever, but had flickered to life just long enough for him to make out where it was in the darkness. Jonah stared at it curiously.

"Light," he experimented.

The light flickered again, longer this time, but then faded out once more.

"Come on," said Jonah with more insistence.

This time the bulb lit for a full ten or fifteen seconds, just enough time to illuminate something in the left corner of the room.

"Whoa," said Jonah. "Um—come on and stay on."

Miraculously, the bulb complied. Jonah was fascinated, remembering what Reena had told him some time back: "*Many Eleventh Percenters have inborn talents that can sometimes be displayed even void of spiritual endowments.*"

Jonah eyed the light as he moved to the corner of the armory. Where had this "inborn" talent been all his life?

He reached what had caught his eye. Between a sheathed sword and a javelin lay a pair of thin, intricate batons. The handles, which were made of polished oak, were fashioned into grooves for their wielder's hands. The rest was made out of a metal that had the dull gleam of steel. Upon further inspection, however, Jonah noticed that it was unlike any steel he had ever seen. It had a smoky, vapor-like appearance that gave the batons an eerie, almost holographic consistency.

Jonah stared at them with interest. On a hunch, he grabbed them both. He knew he'd made the right choice the second he'd touched them. The grooves accommodated his fingers perfectly; the batons felt like natural extensions of his hands. Jonah felt them out with curiosity. He had a notion that they were made for him, and waited all this time for him to find them. Why would he feel that way? Why would that be?

He shook his head. It was a concern for a different day. He pushed the batons into his pocket.

So what did this mean? Was this all he had? Creyton, his lackey, Trip, Howard, Walt, and all the other minions were armed with dark essence from the blocked path. They had five hostages who couldn't defend themselves. With Jonathan MIA on the Astral Plane somewhere, Jonah was alone.

Just what the *hell* had he gotten himself into? He, Jonah Rowe, disgruntled accountant and wannabe aspiring writer, was the only thing between safe, freed friends and a dark ethereal faction bent on killing and manipulating endowments until they made Earthplane some dark, dystopian hellhole?

A light popped on in his head. That was it. It had to be. But if *that* was what he had to do...

He looked at Bast, who had settled herself on a footstool beneath the maces. Her eyes narrowed at him as though she read Jonah's mind and desired saying, *You can't be serious.*

"I have to do it," he said to her in a solemn voice. "It's the only way to save them."

He willed the light off and left the armory. He hoped that the negative affirmation he'd made earlier about words killing him one way or another was wrong. Hopefully, his words would keep him physically alive.

18

Chaos Revisited

Jonah's epic plan hit a snag the second he set foot on the grounds. The minions had destroyed all the cars.

The red Toyota Celica—Reena's car—was overturned. Terrence's black Volvo had an opening through its hood so wide that Jonah could see the ground through it. Bobby's Honda Accord was ... gone. The only evidence that it had ever been there at all was a flattened tire sitting upright on the gravel path.

And his Taurus, his trooper that had survived so much, sat worthless with the brake line slashed and the steering wheel on the ground. There was a crowbar jammed through his back windshield. No doubt Walt took great pleasure in doing that.

Jonah wondered why they hadn't taken him too, but they must have figured he was finished after being crushed underneath the bookshelf and television. They never imagined that those two things would collide and form a shelter over him. Hell, under other circumstances, Jonah wouldn't have imagined it either.

But that didn't matter now. His plan wouldn't work at all if he had no transportation.

A loud meow startled him, and he turned to see Bast scamper away. He hoped that she wasn't expecting him to run the whole way. But he tore off after her. He ran maybe twenty minutes to catch up with Bast and felt a slight stitch in his side and discomfort in his newly healed ankle when he saw her next to a garage with her tabby friend.

There was a truck in the garage that looked older than Jonah. But when he cranked the ignition (the keys had been provided by Bast's friend while Jonah rummaged in the armory), he found it to be in perfect working order. He steeled himself and drove off with Bast in the passenger seat. How he got to his destination so quickly, he'd never know. He was reminded of his notion that whoever controlled time had a mean-spirited sense of humor.

He left the truck and trudged through waist-high grass. He nearly twisted his recently healed ankle twice and almost got lost amongst the tangled and shapeless masses. But Bast was a huge assistance. Jonah kept her in sight as she skittered along a beam of iron that twinkled in the moonlight. He thought of it as some sort of second-rate North Star that pointed him to his destination.

After he tripped, stumbled, and swore more times than he could count, he finally found himself in the center of his destination, which was the only part of it that hadn't been overtaken by time and elements. The journey had been so frustrating that Jonah had almost forgotten his fear. As he took in his surroundings, however, the apprehension rekindled. His eyes fell upon a sign that had yellowed due to years of neglect: *Mandy Realty: Family. Homes. Smiles.* The juxtaposition was not reassuring in the slightest. Jonah could see the highway from here, which had been the very place he'd seen the Mandy Housing site for the first time.

Way with words. He had to remember his way with words.

"Spirits and spiritesses of the Mandy Housing complex, formerly Tilford Cemetery," he called to the area at large, "I kindly and respectfully ask your presence. I face an insurmountable task, and time is of the essence."

There was a rumbling that vibrated the ground underneath Jonah's feet. Reddish dots began to wink into his line of sight. The cool evening's temperature elevated. The reddish dots lengthened and formed body shapes which fused together. As their glow achieved higher and higher brilliance, Jonah felt inchoate emotions that starkly contrasted with his own: rage, pain, bitterness, contempt, envy, longing. He had never felt such emotions in his life, not even when his grandmother had passed into Spirit.

Focus, he scolded himself.

He quickly realized that focusing was going to be about as easy as complimenting Jessica. He forced himself, moment by moment, to increase his attention on the thing in front of him.

Through the bright-red haze, Jonah saw a composite, nightmarish apparition. Half of the head belonged to a dark-haired man with a sea-green eye; the other half belonged to a fair-haired woman whose eye color was pale gray. The parts connected to a partially dark and partially pale neck, which lowered to a mixture of clothing that Jonah couldn't even imagine in one of Reena's most abstract paintings: part work uniform, part dress, part trousers, part suit, and part sweater. The left hand looked to be a calloused male's. The right hand was a female's. The horrible sight culminated with the right foot of an adult and the left foot of a child. It was a truly horrible thing to behold.

"Why have you disturbed us?" The voice was shocking. It sounded as though every spirit on the property had shouted as one. "Why do you trespass here?"

Jonah's heart slammed into his chest with such ferocity that it echoed in his ears. "I need your assistance."

"Another Eleventh Percenter," growled the collection of voices. "Your pride and vanity know no bounds! Rashness has already destroyed one of you in the past; must this misfortune occur again? Depart while your physical life is still intact."

Jonah blinked. "I can't do that. I didn't come here to brag about strength or build up my ego. I humbly ask your assistance in saving my friends, who were ambushed by Creyton and his minions."

The mismatched eyes surveyed Jonah. "Creyton is a monster. His regard for life is nonexistent, and his chaos outstrips even our own. Why face him? Why risk yourself? You may not survive, you know."

"I am only attempting to benefit others," said Jonah. "Sure, I could turn and walk away and keep on going with my physical life. But I couldn't live with myself knowing that I abandoned my friends without even trying. The other Eleventh Percenter sought an endowment to say he bested you. I seek an endowment from you to spare other physical lives."

The composite face regarded Jonah. Their anger was as vivid and profound as ever, but now it felt different. It seemed to be directed elsewhere, at least. "Noble," said the collective. "Maybe you will survive this attempt, Eleventh Percenter. If this is the case, may your endeavor be a successful one. We truly hope that it succeeds. You have been endowed."

Blind rage ambushed Jonah's body. The emotions didn't feel like power; they felt like he had been smashed in the head with a refrigerator. Agonized, he tried to think of boundaries or walls or anything to curtail such volatility, but those mental walls eroded like they were made of paper.

Strength, son! The spirit of the war veteran chided in Jonah's mind. *You are stronger than this!*

Jonah fell to his knees, still attempting to stem the flow, but the effort was pointless. Once again, everything went black.

19

Tripped Up

Confusion. That was the only thing present in Jonah's mind.

He thought that after such a torrent of emotions, he would have faded to nothing. For a wild moment, he thought he actually *was* nothing. But that couldn't be. He couldn't be mist, or he wouldn't feel so heavy and awkward. When he opened his eyes, they came into sharp focus. The collective apparition was no longer present. The only light sources now were moon and the distant orbs that illuminated the highway for several miles.

Jonah felt the endowment within him. It felt like he had consumed thirty espressos at once. Warmth tingled just underneath his flesh; he wouldn't have been surprised if his hands glowed (they didn't). He now possessed an endowment that his body simply shouldn't have been able to handle.

Why, then, had he been able to do so?

The answer to that would have to wait because now he had a new problem. All his thoughts had been focused on how to butter up the Mandy spirits and spiritesses. He hadn't actually given any thought to the fact that he didn't know where Creyton held his friends.

"Wonderful," he grumbled. "I got the Spiritual endowment, and I have no idea where to go to use it."

A meow made him look down. Bast had surrounded herself with even more cats, which all congregated a small distance from him. Bast situated herself in front of the other heralds and locked eyes with Jonah. She intimated thoughts into his mind and then blinked slowly.

Jonah mirrored the action and willed the curtain to open while he took the usual deep breath. When he opened his eyes, the Spectral Sight revealed no spirits around him, which Jonah found strange since it was a cemetery. The grounds should have been littered with them. Then he noticed a silvery mass in front of him gleaming like the moon above. Bast and her friends stood immobile as Jonah frowned at the mass.

"What does this have to do with finding the others?" he asked.

It was like the mass needed the question to be asked. It began separating itself into smaller pieces, morphing from one solid mass to seventeen shapes that evolved further to form letters and numbers. In that moment, Jonah understood. The spirits weren't present in defined forms because they were creating this mist. It was probably taking all of their strength to maintain this work that they didn't bother to form into their own shapes.

Their message gleamed so sharply that Jonah didn't even need his reading glasses to make it out. But there was still one small problem.

"Okay," he said. "Thanks for the location, but I still don't know how to get there."

Instantly, the words dissolved into the shapeless mass again, first gleaming like molten metal, then lightening to a gentle vapor, like steam that rose from a cup of coffee or a bowl of soup. The mist lowered into Bast's head. Her amber eyes alight and determined, she walked to Jonah, and he put the pieces together. He had the location, courtesy of the Spectral Sight that enabled him to see the essence the spirits made, and Bast knew how to get there.

"Well, Bast," he said, looking at her, "now or never."

* * *

Jonah vacillated between speed and caution the entire trip. Bast remained stretched across the seat and kept her paws on his arm; as long as she kept contact with him, he knew what she knew and knew where to drive. While this arrangement was helpful, it made his focus on the road a challenge.

After about an hour of this, he was near his destination, but he didn't drive up to the doorstep. He wasn't sure how he knew, but he was sure that he had to remain hidden as long as possible. The element of surprise was his most valuable asset at this moment. A force of the hand would have disastrous consequences.

He saw a condemned warehouse behind a thick collection of trees, but when he reactivated his Spectral Sight (he'd closed the curtain on the road), he saw that this was a façade. Creyton must have used his powers to disguise it. A Tenth Percenter could pass by and see a wrecked ruin of a warehouse that had been closed for years. But Jonah saw the reality. No warehouse had ever been here. It was a very large house, so aged and creepy that Jonah thought about the houses that scared people in the old horror movies. The house looked like what the Grannison-Morris estate would look like if it had been left to neglect and decay. Jonah counted at least eight windows on the side facing him, but they were gray, unsightly, and hadn't been opened in years. The wood was cracked and looked unstable. The weather vane on the roof was rusted due north. An entryway to the cellar, also visible to Jonah, was sealed by an aged padlock. The lawn was almost as overgrown as the one at the Mandy site. The land was also home to a tree that looked even older than the house, curved with age and twisted in a most grotesque fashion. If Jonah hadn't known any better, he'd have thought the tree was a disguise for some evil entity that was caught in a sort of suspended animation as it loomed over what was once a handsome landscape.

And of course, no haunted mansion would be complete without something to haunt it.

Spirits traipsed the unkempt grounds, but Jonah noticed that *these* spirits didn't look woebegone or sad. They were wary and alert. They functioned like guards, but they didn't need weapons. Their weapons were of an ethereal nature, and in many ways, much more dangerous. Jonah could also tell that they were intangible, which meant that the tangible minions were inside with his friends. And just because these minions outside were intangible didn't mean they weren't dangerous in some other way.

Okay, Jonah, he thought, *you are actually about to run into the haunted house. Nice.*

He grabbed the batons from his belt, and they began to hum as if they'd been plugged into an outlet. A blue current left his fingertips and danced up the batons. It followed the ridges within the metal where the blue light sharpened into focused brilliance. Jonah realized that the batons were utterly mundane until they were touched by spiritually endowed hands. Endowed hands made endowed weapons.

He also realized that the batons lighting up like this had just given away his location to the patrolling spirits.

"Who is there?" barked a harsh voice.

Jonah grimaced. He knew that it would be too much to ask for the minions outside to kindly not notice the two blue currents that suddenly lit up the night, but it didn't matter. He wasn't going to wait for them to converge on him. The goal was to infiltrate the ragged mansion where there were threats worse than the spirits who were in the yard. He fixed his vision on a window directly in his line of sight, readied the batons, and charged out of his hiding place.

If Jonah had given it thought, he wouldn't have run headfirst into a crowd of murderous spirits. If he'd given it thought, he would have panicked because all the spirits were now focused on him. If he'd given it thought, he'd have probably waited for another night.

Luckily, though, he hadn't given the action any thought. He forced himself to put all his focus on the window in front of him. No other thought strayed across that goal. He simply ran. He didn't even think about the fact that he wasn't the most athletic person in the world. Whatever flaws he had didn't register. His body and the Mandy spirits' endowment picked up whatever slack there was. He wasn't aware of what happened around him. Perhaps the minions that were on patrol gave chase. And since they weren't physically limited, they should have caught him with zero effort. But he ran like they weren't there. He glided with each bound, but he didn't dare stop to focus on it. If a watched pot didn't boil, watched feet certainly wouldn't glide.

He leapt at the window. *I won't get cut,* he thought to himself. *I'm not getting cut by the glass.*

As soon as he thought this, a portion of the fog detached itself from the rest near the ground and hovered in front of him like a shield. When he crashed through the glass, the shield of fog prevented all cuts, bruises, and lacerations, just like he had willed in his mind.

The autopilot faded when his feet hit solid ground. He stood on an aged, well-worn rug that was now adorned with shards of glass that glittered in the light of his batons. Five or six minions stood there, shocked at the unexpected arrival that had literally crashed into the room. Without a moment's hesitation, Jonah struck the two that were the nearest to him, and their forms shattered like the glass on the floor.

"*Shock value approaches are lousy for a prolonged plan,*" Bobby told Jonah during a very helpful training, "*because shock is temporary. However, if you actually do catch a threat by surprise, drop him. It works in football; it should work in a fight.*"

It turned out Bobby had been right. As the two vanquished minions faded to pieces, Jonah lunged at a third. The baton caught him in the abdomen, and he exploded in a cascade of illuminated shards. The third Minion's vanquishing jarred the other minions out of their shock. A burly one vaulted over a chair to get at Jonah, a piece of the broken glass in his hand. But Jonah deflected it with a sharp slap of the baton in his left hand, and before the minion could correct his posture, Jonah tagged him with the tip of the baton, and he was done. The remaining minions moved toward him like a defensive line determined to blitz. Jonah swung his batons this way and that and heard shouts and yells that were followed by light spurts that indicated successful vanquishing. He remembered the task at hand and bolted for the door, having no desire to be cornered in some far-flung room. Perhaps it was weakened due to age, or perhaps Jonah had extra strength due to the endowment, but the door was separated from its hinges the second he grabbed it.

There were more minions in the hall, and the few that remained in the room now chased him. He knew he had to be as quick as possible. Even with a spiritual endowment, he still wasn't Rambo.

His attacks brought about more shattering. It seemed like he made some headway. Jonah's arrival had taken most of the minions by surprise, because they fought with a certain amount of disorientation. But Jonah suspected that that might be because they weren't at full numbers. God forbid *that* happened.

He swung the baton at a minion on his left and he felt his knee buckle. His foot had just dipped in a particularly aged part of the floor, and he paid for it. A minion, blade at the ready, took a triumphant swipe, and Jonah felt fire in his shoulder. The pain distracted him, and another blow rattled him further. With a swear, he realized his foot was still wedged. How could it have been so easy to lodge, yet so difficult to detach?

Don't get hit, he said in his mind, and a minion grunted in surprise when he hit a shield as he aimed for Jonah's face. Jonah used the moment of shock to wrench his foot free, and he shoved the angered spirit away long enough to retrieve the baton he'd dropped. He was ready to vanquish the minion that caused him so much trouble when limbs wrapped around him. He had had more than enough experience with this occurrence from his trainings, and he let instinct take over. He elongated his left leg to kick an oncoming minion in the gut. The charger's force into Jonah's outstretched leg sent both him and his unseen captor backward, which gave him a split-second idea. He put an extra push into their already unstable bodies, and they crashed into an ancient trophy case. Glass shattered, and tarnished cups, medallions, and trophies rained down. Jonah felt one of the batons fly from his hand, but he blindly snatched up a heavy silver cup and brought it across the minion's face. When the minion fell to the ground, Jonah was ready. He jabbed the baton he still had into the minion's back. With a yelp, the spirit exploded.

The silence sounded foreign to Jonah's ears after all the crashes, blasts, and shouts. He didn't know where the rest of the minions were, but at the moment, he didn't care. He picked up the silver cup he'd just dented with a scowl. First books had fallen on top of him. Now trophies and medallions. When his mind fell on Creyton and Trip, he shook his head. Was this someone's attempt at a sick joke? How many times were someone else's achievements going to threaten to crush him?

He didn't hear his friends either. If the commotion that had just occurred had not been enough to rouse some type of cries, then they must be under heavy lock and key.

Where were they?

Jonah saw that he was at a heavy door that was adorned with a peripherally angled illustration of a crow's face. Grabbing the knob, he turned to find it would not budge. He inspected it, frowning. After all that battling and patrolling, he was being hindered by a locked door? *Seriously?*

Jonah looked down, and his irritation increased tenfold. There was the detached claw of a crow a small distance away from the wreckage of the trophy case. It looked like the top of a key. Jonah picked it up and was not surprised or pleased to meet an obstruction when he put the small piece to the keyhole.

A minion must have tried to unlock the door when the fight broke out. And in the scuffle that had ensued, the jutting crow's key had been broken in the lock. It made Jonah so angry he could punch something. He wished Trip would accidentally open it, then he could meet him with a spiritually endowed sucker punch to the face—

"Wait," he muttered aloud. The vengeful idea also brought back a memory, one that had made Jonah gleeful when it occurred. He pushed the batons into his pocket and looked down at his right hand. He flexed the scratched, slightly bleeding fingers, and took a deep breath.

"Strength," he said. "I need extra strength."

The same vapory material that Jonah had willed to shield him earlier appeared from nothing and circled his hand. The cloudy glove formed effortlessly on his fingers. He gripped the doorknob with his vapor-gloved hand. It buckled in his grip. Pushing forward, the door moaned loudly and gave way. He smiled as the glove dissipated. Power and strength moves weren't his style, but they sure did have their advantages from time to time.

He was at the end of a long hallway. Jonah paused, unnerved at the familiarity of the setting. Then it dawned on him. He knew exactly where he was. Jonathan had been right; mental clarity was a wonderful thing. This was the darkened hallway that had been obscured in the dream he'd had when he'd heard Creyton's conversation. Jonah walked down the hallway, all senses on edge. Yeah, he was armed, but he was still uncertain about what he'd find. And he still needed to rescue his friends.

He reached the end. Creyton was seated in a high-backed chair that was tipped with a carved crow. His black eyes gleamed with an amusement that Jonah couldn't place.

"Jonah Rowe," he said, steepling his fingers. "So very interesting to see you, *alive.*"

The cold pleasure in Creyton's voice rankled Jonah. It was an anger that wasn't exclusive to Creyton. "I don't have time for your bullshit, Creyton," he snapped. "I'm going to stop you and save my friends. But first, I want to see your bit player. Your little spy. TRIP! I know you're here. I know everything you've done! Come on out!"

There was silence. Jonah heard no footsteps and sensed no movement. Creyton hadn't moved a muscle. His amusement and pensiveness seemed more pronounced, though, as if he enjoyed the rage. Jonah didn't care; it only increased his temper.

"TRIP!" he repeated to the room at large, not realizing that the three bulbs hanging from the ceiling had dimmed. "Come out now, you stupid bastard!"

"What?" grumbled Trip.

Jonah turned in the direction of the hated voice, and sure enough, Trip was there. But something was wrong. Trip didn't look triumphant or gleeful. Now that his face was somewhat visible in the dim light, Jonah noticed that he was a mess. His right eye was badly swollen, his lip busted, and his nose was broken. His shirt was ripped, revealing a freshly scarred torso. The second and third fingers on his left hand stuck out oddly, and it seemed that standing upright caused him pain.

Simply put, he didn't look like a spy who had experienced a job well done.

"What—?" began Jonah, then a muffled thud shuddered Trip's body, and he fell to the floor. Jonah's eyes bulged, his mouth open in horror. Behind Trip's limp form was someone he hadn't expected to see. The room must have lost oxygen because he was no longer able to breathe.

It was Marla.

20: Hell Hath no Fury

Jonah gaped at her. Finally, Creyton laughed.

"But—" Jonah sputtered once he found his voice again. "But, but—"

Marla fixed a contemptuous gaze on him. "You will need to add a noun and a verb to that to constitute a sentence, Jonah," she chided. "One would have assumed you knew that, calling yourself a writer and all."

The insult didn't even compute. Jonah's higher brain functioning was jammed. "Marla ... it can't have been you—"

"Why?" she said. "Because I'm a woman?" Suddenly, tears brightened her eyes. "Because I'm a sad, deprived, wistful spiritess?"

She smiled again, tears fading as if on command.

"But T-Trip," Jonah stammered, "Trip was acting so funny—"

"Ah, well," said Marla, as though she conceded the point. She stepped over Trip's body, deliberately pausing on his already damaged fingers. "That's his specialty, I'm afraid. Trip is a funny man."

"But I heard his voice," said Jonah. "In that dream!"

"Oh, you mean this?" said Marla, but her voice was different. It was distorted, like he'd heard in the dream. "I'm a spiritess, boy. Hasn't Jonathan taught you that spirits aren't three-dimensionally bound? I can do that and more. I knew you might be listening. Ethereal humans sometimes have the ability to traverse in dreams. I certainly couldn't allow you to hear me discussing plans with my master, could I?"

But Jonah still couldn't grasp the reality that was staring him in the face. How could this be? How could Marla have been the spy? Hadn't she appeared to him when his true nature was kick started? Hadn't she cried for help countless times? Wasn't that why the other Eleventh Percenters who'd been killed—

"Oh my God," said Jonah, struggling to breathe. "The Elevenths that were killed. You weren't asking for their help. You were tracking them down for Creyton, like some kind of spiritual flare—"

Marla cackled. "So you're not entirely stupid," she said. "Yes, they were killed because I tracked them. I had conjured the most pathetic story while I pleaded for their aid. 'Please help me. I've been on this plane too long.' The minute they felt pity for me, they were done."

Jonah could see those false tears again. The spiritess had truly played her part well. But it still didn't make sense.

"That day," he ventured, "the one when Jonathan kick started my aura, you showed up—"

"To alert Creyton to your presence," supplied Marla. "But because of Jonathan and that irksome feline, you survived the first attempt on your physical life at your apartment. A magnificent display of beginner's luck, I grant you, but luck nonetheless."

Marla's features no longer looked melancholy and serene. She had the blazing, calculating expression of a murderous enchantress. Jonah still couldn't believe it.

"That night at the bakery?" he asked.

"That was your own fault, fool," spat Creyton, breaking his silence at last. "Though I must admit that the linkage was most beneficial. Jonathan drained himself shielding you from me. Then you wallowed in bad memories and undid all of his work. It would have been amusing if it hadn't been so pathetic. I thank you for your doubts, fears, and worries. They are living things, you know. Living power. So empowering, in fact, that they allow me to grant my minions tangibility and all the things that go along with that."

Jonah heard familiar laughter, and turned to see Howard, Walt, and several other minions materialize. Creyton waved a hand, and their shadowy figures instantly filled in, like an illustration in a child's coloring book. When they all became solid, Jonah could see their weapons had solidified as well. Now he was surrounded by knives, ice picks, daggers, and in the case of Howard and Walt, crowbars. Jonah took in these new threats, and then his eyes fell on Marla. The minions being solid again had stirred a memory.

"That morning at the estate when I summoned you," he said in a voice obstructed with anger, "you sat down in the gazebo and the seat made noise. It creaked because you were tangible. You had weight. Creyton was the one that gave you that."

Marla applauded. "Figured it out at last!" she exclaimed. "Truth be told, Jonah, I'm surprised you didn't figure out it was me that day."

"Yeah?" snapped Jonah. "Why?"

Marla rolled her eyes. "You may recall that I said I had been stuck on this plane too long. I mistakenly told you that I had been stuck since I passed into Spirit, which was decades ago. But our master only blocked the path within the past several months. I made an error, and you *still* didn't put it together."

Jonah realized he was outnumbered. He realized what type of situation this was. But he still bristled with anger. They had all been betrayed by this spiritess bitch.

"So that whole thing was just some bullshit story—"

"Not true," said Marla, the laughter fading from her face. Like the other minions, she had a weapon. It was a sliver blade, small and unassuming, but wickedly sharp, just like her. "What I told you was true. My master did indeed kill my husband."

"She asked me to," chimed in Creyton before Jonah could ask the question. "Dear Marla has always been a valued servant. Women make the best infiltrators."

Jonah was no idiot. There was some meaning in what Creyton said. But he found that he had no desire to even entertain the notion. "Your husband wasn't the villain in your marriage," he said. "*You* were. You evil skank—"

Creyton approached Jonah so quickly that he may as well have disappeared and then reappeared in front of him. "Evil," he snarled. "Such an infantile notion. Jonathan didn't, and *still* doesn't, understand. My former associates never understood. That is why they had to be disposed of all those years ago. Such warped views, such ivory tower sentiments. Good and evil are moot, Rowe. What is looked upon as 'good' is merely adherence to antiquated morals that were thrust upon the meek by so-called 'qualified' individuals. Only the inadequate speak of evil. Evil is the label slapped upon those who embrace the absence of limits and have the wherewithal to take their rightful places above the unworthy."

Jonah took a step back. "Where does Trip fit into all of this?" he asked. "He has to have been on your side. He hasn't acted like an innocent man would at all."

Marla sneered at the crumpled heap behind her. "Titus has a remarkable presence of mind," she said grudgingly. "He is a musician, but you already knew that. Like all of you, he has certain talents. He has a gift with sound waves. He began suspecting me when he started to notice sound anomalies all over the estate grounds. He was hearing my distortion when I communicated with crows but didn't know it at first. When the Eleventh Percenter Abel Ford was murdered, he began putting two and two together, but he couldn't catch me because I played my part so impeccably. He confided, foolishly, in Rebecca Cayce, Lillian Darby, and three other allies he'd gained. But our master's Mindscopes and my tracking of them saw to it that they didn't tell another soul. After that, he withdrew from you all and tried to catch me by alternate means."

Jonah blinked slowly. "Trip wanted to keep us out of the loop to protect us?"

"Of course, Rowe," said Creyton. "Why do you think he was so angry when you spilled your guts about what you'd learned? When you dwell on things, it only makes you more vulnerable to Mindscopes, as you should have learned that night at the bakery."

Jonah felt those lingering feelings of self-deprecation again. Damn, had he messed up. Had Trip been right about him, after all? Was he truly a liability and prone to fatal mistakes? Wait.

"Trip tried to throw me off," he blurted out. "But someone caught him in the act with the pictures—"

"I was wrong," said Marla, frowning. "You *are* entirely stupid. I sent those pictures to you, Rowe."

"What? That was you?"

"Of course it was me," said Marla, shaking her head at Jonah. "Your hatred of Trip caused helpful misdirection from me, so I nursed it along."

"But why did he take them, then?" asked Jonah.

"Because it was the only way he could track who my spy was without making you all vulnerable," said Creyton. "He had been photographing the other Eleventh Percenters to see who would show up in the pictures in attempt to make a connection. That's how he finally figured out it was Marla."

Marla reached into her coat and tossed a stack of pictures at Jonah's feet. He looked down and sure enough, she was in every one of them. With a jolt, Jonah remembered when he'd noticed that there had been missing pictures from the folders. Here they were. It was Marla that had been keeping Creyton informed of their every activity. She had seen to it that Creyton was a step ahead the whole time. She had stolen Trip's pictures, removed the ones that incriminated her, and sent the remaining ones to Jonah with a little note attached. Her actions had not only falsely confirmed Jonah's suspicions but made Trip look beyond guilty.

A lurking doubt in his mind reared itself. "I saw Trip accost you in the woods."

"No, you didn't," said Marla, sounding bored. "You saw him attempting to bully me since I was in Jonathan's domain. Quite laughable."

Jonah felt like sandbags were dumped on him. "The automatic writing. The answer that I sought in the north woods. It wasn't Trip; it was you."

Howard chuckled, as if Jonah was the most stupid person on earth. Jonah ignored him.

"Why did Trip leave the estate, then?"

"Rowe, you are proving the reason right now," said Creyton. "After the incident you witnessed in the woods, he attempted to vanquish Marla and curtail us before your nosing around muddied the waters any further. As though he could stand a chance against me. He will take his place, along with your other little friends, as vessels."

Jonah blinked. "Vessels?"

"That's right," answered Creyton. "Did you think I took your friends to kill them?"

"Well, based on past events—" began Jonah, but Creyton interrupted him.

"The others only died because they served no further purpose," he said.

Jonah frowned. Did Creyton just say the other Eleventh Percenters *died*? Wouldn't he, of all people, know better?

Creyton was still speaking. "Look for yourself," he said, waving a hand in mock welcome, but Jonah noticed that it was a beckon to someone behind him. A minion grabbed Jonah's left arm and pinned it behind him. He also felt the cold tip of a blade at the back of his neck. Walt moved forward and pointed the slightly blunted tip of his crowbar at Jonah's face. The rear captor pushed Jonah forward. With metal at his throat and back, coupled with the fact that his batons were uselessly placed in his pocket, he had no choice but to comply.

"Unwise to be a hero, Blue Boy," whispered Walt.

Despite the situation, Jonah could feel nothing but hate. "I'm going to lodge that in your throat, Casper," he snapped.

During this brief exchange, Creyton had joined Marla next to Trip, who was still motionless on the ground.

"Any volunteers?" he said, a threatening tone in his voice.

Jonah frowned, confused, but one of the minions to his right stepped forward.

"Here, Master," he said.

Jonah grimaced. These wayward spirits were utterly petrified of Creyton and would certainly be vanquished if they disobeyed even his simplest order. For all their power and "lack of limits," they were just glorified slaves.

Creyton extended a hand to the minion, and his solidity faded. Once again, his consistency was something like a milky shadow. Jonah noticed that something about Creyton had changed; there was more of a glow to his frame and more of a gleam in his eye. Weird. Creyton pointed a finger at Trip and ripples of shadow left his form. Trip shuddered and curled up like he was cold. With his hand, Creyton guided the shadow to the minion, who was once again three-dimensional.

"You see?" said Creyton. "Immediately killing your friends would've helped nothing. They will live and serve as outlets for tangibility and power."

"And what long term effect will that have on them?" asked Jonah, glancing at Trip, who didn't look very well at all.

"They'll die, of course," said Creyton indifferently. "The frequent drains of essence will render their hearts useless after a while."

Jonah closed his eyes. So *that* was what Creyton meant when he said the other Eleventh Percenters were killed because they no longer served a purpose. They were taken before they could alert others of what was going on, drained of most of their essence, and then killed when they couldn't sustain the torture any longer. Creyton took advantage of this and used the essence of their tormented spirits to block the path to the Other Side.

It was the same fate that awaited his friends...

"Wait," said Jonah. "What will happen then? Won't their passing into Spirit put you back to square one?"

"Of course not," said Creyton, his eyes gleaming red. "You meddlesome fools infest this world. When the need arises for reinforcements, we'll do what worked best," he snapped his fingers, and Marla's eyes began tearing up again, "and take Marla's show on the road."

Jonah took a deep breath. Marla's façade infuriated him something fierce. "And what's your plan for me?" he asked in a neutral voice. "You want me to be a vessel too?"

Creyton looked at Jonah with such hatred that even Marla shrank away. "No, Jonah Rowe, Blue Aura and Savior," he whispered. "I am finished with you. I have neither the time nor the patience for a self-righteous accident whom Jonathan has force-fed delusions of grandeur. I gave you the chance to walk away, but you didn't heed my warning. Now you will die. As you heard when you spied on us through your dream, you are not a big enough blip on the radar."

Jonah started to respond but froze. Creyton had reminded him of the "blip on the radar" comment. But something else from that dream stirred in his memory too. This was a very difficult situation, though. They were planning to kill *him* immediately. His murder couldn't happen; he had to rescue his friends from unending torture and drainage until they were useless shells. And then there was Trip. They had all been played like absolute fools, and Trip was innocent. Since that was the case, Jonah had to save *him* as well.

An idea began to stir in his mind. It wasn't the greatest option, but it was an option.

"Master, I volunteer myself," said Marla, bringing her knife to the ready. "I'll kill this bumbling idiot."

"Not likely," said Walt, turning to her. "Two times, this boy has made a fool of me. That last time, I was up to my neck in muck. *I* will kill him."

That's right, thought Jonah as he concentrated. *That's right. Keep arguing for just a little while longer.*

"Silence," said Creyton. His tone was quiet but resonated with authority. "Marla, be a dear and leave the boy alive enough for Walt to finish him?"

Though he said it like a suggestion, there was no doubt that it was understood to be an order.

Marla smiled. "Yes, Master."

Walt didn't look too pleased but didn't question Creyton. With a nod, he lowered his crowbar.

"Mallon, drop your blade," said Creyton. The rear captor released Jonah's arm, and Jonah felt the edge leave his back. Marla moved forward with her knife aloft. Jonah steeled himself for two seconds. It was now or never.

He loosed the most vicious bellow he could and willed his own ethe-reality to come to fruition. The flimsy light bulbs exploded and threw the place into total darkness. As an added bonus, the darkness was particularly dense because the study had no windows. Jonah snatched his batons from his pocket and barely waited for his endowment to illuminate them. He whirled them around in desperation, and luck was on his side once more because he heard two wails that were followed by shattering explosions that dazzled in the dark. He ignored the shouts and exclamations and moved toward Trip; he had fixed his position in his mind before destroying the lights. He paused only to tip over two bookcases, whose locations he'd fixed in his mind as well. It was time for heavy books to injure someone else for a change. The crashing made the very floor shudder, but it was mere background noise compared to the minions, Marla's, and Creyton's howls of rage and confusion. Jonah knew he had to move fast. The bookcases were a helpful distraction, but he knew it would only be a matter of time before the blue glow of his batons would lead them to his position.

He put a baton away and groped for Trip, whom he heard groan with pain. Jonah must have grazed an injured limb. Oh well.

"Get up, you bastard," he grunted. "We need to find the others."

Jonah heaved, and Trip was on his feet. Using the bluish light of his baton, they hurried down a hallway. Jonah made sure to put at least a floor between them and Creyton before he burst into an empty room to regroup. Jonah took a moment to rest his back (Trip was heavier than he looked) and wondered about his next move. Trip favored his ribs.

"You're not dead yet?" he whispered. "That's ... surprising."

"Yeah, well, death isn't real, is it?" Jonah fired back.

"Would have been real enough if that knife had gone through your windpipe," mumbled Trip. "Got a new plan, fearless leader?"

Jonah couldn't believe the nerve of this guy. If he were an evil person, he would have left him to be trampled and drained. He knew that if someone had just saved *him,* he'd have gratitude. But with Trip, something like gratitude was clearly too much to ask. Before Jonah could inform Trip of this fact, however, a young girl's voice said, "We can help you if you help us, sirs!"

They wheeled around to see a teenage spiritess with innocent eyes and a long brown plait. Jonah could see the transparent shackles on her wrists, but her face showed a determination that, at the present time, outweighed her fear of Creyton.

"You must save us!" she told them in a shrill voice. "You have been endowed!"

Jonah felt nothing as he was already endowed, but Trip's weaknesses seemed to fade somewhat. The effects of whatever they had put him through hadn't vanished, but he was no longer unsteady or groggy.

"I suppose I ought to thank you, young spiritess," Trip grunted. "The people that Creyton's got hostage. Where are they?"

The girl's face fell. "Cannot help with that, sirs," she said, showing the ethereal chains at her wrists. "What I can communicate to you is limited. Please just help us. Save us from him."

Jonah and Trip looked at each other. They were outnumbered and faced minions that wanted to kill them at every pass. But in that moment, they both knew that if they attempted to work together, they would kill each other before the minions even reached them.

"I'm going to find them," said Jonah shortly. "You—I don't know, just do *something.*"

Trip's eyes flashed, but Jonah backed out of the room before any more words were spoken. An inattentive minion passed the door, which gave Jonah a golden opportunity to vanquish him. He was so shocked by Jonah's presence that he didn't even lift his hands in defense. Jonah hopped the last four steps on the staircase to the first floor and ran into a dining room. There was a table that was magnificent at one time but was now smashed and so thick with dust that Jonah's lungs would protest if he inhaled anywhere around it. But what made Jonah hesitate wasn't the dust that coated the long-forgotten ruin of a table but the footprint on it. Why would there be footprints on the table? But they were there, plain as day, and recently made. Jonah lifted his gleaming baton to the print and saw that it had been made by a cross trainer. A cross trainer that Jonah had no trouble recognizing as he'd seen it coming to his face more times than he cared to count.

He followed the direction of the footprint and raced down more stairs into a wine cellar. He hopped the last couple of steps again, which was a good thing, as the last two steps looked like they were ready to crumble the minute they took the wrong person's weight. There were rows and rows of ancient, dusty vintages. If Jonah hadn't been preoccupied with this rescue, he'd have snagged some to sell.

"Reena!" he called.

"Jonah?" called the familiar voice in surprise. "I'm over here!"

Relief swept through him. He found her shackled with chains similar to the ones that bound the spirits, though these were made of steel and dug into her flesh. He extracted a hairpin from Reena's hair and began picking the locks.

"You know how to pick locks?" she asked, incredulous. "Damn—I have newfound respect for you."

"Save your admiration," muttered Jonah. "I only know how to do it because I kept losing the key to my foot locker I had when I was a kid. Had to have a plan B, just in case."

"Still impressive, though," said Reena. "I'm so glad to see you physically alive, Jonah. I thought that bookshelf was the end of you."

A minute later, her hands were free, and she was rubbing her bruised wrists. "You were wrong about Trip, you know," she told him.

"No, I wasn't," replied Jonah. "He's still scum. He just wasn't the scum that spied on us. Are the others down here too?"

"No," said Reena, who looked as concerned as Jonah. "They knew better than to lock us up together. Don't know where they are. How did you even find *me?*"

"Print of your sneaker," said Jonah. "You cut a path through the dust on the table up there."

"Oh, that." Reena managed a half-smile. "I wasn't unconscious when they brought me in, and I made an attempt to break away—leapt on the table—"

Jonah shook his head. "You jumped on a table that was three days older than God?" he asked.

"In my defense, Jonah, it was a tense moment," said Reena, eyes narrowed. "So what's the current situation?"

"Got a reprieve, now Trip and I are looking to round everyone up," said Jonah. He was about to ask her for ideas but paused when he noticed Reena staring at him in amazement.

"Jonah, your essence is wild," she commented. "Like 'critical mass' wild. What's your endowment? Only thing this chaotic..." Her eyes widened in realization.

"No time to explain," said Jonah hastily. "We've got to find everyone else!"

They ascended the stairs, and Jonah silently prayed that they'd meet no one. He didn't like Reena's chances against some sharp edged weapon while she had no endowment. They crossed to another set of stairs that led to a half dozen doors, two of which were locked and another two that had been smashed in. Reena made to continue but fell forward, shrieking in surprise. Thinking of minions, Jonah turned to see that Reena's foot had caught in the old groove in the floor next to the smashed remains of the trophy case.

"Sorry, Reena, I should have warned you," said Jonah, helping her up. "I've been here already—"

"Hey!" roared another familiar voice. "Who's out there?"

Puzzled, Jonah and Reena followed the call to one of the ruined doors. In a shadowy corner, hands and feet bound to a chair, was Terrence.

"Terrence!" said Jonah. While he was very worried about all of his friends, he was grateful to have found the two that were his closest friends out of the whole group first. It seemed to center him and clear his head. "I have been on this hall before! Why didn't you call then? That door wouldn't have kept me out."

"That's why they put me in this corner," grumbled Terrence. "I could see out, but no one could see me without a light. I was also gagged."

Reena had untied his hands and he indicated a length of black cloth that hung at his neck like an ascot.

"I heard you fighting them earlier, but I couldn't make enough noise with this thing around my mouth," he said. "Took twenty minutes of maneuvering the bottom half of my face in order to work that stupid cloth down."

"Glad you were able to do it, man," said Jonah as he helped Terrence to his feet. "Trip's around here somewhere. Hopefully, he found Malcolm, Liz, and Bobby."

"Where is Creyton?" asked Terrence.

"No idea, but Marla is with him," said Jonah. Oh, what he wouldn't give to jab his baton between Marla's eyes and watch her shatter! "She was the spy, not Trip."

"Yeah, I know," said Terrence as they headed out of the room. "She was gloating about it earlier. But they thought you had gotten killed. We *all* thought that. How are you physically alive? I saw that bookshelf crush you."

"Got lucky," replied Jonah. "The TV kind of jammed up against the shelf and lodged over me. My number isn't up just yet."

They retraced their steps back to the dining room and went into the kitchen where they found a door near a long-retired wood stove. Unlike the dining area, there were no articles of furniture in the kitchen, save the stove.

"This doesn't make any sense," said Jonah, frowning.

"Yes, it does," said Reena. "Spirits don't have to eat, you know."

"Oh, right," he said. "Think they might be—?"

The door they'd just come through was knocked off his hinges, and Howard, Walt, and two other minions swooped in. In unison, Jonah, Terrence, and Reena ran for the opposite door. They narrowly avoided blades that whipped past their heads. The stairs beyond led down to another basement setting that appeared to be a convergence point from another set of stairs. Jonah, Terrence, and Reena made it to the bottom of their stairs and braced themselves to fight. Jonah hoped no further harm would befall his friends. They didn't have endowments. Strangely, Howard, Walt, and the others hadn't given chase. Reena frowned.

"Why—?"

The door at the top of the adjacent set of stairs burst open, and Jonah wheeled around to see Trip, Malcolm, Liz, and Bobby run down. In no time, the group was crowded at the downstairs convergence point. Jonah was relieved to see them all whole, even Trip, but his words of greeting died in his throat when he saw *their* pursuers close in at the opposite door.

There were three minions, faces full of triumph, with Marla at the forefront. Jonah guessed the trick a split second after Reena, who uncharacteristically swore so loudly that they all started.

Marla's lip curled. "You young people and your profane language," she scolded. "Pity you won't have the chance to learn how to better articulate your thoughts."

She raised a lit kerosene lamp. Jonah looked up at Walt, who had just taken a similarly lit lamp from Howard's hands.

"I'm sorry for not bludgeoning you beyond recognition with the crowbar, Rowe," he said, "but given how you escaped Marla, this will do just fine. What's that old saying, Marla?"

The spiritess smiled widely. "Hell hath no fury."

She tossed her lamp in a graceful arc, while Walt pitched his own in a zealous hurl. Jonah watched in horror as Marla's lamp crashed to their left, Walt's to their right. Once free, the flames hungrily ignited everything and quickly illuminated the dark basement. The wood, papers, and cloths proved to be a most efficient kindling as flames encircled them. Within minutes, Jonah stood in the center of a hellish ring, and six other people would burn along with him.

21

Shock Treatment

The inferno grew at an astronomical rate. All around them, objects that caught fire served to bridge the flames.

So far, Jonah successfully held panic at bay, but that wouldn't last. His and Trip's endowments were useless against fire; they were as helpless as their endowment-less friends, who stared at the blaze in terror.

"What do we do, Jonah?" yelled Bobby.

"*Why are you asking me?*" Jonah shot back, but not in frustration or anger. As the fire spread at a speed that made it appear sentient, the mere notion that they looked at him as the leader made him feel, if possible, even worse.

In the midst of his mental tailspin, an idea suddenly reared itself. He had no clue where it came from, and it was a long shot, but it should work. He'd already created a link...

Giving the matter as much attention as possible, he thought, *Spirit! I'm summoning you! I know you're shackled, but we need your help now!*

Immediately, the portly, brooding spirit that he'd beckoned the day he was attacked by Walt appeared before them, his spectral form barely discernible due to the flames.

"Why have you summoned me, Blue Aura?" he asked in an anxious tone. "He'll punish me, don't you understand that?"

Jonah wiped his face impatiently; sweat stung his eyes and obscured his vision. But he glared at the spirit, tired of his whining. "Creyton won't be able to punish you anymore if you help us, spirit," he said. "A young spiritess endowed one of us, and she was shackled just like you. Be brave, and we'll stop him for you and all the imprisoned spirits."

The spirit hesitated, looking at Jonah sadly. "I cannot help you, Eleventh Percenter. You are already carrying a heavy endowment."

"It's not for me!" said Jonah impatiently. "Endow *her!*"

He pointed at Reena, who looked at him in confusion. Seconds later, though, she caught on.

"Will you help us, spirit?" she asked. "Will you endow me so that I may preserve our physical lives?"

The spirit smiled, and Jonah saw that he looked quite peaceful when he wasn't marring his features with worry lines. "I would be honored, beautiful one. You have been endowed."

Jonah saw Reena scowl. Clearly, she was not very keen on the label of "Beautiful One." But she closed her eyes tightly as the endowment strengthened inside and out.

"You guys had better huddle," she warned.

Jonah moved to a petrified Liz and flung an arm over her shoulder. Bobby did the same. They were quickly joined by Malcolm and Terrence. Trip knelt and hugged his shoulders, but did not join their group.

Reena stood straight, swung her hands out as far as they would go, and joined them in a sharp, crisp clap. The environment went to another extreme as the sweltering heat froze. The sweat on Jonah's body felt like ice water. He attempted to give Reena words of gratitude, but his teeth chattered too much to allow it, so he compromised by clapping her on the back. There were no traces of the flames whatsoever. The acrid smell of smoke lingered, but the fire had no home in this sub-arctic area. Reena's cold spot trick had snuffed it out.

"Man," shivered Terrence. "I've never been so happy to be frozen in my life."

"You saved us, Reena," Jonah finally managed. "But please put it back to normal. Any lower, and we'll have to resort to hunting for stray embers."

Smirking, Reena clapped once more, and the temperature elevated. She swayed, and Terrence moved to her side for support.

"What's up?" asked Jonah.

"Nothing," murmured Reena. "The shackled spirit took away his endowment. He must have known Creyton would get to him quickly. He took a big risk answering your summons, Jonah. But I'm glad he did."

Reena's words made Jonah angry. The spirit had helped them even though he knew he would pay dearly for doing it. He thought of the young spiritess's brave but frightened face as she endowed Trip. He even thought of the minion who was all but coerced to abdicate his tangibility because he knew the consequences of not doing so would be dire. For all his power, for all his pomp and circumstance, Creyton was just a bully. And Jonah was done tolerating bullies.

"Reena, t-thank y—" whispered Liz, but then the poor girl fainted. Bobby caught her just in time.

Seeing Liz's limp form whetted Jonah's anger that much more. The girl was barely eighteen, concerned with her bio labs and finals. Not that Jonah was that much older than her, but Liz did not need to be threatened and nearly incinerated.

"You guys get out of here," he told his friends. "The fire didn't burn too long. The stairs should still take your weight."

"And what will *you* be doing?" asked Terrence.

"Going to find Marla and Creyton," Jonah said shortly.

"Say what?" said Malcolm; it was the first time he'd spoken tonight. "They've got knives, crowbars, and dark ethereality, and you are just going to go face-first into it? Are you crazy, Jonah? Do you even have a weapon of your own?"

"Yeah, I do," said Jonah, and he pulled the batons from his belt and showed everyone. He had to admit it was cool to see the blue essence blaze across them.

Malcolm stared at him in shock. So did everyone else. Bobby nearly dropped Liz. Jonah didn't understand. They already knew about all these things, didn't they?

"Y-you have those batons," whispered Terrence, awestruck.

"Yeah," said Jonah, "so?"

"How—how did you get them to work?" demanded Reena.

"I touched them," said Jonah, "but get yourselves to safety. And Bobby," he gave a concerned look to Liz, "get her out of this basement."

He turned his back on his friends and Trip and went upstairs. He made it ten feet when he realized the minions had regrouped.

After a quick glance, he saw that the room he'd entered was the family room and was full of maybe ten or twelve minions. Just when Jonah was about to question his reckless action, a cloud moved somewhere outside the window and illuminated the yard.

Creyton and Marla were out there. Jonah's apprehension faded and was replaced by irritation. Now the bully hid behind his lackeys.

"Fine," he said aloud.

Jonah plunged into the minions and instantly vanquished two of them. The others closed in, but it didn't matter. He jabbed a minion in the heart with the baton. He ducked low and allowed a charging minion's momentum to carry him over his back in a back-body drop fashion. Then he jabbed the baton behind him. He knew he would hit his mark before he saw the spirit shatter. Maybe the minions were still disorganized. Maybe they didn't expect the fight to be so intense. Maybe Jonah was lucky. He honestly didn't know.

What he did know was that when he stood to catch his breath, only Howard and Walt were left. They stared at each other and then looked at him. They realized that their dream to bludgeon him might come to fruition after all. But Jonah wasn't going to indulge them. He wasn't even focused on the two fools as they approached. He didn't pause to consider what he was about to do, he just ran between them and tossed the batons, one at Howard, the other at Walt. He timed it perfectly, and they both got hit full in the face. *Back*, he thought in his mind, *come back...*

His endowment responded, and what looked like blue current whipped from his palms and wrapped around the handles of the batons, and they were back in his hands even before the final note of Walt's anguished wail pierced the air.

As much as Jonah would have liked to pause and savor Howard's and Walt's vanquishing, he didn't. Once again, he burst through a window and remembered to take the impact with his knees bent. He was thankful for the open air, where the smoke and moldy odors in his nostrils were chased out by the scents of grass, wildflowers, and wood.

It was only after the fog thinned that he realized that he was standing in a graveyard. Despite all that had happened, Jonah was surprised. Wasn't a graveyard behind a haunted house a little overkill?

It was clear that Creyton was angry about the minions' failure, but Jonah swore that he, too, registered surprise when he saw the batons. Marla was terrified but tried to hide it by sneering.

"Well," she said in a voice that betrayed no one, "I will get to kill you after all!"

"Whatever you say, Marla," said Jonah. He noticed that the spiritess trembled when she saw him, and despite the situation, he fought the urge to laugh. Through all her evil, all her treachery, she was pathetic. She was a joke.

The moment Marla swung her dagger, Jonah realized something. Marla might have been dangerous as a spy, very manipulative and cunning. But her fighting skills were nonexistent. Jonah wasn't some inveterate pro, but he was better than *her.*

After several uneventful minutes of absurdity, Marla lunged awkwardly. Jonah took advantage of her mistake, clutched her wrist, and flung her to the ground. Creyton stood motionless and indifferent as Jonah pinned her arm behind her and lowered his knee to her lumbar area.

Marla's eyes bulged in terror. "No! No, please … Master!"

Jonah lowered his baton to the back of her neck. "You aren't betraying anyone else, bitch," he told her. "Your 'show' is done."

He directed his anger as the blue baton connected with her form. Her cry was even more high-pitched than Walt's as she disappeared in a cloud of shards.

Creyton hadn't lifted a finger in protest while this happened, which Jonah found odd. If she had been so loyal for so long, why would he let her be vanquished?

He lifted his head but didn't see Creyton. His puzzlement over this lasted for only a moment.

A vicious strike propelled him forward with such force that when he collided with a headstone, his impact cracked it. Remarkably, he was still conscious, but in a very pained daze. He rolled to see Creyton standing over him, his crow-tipped staff now encased in a sinister dark vapor.

"Sending minions to do a Reaper's job," he rasped. "Whatever was I thinking?"

Jonah inwardly begged his head to clear when the staff came toward his midsection, connecting with such force that Jonah's ribcage would have been smashed had it not been for his endowment. As it was, he knew that some of the ribs were cracked. They felt like pinpricks underneath his flesh. Creyton swung again, but Jonah managed to raise a baton and deflect it. The maneuver aggravated his injured ribs but was forceful enough to make Creyton stagger. Jonah had just enough time to get back to his feet, but Creyton was on him again with the swiftness of a snake. He swung his staff again, and though Jonah got a baton in the way of it, the force still made him stagger to his right. He attempted to buy himself some time with a swing at Creyton, but Creyton dodged it easily. Jonah straightened once more, prepared for another swing, but Creyton tricked him. When Jonah focused to his right, Creyton opened his right palm and an invisible force impacted Jonah's exposed left side. The blast sent him into another headstone. Jonah was dazed and hurt, but he was able to register a crackling sound from Creyton's staff. The crackle sounded similar to the one Jonah heard before the front of the estate had been destroyed. Allowing his instincts to take over once more, he flung himself clear and missed a concussive blast that gouged a crater into the hard-packed dirt.

"You're in over your head, boy," said Creyton. "Jonathan has taught you very little. That much is obvious. I can see by your fighting that he still allows his unofficial wards to teach amongst themselves. Unfortunate."

Creyton grabbed Jonah by the throat. Before his stranglehold tightened, however, Jonah lodged his foot in Creyton's midsection and kicked out. The counter was meaningless; Creyton had returned to him before Jonah could regain his bearings. He achieved perfect purchase at Jonah's jugular this time and punched him across the face twice. After the second punch, Jonah had the taste of copper in his mouth again, and lights danced across his eyes. Creyton drew back for a third, which would have surely knocked Jonah unconscious, but Jonah made a reflexive gesture, and Creyton's pale fist connected with a baton's blue current.

Creyton roared in agony, and—was it Jonah's imagination?—something about his form changed. What was that about?

The shock had really disoriented Creyton, but Jonah couldn't take advantage. The facial strikes felt as though they had scrambled his brains. Creyton seethed as he retrieved his staff, but Jonah noticed it just in time. How did he know what Creyton was about to do? But he knew, beyond a shadow of a doubt, that Creyton had planned to pivot his staff and freeze time. Jonah knew that he'd never reach Creyton in time; he'd be in suspended animation before he'd taken two steps. Without thinking, he hurled a baton. It hit Creyton's wrist and clattered to the ground.

When the second current met Creyton's flesh, he twitched violently, and Jonah realized what had happened. One of the endowments Creyton had stolen left him. Jonah already knew that Creyton was powerful because of spiritual endowments he'd usurped. He had kept himself at full strength through this practice and had even delegated some of it to his minions. Now Jonah realized that Creyton's deed had taxed his power. It was too much. The reason he staggered, his "minor irritant" in Jonah's dream, was now clear. Creyton had never released any of those endowments, and it put a strain on him. That was why he'd needed the vessels. With his plan foiled, however, Jonah's batons forcibly extracted the endowments from him.

It appeared to Jonah that Creyton was aware of his realization because he lunged for his staff again.

"No!" shouted Jonah, throwing his other baton at Creyton. Once again, it hit, and Creyton's form twitched again. It was as if the weaker he got, the less pronounced his sinister glow was. That could only mean one thing. Jonah willed the batons back in his hands and raced at Creyton. No holding back now.

He struck Creyton, hard, in the midsection. When he doubled over, Jonah whacked him hard across the face, careful to make the essence's current connect with Creyton's skin. He struck Creyton again and again, focused only on his goal. He inflicted one final strike before he had to double over himself from the injury to his ribs.

Despite the need to back off, he had achieved his goal. For the first time in who knew how long, Creyton had no spiritual endowments. Jonah hoped those released spirits and spiritesses, wherever they were, could finally have some peace.

A sudden movement brought Jonah's attention back to Creyton. He had collapsed to his knees in the fog. Though rage was evident in his pale, harsh features, he was completely thunderstruck about what Jonah had done. "You're weak," he growled. "Insignificant. No threat at all."

Jonah walked toward Creyton, wondering how he was upright with the bad ribs. Then he remembered that the endowment increased everything. Even so, he knew that it was supplemental. The actions were his own. "I'm still standing," he said. "That counts for something."

Creyton rose to one knee but didn't stand. "You view yourself as better than me, is that right? You think a shade of righteousness makes you better?"

Jonah stared into the dark, lifeless eyes. How could a person be so evil? Jonathan was so different. What had happened with Creyton?

How did he stray so far? How could he be so focused on ambition, destruction, and decay?

"I'm not trying to be better than you, man," Jonah told him. "I'm simply not a destroyer or a deterrent."

"Destroyer?" demanded Creyton. "*Deterrent?!* What gives you the right to judge me, boy? Is ambition wrong? Is a desire to transcend limitations wrong? To be powerful, to cast aside the fetters that an ignorant populace have placed upon themselves? This is what gods deserve."

Jonah took another wary step toward Creyton, who hadn't risen. Why was he still on the ground? "You're not a god, Creyton," he muttered. "From what I've been told, you lost your conscience forever ago. Sure, people limit themselves. There is no denying that. But you never had the right to take it upon yourself to decide for them! You've been usurping spirits and hoarding endowments for yourself! You blocked the path with the essence of Eleventh Percenters you killed for power. You used spirit essence to keep you young. You drained Eleventh Percenters dry and then killed them, just for personal gain! Violating nature isn't ambitious."

Finally, Creyton stood. He had no endowments and was without allies. So why was Jonah still wary of him? Why did he still feel inclined to be cautious?

"You heroes are misinformed," said Creyton. "The archaic notion of good over evil, while refreshing, is a delusion. I did those spirits and spiritesses a favor."

Jonah pulled a face. Would Marla agree with that statement after Creyton just stood there and let Jonah vanquish her?

"They were thankful to have the path halted because they feared the beyond," Creyton continued. "There isn't a single person, alive or dead, that does not fear the Other Side. Think, Rowe. Take advantage of a golden opportunity, or embrace limitations under the guise of heroism? No sane person would choose the latter. No one would bend over a dollar to pick up a dime."

Jonah frowned again. Why did Creyton keep saying people were "dead?" Although he was confused by that, he still felt that Creyton had something planned. He just had to prepare himself. But how did you prepare yourself against the unknown?

"You're better off joining me, Rowe," said Creyton. "Allow me to aid you in harnessing your strengths. Spirits can be very chaotic, after all."

Jonah was distracted by the abrupt offer, but in that second, something in the air changed. Creyton glanced over Jonah's shoulder so quickly that Jonah almost didn't catch it. The hairs on his neck stood on end, and the temperature at his back dipped about ten degrees.

Reflexively, Jonah willed the fog near his feet to become tangible vapor. The milky white wisps flattened into a cushioned sheet, and he flung himself on it, resigned to the fact that his ribs wouldn't respond well to slamming on the ground like that.

Not a second too soon. Creyton had indeed planned something during his monologue. He'd manipulated the water vapor in the fog behind Jonah, using it to create sharp-edged projectiles. They flew toward Jonah's back when the prickle of danger forced him to make a split-second decision. Jonah jumped clear, which left the daggers' path wide open.

The daggers Creyton had just made impaled him all at once. He took a sharp intake of breath.

Jonah didn't know whether to feel pity or not. Creyton's own evil had just destroyed him. He looked down at the blood that ran down his torso in dark rivulets. He keeled over, and for a fraction of a second, Jonah thought that Creyton had flung a handful of blood against a headstone. That couldn't be. It simply flew that way when he dropped, that must have been it. Creyton finally seemed to register that his physical life neared its end. Anguish was etched on his face as his ragged breaths faded.

The monster was gone.

Seconds later, Creyton's corpse became hollow. A darkened mass rose from the pale heap, forming the indentation of a man. Then the mass attained definition, substance, and features, and Creyton's spirit appeared, standing at the feet of his remains.

Jonah's eyes widened. Creyton was an Eleventh Percenter, which meant that Jonah shouldn't be able to see his spirit. What was going on now?

"What—?" said Creyton, awestruck. "What is this?"

"Your number's up," said Jonah, still shocked about what he saw. "You've lost."

Creyton shook his head. "I do not accept this!" he shouted. "I am an Eleventh Percenter! I still have the ability to walk the earth. You aren't rid of me."

Jonah looked down at Creyton's body, now feeling the pity that was absent moments before. "I don't think that's how this is going to work."

"You know nothing, Rowe," said Creyton, his voice heavy with defiance. He tried very hard to keep his eyes away from the body that lay at his own feet. *His* body. "I will plague you for the rest of your days. Just like your beloved mentor, Jonathan, I will never leave. I will achieve tangibility and finish what we started here—"

"Do you not see what I see, Creyton?" said Jonah. "You aren't messing with anybody! Jonathan walks on Earthplane because he chose to become a Protector Guide and do some good. He respects the laws of nature and follows them. *You,* on the other hand, gave up that right when you abandoned your morals. It's time for you to piss off."

Enraged, Creyton moved forward, but Jonah had finally overcome most of his shock and was ready. He lifted his hand, as he'd done that very first night, and the fog engulfed Creyton's spirit in a spectral net. Creyton struggled to no avail. He looked Jonah square in the eyes, his face a mask of pure, undiluted loathing.

"You won't be rid of me, Jonah Rowe," he promised. "I'll find a way. You will rue this day, so help me."

"Whatever, man." Jonah shook his head. "Now, just fuck off."

The current from his baton came to rest in his other palm. He pitched the blue, crackling mass at Creyton, who was instantly overtaken. Jonah intensified the current and allowed it to become almost unstable, and Creyton's spirit burst like a disposed wineglass.

There was silence. The night was completely still. Jonah took a deep breath to help his heart regulate itself. A twig snapped behind him, and he turned to see Terrence, Reena, Bobby, Malcolm, and a recently roused Liz. All of his friends. And Trip.

Terrence stared at him in awe. "Now *that* was impressive!" he exclaimed.

Jonah opened his mouth to reply, but at that moment, the Mandy spirits' endowment left him. The fatigue that set in was so sudden and all-consuming, he collapsed much like Liz had earlier.

Jonah awoke to find the sun's reflection on his feet. It was the most pleasant-feeling part of his whole body. The rest of him was sore as hell.

A soft thump on the chair next to his bed prompted him to turn in that direction, and he was unsurprised to see Bast curled there like she owned the place. He *was* surprised, however, to see Jonathan standing by the windowsill.

"At last, he wakes," he said, relieved.

Jonah sat up and noticed that he wore a large comfortable T-shirt that covered, once again, one of Liz and Reena's snug wrappings around his ribs. "And at last, you're back," he grumbled.

"I deserved that," sighed Jonathan. "I truly did."

Jonah would come back to that, but there were other matters on his mind. "How is everyone? And what about the damage to the estate?"

"All is well," said Jonathan. "As for our home, that isn't a problem either. The repairs have already been made."

"They have?" said Jonah, stunned. "But—how long was I out?"

"Oh, three days," said Jonathan.

"Three—the repairs were made in *three days?* How did that happen so quickly?"

"This isn't an ordinary dwelling place, Jonah," said Jonathan. "And time doesn't exist where spirits are."

Jonah didn't know how to answer that, so he let it pass. "And I missed it all—I guess I, like you, can vanish most efficiently."

Jonathan looked at him, but there was no anger in his expression. "You must understand, Jonah, that interference from Protector Guides is forbidden. We can't tell you what to do or personally influence your decisions. I've chosen the capacity of Protector, mentor, and trainer. As such, I must allow pupils to navigate their own way, explore their own boundaries and strengths. This can be very frustrating, but when I see my pupils go forward and succeed..." he fixed a proud smile on Jonah, "that's the best part. By far."

"Did you really have to leave us completely in the dark?" asked Jonah.

Jonathan chuckled. "But I didn't, Jonah. I left you some seeds. Do you not recall our last talk?"

Jonah frowned. "Are you talking about the cryptic stuff about creation being great and placing our own meanings on things?"

"The very same," said Jonathan, nodding. "I didn't leave you totally in the dark, now did I?"

"Um, Jonathan—"

"When Creyton took your friends, you were at your wit's end," said Jonathan. "You felt lost and out of options, so you *created* a way to help them. From a formless void of doubt, you created a rescue. With an endowment from the Mandy spirits, no less."

"Yeah..." said Jonah, suddenly curious about something else. "Terrence told me that an Eleventh Percenter, Aaron Miles, attempted an endowment from the Mandy Spirits and paid for it with his physical life. How did *I* manage it? I was desperate, I know, but why did it work?"

Jonathan smiled again. "I was hoping you'd ask that. Has anyone informed you on the finer points of being a Blue Aura?"

Jonah raised an eyebrow. "Yeah, Reena. She told me a lot, but the main thing was about balance, or something."

"Precisely," said Jonathan. "You have powers that are still very raw to you. Inside and out. In this particular case, when the Mandy Spirits bombarded you with such an immense, chaotic essence, your powers balanced the endowment in your system. It may have taken a few moments, I'm sure, but it happened. That's how you survived it."

Jonah thought on that. It might not be as great as pyrokinetic power or superhuman strength, but it was useful in its own way. Seeing as how the balance saved his life, he couldn't help but be grateful.

"Also," continued Jonathan, "you knew what Terrence had told you, which built resistance and fear inside you. Yet you went thinking you could reason with them and withstand their powers. That was the other clue I gave you. You placed your own meaning on the situation instead of the meaning provided. And in so doing, you saved your friends."

Jonah said nothing. He wondered how often Jonathan would spout some farfetched philosophy that he would have to grin and bear when it turned out to be accurate.

"I must admit, Jonah," said Jonathan, "that I am surprised that we haven't reached the question that must be burning in your mind."

"I'm getting to it, don't worry," said Jonah. "Where was Trip all that time?"

Jonathan smiled, obviously pleased that they'd reached that. "Titus. He is especially gifted with sound. Quite the authority on the matter, once you get to know him."

Jonah scoffed, but Jonathan took no notice.

"Titus began sensing and recording disturbances in sound all around the estate," he continued. "Quite a useful talent, considering that spirits sometimes use sound anomalies to communicate, such as white noise. I'm sure you wondered what he was doing the day you saw him inspecting the air near the trees. He'd just witnessed Marla scouting the ethereal defenses. There was darkness in the usual sound vibration, due to the crows, which function as Creyton's familiars, cawing to alert the minions. You saw Titus cupping air samples because he hoped to track the source and stop it. That is what he meant when he said it 'had to end quick.' "

Jonah made a non-committal grunt. Maybe Trip had actually been trying to help, but it didn't change the fact that he was a caustic asshat. "I am truly sorry about the ones that were lost, Jonathan," he said. "I know you taught three of them, but I feel for those other ones too."

"I am sorry too," said Jonathan, sighing again. "But they will never be forgotten. Their spirits are no longer being usurped. Peace and blessings to them. We will all meet again."

"They crossed on?" said Jonah hopefully. "So the paths have been unblocked? All the spirits and spiritess are free?"

Jonathan looked solemn. "Things won't reverse instantly, Jonah. Creyton's damage didn't occur overnight, and it won't be undone overnight. The spirits and spiritesses who were being usurped are indeed free, but there is always work to be done. His blockade has been greatly weakened, but it hasn't completely faded yet."

Somehow, Jonah had expected it to be something like that. He was thankful that *some* progress had been made, though. "Jonathan," he said slowly, "Creyton said that people 'died.' He said 'death' quite frequently. I assumed that he, of all people, would know better than that."

Jonathan looked away. "Jonah, Creyton never understood all the nuances of life," he said. "He never could bring himself to accept that the form of flesh wasn't all there was. He believed that if you weren't in the flesh, weren't physically alive, then you were merely an imitation of life. He was inflexible in that belief, as false as it is."

Jonah nodded. "Can you tell me why I was able to see his spirit?"

Jonathan shook his head, looking troubled. "I'm sorry, Jonah, but I cannot. It is quite astounding that you *did* see it, but I have no idea why."

Jonah looked Jonathan in the eye. "Creyton promised me that he'd be back. He said he'd find a way. Can that happen? Is it possible for people who have passed into Spirit to come back?"

"Remember, Jonah, life cannot end," said Jonathan. "It only changes form. But to answer your question—" Jonathan hesitated for a second; was he hiding something, or did he truly not know? "Life holds many mysteries, Jonah, but spirits cannot re-enter the flesh. Creyton may have been powerful, but he was still a mortal, which meant he had to adhere to the laws of nature. And those laws are irreversible."

That sounded all well and good to Jonah. But he still had doubts. Creyton was adamant about finding a way back. For some reason, it made Jonah think about the dream with the crows, where the guy said something about a coming storm. Were they connected? Did Jonah believe that it was possible, or had his recent experiences simply brought about a reasonable amount of paranoia?

"Do not dwell on these matters so heavily, Jonah," advised Jonathan, who sensed Jonah's misgivings. "Know that you have achieved a great victory, and have righted many wrongs. Our friends, physical and spiritual, are no longer doomed to be usurped and voided, and the spy has been vanquished. You have done well, son. Very well indeed."

Just then, the door creaked open, and Terrence peered in. "Great, you're up!" he said. "Just in time for food!"

"Ah, yes," said Jonathan. "I believe Reena has seen fit to throw you all a bone? Pizza, I think?"

Jonah's eyes widened. "Pizza? *Reena?*"

"Yep," said Terrence. "A Triple XL from the Pizza Plant."

"Sounds great," said Jonah but noticed Terrence didn't look very thrilled. "What's the problem?"

"I wouldn't get too happy if I were you," said Terrence. "Reena threw us a bone, sure, but that bone was a wheat-free Veggie Delight, with Caesar salad on the side."

Jonathan laughed as Jonah's face fell. Jonah glared at the cackling spirit, very annoyed, but secretly jealous of his lack of the need to eat.

The next few days passed much too quickly for Jonah's liking. Since his ribs were on the mend, he couldn't train with the others, but Terrence and Reena put him through some helpful paces to avoid total inactivity. Jonah thanked Liz for her ministrations the first chance he got. Though still rather shaken by their experiences, she flashed a bright grin and said, "I'm a Green Aura; that's what I'm here for."

Bobby was extremely appreciative of what Jonah had done, and was most intrigued by Jonah's choice of weaponry ("No blade, huh? You prefer blunt force, just like me!"). Bobby also volunteered to be Jonah's pseudo-personal trainer when his ribs finally mended. Jonah told him that he would think about it. Malcolm wasn't as vocal about recent events, but Jonah had already gleaned that this was just Malcolm's way, so he respected his silence. When Malcolm discovered that Jonah had saved his breadbox from looters, he had smiled appreciatively and said, "It's not as great as you make it out to be, but it's pretty okay."

Jonah shook his head and let the matter drop.

If Jonah had expected Trip's demeanor to change after he'd rescued him, he was sadly mistaken. Jonah saw Trip at his usual spot in the kitchen the day he'd awakened and rejoined everyone. Trip barely acknowledged Jonah's presence when he walked near him.

"The fact that you didn't get yourself killed was a success in itself," he said.

"Yeah, well, I had to save your life," Jonah retorted. "So it wasn't a *total* success."

They didn't say another word to each other.

There was one thing Jonah still didn't understand, and he asked Terrence and Reena about it after a low-impact workout one night.

"Why were you guys so shocked that night when you saw me with those batons?" he asked them. "I would have asked you then, but we were all pretty busy at the time—"

Reena still looked mystified over it. "Those batons have never been used by anyone, Jonah," she told him. "They would never activate for any of us when we touched them. They just sat there, collecting dust because no one could use them. Until you."

Jonah wondered if there was more to that story and remembered his intense notion that the batons had been waiting for him. Given recent events, however, he decided that that story needed no further elaboration.

It was with the utmost reluctance that Jonah prepared to leave for the city again, placing his duffel bag in the truck that Jonathan allowed him to borrow. As he had told his insurance company that a wreck had led to the appalling damage to his car, he was going to be covered. He was glad and thankful that he wouldn't have to drive this antique truck for too long.

"Look at it this way;" said Terrence, "you're borrowing the truck, so you have to come back here."

"Plus, you've got to meet everyone else," added Reena. "The estate will probably never be this empty again. Now that Creyton's gone, people will probably find excuses to crash here long-term."

Jonah wasn't surprised by that at all, surveying the vast premises.

"Why are you so down, Jonah?" asked Reena with a laugh. "I thought you'd be pleased to have some time away from my healthy eating and the exercise."

Jonah cracked a smile. "Are you kidding? Rabbit food is all my stomach will accept now!"

With another shared laugh and wave, he headed down the gravel driveway.

"Sit down, Mr. Rowe."

Jonah seated himself with a pleasant expression that baffled Mr. Langton. He couldn't help it; if this had been as recent as a week ago, he'd have probably had a gut full of dread, but after explosions, fire, endowments, and vanquished minions, this obnoxious, fat fool just didn't register any apprehension in him.

"I must admit that I'm disappointed, Jonah," said Langton. It was clear that he was confused by Jonah's light-hearted demeanor and hoped to gain a leg up. "Many questions have been posed about your commitment to this company by staff—"

"No they haven't, sir," interrupted Jonah, his voice pleasant.

"I'm sorry?" said Mr. Langton.

"We aren't talking about the staff here, Mr. Langton," said Jonah. "The only employees you are referring to are Jessica and Anthony. We may as well be honest here."

Langton frowned. "Miss Hale was understandably shaken by your, forgive me, tactless and vicious tirade."

"Good," said Jonah, indifferent. "Her bubble needed bursting."

"Essa, Langton, and Bane is about cooperation, Mr. Rowe," said Mr. Langton, displeased with how this was going. "We need people that are on the ball, people who are respectful to their colleagues. To be a member of this team, you must possess an Essa, Langton, and Bane mindset—"

"You're right, Mr. Langton," said Jonah, doing a much better job of keeping the irritation out of his voice than Langton. "And that mindset you are speaking of entails being an ass-kissing automaton who takes your word as law because you have your finger on the trigger. A good job requires working together, appreciation, and respect for various opinions that contribute to the whole. That is not the case here. You expect people to be productive in a fear-based setting. That doesn't fly with me, and I'm tired of dealing with it."

Langton blanched. "What are you trying to say, Rowe?"

Jonah stood up, expression still polite. "I'm not *trying* to say it. I'm telling you I'm done."

Langton had been trying to look impassive, but when Jonah said that, his face hardened. It was clear that his plan was to regretfully inform Jonah that his employment wasn't working out. He probably expected Jonah to grovel and beg. Jonah waited until the right moment and stole Langton's thunder. Langton didn't know how to take it, and it was hilarious to see.

"You're quitting—?" he began angrily, but Jonah was done with the corporate vocab.

"I'm removing myself from a situation I've outgrown," he said. "I wish you the greatest success. I really do. But I cannot and will not accept these work conditions. They are counterproductive on every level. Goodbye, man."

Jonah left Langton's office. The walls were thin, so everyone heard the conversation. Jonah saw several faces that were full of admiration and awe. Nelson beamed and flashed him a thumbs up.

But there was one pair of eyes on Jonah that were neither admiring nor pleasant. Their owner didn't remove them as she barred his path to the exit.

"Who the hell do you think you are?" Jessica hissed.

Jonah maintained his composure. "Don't worry, Jess. Anthony will gladly take the role as your new scapegoat."

Jessica looked homicidal. "You will never be noteworthy, Rowe," she whispered. "Your grand plans are going to fail."

"Maybe," shrugged Jonah. "But the one thing I know for sure is that I'll never find out if I keep rotting away in that fucking cubicle. Now if you'll excuse me."

Jonah pushed past her and smiled at Mrs. Souther. Jessica's interruption had almost made him forget one last thing.

"Take care, Mrs. Souther," he said. "Your husband is so proud of you."

She looked surprised but very pleased. "How would you know that, darling?" she asked.

Jonah glanced at her husband's spirit, who winked at him over her shoulder.

"Just trust me on it, ma'am," was all he told her.

With one last smile, he walked out of the door, grateful that this was the last time he'd hear its entrance and exit chime.

Dear reader,

We hope you enjoyed reading *The 11ᵗʰ Percent*. Please take a moment to leave a review, even if it's a short one. Your opinion is important to us.

Discover more books by T.H. Morris at
https://www.nextchapter.pub/authors/th-morris

Want to know when one of our books is free or discounted? Join the newsletter at http://eepurl.com/bqqB3H

Best regards,

T.H. Morris and the Next Chapter Team

The story continues in:

Item and Time

To read the first chapter for free, please head to:
https://www.nextchapter.pub/books/item-and-time

About the Author

T.H. Morris was born in Colerain, North Carolina in 1984 and has been writing in some way, shape, or form ever since he was able to hold a pen or pencil. He relocated to Greensboro, North Carolina in 2002 for undergraduate education.

He is an avid reader, mainly in the genre of science fiction and fantasy. He is a fan of body ink culture and loves all genres of music, which aids him with his creative writing process. He is also a gamer, loves working out in the gym, Netflix binges, long walks—which is another thing that assists him with creative thoughts—and meeting new people. He began to write *The 11th Percent* series in 2011 and published Book 1, *The 11th Percent*, in 2014.

After living in Greensboro, NC for fifteen years, he relocated to Denver, Colorado with his wife of ten years (and partner for fifteen), Candace.

Connect Online!

Twitter: @terrick_j
Instagram: Instagram.com/j_morris11th
Author Page: www.facebook.com/authorthmorris
Website: thmorris.weebly.com

By *T.H. Morris*

The 11th Percent (The 11th Percent Series, Book 1)
Item and Time (The 11th Percent Series, Book 2)
Lifeblood (The 11th Percent Series, Book 3)
Inimicus (The 11th Percent Series, Book 4)
Gaslighter (The 11th Percent Series, Book 5)

Coming Soon
Grave Endowments (with Cynthia D. Witherspoon)

The 11th Percent
ISBN: 978-4-86747-514-0

Published by
Next Chapter
1-60-20 Minami-Otsuka
170-0005 Toshima-Ku, Tokyo
+818035793528
28th May 2021